# MISSION TO
# CHARA

To Joe ~

Lynn M Bap...

# MISSION TO CHARA

Lynn M. Boughey

North American Heritage Press

MISSION TO CHARA
Copyright 2001
by Lynn M. Boughey.
All rights reserved.

This is a work of fiction. Although some names and numerous locations are actual for the limited purposes of this genre, all characters and
the plot are fictitious, and any resemblance to actual events, locales,
organizations, or persons, living or dead, is entirely coincidental and
beyond the intent of the author or the publisher.

As a recognition of the former commanders of the Fifth Fighter
Interceptor Squadron, the author has employed only the surnames of
the former commanders of that squadron, as well as the surname of
one former Air Division Commander assigned to Minot Air Force
Base who has unfortunately passed away; nonetheless, all aspects of
those characters are fictitious.

This manuscript has been cleared for open publication by the
Directorate for Freedom of Information and Security Review,
Department of Defense [SAF/PAS Doc. Nos. 99—0292 and —
0292A, and 99-S-1627 and -1783]. The views expressed in this book
are those of the author and do not reflect the official policy or position
of the Department of Defense, NASA, or the U.S. Government.

North American Heritage Press

Distributed through
Heritage Place Publishing
1-800-256-7977

ISBN: 0-942323-32-7

*To my wife, Lanette,*
*who makes everything possible*
*and everything worthwhile*

# LIST OF CHARACTERS

## The White House

Frank Jenkins, National Security Advisor
Paul Fuller, Deputy National Security Advisor
Gail Smith, Assistant to the National Security Advisor

## The Pentagon

Gen Scott, Chairman, Joint Chiefs of Staff
Admr Matthew Hacker, Vice Chairman, Joint Chiefs of Staff
LtGen Richard A. Williams, J-3 (Operations), Joint Chiefs of Staff
Col Allison Markham, Executive Officer, J-3, Joint Chiefs of Staff

## The Planning Team

Col Joseph Sandstrom, Director of Plans,
    AF Special Operations Command, Hurlburt Field, Florida
Col Jody Harper, 67th Information Operations Wing,
    Kelly AFB, Texas
Col Vander Parsons, 50th Space Wing,
    Peterson AFB, Colorado
Col James Coe, Operations Officer, 49th Fighter Wing,
    Holloman AFB, New Mexico
Col Richard Dobson, Deputy Operation Officer,
    9th Reconnaissance Wing, Beale AFB, California
Maj James Hanna, 353d Special Operations Group,
    Kadena AB, Japan
Maj Daniel Maki, Operations Officer, 18th Wing,
    Kadena AB, Japan

# The CIA

Phillip Jackson, Deputy Director for Operations, Langley, Virginia
Thomas Myers, Senior Case Officer, Langley, Virginia
Dave Mobbs, CIA Station Chief, Moscow
Riana Kovapiova, Russian CIA Operative, Moscow

# Defense Threat Reduction Agency, Dulles, Virginia

Dr. Jay Allen, Director, DTRA
David Eliker, Chief, Public Affairs, DTRA
Lt Cmdr Ike Watson, Public Affairs Officer, DTRA
Maj Brent Franklin, pilot, Open Skies Directorate, DTRA
Col Randy Broughton, Air Attaché and START Compliance Officer,
    American Embassy, Moscow

# NASA Dryden Flight Research Center, Edwards AFB, California

David Heckman, NASA Blackbird Project Director
Marta Whisenand, NASA flight engineer
Robert Holdiman, NASA flight engineer
Ed Empey, NASA Blackbird pilot
Rogers Karr, NASA Blackbird pilot

# North Dakota

Col Richard Linhard, Commander, 5th Bomb Wing, Minot AFB
Col Mike Garland, Commander, 119th Fighter Wing, Fargo
Capt/Maj/Lt Col Jack Phinney, F-15/B-52 pilot, Minot AFB
Lt Thurman Waddle, F-15 pilot, 5th Fighter Interceptor Squadron,
    Minot AFB

# Whiteman AFB, Missouri

BGen Tom Robertson, Commander, 509th Bomb Wing
Maj Keith Payne, B-2 pilot
Capt Ward Swigler, Public Affairs Officer, 509th Bomb Wing

## Other American Locations

Gen Wodstrchill, Commander, Air Combat Command,
        Langley, Virginia
RAdmr J. Howard Bryson, Command Director,
        Cheyenne Mountain, Colorado
Maj Marshall Cothran, Mission Crew Commander,
        E-3 AWACS plane, Tinker AFB, Oklahoma
Richard Defresne, Photographic Analysist,
        National Reconnaissance Office, Arlington, Virginia
Prayoot Selfridge ("Pry Sing"), 67th Information Operations Wing,
        Kelly AFB, Texas

## Japan

CMSgt Hadley Fowler, 2920th Electronic Security Group,
        Misawa AB
Sgt Steve Deaton, 2920th Electronic Security Group,
        Misawa AB
Capt Thomas Bennett, C-21A pilot, Yokota AB
Capt Allan Erickson, C-21A pilot, Yokota AB
Lt Gen Marcus Spetman, Commander 5th Air Force, Yokota AB

## Moscow

Aleksei Kalganov, Deputy Minister of Defense and
        Commander-in-Chief, Soviet (now Russian) Air Forces
Grigoriy Pavlovich, Director, Second Directorate, KGB (now FSB)
Col Alexander Konesky, Russian START Compliance Officer
Vagan Zaykov, Russian Counter Intelligence Officer,
        Second Directorate, FSB
Andre Ruschev, Director, Special Materials Extraction Directorate

# MAPS

Russia

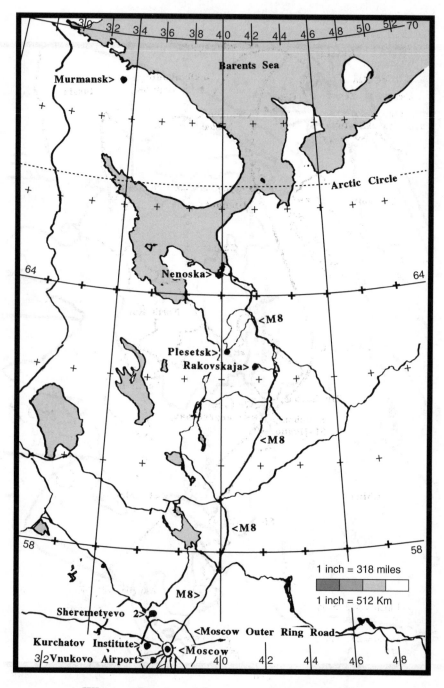

Western Russia – Moscow to the Barents Sea

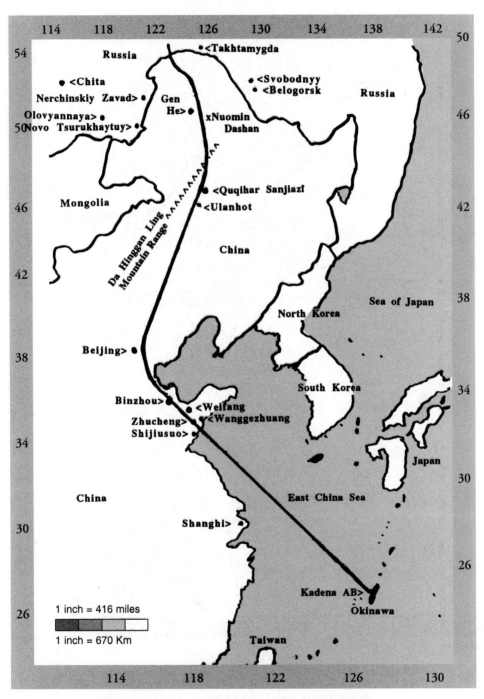

Eastern Asia – Okinawa to Russian Border

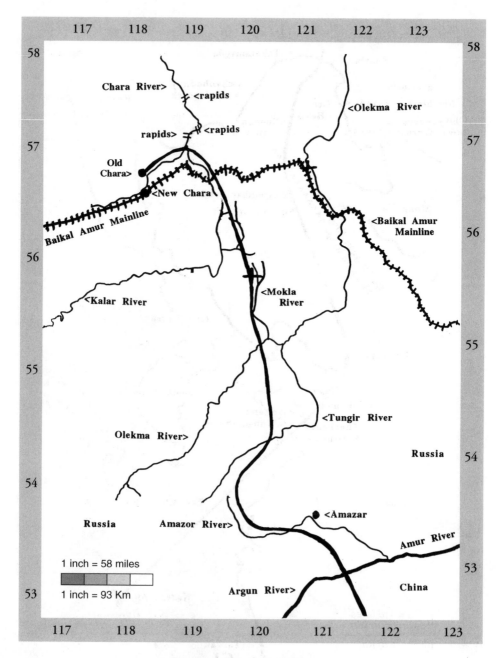

**Russian Border to Chara**

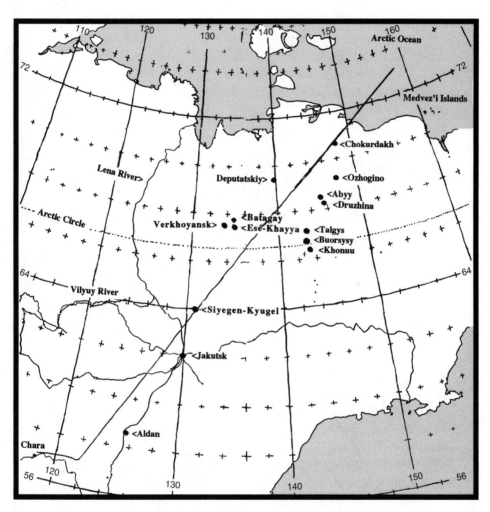

**Eastern Russia – Chara to the Arctic Ocean**

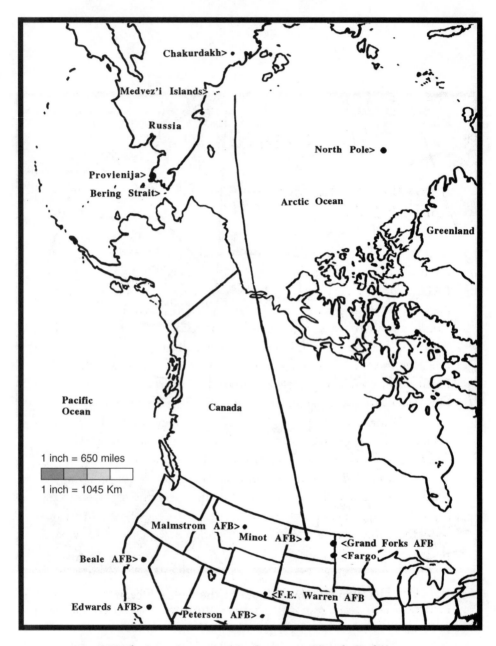

North America – Arctic Ocean to North Dakota

# CHAPTER 1

## Above the Atlantic Ocean
## April 17, 1983

Flying at thirty thousand feet as dawn approaches one cannot tell if the ocean reflects the blue of the northern sky or the gray of the darkness above. At times it alternates, once looking bluish, later looking gray, or even green. Finally, each reflection from the moon-filled clouds allows the ocean to be all of these colors at the same time, depending on where one looks and at which angle is obtained along one's flightpath. Some say this is the nature of flying . . . and of life. Phinney only knew that he was flying east southeast toward the intercept of an unknown plane, most probably Russian.

"Yankee Foxtrot, we have incoming bogey, heading two three zero, Angels 25, three twenty knots, range twelve hundred miles from coast, possible unknown. Vector one one zero for interception."

Captain Jack Phinney adjusted the radar elevation control to bracket twenty-five thousand feet while he angled his F-15 to a heading of 110 degrees, or almost southeast. Moving his left hand back onto the throttles, he slid the microphone switch forward with his thumb.

"Roger, Scan Man," Phinney replied to the E-3 AWACS aircraft that was directing him and his wingman to the target. "Yankee Foxtrot heading one one zero. Will confirm when radar contact with bogey."

Phinney looked down at the left side of his cockpit panel, waiting for his radar to locate the unknown aircraft. It was three hours ago—at 0200—that the alert klaxon had awakened Phinney and his wingman, 1st Lieutenant Thurman Waddle. Temporarily assigned to the alert detachment at Loring Air Force Base, Maine, the pilots had waited anxiously the last two weeks for the chance to intercept a Soviet bomber. Just five weeks ago, two other pilots, Major Rick Evans and Captain Paul Sparkman, made the first interception of a Soviet bomber by the Fifth Fighter Interceptor Squadron. Normally stationed at Minot Air Force Base, North Dakota, Fifth Fighter pilots rarely had the opportunity to test their intercept skills on the real thing. Evans and Sparkman had the great fortune of catching two "Bear" bombers—as well as winning the prize for the first interception, a case of champagne. Maybe we won't win the champagne, thought Phinney, but a touchdown's a touchdown, even if it isn't the first.

"See anything yet, Ducks?" Phinney asked his wingman over the squadron common frequency, which was used for interplane transmissions. Waddle, fresh out of the F-15 combat flying school at Tyndall AFB, had impressed Phinney in the short time he had been assigned to the Fifth Fighter. From what Phinney saw so far, Waddle was a gifted pilot and a bright officer. Nonetheless, this was his first mission, and Phinney knew he would have to watch him carefully.

"Negative, sir," Waddle replied. "Still scanning at twenty-five thousand."

"Roger. Maintain speed and heading. I'm going topside, left."

While Waddle alternated among the radar's three fields of vision, Phinney banked his F-15 up and to the left while leaving his radar on the more narrow, and more accurate, fields of vision. With his intercept heading 110 degrees and the unknown aircraft heading 230 degrees, Phinney knew that the bogey had to be coming at him generally from his left. Suddenly, the target symbol appeared on Phinney's radar scope.

"There!" Phinney said over the open mic to his wingman, "I've got him." Phinney then switched the mic to general frequency so that both his wingman and the AWACS plane could hear the traditional "BRA" report, listing bearing, range, and altitude of the unknown craft. "Scan Man, we have contact, zero nine zero degrees, one-twenty miles at Angels 25. Closing speed ten-fifty knots. Ducks, follow my bearing zero eight five, close in right and aft." Waddle regrouped behind and to the right of Phinney, and then followed

Phinney's aircraft as it banked slightly left to a heading of zero eight five degrees.

The signal on Phinney's radar screen remained steady as it moved to the right. Thus, the unknown plane was not attempting to jam Phinney's radar or to modify the return signal by electronic countermeasures, referred to by the pilots as "music." Phinney activated his microphone. "Scan Man, we have no music, no evasive maneuvers." Due to the lack of evasive maneuvers and electronic countermeasures, Phinney concluded that the plane was probably a Soviet bomber on a training mission. He knew that most of the Soviet bombers were sent up to test the readiness of the Air Force air defense squadrons and to conduct reconnaissance missions. It was a game, of sorts, like cat and mouse. But everyone involved knew that the next time it might not be a game.

With the beginning of dawn approaching from the east, Phinney decided to try to get a visual identification on the aircraft. Leaning forward in the cockpit, Phinney looked through his Eagle Eye, a rifle scope mounted to the side of the head-up display (HUD) bracket. "Damn," Phinney said out loud, "can't see a thing." It was times like these that Phinney wished that the F-15s were equipped, like the Navy's F-14 Tomcats, with long-range TIESO cameras (meaning Target Identification Electro-System Optical) or an infrared search and track system. Maybe President Reagan's infusion of money into the military would change that, but for now he still couldn't see a damn thing. Pressing the mic button, Phinney gave the AWACS plane his report: "Scan Man, unable to confirm bogey by visual. No response to IFF; unknown is flying passive. Will proceed." Phinney paused as he pushed the mic button back to squadron common. "Ducks, when I engage follow my bearing left to two three zero. We'll get underneath, altitude Delta 5." Phinney once again looked at the closing speed, made a quick calculation, then relayed the estimated time of interception to the AWACS plane. "ETI ten minutes," Phinney radioed.

Ten minutes, thought Waddle, ten minutes until my first intercept. Although the adrenaline was rushing through his body, Waddle concentrated on keeping his breathing steady, well-controlled.

Breathing, he knew from his years of karate, was everything—in stress, it would calm you; in combat, it would sustain you.

In, out—in, out—like the ticking of a clock, or the steady waves of the ocean coming to shore, bringing calmness by its constant and unchanging rhythm. As the time passed it seemed like ages to Waddle, but when it was over, it seemed like there had been no wait at all.

"Yankee Foxtrot Two," Phinney radioed to Waddle, "assume double attack formation, check high deck." Waddle moved his F-15 forward so it was abeam and to the right of Phinney's plane, and then began scanning the area above the unknown plane with his radar. At the same time, Phinney adjusted his radar to check the airspace below the unknown plane. If it was a Soviet bomber, as they suspected, he wanted to know now if it was flying with another bomber; it was also possible that the bomber had fighter support, especially if the Soviets were running a mission to Cuba with one of its "Midas" long-range tankers. Seeing no other planes, Phinney once again focused the radar on the twenty-five thousand foot mark—the level of the unknown.

"Ducks, we're even with the bogey. Bank right on my mark; engage." Phinney followed the intercept instructions supplied by the computer on the HUD. Aiming the plane toward the allowable-steering-error target shown on the screen, Phinney banked his plane to the right and downward, obtaining an intercept position behind and five thousand feet below the unknown plane.

"Scan Man, this is Yankee Foxtrot One," radioed Phinney. "We are Delta five, six o'clock position, but cloud cover."

"Affirmative, Yankee Foxtrot One."

Phinney relaxed, waiting for the cloud cover to break. His HUD showed the target ahead of him at a range of eight thousand feet. Phinney switched the display from air-to-air gun mode back to the air-to-air medium range missile mode, which showed his closing speed to be just over ten knots. Good, Phinney thought, we'll ease up on him until it gets clear. With the bright moon and the beginning of dawn coming from the right side of the plane, it will be easy to identify the bogey.

As the clouds broke Phinney could see the silhouette of the plane, and then something dropping from it that looked about twenty feet long. The falling object showed up on the HUD, accelerating downward from the unknown craft. Within seconds, it was below Phinney's display screen. Phinney quickly reached down to the left side of his throttles, adjusting his radar downward to focus on twenty-four thousand feet. "Gotcha!" Phinney shouted to himself as he locked his radar on the falling object.

"Scan Man, this is Yankee Foxtrot One. We have a free-falling, forty two/twelve/zero three West, forty/zero-nine/aught North. Am in pursuit. Ducks, continue coverage and obtain ID."

Phinney dropped his three outboard fuels tanks and yanked his F-15 to the left and downward, angling it into a tight defensive spiral. As the plane plunged toward the Atlantic Ocean at 650 knots, Phinney searched the gray-blue waters below for the tell-tale flame of a Russian cruise missile.

★     ★     ★     ★

Major Marshall Cothran, mission crew commander of the E-3 AWACS plane that had directed Phinney and Waddle to the unknown plane, turned to his deputy control officer sitting immediately to his left. Assigned to the 964th Airborne Air Control Squadron, Tinker Air Force Base, Oklahoma, Cothran had spent the last three years in command of one of the most sophisticated planes ever built. Able to provide all-weather surveillance, command, control, and communications while in flight, the modified Boeing 707/320 airframe was famous for its huge, saucer-shaped radar antenna that rested above the airframe just in front of tail section. Thirty-feet in diameter and six-feet thick, the rotodome contained a powerful radar antenna capable of transmitting a low-PRF signal used for long-range detection while at the same time transmitting a high-PRF pulsed-Doppler signal used to supply altitude data on the target.

"On speaker, " Cothran ordered, and then turned to his radar control officer. "Radar control, find free-falling." Looking at another radar operator, he said, "I want infrared, fifty mile radius of drop point. If there's a flame, I want to know immediately."

Turning back to his deputy, Cothran ordered him to give the National Military Command Center, located deep inside the

Pentagon, a status report. If this was a start of a war, he had to make sure that they knew what was happening. He knew that if the Bear was flying with interceptor cover and a yet unseen MiG fired an air-to-air missile at the AWACS plane, he may not have another chance to provide a report.

The major next spoke into his headset to his intercept communications officer (CSO) seated near the front of the plane. "CSO, Tell Yankee Two to give us ID as soon as possible. Have him move up closer. Four thousand feet or so."

While the communications officer gave Lt. Waddle his instructions, Major Cothran turned back to his deputy. "Request ID and intentions."

The deputy control officer pressed his mic button and spoke into his headset: "Unknown aircraft, bearing two three zero, altitude two five zero, please identify and state intentions."

Static.

"OK," the major said, "let's have the CSO try all Warsaw bands, and in Russian." The deputy control officer relayed the order to the CSO.

Near the front of the plane, just behind the air crew, Senior Airman Rob Hodges flipped through a notebook, looked up the various WARSAW frequencies, and rolled each of them into the console instruments in front of him by spinning the frequency knobs. Following high school, Rob had spent two years getting an associate degree as a computer network technician, and then joined the Air Force. Only twenty-two-years-old, he had already been all over the world, and had even had the chance to fly support once for Air Force One as it crossed the Atlantic Ocean. But this was Rob's first intercept of a possibly hostile aircraft, and he could feel his pulse quicken as he pressed a button on his console, activating the four Warsaw Pact frequencies currently in use.

"Unknown aircraft," Rob stated in Russian, "compass heading two three zero, altitude seventy-nine hectometers, please identify and state intentions." Still, only static came across the airwaves.

Major Cothran waited a few more seconds, then turned to his deputy. "Tell Yankee Two to close in to two thousand feet."

Major Cothran realized that a Soviet "Bear" bomber could easily shoot down an F-15 with its tail gun at that range, but there was no choice—he had to have a positive ID before the falling object reached the surface of the water.

★        ★        ★        ★

Captain Phinney leveled off his plane at five hundred feet above the rolling surface of the Atlantic, aiming back toward the point where the plane, now miles ahead, had dropped its cargo. Pushing his speed brakes out slightly, he slowed his plane to just above its stall speed; Phinney then lowered his flaps while increasing his throttle-setting, keeping a steady distance from the water while maintaining a high angle of attack. Now in position, he began searching the sky with his radar for the falling object. Knowing the rate of acceleration of a free-falling body and the time and height at which the object was released, Phinney estimated that the object would now be at about fifteen thousand feet.

According to NATO intelligence, Phinney knew that Soviet cruise missiles free-fall until about three thousand feet, at which time their engines are ignited by the ram air. Of course, if the Russians had ignited the cruise missile upon release, it would be well past him and headed toward the American coast. Still, if that was the case, he would be able to use his afterburners to catch up to the subsonic missile and destroy it with one of his four Sidewinders.

Phinney watched the radar screen intently as he moved the angle of his radar from fourteen thousand to eighteen thousand feet. Was that a glimmer at fifteen? he thought to himself. Focusing between fifteen and fourteen thousand feet, Phinney once again saw the faint blip on his screen. The object was still free-falling downward at a constant rate of speed, apparently having already reached its terminal velocity, where the force of air prevents further acceleration. Phinney armed the missile as he carefully manipulated the target designate control on the front of the right throttle. Watching the radar screen, he placed the acquisition symbols, called "Captain's bars," directly over the target, Phinney momentarily pressed the target designate control downward into the right throttle; as he did so, the "Captain's bars" switched to a computer-generated target symbol.

"Scan Man, this is Yankee Foxtrot One. I have radar lock on free-falling. Just under Angels 15, estimate 45 seconds before impact. Range twelve miles vector ONE NINE ZERO. Request instructions."

★          ★          ★          ★

Major Cothran considered the situation. The decision was made easier since Yankee One was able to locate the potential cruise missile. We'll wait, he told himself. Let's see what happens.

Cothran reached down to his control panel and switched on his mic button. "Yankee Foxtrot One, can you identify the free-falling?"

"Negative, Scan Man. Too small for long-range visual."

Major Cothran turned to one of his radar operators. "Have you got it?" he asked.

"Yes, sir," the operator replied. "It's reached terminal velocity, same speed known for Russian cruise missiles test drops."

In other words, Cothran thought to himself, it's probably an air-launched cruise missile. "Tell the pilot to maintain distance, watch for flame, and await instructions."

As the radio operator relayed the orders to Phinney, Lt. Waddle's voice came over the speaker. "Scan Man, Yankee Foxtrot Two here. Clouds are clearing. Yes, I can see it. Have positive ID: One 'Bear' Hotel. Do you want door numbers?"

Major Cothran muttered "Damn" under his breath. If it had been any other type of "Bear" bomber, he might have been able to relax and have the pilot close in to get the plane's ID numbers for the recon purposes. Cothran, like everyone else on board the AWACS plane, knew perfectly well that the Bear-H version of the Tupolev Tu-142 was capable of carrying eight AS-15 "Kent" long-range cruise missiles. If one was headed downward toward the sea right now, there would be seven more missiles to worry about. He could no longer risk the F-15 trailing the bomber.

"Have him fall back," General Cothran ordered. "Tell him to arm and lock, but do not engage. Get a confirmation on negative engagement."

"Yankee Foxtrot Two," the deputy stated, "resume shadow, arm and lock. Do not engage. Repeat, permission to arm and lock, negative engagement. Confirm."

"Roger, Scan Man. Yankee Foxtrot Two pulling back. Authority confirmed to arm and lock. Negative engagement."

"Yankee Foxtrot Two, instructions confirmed."

There was a slight pause. "I have radar lock," Waddle radioed back. "Missiles armed and locked."

Major Cothran pressed his internal mic. "Navigator, what's the range to our coastline from the drop point?"

"Eighteen hundred miles, sir."

"And their 'Kent' cruise missiles have a range of 1,850," Cothran thought out loud. "If infrared sees a flame," he ordered aloud to everyone, "we'll recommend DEFCON 2 and splash the 'Bear.'" Cothran turned to his deputy control officer. "Request again."

"Unknown Soviet bomber, bearing two three zero, altitude two five zero, identify and state intentions. Repeat, identify and state intentions."

The speaker crackled, and then came to life. "This is Soviet aircraft Kilo Lima three four five," the barely accented voice said in almost perfect English. "We are in international airspace on training mission. Please state *your* intentions."

Cothran noted the Russian officer's fluent English. Had they planned on being intercepted? Or are they just trying to gain time, time to shoot down the trailing F-15 and then launch the other seven cruise missiles? Major Cothran reached down and activated the microphone. "Kilo Lima, we are concerned for your well-being. Our pilots noted something falling from your plane. Do you need assistance?"

There was a pause. If they were going to fire, Cothran thought, now is when they would do it; now would be their only chance to shoot down the F-15 and drop the other missiles. Instead, the Russian voice came over the speaker; the voice was calm, almost apologetic.

"Negative. We are not in need of assistance. We have merely jettisoned our extra fuel tanks. Thank you for your concern."

Cothran turned back to his deputy. "Ask Yankee One if he has two falling targets."

"Yankee Foxtrot One, do you have two targets on your screen?"

Phinney scanned his screen, adjusting the radar altitude setting on his throttle, checking both above and below the free-falling object that he already had radar lock on. No other objects appeared on the screen.

"Negative, Scan Man. Only one target dropped; one target on lock."

Cothran paused for a moment in thought. As far as the West knew, the Bear-H bomber did not have external drop tanks. Thus, the reference to fuel tanks was probably a lie. If the falling object was a cruise missile, Yankee Two would destroy the bomber seconds after the missile ignited. If this was indeed the beginning of a war, they should have already shot down the F-15. Perhaps, Cothran asked himself, they were dropping a package for a Soviet sub? Package or missile, he wanted the object destroyed. Besides, Cothran reasoned, the Soviets couldn't complain about the destruction of the falling object; according to them, it was just trash, a jettisoned fuel tank.

"Tell the Yankee to splash the free-falling."

The deputy pressed the mic and spoke into the headset. "Yankee Foxtrot One, splash the free-falling. Foxtrot, foxtrot, foxtrot. Repeat, permission to fire. Confirm."

"Scan Man, Yankee One, confirms permission to splash free-falling."

★      ★      ★      ★

Captain Phinney skimmed the water at five hundred feet, travelling at 120 knots at a high angle of attack, all the while keeping the target on his head-up display. His radar screen showed the object at four thousand feet, headed downward toward the water at a constant speed. He glanced forward at the HUD, making sure that the short-range, radar-seeking missile was armed and locked on the target. By his estimation, the target would hit the water in less than twenty seconds. Phinney activated the Airborne Video Tape Recorder, and then moved his thumb over the red firing button on the front of the control stick, and pressed.

The AIM-7F Sparrow air-to-air missile streaked toward its target, accelerating almost immediately to more than three times the speed of sound. Phinney watched as the missile's exhaust trail angled slightly, showing that its guidance system was operating and had made a slight correction. Within a few seconds after launch, the missile drove its eighty-six pound blast fragmentation warhead into the target. The flash momentarily turned the dawn into day, then the calmness of dawn once again returned.

Captain Phinney pressed his mic button. "Scan Man, this is Yankee Foxtrot One. The target is destroyed. Repeat, the target is destroyed."

★          ★          ★          ★

Back in the E-3 AWACS plane, Cothran looked down at the radar screen that displayed the "Bear" bomber, with Yankee Two immediately behind it. If the object had been a cruise missile, the bomber's only other chance to complete its mission would be now; it would have to gun down Yankee Two and drop its remaining cruise missiles before Yankee One returned to fly cover.

"Scan Man, Yankee Foxtrot Two here. Bear is breaking off to the left, executing a one-eighty, aiming back toward the Iceland Gap. Appears headed home."

"Roger, Yankee Foxtrot Two," Cothran replied. "Fall back to shadow. Release missile lock. Repeat, release missile lock. After Yankee Foxtrot One returns, get door numbers and snapshots for the boys back home."

"Roger, Scan Man."

Cothran was all smiles as he congratulated his crew. "Well, gentlemen, if that was a test to find out if we can shoot down cruise missiles while they're free-falling, we certainly answered their question."

# CHAPTER 2

## Moscow, U.S.S.R.
## Two days later

Aleksei Kalganov, Commander-in-Chief of the Soviet Air Forces and Deputy Minister of Defense, walked quickly along the red brick road of the Kremlin, past the State Council building and towards the exit at Spassky Tower.  He was a large man, broad shouldered, tough looking; every bit a general.  His eyesight, it was said, was still perfect, his stamina legend.  He claimed that he could still fly every plane in the Russian Air Forces inventory; it's just that he no longer had the time.  Kalganov pulled his wool coat upward, thrusting the lapels into a tight fold covering his neck.  It was cold, and getting colder.  Kalganov looked up as he walked past the large black statue of Lenin sitting forward, his left arm resting on his knee, his serious countenance silhouetted by the evergreen trees behind him.

Large snow flakes fell softly upon Kalganov's coat as he entered Spassky Tower.  The guards recognized him, of course, even though he was wearing civilian clothes.  Although General Kalgonov's silver-white hair, receding hair-line, and weathered face showed his advancement of years, the general's physical prowess and strength still showed.  Although in his sixties, Kalganov still kept up with his rigorous exercise program, including one hundred sit-ups each morning and a five-kilometer run each weekday afternoon.  The soldiers made sure that no cars were entering the gate from either direction, and then saluted the general as he walked by them.  Kalganov was silent, ignoring the soldiers entirely.

Walking out of the Kremlin into Red Square, Kalganov noted the heaviness of the snow as twilight beckoned toward the night.  To his right he glanced at the Cathedral of St. Basil, prefaced by Martos' statue of the butcher and the prince. Kalganov walked quickly upon the red brick of Red Square towards the east entrance of G.U.M., the large government-run department store. Passing the entrance to the G.U.M., Kalganov walked along Ilyunka Street for a block, then turned left on Kuibishevskiy Street. He continued walking past Building Six, then turned left again into what appeared to be an alley. He did not even look up at the sign on the left that read "12•21" or the one next to it that read "Cafe•Bar." Knowing the area well, he walked down the stairs into the dim, smoke-filled bar.

Kalganov walked past the bar and serving counter, continuing on to the far end of the small bar. Placing his plain wool coat on a peg on the back wall, General Kalganov sat down at a table with his friend, Grigoriy Pavlovich, who had been waiting for the general to arrive. Without saying a word, Pavlovich—despite his almost bookish looks due to his thin face and small metal-rimmed glasses—opened the bottle of vodka that sat on the table, pouring out two shots. Although he was close to the same age as Kalganov, he looked younger due to this continued brown hair; his broad smile exhibited friendliness, but also an air of cunning. After pouring the drinks, Pavlovich set the bottle down gently, so as not to pierce their weekly ritual with a dark thud of reality.

"To Mother Russia," Pavlovich said, looking directly at Kalganov. Kalganov ate from the tray of bread and sausage set on the table before them, then lifted his drink.

"To Mother Russia," Kalganov repeated, both of them downing their drinks in one easy movement. They paused, allowing themselves to ease into the steady noise of the bar. It was this way every late Saturday afternoon; the same bar, the same time of day, and the same table, far enough away from the uninterested ears of the usual patrons.

"So, Aleksei," Pavlovich said, "I see that I must once again arrest you for treason." Grigoriy Pavlovich often began the conversation this way after discovering anything he regarded questionable about General Kalganov, such as a loss of funding on a project, a failed test program, or even a new mistress.

"Is that so Grigoriy?" This time Kalganov poured the drinks; they silently toasted each other, then let the warm vodka once again ease into the back of their throats. "And what profound news does the head of the second directorate know today?"

"Today, my friend, is different from any other day. Today, Aleksei, I truly could arrest you for treason."

"Well," Kalganov sighed, unconcerned, "in that case, I am pleased." He watched as his friend poured another drink. "I am indeed tired, Grigoriy, tired of being an old general." Kalganov smiled as he looked up at his friend. "I could use a vacation."

"Yes, yes, Aleksei, I know; but this time I have you." Pavlovich set his glasses on the table and looked directly into the general's crystal blue eyes, and then raised his drink. "To Operation Daedalus," he said simply.

Kalganov paused for a moment, then raised his own glass and drank the vodka slowly, his mind racing. "So," the general replied as he ran his fingers along the rim of the glass, "you know about Daedalus." He paused, looking down at the empty glass, helping himself to more bread and sausage. "So what's to know?" General Kalganov continued. "A simple military operation; the Americans reacted as I expected, and they demonstrated their ability to shoot down a falling cruise missile. They proved my point that we need more bombers, and that they should be given full fighter support. Now perhaps the chairman will listen."

"Yes, Aleksei, I know what you showed, and I know what you proved. But I also know *why* you did it." The head of the most powerful directorate of the KGB paused as he once again poured from the bottle.

"Then please enlighten me, Comrade Pavlovich. How can doing my duty be an act of treason?" The two men stared intently at each other as the seconds passed.

"It is treason, my dear Aleksei, when it is done for the purpose of getting one of our bombers shot out of the sky by some trigger-happy American pilot."

General Kalganov smiled. So, he thought, it is out. But how did he know? Or is Grigoriy just making an educated guess? "But my dear friend," the general said as he poured another set of drinks, "we both know that it is not a crime for a general to send a man to his death. And besides, they did not die."

"Yes," Pavlovich persisted, "but did they know that you actually wanted them to be shot down?" The general swallowed hard, envisioning the cells he had toured fifty-some feet below Moscow's city streets at Lubyanka prison. Kalganov decided to ignore the question and started to raise his drink to his lips. As he did this Pavlovich reached over and placed his hand firmly on the general's wrist, pressing Kalganov's arm against the table and bringing himself within inches of the general's face. Pavlovich spoke in a whisper that even Kalganov could barely hear. "And did they know that by being shot down, you had hoped to prevent the chairman from giving the Americans more military advantages? And maybe get rid of the chairman himself?"

Both men looked evenly at each other; General Kalganov waited, sweat beginning to appear on his brow. The room felt hot, the air musty. Pavlovich had him and both men knew it.

Pavlovich leaned backwards into his chair and began to smile. "Those of us at the directorate were most fascinated with your ploy. Indeed, my good friend, we were sorry that it did not work." After hearing this, General Kalganov relaxed into an uncomfortable smile, waiting for Pavlovich to continue. "True, we don't care that much about the reduction of your military power, but we too believe that *glasnost* has gone too far. Unlike us, the chairman does not understand the effect of uncontrolled liberty on the masses. These changes are dangerous. Like Pandora's box, once they are in place, we will never be able to go back to the way it was. The masses will want more—things that we cannot give them. Freedoms that they cannot handle." Pavlovich paused as he filled the shot glasses. "But you, Aleksei, you have given us an idea. Your plan was good, almost perfect. But we have thought of something better; something on a larger scale. And, my friend, it concerns you."

# CHAPTER 3

## Minot Air Force Base, North Dakota
## Two weeks later

Jack Phinney unlocked his door to his duplex on Sirocco Drive, Minot Air Force Base. Not a good sign. Rarely would she and he lock the door—one of the benefits of living in a place as safe as Minot. It took people from the bigger cities quite awhile to get used to an environment where there may be ten murders a year in the whole state that has a population of only six hundred thousand, and where everyone leaves the car running and unattended outside the grocery store or the mall when the temperature falls below zero during the winter.

The missing knickknacks should have given it away. But Phinney didn't notice their absence for several days. She always said it was the little things that bugged her, not the big ones. The little things must have added up though, for sitting on the dining room table were the documents and a sterile note: "Here are the papers. I've already signed and taken my stuff. Sign it and take it to my lawyer's office, or get one of your own. It doesn't matter."

It doesn't matter, Phinney thought to himself. No shit. You're gone, you've taken whatever the hell you wanted and left me the papers. No shit it doesn't matter. Phinney sat down at the table thinking. Sure there were good times. Sure he was gone a lot. It was the nature of the job. What about duty? What about commitment? Instead, he got the "I've given all I can give, there's nothing left" bullshit. Maybe she had. Maybe he hadn't. He didn't know. All he knew was she was gone, that he still loved her, and part of him had left with her.

And yet, in a way, he was relieved. No more arguments, which actually had been few and far between for the last couple of months; they had been replaced by the constant tension, which in turn had been replaced by silent and mutual indifference. After a while Phinney thought it best to leave it that way, to see if she would come around, figure out that she had it pretty good, figure out what it was she needed to be happy. Phinney already knew he couldn't make her happy, that happiness comes from the inside and was something he couldn't control or guarantee. At least that's what he told himself as he watched her day after day becoming more distant and unhappy.

Phinney grabbed a beer from the fridge and sat back down at the table to read over the papers. The hell with her, he thought to himself, and signed the papers.

That evening Phinney went to the O'Club and tied one on, playing crud (a full-contact billiards game often played at officer clubs throughout the Air Force), bat hanging (drinking shots while hanging upside down from a helicopter landing pad attached to the ceiling in the crud room), the works. He shared his case of champagne that he had won for the Bear sighting with his fellow green-baggers. The old Phinney was back; no more running home to "the Mrs" trying to make her happy. From now on it was work hard, play hard. And he did both with a vengeance during the next few years—almost to the point where he didn't think about her every moment. Years later he found, inside the back cover of his copy of *Les Miserables*, something he had written down before she had left him:

> I shall not have silence in my home. I would rather have arguments than silence, for silence is the shepherd of indifference, and indifference the destroyer of love and the harbinger of misery to come. So let there be words in your home, even if they are occasionally harsh. And if, with this in mind, you find yourself repeatedly assailed and harassed by words devoid of love and you find yourself desperate for silence, then it is time to depart for good in search of kindness and soft words of love.

There would be no more silence in his life, Phinney had decided. He would enjoy life to the fullest and be with the people who wanted to be with him. And soon everything revolved around the long hours at work and the uncomfortable blur of wild weekends gone by.

# CHAPTER 4

## Biysk Rocket Facility, 52 34N 085 15E
## 1986

The colonel looked tired. The smoldering remains of the Biysk solid propellant missile factory was as bad as it looked. The fire had destroyed at least two hundred RSM-52 three-stage missiles that were ready for shipment to Nerpichya. The fire could not have happened at a worse time. In another week the missiles would have been in transit to another base, outside of the colonel's jurisdiction and concern.

How could such a thing happen? the colonel wondered to himself. Certainly sabotage was a possibility, but there was no indication that anyone got anywhere near the heavily-armed guards surrounding the building. Especially these guards. General Prostiakova, the head of the Russian rocket forces, had sent them himself to protect the facility and escort the missile convoy during the transfer stage. Perhaps, he thought, that would be the only reason his life would be spared: The blame would fall, at least in part, on the general. And as such, General Prostiakova would be less inclined to desire the traditional full investigation, normally followed by a court martial. Yes, it was fortunate indeed for the general's troops to be on hand when the catastrophe occurred.

The colonel watched as the ZiL black limousine approached the fire site from the exterior gate—obviously General Prostiakova coming to see the damage and receive personally the colonel's report and attempts at explanation. But there was no explanation, the colonel thought. Nothing made sense. How could this have happened? How could it be worse?

As the limousine drove up to the site, the colonel came to attention. As expected, General Prostiakova exited the vehicle, his great size known to all. The colonel watched with disbelief and then horror, however, as he watched General Kalganov himself, the Deputy Minister of Defense, follow General Prostiakova out of the limousine, his massive body as large as it had been described to him.

The colonel remained standing at attention, convinced now of the court martial and speedy execution; for he now knew that he was a dead man and nothing he could say would change it.

"Colonel," General Prostiakova began, "this is General Kalganov. He has come here for a full report on this tragedy. You will of course tell him everything you know. Do you understand, Colonel?"

"Yes, sir. Absolutely."

General Prostiakova waited a moment as he watched the colonel's forehead begin to sweat. "Well?" he asked once his patience was gone.

"Ah, yes, sir. Yes, sir. Ah, General, as you are probably aware the rockets were scheduled to leave the plant sometime this week. They were scheduled to be taken by truck to Nenoska for testing, and then deployed at the Northern Fleet submarine base at Nerpichya."

"In other words, Colonel, the rockets were meant for our new Typhoon submarine. Correct?"

"Yes, sir."

"And how many of the rockets were destroyed?"

"All of them, sir."

General Kalganov turned pale; his bottom lip quivered as he walked up to the colonel's face. "'All of them?'" he yelled. "What do you mean, 'All of them'?"

"Sir, I regret to report that all 207 rocket motors completed thus far were destroyed in the fire."

"But how can that be, Colonel? Do we not have safety precautions? Separate storage facilities? People guarding them?"

"Yes, sir, we do. But all of the missiles were consolidated to this storage facility for preparation for transfer."

"And who came up with that wonderful plan?"

General Prostiakova stepped over to General Kalganov's side. "Sir, if I may interrupt?"

"What is it?" Kalganov yelled.

"Sir, the decision to consolidate the missiles for preparation for transfer was made by my men. It was necessary in order to guard the rockets during loading onto the transport trucks, pursuant to your order of January 1984 on missile transport and protection."

The colonel watched General Kalganov try to gain control of his famous temper. He quickly turned away from both of the junior officers and walked toward the smoldering fire.

"Colonel," Kalganov yelled back at the two men as he continued walking, "what the hell happened here?"

The colonel ran to catch up to General Kalganov, with General Prostiakova doing his best to keep up. "Well, sir, at 0200 last night there was a massive explosion in Building 508, the building where all of the missiles were being prepared for shipment."

"Was the building under guard?"

"Of course, sir. General Prostiakova's own men were stationed all along the perimeter and, during the day, were in charge of supervising the preparation and loading."

"How many men were inside?"

"We lost seven men, sir."

Kalganov stopped and turned on the younger man. "Colonel, I don't give a damn how many men you lost! I want to know how this happened!"

"Yes, sir. I understand, sir. We don't know how it happened."

"Well, any survivors who were inside?" the general asked with a little less anger as he once again began walking toward the rubble.

"No, sir."

"I take it from the spread of debris that the explosion was substantial."

"Yes, sir. Very substantial."

"And no one survived who can tell us what happened."

"No, sir. No survivors."

"Prostiakova, how about your men? Any survivors?"

"Yes, sir, but none were in the building at the time it occurred."

"So, Colonel. What happened?"

"Sir, I believe that the solid propellent on one of the missiles became unstable, that it ignited and then ignited the other rockets. As you know, we have had instability problems before."

"And the rocket motors themselves?"

"They of course survived the fire, sir, but they are not usable due to the charing of the debris around the metal."

"So what you're telling me, Colonel, is that every RSM-52 designed for operation on our new Typhoon submarine is destroyed, and that we have to start the production cycle all over, is that right Colonel?"

"Yes, sir. I am sorry to report that that is correct, sir."

The general swore, muttering under his breath. "How am I to equip the new Typhoon submarine? Now it would be years before a Typhoon will become fully operational. Years!" General Kalganov kicked at the black rubble at his feet. "My God, this is as bad as the destruction of the R-1 and R-2 depot in 1953."

The colonel and General Prostiakova both knew very well to what General Kalganov was referring. The early Soviet rocket program was set back years in 1953 because, of all things, a warm winter! In January the snow around the main storage depot melted; the fields surrounding the depot flooded and the rats and other rodents sought dry ground at the higher level depot site. Unfortunately, the rats found the fabric insulation around the electrical wiring quite tasty and thereby ruined all of the rockets stored there. It was a disaster. General Gaydukov personally visited the site, firing General Volkodav on the spot.

"Until today," General Kalganov said sadly, his anger coming back to him, "I never thought we would ever have such a catastrophe." The colonel watched in trepidation as General Kalganov's anger quickly returned. "And certainly not while I was in charge!" Kalganov stated quickly as he walked toward General Prostiakova, his teeth clinched, his face turning red.

"General Prostiakova," Kalganov screamed, "I will hold you personally responsible for this accident!"

"But, sir . . . ."

"General, do not even think about saying a word! Look at this! What was going to be the most important modernization of our rocket force lies here at my feet, smoking and burning and smoldering like the career you once had, General! How could your scientists be so sloppy? Imagine if one of these rockets had been placed inside the submarine and then did this? This building I can replace, but I will never be able to replace one of my Typhoon subs! I will have your head, General. Your head!"

And with that statement the colonel watched General Kalganov storm off back to the limousine with General Prostiakova following closely behind him, not daring to say a word. But the colonel was already thinking about what to do next. Secure the area. Box up the debris and store it in a secure building. Little remained, but it still must be protected. Perhaps Building 407 could be transformed into the new production facility? he thought to himself.

The colonel watched as the limousine drove away, its mirrored windows not allowing him to observe what he assumed to be the last moments of General Prostiakova's career. He would blame the fire, of course, on the instability of the solid propellant. But it will not matter since the general was also in charge of all aspects of the production, including the design teams and the chemists who manufactured the rocket propellent.

Yes, the colonel thought, better a building destroyed than a Typhoon submarine. Perhaps he would even be allowed to continue to manage the operation. Yes. Possibly. Especially since Kalganov's anger is entirely directed at General Prostiakova and his inept scientists. The colonel welcomed the fact that he could survive this fire as he began issuing orders for the clean-up.

# CHAPTER 5

## Kurchatov Institute, Moscow, Russia
## Two days later

The twenty-foot steel sculpture of Igor Kurchatov's face seemingly stared into General Kalganov's eyes as his driver approached the Kurchatov Institute. General Kalganov's limousine glided off of Pehotnaja Street, jogged right and then left as it made a half circle around the deep-black statue. From the outside the Institute looked deceptively small, its yellow entrance building, bordered in white, reached only one hundred feet across and three stories high. General Kalganov always thought it strange that the Institute was painted the same ugly pale-yellow of the American Embassy.

Immediately prior to pulling up to the entrance building the general's vehicle made a sharp right, thus facing the steel gates that stood between the adjacent guard houses. With a short honk of the horn the gates were opened; there would be no need to show his identification since all of the guards knew the general's vehicle. Moving forward the vehicle passed several yellow buildings to the right, stopping at the south end of the building that originally contained Kurchatov's office.

General Kalganov stepped out of the vehicle, took a deep breath of the cold January air and stretched his arms high as he looked westward into the midst of the unleaved forest before him. As a young officer he spent many years working at this place, inside this very office building. He loved the place, especially in the late spring when one could stroll through the forest with friends as they relaxingly planned the destruction of the world by nuclear bombs as if they were talking about last week's hockey scores. It was indeed a peaceful existence, despite the topic.

Walking into the building behind the main office building General Kalganov bounded up the four flights of stairs and down the hallway past office after office of scientists dealing with the intricacies of critical mass, isobaric analogue resonances, Coulomb repulsion, and such other niceties of nuclear physics. Reaching the end of the hallway General Kalganov did not even pause as he burst through the partly opened door.

"Pavel!" he cried out. "Where is that young scientist of mine?"

A young man looked up from his desk smiling. "Uncle Aleksei! What a surprise! Why didn't you tell me you were coming, I could have had tea and cake brought in."

"No need, no need, Pavel. Besides, I would rather walk, if you would be kind enough to join me."

"But of course, Aleksei, of course. Just let me grab my coat here and we can go. Natasha!" Pavel Kerlov waited a moment, then yelled again. "Natasha!"

An even younger woman stepped in from another door. "Yes, sir?"

"I will be leaving with General Kalganov for a while." Pavel looked up at the general. "Will we be long?"

"Perhaps," he replied smiling. Pavel understood.

"I will be gone the rest of the day, should the director ask."

"Yes, sir," Natasha confirmed sheepishly. "I will tell him, if he asks."

Within minutes General Kalganov and his "nephew" Pavel were walking down the tree-lined road, the general's limousine trailing behind them at a discreet but appropriate distance. The general stopped.

"One moment, Pavel." The general walked back to the driver's window. "Meet us at the house. Yes, Kurchatov's house." Pavel watched as the limousine pulled away. To have such power, he thought to himself. If only I had such power.

"So, my dear Pavel. How are you doing?"

"Very good, Uncle Aleksei," Pavel Kerlov answered as they walked along the trees, a car occasionally driving by. "Very good, thank you."

"It is so good to see you. So how are things going in the lab?"

"All right." Pavel paused for a moment. "But also not so good. The money is very short. We are down to five hundred scientists, and there is talk that they may even close the lab down in its entirety. It is so unbelievable! Our work is so important, and yet it is falling away by the wayside."

"That is indeed unfortunate, my dear Pavel."

"How can you let them do this? Don't they know what they are doing to our scientific community?"

"I too am very dissatisfied with what is happening. Tell me, Pavel, what do you think of it from a military standpoint. You grew up around the military. You and your father—who I still miss greatly—had many talks about the world. What do you think of all of this from that perspective?"

"Between us?"

"Of course, Pavel, between us."

Pavel leaned closer to General Kalganov, speaking quickly and forcefully. "We are giving up and giving everything away at the same time! At the rate Gorbachev is going with his unilateral asymmetrical cuts, we'll be lucky if we have any nuclear weapons ten years from now. The morale at the lab is the worst that I have ever seen. We have spent our whole lives learning how to make bombs, and now we are obsolete! Aleksei, we don't know how to do anything else. Nor do we want to learn anything else. This is what we are good at. This is what we have trained for all these years. Can't you do something to make them understand that they are giving everything away?"

"That is what I thought you would say, Pavel. You have the patriotism of your father and the scientific genius of your grandfather. No, no. It's true. I knew them both. And I have known you from the day of your birth, Pavel. True, you do not hold the place in history that your grandfather does, but who could? He is rightfully known as the father of the Russian missiles. He was a great man. A very great man."

"Yes, Uncle Aleksei, I know. But there are days that I wish I was as great. Days that make me feel that history has passed me by. Here we are, standing in front of real history." Pavel pointed at the pinkish brick building before them, looking up at a brown-granite plaque showing the date of December 25, 1946, and depicting the splitting of an atom. General Kalganov knew the building well, had witnessed its construction, the arduous task of building the graphite mound interspersed with uranium cylinders. Downstairs, next to the engineering station that controlled Russia's first operational nuclear reactor, was the mound. Based on stolen plans of the American Hanford 305 test reactor, the F-1 was Kurchatov's first attempt to create a controlled chain reaction. He succeeded on December 25, 1946, and henceforth became Russia's most famous scientist. Pavel continued to stare up at the date chiselled into the marker.

"I too had hoped to change the world," Pavel stated, "to make a difference. All I do is live in shadows, shadows of him, and my father, and my grandfather. Especially since I chose science as my profession."

"Of course you do, Pavel! And perhaps your father was right in choosing the military as his career. He too knew the length of your grandfather's shadow. He accepted it and went on to be a great soldier. His death in Afghanistan was especially troubling to me. You know that I loved him as a brother."

"Yes, I know Aleksei. I know." Pavel thought of his father's fiery death, visualizing in his mind an American Stinger missile arcing up toward the Mi-24 HIND-D helicopter as it surveyed that mountainous terrain. Just the thought of the capitalist missile killing his father brought a wave of anger. General Kalganov observed this, and was pleased.

The general pointed up at the date chiseled into the marble. "You know that I was in there a few weeks after that famous day. I was then, of course, a very young officer." The two men began to walk along the road away from the building toward Kurchatov's former residence. "I worked as an executive officer for General Pavlov," the older man continued, a fact well-known to Pavel and told to him by Kalganov on numerous occasions. "Kurchatov was so excited with the success of his project that he invited Beria himself to witness the reactor in operation. So Beria sat down in the control room, Kurchatov initiated the reaction by inserting the rods, and the Geiger counter clicked away. And Beria, the fool, wanted more proof! He actually asked to go inside and see the reactor itself, after just being operated.

Can you imagine? Luckily Kurchatov convinced him of the danger, but the master-spy still wasn't satisfied that it wasn't a trick. So he insisted that Kurchatov write Bohr himself and confirm that the Americans were using plutonium for their bomb. Of course Bohr had no knowledge of the American's decision to use plutonium, and it was a waste of ink and time. All of that angst for nothing! Beria knew full well from his spies that the Americans were using plutonium." General Kalganov realized that he had been rambling like an old man as they walked and decided to be quiet for awhile.

"So, Pavel," he continued after a bit, "the money is going away. The morale is low. What do you think we should do?"

"There is nothing to do," Kerlov answered dejectedly, kicking away a stone as he walked. "We have no control. We will all be done within the year. Another five hundred people out of work. They have no need for us theoreticians anymore."

"But you have done more than theoretical physics, haven't you?"

"Yes, of course. But that is my weakness. The generals who paid for my education and moved me from place to place thought I'd blossom like my grandfather. Then 'poof' I'd be suddenly inventing new missiles like he did. New means of destruction. New areas of science. But I did not."

"But you did well applying the new technology to the old, did you not? Your work in solid propellants was very good, I heard. And you also worked on other practical things, such as silo designs for cold-launched boosters, initiation sequencing, even some targeting and navigational systems."

"Yes, I did those things. But I only applied what was there, merged it into a working system. I did not invent anything new."

"Invention is a fine thing, Pavel. But sometimes it is just as good to stand on the shoulders of giants," alluding to Newton's famous comment to his friend Robert Hooke: "If I have seen further it is by standing on the shoulders of Giants."

The two men approached Kurchatov's residence. The simplicity of the building befitted the simplicity in life that Kurchatov himself had insisted upon. Placed in the middle of the forested area of the

Institute, the square, two-story building sat calmly and quietly in its humble domain.

"Come," the general told Pavel, "let's go in. I called ahead so they expect us." The front door opened even before the two men reached it.

"Hello, General," spoke a woman as she stepped out to greet the general.

"Hello, Olga. How are you?"

"Fine, fine. It is so nice to see you. You honor us with your presence." The three of them entered into the house. "No, no, you need not wear the slippers, General. Please, just step in. The snow is clean. It will be fine. And how are you, my sweet Pavel?"

"I am fine, Olga. Fine, thank you."

"You too, Pavel, need not worry about the slippers. Come, come in. I am making the tea as we speak."

"Thank you, Olga," General Kalganov replied with genuine warmth. "You always treat me so well. How will I ever repay you?"

"No need, my friend, no need. You have helped us so much over the years, and, perhaps, you are here to help us again. They have let go so many. I did not think the mere talk of peace would undo so many. It is quite trying."

"Yes," General Kalganov replied, understanding her allusion to Dante's *Inferno*, "that is what Pavel has been telling me. Might we have the *chi* in the sun room?"

"But of course. I shall bring it to you immediately. Please, go on in."

General Kalganov and Pavel walked into the living room, Pavel hoping that he would have a chance later to go upstairs and look at the brilliant man's desk. The eye glasses, the opened notebook, the simple quill pen that he used, all showed the simplicity of Kurchatov's existence. All around them stood simple furniture—grand and expensive, but simple nonetheless. Simple lines. Simple patterns. Staid, direct calmness befitting the brilliance of his mind, and the love of his wife, Marina.

Pavel walked past the cabinet filled with statuettes of animals that Marina had collected during her life and so loved. Outside the sunny room were hundreds of plants and trees. Kurchatov's team of scientists called the house "Forester's Cabin," and rightfully so. For fourteen years Kurchatov lived here with Marina, surrounded by his forest and the silver firs, birches and oaks that he had personally planted around the house. Kurchatov lived here from 1946 until his early and untimely death in 1960 at the age of fifty-seven.

General Kalganov and Pavel continued through the dining room and entered the general's favorite place, the sun room. The two sat down and within moments Olga arrived with the tea. Looking outside Pavel observed the large yard and the forest behind it. It was as if they were nowhere near Moscow, nonetheless only eight miles from its center. Olga left as soon as she had delivered the tea, apparently sensing that the two had work to discuss or problems to solve. The scientist and the general paused as they sipped their *chi*. Pavel said nothing as he watched the flakes of snow occasionally hitting the warm window-pane, the snow turning into liquid and forming droplets that converged as if pulled together by a mysterious attraction, forming first tributaries and then small rivers of water downward along steadfast borders that remained fixed and unseen. Within this scene, thought Pavel, are all of the answers to science's unanswered questions: the secret of conversion from solid to liquid, mutual attraction, gravitational pull, molecular cohesiveness. All here. All before him. All but inches away from his mind, a mind that inquires but cannot see; a mind, like any scientist's, that tries to see inside nature, that looks for connections, infers subatomic nuances. To see truth. To understand reality. To see God.

General Kalganov finished sipping his tea and leaned back into the green upholstered chair that matched the color of the plants that were sprinkled throughout the sun room. "Tell me, Pavel, how long have you been doing theory alone?"

"Five years."

"Why did you switch to theory?"

Pavel shrugged his shoulders. "I don't know. Mainly because I enjoy it the most. I tried to get them to let me do theory from the beginning, but they insisted it had no value. It was the concrete that they wanted. Something they could use now, not ten years from now."

"Yes, I know Pavel. And I too may be partly to blame for that decision. The shadow of your grandfather had us all transfixed, looking for new types of delivery systems, new types of weapons. But, I wonder, would you be willing now to go back to something more practical, to give up theory for a while?"

Pavel thought for a moment. "I suppose so. As long as I could continue to work on my theories on the side. Why? What do you have in mind?"

"I am working on a project. A very secret project. One that I think you would like. I would like you to be the director. And we will need to employ your friends, but only your closest friends, the ones who you can trust absolutely and who think like you do."

Pavel smiled broadly, having difficulty in restraining the excitement he felt building. "And what would I be doing?"

"Changing history, Pavel, changing history."

Pavel liked the way that sounded. He had always thought about being a director of a research facility, in charge of people, making decisions that only he could make, giving fatherly advice, surrounded by his friends who were working there only because of him, because they were lucky enough to be his friends. He liked these thoughts as they flowed quickly through his mind.

The general, of course, observed all of this, each of these thoughts, for he knew Pavel well, and believed he could read his innermost desires given the many years he had known him. General Kalganov smiled as he watched Pavel thinking, the initial burst of excitement changing steadily into calm elation and quick analysis.

"Where would the facility be?" Pavel asked. "Would we do it here?"

"No, it is much too secret for that. We must be away from people, away from Moscow."

"Where then?"

"North of here. Quite a ways north. But do not worry. You would be taken care of well. Your own apartment, a large one, lots of food. Lots of responsibility."

Pavel thought for just a second. "I do not care if I'm here in Moscow or in the middle of nowhere. If I can do my work and be with my friends, I will be happy."

General Kalganov was pleased. "As director you will be very busy, at least until the project is completed. But then you and your friends can sit around and work on whatever theories you want, and as long as you want. All you will need to do is keep the project operational once it is built, and that will take some time, perhaps five years or so."

Pavel stood up from the chair and walked over to hug the general. "Uncle Aleksei, you are a savior! A true savior. I accept even though I do not yet know what it is you want me to do."

Three hours later Pavel exited Kurchatov's house with General Kalganov. He looked thoughtful but pleased. "Can I give you a ride back?" the general asked.

"No, thank you, Uncle Aleksei," the younger man replied. "I will be fine. I would rather walk."

"Very well. Will you be able to get the other scientists to join?"

"Yes, I think so. I will convince them just as you have suggested. They will assume it is a secret military project. It will work; they do not know anyone who would tell them otherwise."

"Excellent, Pavel! Make sure you tell them that they will be paid well, very well. That should be enough to convince them. Goodbye, Pavel. We will talk soon."

Pavel said nothing as he watched General Kalganov get into his limousine and drive away. The sun glittered on the fresh snow, sparkling, Pavel thought, like diamonds on sand. Life is good when it is going right—very good. Somehow the cold snow now looked warm, the day exceedingly less dreary. Pavel walked back to his office quickly, his mind racing through the hundreds of things he needed to do.

# CHAPTER 6

## Langley Air Force Base, Virginia
## 1993

The security police sergeant assigned to the West Gate of Langley Air Force Base aimed his flashlight at the younger looking man. Clearly an officer, probably a hot-shot fighter-jock. No matter. He could smell the scent of alcohol, could see the bloodshot eyes, hear the slight slur in his language when he had responded to his preliminary questions.

"Could you step out of the car, sir?"

"Absolutely," the man responded, fumbling slightly as he reached for the door handle of the black Honda Prelude.

"Do you own this car, sir?"

"Yes, I do." Again the smell of booze.

"Can I see your military ID, license, and registration?"

"Certainly!" The man reached back into the car through the open driver's-side window to get his registration out of the glove compartment, losing his balance slightly in the process.

"Sir, I stopped you because I noticed you weaving slightly as you approached the gate to leave. Were you headed home, sir?"

"Yes, as a matter of fact I was." Too many words, and still the slight slurring of those words. The policeman looked down at the driver license.

"Major Phinney, I show you as living at Newport News. Is that correct?"

"Yes, it is."

"Have you had anything to drink tonight, sir?"

"Sure, I had a couple at the Club." At least he's honest, the sergeant thought to himself.

"Well, sir, we're going to need to do a few sobriety tests."

"Fine with me."

Phinney failed the tests, partly due to the amount he had consumed, but also because he failed to understand the inherent subterfuge contained within those tests. Sure he put one foot in front of the other for seven steps and then turned and came back with the same number, but what the cop was really watching for was if he lost his balance when he turned around, which he did. And sure he counted backwards from 78 to 68 just fine, but he forgot to stop at 68 and kept going to 58.

"Sir, I'm placing you under arrest for driving under the influence of alcohol. We'll need to leave your vehicle here and go down to the LE desk and do a breathalyzer."

"Shit," Phinney said simply, thinking to himself, there goes my career down the tubes.

    ★        ★        ★        ★

Major Jack Phinney stood at attention immediately in front of the desk of the commander of Air Combat Command. This alone was a rarity for Phinney; normally the four-star general and his aide would be relaxed sitting on the couch in the general's office discussing the speech he was preparing for the AFA or some other group, or talking about this senator or that senator and what needed to be done to get Congress to grant funding to leave the B-2 production line open for another year in the hopes that eventually the Air Force could build more than the twenty thus far allotted by Congress.

No, this was no normal situation, and Phinney felt like shit about it. The hangover from the night before was a bitch, but it was nothing compared to what it felt like now. As he watched the general reading the report—undoubtedly the report on his DUI the night before—Phinney felt like crying. He wouldn't, of course. He'd take it like a man. But God he felt like shit; all he could think of was how he had let the general down, that he had become, God forbid, an embarrassment to his boss, a man he loved like his own father, a man he would do anything for.

"Damn it, Jack, what the hell was going on in your head?" Phinney knew it was not a question to which an answer was expected; he remained at attention, saying nothing. "You know this could be the end of your career. Hell, in the old days we could get one of these every other week and nobody cared. But that's the old days. You can't trip the wrong direction without getting fired nowadays."

Of course Phinney knew all of this, and the general knew he knew it, too. But it seemed right for both of them that it had to be said.

"Do you have anything to say for yourself, Major?"

The word "Major" stung Phinney like a slap in the face. The general almost always referred to his staff by their first names. Phinney had worked for General Wodstrchill for almost two years now as his aide, holding his speeches, getting him a gin and tonic at the many receptions he had with civilians and dignitaries, setting up his golf times at the Langley course or a morning run with the vice president— who, by the way, stayed at Langley as opposed to Norfolk Naval Base, even though he was there for a Navy matter, a point noted by all the military. As commander of Air Combat Command, the general had over one hundred thousand men and women under his command, not to mention the fifteen hundred planes and thirty-five bases throughout the country, all of which were his personal responsibility, his personal problem. But right now his problem was more immediate, and standing in front of him.

"Well, Jack, do you have anything to say?" Explanation time, Phinney thought. Excuses time. Sure he could blame his ex-wife. Or those extra shots of Jeremiah Weed during the crud game. Or a host of other things, all of which were bullshit. No, he thought again, he'd take it like a man. He screwed up, big time. And, the way Phinney had it figured, in about ten seconds the whole world was going to come down on him. And deservedly so.

"No, sir. I screwed up. I have no excuse. I'm sorry that it happened, particularly that I let you down, sir, that I became an embarrassment."

Good, the general thought to himself. No excuses. No crap. No "please-give-me-another-chance" shit. He's a good officer. A good pilot. Wodstrchill decided he was right to have hired him after the

"Bear-H" incident. He knew that long ago. Phinney had always been a good sounding board and had a way with words, as the general well knew since he used Phinney as his final editor of his speeches. A good man.

"Jack, you know that I can't keep you here after this. You understand that, don't you?"

"Yes, sir," Phinney said automatically, knowing it was true. Can't keep me here? A glimmer of survival peeked through the darkness of Phinney's situation. But his mind couldn't think fast enough to figure out what might be happening.

"Go see Colonel Johnson," the general said matter-of-factly. "He'll take care of you."

"Yes, sir." Meeting over. Phinney saluted, about-faced sharply, and left the room, thinking to himself, no goodbye, no "thanks for all the work." Just like it should be. I did my job, just like I was supposed to. I was given one of the best jobs in the Air Force. An opportunity to see where the action is. To see the big picture. To see the big boys—the *really* big boys. And I screwed the pooch. Phinney walked across the commander's anteroom to the director of staff's office.

"Colonel Johnson," Phinney said to the director of staff, "General Wodstrchill said I needed to speak with you."

"Yes, Phinney. Come on in. Would the rest of you excuse us for a moment?" The others left the room. Not a good sign. The worst. Phinney once again stood at attention. The director of staff, as everyone knew, had a lot more important things to do than deal with a miscreant major. He was, in every sense of the word, General Wodstrchill's gatekeeper. Nothing reached the general's desk without being seen by Colonel Johnson, and 90 percent of what Colonel Johnson saw never reached the general's desk. He took care of it. He dealt with it. That was his job, and he loved it. Except this part. Dealing with screwups. They rarely happened—the people who worked for General Wodstrchill were too good, knew exactly what to do and what to avoid. So it was rare that he had to act as disciplinarian, and when he did, everyone knew that he was the worst. "No mistakes. No prisoners." They all heard it a thousand times from him. It was his motto. His mantra, if you will.

"Major Phinney, I am obliged to relieve you of your duties."

Obliged, Phinney noted. In other words ordered. In other words Wodstrchill himself decided this one. Christ, I'm really dead meat. I'm out. Done. A mort. "Yes, sir. I understand, sir."

"You also understand, I assume, that I have the option of issuing you an Article 15 court-martial for conduct unbecoming an officer?"

"Yes, sir. I understand, sir."

"Well," Colonel Johnson almost yelled, "what the hell do you have to say for yourself?"

"Nothing, sir, except that I intend to plead guilty to the DUI and take the consequences, whatever they are."

"You damn right you'll take the consequences! Our country let's us be in charge of nuclear weapons. Our country gives us the privilege—the sacred privilege, damn it—of defending its borders. To let you fly multi-million dollar planes."

"Yes, sir. I'm sorry, sir."

"You damn right you're sorry." There was a pause. The colonel had said what he had to say. He let it sink in, let the major twist slowly in the wind.

"Jack," Colonel Johnson continued now in a business tone, not in anger, "you did a helluva job here. You served the general well. And you're a damn good pilot." Another pause. "Stand at ease, soldier. Let's talk."

Phinney went to at ease, unsure of what was happening.

"I've looked over the report. The civilian authorities haven't been notified yet. It turns out that the security police, when he gave you the breathalyzer, didn't realize that you were chewing gum within the last ten minutes prior to the test. I'm told that that invalidates the test."

Chewing gum? Phinney thought. I haven't chewed gum in ten years!

Colonel Johnson continued: "But that doesn't get you off the hook with me. I don't give a damn if they can't prosecute you downtown on this one. You're guilty as hell. You know it. I know it. So here's the deal. I checked with the Judge Advocate and he tells me that if this thing had been done right you would have been fined $500, your license would have been suspended for sixty days, and you would have been required to have an alcohol evaluation. Plus one hundred hours of community service. You understand?"

"Yes, sir."

"Well, all of that is still going to happen. I'm giving you a LOR today. You got a favorite charity?"

Phinney's mind was spinning. A letter of reprimand? I'm not out? "Ah, well sir, how about the Airman's Attic?"

Colonel Johnson was pleased. Thinking about the little guys—the crew dogs who keep the plane flying, the ones standing outside when it's cold as hell for hours fixing the aircraft scheduled for the next day. This kid's all right, Johnson thought. "That'll be fine. You got five hundred available now?"

"Yes, sir."

"I want that check made out to the Airman's Attic on my desk today by noon."

"Yes, sir."

"Your driving privileges on all ACC bases are revoked for sixty days one week from today. Make whatever arrangements you need to make."

"Yes, sir."

"Here are your orders. Clear off your desk by noon today, and be off base and on your way to Barksdale by noon tomorrow. Can you handle that, Major?"

"Yes, sir. Thank you, sir."

"You'll be working for the Commander, 8th Air Force. He'll decide what to do with you. You report a week from today. That gives you a week to get your act together. You understand?"

All too well. "Yes, sir."

"And, Jack . . . ."

"Yes, sir?"

"Don't let the general down."

He might as well ended the sentence with the word "again," but it was implied, and both men knew it. "Yes, sir. I won't, sir."

"Dismissed."

Phinney left the room in shock. He was being given another chance. He was being sent to Barksdale to work for the general's former vice commander. The general had saved his butt, and he knew it. The first thing he did when he got back to his apartment was to dump every ounce of booze down the drain. He never drank again.

# CHAPTER 7

## Plesetsk Rocket Facility, Russia
## The present

Professor Dmitri Tsinev quietly sat behind the group of minor Moscow officials receiving their annual accolade, a tour of the military rocket facility at Plesetsk. The bus tour of the cosmodrome was a great honor for the officials, especially since it was not long ago that Russia had finally acknowledged even the existence of the Plesetsk facility.

Sitting near the rear of the bus, the tall, middle-aged professor kept to himself. The task was somewhat easier due to the combination of the Tsinev's general appearance as a Westerner—resulting from his short, blondish hair and the modern, plastic lensed glasses—and the dark-green overcoat he wore. Each of the officials immediately recognized Tsinev's coat as the traditional coat previously worn by KGB agents. Tsinev had counted on the recognition of the coat. Although he knew it would engender curiosity, it would also serve to distance himself from the others.

The thirty directors of the *rayony*, the administrative districts used to organize the city of Moscow, knew enough not to question a KGB agent. Although many in the West thought that the KGB had been dissolved and disbanded under the Yeltsin administration, these Russians knew all too well that the KGB still existed, still went to work every day inside the Lubyanka buildings in downtown Moscow and at the dreaded Lefortovo Prison. Indeed, now that Putin was in charge, the old KGB probably had more power than at any time in the last decade.

True, after the collapse of communism the domestic divisions were initially organized as the Federal Counterintelligence Service (or

FSK) by an edict signed by Yeltsin in 1994. A year later, the name of the FSK was changed yet again to the FSB. To most the change seemed inconsequential, but in reality the change was substantial, involving a total restructuring of duties and powers, providing the FSB—now headquartered at Lubyanka—with broad investigatory powers, renewed control over the fourteen investigative detention prisons, and the assignment of several special troop detachments. The old KGB was back even under Yeltsin, in many cases run by the same people, still using many of the same tactics that had made them so famous. One Russian newspaper, the *Moskovkii komsomolets*, went so far as to declare in 1995 that the new service was far more powerful than the old KGB. And, of course, all of the *rayony* directors were well-aware of those new powers. Thus, their willingness to leave Tsinev alone was not surprising.

Earlier, while waiting for the bus that was to take the Moscow officials through the facility, some of the bolder directors speculated, albeit in whispers, that the Westerner was an American who must have forgotten to bring his opulent fur coat. Some foolish Russian FSB agent, so the speculation went, must have loaned his coat to the stupid American so that he would not freeze so close to the Arctic Circle. Another director complained about the new freedom foreigners were being given. Allowing Westerners into Moscow to spend their blood-soaked money was one thing, but to allow them to tour military bases in Russia was beyond foolishness.

After overhearing some of the directors' comments, Tsinev concluded that he had made the right choice by not travelling from Moscow to Plesetsk with the *rayony* directors; his presence on the Antonov An-26 transport plane would have resulted in even more unwanted attention. Worse yet, one of the directors might have become friendly toward him as time went by, making it more difficult to separate himself from the group when it came time to fulfill his mission. During the twenty-minute bus ride from the Plesetsk Airport to the rocket facility, the discussion about the "strange American" dwindled, naturally replaced by a haphazard mix of Party gossip, superficial boasting, and discussion of general matters relating to administrating a *rayon*. As Tsinev had hoped, any remaining concerns about him were lost entirely upon entry into the core facility and the beginning of the twenty-five mile ride along the seemingly endless stretch of launch pads, huge buildings, and circular fuel tanks used to store liquid oxygen.

As the military tour guide rambled out numerous facts and figures, the *rayony* directors strained to see as much of the facility as they could. The directors were awed by the length and breadth of the facility. It is no wonder, Tsinev thought, that Eisenhower was willing to risk another U-2 flight over the Soviet Union a mere two weeks before the Paris Summit of 1960. The Plesetsk Cosmodrome was considered the most vital target of the ill-fated mission flown by Francis Gary Powers, primarily because the United States suspected—correctly, it turned out—that this was the location where the Soviets were deploying their first operational intercontinental ballistic missiles.

After a tour of the base at large, the Party officials and Tsinev were taken to see one of the launch sites first-hand. Tsinev waited for the bureaucrats to exit the bus ahead of him, and then followed the group toward the launch pad. The huge missile, which was scheduled for lift off in three weeks, towered imposingly toward the light-blue sky. Soon the rocket would cut through the Earth's thin layer of air and plunge itself into the dark reality of space.

"No pictures until we enter the bunkerhouse," warned the tour guide, looking particularly at Tsinev. Professor Tsinev nodded his head, letting the young military officer know that he understood what he had said. Tsinev left his "camera" in its case; viewing the rocket was no great concern to Tsinev except for the desire to appear interested.

The rule concerning the taking of photographs was unnecessary. Tsinev knew that unless a person got within ten feet, everything visible to the onlookers had already been photographed by satellites and reviewed time and time again by CIA intelligence officers. The United States had two KH-11 satellites assigned specifically to the Plesetsk complex, one that maintained a geostationary orbit always directed at the facility and another that flew past at various angles to allow accurate interpretation of heights and distances. By this time, some seven days after the rocket had been moved by rail car to the launch pad and erected to a vertical position, experts in Washington had obtained hundreds of photographs of the missile from almost all angles. Now these same American satellites were poised to recover the electronic data sent back from the rocket to the flight control center at Kaliningrad, a suburb some fifteen miles northeast of the center of Moscow.

Tsinev looked upward—not so much at the tip of the rocket, but toward the American KH-11 satellite that he hoped was still operational. He was counting on the continued operation of the satellite circling above him, particularly its ability to pick up a weak VHF signal sent from the device hidden in his camera case.

Professor Tsinev was surprised how much the launch pad reminded him of an off-shore oil rig. The rectangular slab of cement jutted out across a deep, concrete crevice designed to receive the rocket's flames and redirect them away from the rocket when it began to climb away from the ground. Two huge towers, one on each side of the launch pad, reached over one hundred meters into the air. The towers, which looked like radio-station antennas Tsinev had seen in the States, served as lightning rods to divert electrical charges away from the rocket and its highly volatile fuel. Technicians dressed in heavy garb scurried around the launch pad while the *rayony* administrators craned their necks backwards to see the top of the rocket.

The tour guide waited for the group to converge around him, and then began his detailed explanation of the rocket and the technology that surrounded it. He recited his memorized litany without emotion, although he occasionally included emphasis at the required moments of patriotic bravado. He spoke of the great power of the SL-12 rocket booster, informing his listeners that it stood over fifty-three meters high and consisted of four stages. He described how the rocket, nicknamed Proton, could place a twenty-one hundred kilogram satellite into a geostationary orbit, and how its three stage version, the SL-13, could place a satellite weighing over 19,500 kilograms—such as a Salyut space station—into a low orbit around the earth. But according to the tour guide, even these rockets were dwarfed by the huge Energia rocket, that at this moment stood ready for yet another launch into space from the Baikonur Cosmodrome, the place from which Comrade Yuri Gagarin began his epic flight in 1961 to become the first man in space.

"The Energia," concluded the tour guide, "is the most powerful rocket in the world and will lead our great Russia into a new age of space exploration, including the establishment of permanent space stations, such as the new international space station recently put into orbit. The Energia," he said proudly, "is much safer than the American space shuttle, and can lift much more."

The guide did not need to remind his listeners of the accident some years ago in which the entire crew of the American shuttlecraft was killed during lift off; the former Soviets were well aware of the *Challenger* tragedy, as well as their own space-related tragedies over the years. Most demoralizing to the Soviets was the return of the triumphant Salyut 1 crew in 1967 that had circled above the earth in the Soviet Salyut space station for almost six hundred hours, setting a new duration record that almost doubled the previous record set by the Americans in Gemini 7. Following what appeared to be a perfect reentry, the Soviet recovery crews opened the Soyuz 11 spacecraft only to find the three dead Salyut crewmen staring into blankness, victims of a faulty valve that had allowed their oxygen supply to escape during reentry.

"We will now go to the bunker," stated the tour guide, "where you may take pictures if you so desire." The bunker, which in reality was a large concrete-reinforced building positioned approximately one hundred yards away from and slightly below the level of the launch pad, served as a protection area for the workers who must stay close to the rocket until moments before ignition. The bunker also served as the closest location to the rocket that the GRU—the Russian military intelligence agency—would allow the taking of photographs.

The bureaucrats walked quickly into the bunker, lining up with anticipation along the protective windows to get the best possible photograph to frame and place in their offices, a symbol of their great prestige and importance to the government. The officials were so entranced with the technology and the quest for the perfect photograph that none of them noticed the absence of the Western-looking FSB agent.

Tsinev, standing outside the building, paused to make sure he had not been seen. Positioned in the shadow of the bunker, Tsinev reviewed his surroundings. A few moments earlier, as the tour group had entered the bunker, Tsinev had nonchalantly walked along the outside of the building to the side facing away from the rocket. The location was perfect. The bunker had no windows facing to the north, and he was completely shielded from the view of the guards assigned to the launch pad.

A large barren field spread outward toward the north end of the complex. At the end of the field, some three hundred meters away, stood a fence. Although Tsinev could only see the beginning of a forest on the opposite side of the fence, he knew from looking at a detailed Defense Mapping Agency map years before that the Yemtsa River flowed between the fence and the forest, eventually yielding its ice-cold water into the Arctic Sea.

Tsinev moved the camera to his side and opened his coat, removing a thin cylinder taped to the inside seam. He opened the cylinder and carefully removed a silver object some ten inches long and the thickness of a pencil. He unfolded the object, which looked like a small, upside-down umbrella, its thin, metal ribs holding open the silvery reflective paper. Tsinev next unscrewed the lens from his camera and inserted the "umbrella" directly into the opening, clicking the antenna into place.

Reaching inside the beltline of his trousers, Tsinev withdrew a small box containing a miniature cassette tape. After attaching the box to the camera's hot shoe to which a flash would normally be attached, he aimed the antenna straight up and pressed the camera's shutter release, illuminating a light-blue piece of plastic located on the box containing the cassette. The light remained on while Tsinev's message was being sent.

While looking down at the device, Tsinev suddenly noticed a flash of light coming from the forest on the other side of the river. The flash was very bright, undoubtedly a reflection of the sun. Tsinev hoped it had been caused by a passing car, but after seeing a second flash of light from the same location, he knew that it had to be a reflection caused by a camera lens, binoculars, or perhaps even by a scope on a high-powered rifle.

Continuing to hold the signaling device steady, Tsinev looked back down at the camera and saw that the transmission of the message had been completed. He then reassembled the camera, placed the signal box inside the antenna, and crushed the antenna snugly around the box. Placing the ball of crumpled paper into his coat pocket, Tsinev moved toward the sound of the directors as they began leaving the bunker. Easing into the group, he boarded the bus that was to return them to the Plesetsk Airport.

On the way to the main gate of the facility, Tsinev nonchalantly glanced back several times to see if a security vehicle was following them. He did not see any, but knew that this did not mean much. They could be waiting at the entrance gate. But when the bus was allowed to exit the missile facility after the counting of passengers and receiving the best wishes of the military tour guide, Tsinev relaxed considerably. More than likely he had not been seen, and even if he had been, at least it was not by the GRU.

When the bus reached the Plesetsk airport, Tsinev walked with the *rayony* directors into the terminal building. Following several of them into a bathroom, he washed his hands, and then, while drying his hands with a paper towel, he slipped the crumpled antenna inside the used paper towel and calmly threw the crumpled mass into the trash. Exiting the bathroom, he nodded goodbye to one of the directors and walked away from the airport gates and toward the airport parking lot.

Tsinev walked to his car at his usual pace, noting a single set of footsteps behind him. As he opened the trunk of his car and reached down to get his briefcase, he once again heard the footsteps. Keeping his right hand on his briefcase, he carefully reached his left hand inside his open coat and withdrew his pistol from its shoulder harness. The gun, with its silencer already attached, was longer than normal, making it difficult to maneuver underneath Tsinev's coat. Tsinev aimed the gun generally to his right keeping it unseen beneath his coat. Just as the footsteps stopped, Tsinev felt a hand on his right shoulder.

"Excuse me, sir," the man spoke in Russian. "Federal Security Service. I would like to talk with you."

Tsinev looked up at the man's face. He had often seen such a face in the ranks of the old KGB: young, patriotic, and so fervently into "the cause" and his new-found power that he was devoid of common sense and sound reasoning. Tsinev looked down at the agent's open right palm that held the crumpled antenna he had just discarded; the agent's left hand rested flat on Tsinev's shoulder. Tsinev looked at the agent who, though trying to look serious and forceful, could not suppress a slightly superior smile of victory. A camera, with its tele-photo-lens, dangled from his neck, once again glistening in the bright sun.

A good agent, Tsinev thought, would have simply reported a traitor to his superiors, carefully following him until given further orders. There was no rush; double agents were often known to be will-ing to assist the spy agency when caught. But this one wanted to be a hero, to make the arrest alone. The fool hadn't even had the good sense to shield his camera from the sun when he was taking the pic-tures of Tsinev sending the message. But worse yet, and to Tsinev's utter amazement, the young agent failed to have the foresight to draw his gun as he made the arrest. Whether due to ego or forgetfulness, it was stupid just the same. Tsinev released the briefcase and stood up from the trunk, glancing quickly around the parking lot. As he had expected, the young agent was indeed working alone.

"You idiot," Tsinev said in Russian as he placed his right hand on the young man's back. "I'm also FSB." As he finished the sentence, Tsinev fired his gun twice through his coat into the young man's chest. With the help of Tsinev's right hand, the man fell smoothly into the trunk. Tsinev shut the trunk as he returned the pistol and its silencer to the shoulder holster, and then calmly went around to the driver's side of the car. As he unlocked his door, he looked again for any sign that he had been observed. Seeing none, Tsinev casually drove out of the parking lot and toward the forest to the north, where he uncere-moniously dumped the body and the now bloody flooring into a thaw-ing tributary of the Yemtsa River.

An hour later Tsinev returned the rental vehicle to the airport and purchased an Aeroflot ticket to Domodedovo Airport south of Moscow.

# CHAPTER 8

## Misawa Air Base, Japan

Deep in the basement of the windowless, three-story building housing the 2920th Electronic Security Group at Misawa Air Base, Staff Sergeant Stephen Deaton glanced up at his computer console, which had just begun flashing "RP23." Deaton hit the reset button to confirm the message. The screen went blank as the huge CRAY-2 computer reran the frequency control program. A few seconds later, the message reappeared on the console, flashing on and off in one-second intervals. Sergeant Deaton removed his headset, picked up his phone, and pressed three buttons on his console.

"Chief Fowler, this is Steve. I have an RP signal, received 1638." Deaton waited needlessly for a reply, knowing that Chief Master Sergeant Hadley Fowler would not waste words—or time—with the usual, "Thank you, Sergeant," or "I'll be right there," or even an "OK." Fowler's aversion to small talk was known throughout the 2920th, so much so that when Fowler did speak, everyone, including the officers, shut up and listened. As Deaton expected, the short silence at the other end of the receiver was followed by a firm "click."

As he waited for Chief Fowler to arrive at his console, Deaton thought about the hundreds of "RP" signals he had received while he had been stationed at Misawa. As a senior listener, Deaton spent most of his time listening to and translating high-level Russian military transmissions. In addition to his assignment to monitor Russian high-command frequencies, Deaton was also assigned to all RP frequencies. Although no one at Misawa knew what the abbreviation meant, the six senior listeners all assumed that "RP" stood for "Russian Priority" signals sent by friendly agents from inside Russia. Deaton studied the flashing signal, pondering the fact that he had never seen a two-digit RP code before; all previous RP signals that Deaton had observed had been followed by a three-digit number. Deaton knew, of course, that in code-making and in security hierarchy, the lower the number, the higher the priority. This, thought Deaton, might be something special.

Immediately after hanging up the receiver, Chief Master Sergeant Douglas A. Fowler walked through the open door of his office and down the several steps to the command center. Fowler's office overlooked the seven rows of operators sitting at their consoles, listening intently to their earphones.

For twenty-five years Fowler had been stationed at Misawa. In those twenty-five years, Fowler had witnessed seventeen major overhauls of computer and receiving equipment. Initially designed to pick up relatively minor military radio signals emanating from mainland China and the Russian naval base at Vladivostok, the importance of Misawa increased with advances in technology. From 1958 to 1965, the 2920th's stock of equipment and commensurate duties had increased exponentially, primarily due to the Soviet's use of Sakhalin Island and the Kamchatka Peninsula as target points for Soviet ICBM tests. Fowler arrived on the scene in 1963, a young sergeant fluent in Russian and knowledgeable about computers. Within twelve years he reached the position of senior analyst, acting as the "SW" (surveillance-and-warning supervisor) during day shifts. It was Fowler's job to realize when something important had been received, and to send it on to Washington immediately. Interestingly, the task of listening to incoming signals was left to noncommissioned officers and their noncom supervisor; except for the commander of the 2920th, who would be informed of important communications after the supervisor relayed the information to Washington, officers were used only as interpreters, synthesizing the thousands of important signals into an intelligible theory.

Chief Fowler walked over to Deaton's station holding the SW manual and his plastic clipboard in his right hand.

"Have you confirmed the signal, Mr. Deaton?"

"Yes, sir."

As long as anyone could remember, Chief Fowler spoke to enlisted personnel without reference to their rank. Some thought this minor deviance in protocol showed Fowler's respect for the enlisted personnel, many of whom had more education than the officers in their unit. All enlisted personnel assigned to Misawa were in the top 5 percent of Air Force enlisted personnel based on intelligence quotients and had had intense specialized training in languages, code-breaking, and computer technology.

Fowler opened the SW manual, even though he knew the procedure for RP receptions by heart. One of the first rules of the 2920th was never, absolutely never, rely on your memory when it came to procedure; failure to use the books at any point in the process was grounds for suspension or transfer. Everyone stationed there knew that the smallest mistake in procedure could result in the misinterpretation of a message, or even make it impossible to transmit the message on to Washington. Even more importantly, some subtle changes in procedure were actually used to convey a separate internal message. Thus, at the 2920th, procedure was king, and the manuals God.

"Length of message?" asked Fowler as he flipped through the pages of the manual.

Sergeant Deaton pressed the letter "L" and "ENTER."

"Fifteen seconds." Fowler had not seen an RP message of this length in over twenty years. Since the advent of digital transponders that were used to send compact "burst" messages, the average length of a message was now measured in hundredths of a second. Christ, Fowler thought, in fifteen seconds he could send us the text of *War and Peace.*

"Frequency?" Fowler asked.

Deaton pressed the letter "F" and "ENTER." The screen went blank, then showed a five-second countdown. During the countdown Chief Fowler inserted a five-digit code into the push buttons on the console. A few seconds later a set of letters signifying the frequency appeared on the screen.

Fowler read the frequency code and then looked down at his SW manual. "Packet T-14."

Deaton reached forward and unlocked the metal cabinet to the left of his computer console. As he unlocked the cabinet a red light on the top of Deaton's console began flashing. Fowler pushed five more digits into the panel of the console, and, as the light went off, the cabinet opened mechanically. Deaton checked through the alphabetized envelopes that contained the coding and process instructions, pulling out the one marked "T-14." As Deaton placed the envelope on the desk, the cabinet, which was designed to allow the removal of only one envelope at a time, automatically closed. Chief Fowler continued following the instructions from his manual.

Deaton followed the normal RP procedure; he broke the seal, removed the 3x8 plastic card and placed it face up between the two sergeants.

Chief Fowler read the contents of the card out loud in a low voice that only Deaton could hear: "Mr. Deaton, I show a transcribe, internal encode, encrypt by random sequence, and pouch stat. Do you concur?"

"Yes sir. I confirm the instructions as 'TRANSCRIBE, IN-ENCODE, ENCRYPT ASTERISK, POUCH STAT.'"

Deaton and Fowler were both surprised by the message. On all previous RP signals, they were merely instructed to transfer the digitized signal to Washington by encrypting the untranslated message and sending it on to the National Security Agency by radio on a pre-arranged, random-based modulating frequency. Here, however, they were being told to actually transcribe the message, and then forward it to Washington not by radio but by hand delivery. Neither Deaton nor Fowler had ever been required to do this before.

Chief Fowler paused, looking down at the INSTRUCT card. "Before we translate this puppy, why don't we double check the INSTRUCT card?" Both Fowler and Deaton knew that after transcribing an RP signal they would be confined to the communications command center until further notice, which meant waiting days, and sometimes weeks, for release orders from Washington. Neither Fowler nor Deaton relished the idea of being under the equivalent of house-arrest, even if it was for their own protection.

"Reconfirm the signal, Mr. Deaton."

Sergeant Deaton entered "RESET" and watched as "RP23" once again appeared on the screen. Deaton then once again requested a frequency readout from the computer. Once the frequency code was displayed, Fowler reopened his SW manual to the appropriate page and confirmed envelope "T-14." He then picked up the plastic card and assured himself, by looking at the printing at the top right corner of the card, that Deaton had selected the correct envelope.

"Request digital transcription, Mr. Deaton."

Deaton typed in "DIGTRAN" and pressed "ENTER."

The screen went blank, then read "Inappropriate command."

"Explain," Fowler said.

Deaton typed in "EXPLAIN" and pressed "ENTER."

The screen flashed its green-tinted message: "Incoming signal not digital. It is audio."

Deaton began to whistle softly, but was cut short by Chief Fowler's firm but quiet voice.

"Request audio RP23." Deaton did so, and watched the screen once again go blank.

While waiting for the computer to locate the transmission, Fowler wondered how anybody could get away with sending a nondigitized, audio transmission out of Russia. Several possibilities came to mind. Perhaps the agent's digitizer had failed. This possibility, however, was rather unlikely; digitizers are relatively simple devices that were one hundred times less likely to fail than other radio parts. Perhaps the agent had to construct a radio out of scratch; but how could he have obtained a crystal which would be set precisely on this particular top secret frequency? No, the radio crystal had to have been brought into Russia by the agent or a courier. And if he was able to sneak in the crystal, he should have also been able—not to mention required—to sneak in a digitizer. The only other possibility left was that the transmitter, or the agent, had been in place prior to the time when miniature digitizers were developed. If so, the agent must have been in the Soviet Union a long, long time.

Deaton interrupted Fowler's thoughts: "Audio ready, sir."

Fowler looked down at the console screen that required the inputting of his ten-letter personal code which would allow the computer to playback the RP audio transmission. Fowler and Deaton plugged in their earphone jacks and pulled out their clipboards and markers. Fowler then inserted the code and, leaning over the console, began writing the message onto the clipboard in tandem with Deaton.

When the message was completed, the two men silently compared messages. Fowler initiated the formal double check.

"Mr. Deaton, do you find the messages identical?"

"I do," Deaton replied. "Chief Fowler, do you find the messages identical?"

"I do. Type the message into the subauxiliary system, Mr. Deaton."

"Message typed on screen, sir. Do you confirm?"

Fowler compared the computer display with the message written on his clipboard. "I confirm typed message. Encode, Alpha Two."

"Encoding complete, sir."

"Digitize, using 2461."

Deaton ordered the computer to digitize the encoded message, employing one of the four-digit modem codes assigned to Fowler that told the computer which encrypting code to employ. Once the message was received at the National Security Agency, the massive CRAY-2 computer at Fort Meade would feed in each of the matrixes until it came across the matrix used by Fowler.

"Digitizing complete, sir."

"Request readout."

"Readout requested and printing."

To the right of Fowler and Deaton, a laser printer pushed out a listing of numbers that covered the entire page.

"Purge the auxiliary system, Mr. Deaton." Sergeant Deaton typed "AUXPUR" and pressed "ENTER."

"Auxiliary system purged." The typed transcription of the message disappeared from the screen and, coincidentally, from the auxiliary computer.

"Compartmentalize transmission, Code A2." By compartmentalizing the transmission, access to the audio tape and RP code-number was limited to a narrow subgroup of the 2920th. "Code A2" meant that only the senior officer, the commander of the 2920th, had access to the material just compartmentalized.

"Transmission compartmentalized, Code A2, sir."

Deaton and Fowler walked over to the printer. With Deaton watching, Fowler pulled out the printed digitized message, folded it in quarters, and placed it into a small, plastic folder that had the appearance of black leather. Fowler then placed the plastic folder into a small press machine which thermal-sealed all four sides. Deaton picked up his phone and requested a courier. A few moments later, Fowler withdrew the pouch from the sealing machine as two armed guards and a captain appeared at the panel window of the control room. Fowler walked over to the control room's only door, entered the code into the electronic lock, opened the door, and handed the pouch to the captain. No words were needed because the captain, through the color of the pouch, knew immediately that he was to deliver the pouch to the C-21 constantly on alert on the runway, ready to fly essential documents to the National Security Agency and to the Pentagon at a moment's notice.

# CHAPTER 9

## CIA Headquarters, Langley, Virginia

Thomas Myers completed the security check and entered Phillip Jackson's office at CIA headquarters at Langley, Virginia. Myers walked over to Jackson's administrative assistant, asking her to inform Jackson that he needed to see him. She immediately left her desk and entered the deputy director's office. Jackson had been the deputy director for operations for the CIA for about one year. Although considered bright and capable, he was generally disliked.

Jackson's assistant returned almost immediately. Holding the door open for Myers, she stated, "The director will see you now."

"Be with you in a minute, Myers," Jackson said as Myers entered through the doorway. Myers sat down in front of Jackson's desk and waited, noticing Jackson's initials embroidered onto the cuffs of his tailored-made shirt, yet another confirmation to Myers of Jackson literally wearing his blue-blood, Harvard background and his substantial wealth, primarily through a fortuitous marriage, on his sleeves. Jackson continued to review the stack of documents at his desk, barely looking up at the lower-ranking Myers. Myers had spent the last twenty-five years seeing these types come and go, but usually they were placed in the political realm of the agency instead of operations. At least in the other areas, Myers thought to himself, they were relegated to just screwing up the budget and looking important. Mistakes in operations, however, costs lives, which made Myers all the more careful around Jackson, even if he was his boss.

"Okay, Myers," Jackson said barely looking up from his papers, "what do you have?"

"A Class 1 message from a Zebra agent."

"Which agent?"

"Zebra 25," Myers answered. The deputy director set aside the document he was reviewing and finally looked directly at Myers.

"Let me see the text." Myers handed him a light-blue sheet of paper.

"It's from an old Elvis Presley song," Myers commented as Jackson read the message. The CIA had often used the lyrics of well-known songs for messages in order to make it easier for agents to memorize the numerous messages they needed to know.

"I know that, Myers," Jackson responded coldly. "But what does it mean?"

"Well, sir, for this particular agent, 'one for the money' means he has Class 1 information; 'two for the show' means he's under surveillance and can't get out by normal means; 'three to get ready' means he is asking to be retrieved three weeks from the date the message was sent; and 'go man go' means he has to be picked up by a plane inside Russia at the prearranged landing site."

"Which is?"

"For Zebra 25, the site is Chara, a small town in southeastern Siberia, just north of Mongolia."

★          ★          ★          ★

## Office of the National Security Advisor, The White House

"How can I help you, Mr. Jackson?" Frank Jenkins asked the CIA deputy director for operations.

"We have received a priority message from one of our agents in Russia," Jackson began. "The message indicated that he has Class 1 vital information, and that he can't get out through a border because he is under surveillance. He therefore has requested a fly-in pick-up at a prearranged point."

The national security advisor sat relaxed behind his desk, while his deputy, Paul Fuller, sat on a couch at the side of the room taking notes. Jenkins and Fuller had been through much during the last six months; both men were relatively new to their jobs, due to the sudden departure of the former national security advisor and his deputy. The last national security advisor had been forced to resign, the sacrificial lamb of yet another botched, not to mention illegal, arms sale. Jenkins had been brought in to provide integrity and stability at the National Security Council, the primary entity established by the National Security Act of 1947 to provide advice to the president. The NSC, consisting of the national security advisor, the president, vice president, secretary of state, and secretary of defense (with the participation of the chairman of the joint chiefs of staff), was in charge of reviewing and directing all foreign intelligence and counterintelligence activities.

One of Jenkins' first acts was to remove the NSC from the practice of initiating and directly planning actual operations. Instead, the NSC had returned to its role of advising the president and looking at the "Big Picture." Nonetheless, the national security advisor remained an important link in obtaining approval for covert operations; only the president has the authority to approve such operations, and before the president approves any covert activities, he looks to the National Security Council for its recommendation. And Jackson knew that during the last six months, the president had given the go-ahead only to those operations that Jenkins supported.

Jackson's presence meant two things to Jenkins. First, a major operation was in the works, and second, the operation required presidential approval. Now, in the midst of congressional investigations and talk of indictments, the last thing the NSC needed was an operation to go wrong.

Jenkins, having completed a three-year term as the second in command at the CIA some ten years ago, remembered Jackson well. At that time Jackson was in charge of the Soviet Intelligence Division. Although a capable man, he was known to throw his weight around. While serving as the deputy director of Central Intelligence, Jenkins had heard numerous complaints about Jackson. Many were trivial personality conflicts; but there were also complaints of substance, complaints about Jackson's failure to listen to the other side or spot weaknesses in a plan, especially when Jackson thought he was right. And, of course, Jackson—like many operators at the CIA—was prone to exaggerate his importance, and the importance of his agents in the field.

Jenkins also knew because of his experience at the CIA that Class 1 information was defined as information vital to the immediate security of the United States. And although Jenkins had never been informed of the details of the high-level mole inside the former Soviet Union, he knew from reading the compartmentalized special insight reports that the United States had a friend very high in the old KGB, someone who had access to extremely sensitive civilian and military information. Jenkins was personally aware of at least twelve incidents where the reports suddenly pointed the CIA to Russian agents and American spies who were providing information to Russia. No one had to discuss either the source or the method. Only high-level HUMINT (human intelligence) could have provided this type of information. So such a message made sense to Jenkins. Perhaps this is the man the CIA wanted to get out. Why else would Jackson dare to suggest such an operation at such an inopportune time?

"How do we know he really has Class 1 information?" Jenkins asked. "What if he just thinks that he's in danger and wants out?"

"That's very doubtful," Jackson replied. "He's been in there for over twenty years. He's risen to great heights in their bureaucracy." Jenkins smiled at the veiled euphemism for the KGB and its replacement agency. "He's had numerous opportunities to get out—in fact, he's scheduled to come to the West six months from now."

"Then why the rush?" Jenkins asked.

"That's just the point. It must be something very important. He has access to almost all military and intelligence operations. He's very deep cover. He's never even been assigned to one of our station chiefs or a case officer. Only the head of the agency and myself know of his existence as an operative."

Lieutenant General Paul Fuller, Jenkins' deputy, spoke up from the couch: "Can't we get the information through a contact?"

Jackson turned toward General Fuller. Realizing that the Army general was relatively new to the business of espionage, Jackson accepted the fact that he would have to explain some of the underlying rationale to General Fuller. Nonetheless, Jackson also knew that Fuller was not to be underestimated. Hand-picked by the president to be Jenkin's deputy, Fuller initially declined the appointment, preferring to remain as commander of the Army's Fifth Corps in Germany.

Over the years Fuller had served throughout the world, including two tours in Vietnam. In Vietnam he received two of his eleven medals for rescuing several of his men from a burning plane.

"No," Jackson explained, "we can't use a contact to get the information out. The agent has no contact inside Russia, and according to the type of message he sent, he is under surveillance. If he's under surveillance, he's under suspicion. And that means if we send a contact to meet him, our man would just suspect it was a trap. In addition, for all we know the information may relate to a double agent on *this* side of the water. If that's the case, he won't talk to anyone, not even our boys."

"All right," Jenkins continued. "So we can't get to him. But he got to us. How did we get his message."

"By satellite—audio, high-frequency modulation, prerecorded." Jackson knew the next question. "He doesn't have any other equipment. He has ten different emergency signals he can send, all prerecorded. His purpose as an agent is to learn as much as he can in deep cover, and then when appropriate, get back out. Normally that's done by having him 'defect' the next time he's in the U.S. or a friendly country. Apparently he won't be able to do that in this situation. Either they're on to him, or he has something that's so important that he has to get it to us immediately."

"Doesn't he have any other sending equipment? A sender, or even a code key?"

"No. The prerecorded audio equipment is all we dared to send in with him at that time."

"Great!" Jenkins paused. He was unconcerned about the danger of sending in someone to get the agent. Whoever accepted the mission would know the risks. What bothered him was the potential repercussions, particularly after Pope's recent conviction as a spy. Even if the plan succeeded, there could be problems. The old Soviet Union, more so than any other country, considered its borders sacred. To cross them without permission is an insult of more than international magnitude. And if it failed? There must be another way, Jenkins thought. "Why can't he just get us the information by a drop or something?"

"He can't be seen giving us information. We assume that if he leaves a package, a paper, anything at all, they'll grab it."

"Any chance we could have a drop at the embassy?" Fuller asked.

"Very unlikely. Being under surveillance, he probably wouldn't get within two hundred yards of the embassy. Once in, they would know that he's a double agent, and he would have to stay there the rest of his life. They certainly wouldn't let one of their own leave the country, especially someone this high up."

"If what he has is that important," Fuller continued, "he should be willing to do that." General Fuller knew that double agents are in reality merely high-risk soldiers, soldiers who know their duty and have to be willing to make whatever sacrifice is necessary.

"He probably is willing to do so," Jackson replied, "but we're not. That would be most disastrous for our espionage program. One of our best selling points is that when they're through, they can defect to the United States and live in luxury, at least compared to their standards. Just as everyone will know that he came to the United States if we get him out, everyone will also know if he was forced to give his information to the embassy and then left there to rot. He is instructed to try to get out and to use the embassy only as the very last option."

Jackson, thinking that he might be losing the momentum, tried to turn the focus away from the method of getting the agent out and direct it back toward the reason for getting him out. "He wouldn't send a call-out message unless it was of the utmost importance."

"Hmmm, hmm." Jenkins didn't sound convinced, but his job was to be a skeptic, to question everything. "Okay. If we did go with the pick-up, how would we be able to confirm the pick-up location and date?"

"The date is predetermined; three weeks from the date the message was sent."

"If it's such a huge priority," Fuller asked, "why wait three weeks?"

Jackson was impressed. What he had heard about Fuller was true. Fuller may not know the intricacies of espionage, Jackson thought, but he sure knows the right questions to ask. "There's a message that could have been used for an immediate pick-up," Jackson explained. "It can only be used when necessary to prevent an 'ultimate mistake,' such as a first-strike nuclear attack. Otherwise, we have found through experience over the years that three weeks or so is the most appropriate delay. When an agent sends out the signal, there is a chance that it will be picked up. If any part of the signal is picked up, the first two weeks are high risk, for him and for us. After two weeks, their guard normally drops substantially. In addition, we alternate the actual number of days with each agent so there isn't a pattern. This agent is assigned exactly twenty-one days." Jackson paused, turning back toward Jenkins. "It also gives us time to prepare a workable plan."

Jenkins considered the matter in silence, resting his feet on the corner of his desk, his head angled toward the ceiling. How would it be presented to the president? If the mission were approved, when would we inform the Senate and House committees on intelligence? Could we waive congressional disclosure by executive order? Could a feasible plan be developed in the short time available?

Jenkins turned back toward Jackson. "What about the location?"

"The location was previously selected. Each agent is given three border locations, three coastal locations, and one airfield. By the message he sent—which includes reference to close surveillance—it is clear that he will not be allowed to get near a border or near a coast without being detained. That only leaves an air pick-up."

"What if that location won't work?"

"We can pick another by leaving a marked map or the name of the location of the pick-up. Leaving him information isn't really a problem; that's relatively easy to do. Of course, it also has its risks. Someone could intercept the map or message. In any event, I've already looked into the prearranged location, and it seems to be perfect."

"When would we have to leave a drop to give a new location?"

"Anytime, though preferably within the first week after receiving the signal. He will have to make some arrangements to get to the spot."

"What about his surveillance?"

"Usually there are only one or two FSB agents assigned to an inside man when he is under suspicion and not near a border. It's when our people head for a border that the old KGB would bring in reinforcements. We assume they have kept the same basic precautions. It would be the agent's responsibility to terminate the tag-a-longs, preferably right before the pick-up—so as not to arouse suspicion, missed check-in's, that type of thing."

"Well, I'll tell you this, Jackson. I'm not taking this to the boss until we've checked into it. I want your people to thoroughly check this thing out. I want to know everything about the agent. Have his complete folder put on my desk by tomorrow. You guys run an intelligence scoop on him. I want to know what you know, what you don't know, and what you think. I want the CIA's assessment, and I want the J-2's assessment. If anything smells funny, we don't go. While your people are doing that, let's have some of the fly boys look into the feasibility of flying in without being detected. The last thing we need is another Gary Powers or Pope incident."

"Well, sir," Jackson said nervously, "we hadn't planned on using the Air Force, except maybe for support. We've already begun setting our people up to fly in."

"Yeah, I bet you have. You CIA guys are good at cloak and dagger, but you and I both know how often you've flown into Russia lately. No, we'll leave this to the experts. Besides, they won't be as gung-ho; if it can't be done, they'll tell me." Jackson cringed slightly at the obvious insult. "If, on the other hand, they say it can be done, then I'll consider taking it up to the committee." In other words, the National Security Council, with the president, the vice president, the national security advisor, the secretary of defense, the secretary of state, and the chairman of the joint chiefs of staff participating.

"There's one other thing, sir."

Jenkins smiled to himself. You weaselly bastard, he thought, what had you planned on leaving out? "Yes?"

"The pick-up has to be by someone he knows. That's part of the signal. If the pilot isn't someone he knows, he's supposed to terminate him and find another way out."

"Great!" Jenkins replied. "Well, I'm still going to use the Air Force. You better hope they have a pilot who knows this agent, or he'll have to swim home."

So, Jackson thought, Jenkins is going to be a pain in the ass. So be it.

"Anything else?" Jackson asked as he closed his folder.

"No, except be thorough on this one, Jackson. We've had too many fiascos already in the last year. I don't want another one, especially with treaty signings possibly coming up in the next few years. The president won't be too happy if that gets screwed up. Get me your personal report before the weekend, with the file on the agent. I'll ask the chairman to get someone from the Air Force ready to brief me on Monday morning on the preliminary plan and its feasibility. I would suggest that your next stop should be the chairman's office."

"Yes, sir."

Jenkins looked down at his desk, ready to begin work on other matters, as Fuller escorted Jackson to the door. "And Paul," Jenkins added, looking up at the two men, "I think you should ask someone from here to go with Jackson when he briefs General Scott, just so they understand the importance of this mission. Why not send Gail Smith; she's excellent on Russian intelligence, and she understands covert ops."

"Yes, sir," General Fuller replied, knowing all too well that Smith was being sent to keep an eye on Jackson and to make sure the military was given free rein to reject the operation if they thought it wouldn't work. Jackson also knew that sending Smith to the briefing was a definite blow directed at him, showing how little Jenkins trusted Jackson. Fine, thought Jackson. I'll just run it by the president's chief-of-staff. I've known him for years. He'll listen to me. The hell with Jenkins. My view will be heard by the president. One way or the other. But first, I've got to get the national security advisor to recommend the mission to the president. The rest, Jackson thought, would be easy.

# CHAPTER 10

## The Moscow Conservatory, Russia

Randy Broughton, air attache to the American Embassy, milled about among the crowd as he nonchalantly looked for Falcon. The upstairs area of the Conservatory was filled with people as they walked along the hallways bordering the various entrances to the balcony. The concert, at least thus far, had been a good one, as Broughton had expected since Igor Zhukov served as the conductor. The second set had been Mozart, violin concert in G major KV 190. Zhukov was superb, and of course very Russian. Broughton loved Russian conductors; their profound and exaggerated movements alternated between a forceful ballet and a fist fight with an unseen overpowering enemy. At one point an usher—at the farthest corner of the farthest right balcony—spoke too loudly while seating a late patron. The perfect acoustics of the French-style concert hall carried her voice throughout the audience, even to Zhukov's ears as he conducted the seventy-five piece orchestra. Turning backward and to his right, Zhukov's body twisted, his eyes filled with fire and rage at the sound. A slight pause in the music resulted—perhaps no more than an eighth of a beat—but more than enough to demonstrate Zhukov's fury. Russian passion, and Russian anger, at its best, Broughton thought to himself as he smiled at the moment.

At the intermission Broughton walked over to the long line of people waiting to buy juice or ice cream bars. Unlike the rock concert he attended just a few nights ago, no wine or champagne would be served. Broughton smiled at the thought of attending his first Russian rock concert back in 1994. The still reserved Moscow audience sat absolutely still as the concert progressed, seemingly ignoring the wonderful beat. But now, Broughton thought to himself, thanks to MTV being played on Russian television, all of this has changed. Broughton's thoughts were interrupted, however, by a man in his late-fifties who walked directly up to him and joined him in line.

"Thank you for waiting for me," he said as if the two had attended the concert together and the latter had just returned from the bathroom. Broughton himself did not know his true name, only his call-sign: Falcon. Nonetheless, he had been told by his intel briefers to use the first name of Victor, and did so.

"My pleasure, Victor," Broughton replied in a normal voice, without missing a beat. "Wasn't Zhukov's rendition of Mozart superb? I can hardly wait for his Tchaikovsky."

The older man glanced around casually as he cleaned his glasses on his silk handkerchief. Now he lowered his voice slightly so only the two of them could hear each other easily. "Yes. Yes. Me, too. How have things been going?"

"I have had a touch of the flu lately," Broughton replied noting Falcon's repetition, "but it will pass."

"Indeed it will. Indeed it will."

Once again a repetition, Broughton thought. "And how is your family?" Broughton asked, also casually looking around as if bored.

"Very well, thank you."

"And work?" Broughton inquired now looking at Falcon directly.

"Work is work."

"Yes. I suppose it is." Okay, already, Broughton thought to himself, I've got the point. Enough with the repetition. Tell me what the message is.

"At least I got to go fishing lately, but unfortunately I have not had much success."

Broughton didn't understand. He had only known Falcon for a few months, knew he was considered the Embassy's most important contact, especially following the Ames' spy scandal. Luckily, Ames never knew about Falcon; his existence was kept to only a few people within the CIA. With so many agents dead thanks to Ames, Falcon's importance had quadrupled in the last few years. Broughton knew that he had to memorize every word, every nuance. But fishing? What the hell did that mean? "That is unfortunate," Broughton replied, feeling it was a safe, albeit lame, response.

"Very unfortunate," Falcon continued. "The sturgeon don't seem to be biting at all."

Sturgeon! Finally something he understood. "True," Broughton replied without showing an ounce of emotion. "But those are supposed to be rather rare."

"That is just the thing," Falcon said matter-of-factly as he angled his head downward so no one could read his lips. "There seems to be a great shortage this year."

"Haven't you had any luck in the usual places?"

"Oh yes, certainly." Falcon paused as he brought his handkerchief upward to his mouth, as if to cough. "But there should be many more," he mumbled quietly through the handkerchief.

Broughton immediately understood Falcon's point. "Perhaps the fisheries are well-stocked."

"That's the surprising thing. The fisheries have done very well, but it seems that not all of them made it to the sea." Falcon shoved his hands into his pants pockets and turned to the side, now adding the look of impatience at standing in line to his studied demeanor of boredom and normalcy. "Apparently there was a problem some years ago in transferring them to the water."

"Oh really?" Broughton paused, thinking. If this were true he needed more information. Much more information. What to ask? He wasn't a spy! He was a pilot, a bomber pilot. He tried to think quickly sensing that Falcon had finished saying what he wanted to say and was preparing to leave. "I understand that if the temperature is too different there can be problems. Have many fish died in the process?"

For the first time Falcon looked directly into Broughton's eyes. "Several dozen. Maybe more."

Broughton suppressed the urge to say "Shit." "That's especially unfortunate if they're ready to lay eggs."

"Yes," Falcon said calmly. "That is also possible."

Broughton studied Falcon as they paused. He seemed relaxed, no longer in a rush to leave. "So tell me," Broughton continued still trying to get more information, "do you have a favorite fishing spot?"

Falcon appeared thoughtful, at peace in the crowd and the situation. "No. Not any more. Although I'm sure I'll be able to find one in the general area. I just hate to ask my friends if they know of one."

"Why not?" Broughton asked as they approached the counter.

"I do not think they know anything about it. And if I were to ask they will think I have too much time on my hands. Even a rumor of that would be very costly." Falcon paused as he paid two hundred rubles for the ice cream cone. "It seems that I'll just have to find the fishing spot on my own, or take up hunting instead, perhaps up north." Falcon nodded, indicating the conversation was over.

"Well, good luck, my friend," Broughton said as Falcon picked up a napkin off the counter. "I look forward to seeing you again soon."

"Thank you. Please tell your staff hello for me."

"I will," Broughton said as Falcon walked away. You're damn right I will! he thought to himself.

# CHAPTER 11

## CIA Headquarters, Langley, Virginia

CABLE 1093:  TOP SECRET/COMPARTMENTALIZED
DIRECTOR AND DEPUTY DIRECTOR EYES ONLY
FROM:  Moscow Foreign Affairs Office
RE:  Transcript (Unrecorded) of discussion with Falcon

| | |
|---|---|
| FALCON: | Thank you for waiting for me. |
| CONTACT: | My pleasure, ————-.  Wasn't Zhukov's rendition of Mozart superb?  I can hardly wait for his Tchaikovsky. |
| FALCON: | Yes.  Yes.  Me, too.  How have things been going? |
| CONTACT: | I have had a touch of the flu lately, but it will pass. |
| FALCON: | Indeed it will.  Indeed it will. |
| CONTACT:: | And how is your family? |
| FALCON: | Very well, thank you. |
| CONTACT: | And work? |
| FALCON: | Work is work. |
| CONTACT: | Yes.  I suppose it is. |
| FALCON: | At least I got to go fishing lately, but unfortunately I have not had much success. |
| CONTACT: | That is unfortunate. |
| FALCON: | Very unfortunate.  The sturgeon don't seem to be biting at all. |
| CONTACT:: | True.  But those are supposed to be rather rare. |
| FALCON: | That is just the thing.  There seems to be a great shortage this year. |

| | |
|---|---|
| CONTACT: | Haven't you had any luck in the usual places? |
| FALCON: | Oh yes, certainly. But there should be many more. |
| CONTACT: | Perhaps the fisheries are well-stocked. |
| FALCON: | That's the surprising thing. The fisheries have done very well, but they do not make it to the sea. Apparently there was a problem some years ago in transferring them to the water. |
| CONTACT: | Oh really? I understand that if the temperature is too different there can be problems. Have many fish died in the process? |
| FALCON: | Many dozen. Maybe more. |
| CONTACT: | That's especially unfortunate if they're ready to lay eggs. |
| FALCON: | Yes. That is quite possible. |
| CONTACT: | So tell me, do you have a favorite fishing spot? |
| FALCON: | No. Not any more. Although I'm sure I'll be able to find one in the general area. I just hate to ask my friends if they know of one. |
| CONTACT:: | Why not? |
| FALCON: | I do not think they know anything about it. And if I were to ask they will think I have too much time on my hands. Even a rumor of that would be very costly. It seems that I'll just have to find the fishing spot on my own, or take up hunting instead, perhaps up north. |
| CONTACT: | Well, good luck, my friend. I look forward to seeing you again soon. |
| FALCON: | Thank you. Please tell your staff hello for me. |
| CONTACT:: | I will. |

**END OF TRANSCRIPT**

The director was not impressed. "So what? They're talking about fishing spots. Why should I call an NSA meeting because of this?"

"Well, sir, as I mentioned, we interpret this to be a very serious matter."

The intel officer looked decidedly nervous today, the director thought. So much mumbo jumbo in this spy crap. I should have stayed a judge; how the hell am I supposed to know whether this is a bunch of bullshit? "Okay. Then tell me what the hell it means."

"Well, sir, when he repeats words like he did at the beginning that means he has a message. If he doesn't do that the contact leaves as soon as possible to prevent any suspicion."

"All right. What else?"

"By repeating words two times, actually three times, he is signally the importance of the message. Usually they use the repetition signal only twice, but since this was a new contact we think Falcon did it a third time just to make sure he didn't miss it."

"You mean we're dealing with a new guy here?"

"Yes, sir. But he's Air Force, very well-trained, and has a particularly good memory for details. We believe the transcript is extremely accurate, probably word-for-word."

"Okay," the director replied in a bored tone. "So what does the rest mean?"

"Well, sir, the initial reference to fishing seems to be just an introduction to the topic that he raises in his next statement."

"The statement about the sturgeon?"

"Yes, sir. We believe the reference to 'sturgeon' is clearly a reference to the Russian's SS-N-20 solid-fueled, sea-launched ballistic missile."

"Because of the NATO designation?"

"Yes, sir."

"He says the sturgeon don't seem to be biting."

"Yes, sir. That, combined with the reference to the shortage, refers, we believe to the source's statement that the Russians are missing some of their SS-N-20 missiles."

"Missing?"

"Yes, sir," the younger man said nervously. He knew the director's reputation of not wanting to hear bad news, especially if he could construe that bad news as speculation.

"Well, where are they supposed to be?"

"Sir, until we received this report we believed that all 120 SS-N-20s were aboard the Russian's six Typhoon subs, and the additional ten or so were in the depot outside of Nerpichya. However, based on this conversation and the repeated reliability of this Russian contact, we believe that, at the very least, there is a good chance that that assumption was incorrect."

"Are you telling me the Russians pulled the missiles out of their subs and put them somewhere else?"

"No, sir. We have reason to believe that the subs continue to be fully equipped with all of the SS-N-20s that we knew of. That is why our contact mentions the rarity of the missiles, and the contact replies that there seems to be a shortage this year, that they have looked in the usual places, and that there should be many more."

"So?"

"We had assumed that there were only 130 operational SS-N-20s in existence, but that was assuming that the initial one hundred or so that were produced were destroyed in the fire at the Biysk production plant in 1986. Our contact asks whether the fisheries, meaning the rocket facilities that manufacture the missiles, are fully stocked."

"And?"

"The contact states the fisheries 'have done very well, but they do not make it to the sea.' Since we know the subs are still filled with the 120 SS-N-20s we knew about, we are forced to assume there are some SS-N-20s we didn't know about, and that those missiles did not reach the subs or the sub storage facilities. Our contact understood what Falcon was saying and asked for a number, and was told 'Many dozen. Maybe more.' And that is the amount previously thought to have been destroyed in the fire at the Biysk plant."

"So you're telling me that the Russians are missing one hundred or so intercontinental ballistic missiles?"

"That's a very real possibility, sir."

"And the reference to 'laying eggs'?"

"An inquiry to whether the missiles have been equipped with reentry vehicles. And Falcon's answer is, 'apparently,' meaning it appears that whoever has the missiles may also have the warheads to go with them."

"And, I suppose he doesn't know where they are?"

"No, sir. Falcon states that he doesn't have a favorite fishing spot—that is, that he no longer thinks they are on ships—and that he is now looking on land, thus the reference to taking up hunting instead of fishing."

"Great. So what you're telling me is that I'm supposed to tell the national security advisor that we think the Russians have lost about one hundred ballistic missiles that may be armed, with what, ten warheads each? Right?"

"Yes, sir, that's what we believe."

"And what steps are we supposed to take to find them?"

"Apparently none, sir. Falcon is trying to locate them through his contacts in the G.R.U.."

"But he says here that he hates to ask his friends, I assume his military friends, where they are. What does that mean?"

"It means we have to hold this close hold, sir. Very close hold. And wait to see what he comes up with."

"So why did he tell us, then?"

"Because he knows we have other contacts, other counteragents, that may have the right information, now that we know what to ask about, or, in the alternative, what to look for from the sky."

The director thought a few moments about the possibility of one hundred intercontinental ballistic missiles missing since 1986, presumably fully armed with nuclear warheads.

"Why would Gorbachev and Yeltsin sign all those treaties if they were hiding missiles? Especially after giving us inspection rights?"

"Well, sir, they may have signed knowing full well that they had missiles that they weren't going to tell us about, and that we would never learn about them. That's one possibility."

"But we'd still have the right to inspect."

"Yes, sir. But we have the right to inspect the sites listed in the treaty; to inspect any other sites we would have to go through a formal process of requesting access."

"And they could either destroy the site or relocate the missiles, right?"

"Yes, sir. But moving them would be very difficult once we know the location; we would just use our satellites to see if they tried to move them, and if they did, where they moved them to. Given all of this, it seems more likely that the Russian leadership does not know about the missing missiles."

"So then, how the hell does this guy know anything?" the director asked, knowing full-well that he was now delving into methods and sources.

"Falcon is G.R.U., sir. He hears lots of things, sir. Lots of things that otherwise we'd never hear. If he thinks there's a secret base, there's most probably a secret base."

God, the director thought leaning back in his chair, some days I hate this job.

# CHAPTER 12

## The Pentagon, Washington, D.C.

Lieutenant General Richard A. Williams, Director of J-3 (Operations), Joint Chiefs of Staff (JCS), arrived at the River Entrance of the Pentagon at his usual 0530 hours. As head of J-3, Williams was in charge of implementing and monitoring any operations selected by the Joint Staff. Normally such missions would be initiated at the direction of the chairman of the joint chiefs of staff, with the approval of the president or the secretary of defense, who would inform Williams of the goal of the mission and its parameters. The J-3 would then select the appropriate mission profile and assign the mission to a particular CINC. As an officer on the Joint Staff Williams did his best to set aside any preferences toward the Air Force, despite his thirty-some years of service in that branch.

General Williams entered the large doors into the Pentagon, walked past the unmarked wood doors immediately to his left, which he knew to be the entrance to "The Tank," and continued to walk into the depths of the nerve center of the Pentagon, the National Military Command Center (NMCC). Walking the additional thirty yards or so past the framed picture of one of the four 747s that serve as an alternative flying command center and the lettered quotations on each side of the narrow hall, Williams walked past the security guard, past the first outer corridor of the NMCC, turned right down the next corridor, and walked the twenty yards to his office door.

"Good morning, sir," another security guard stated. This guard, at Post 7, was stationed immediately across from Williams' office door and controlled the access into the actual working area of the National Military Command Center. Whenever Williams needed to enter the command center he would simply exit his office and walk right into the NMCC through this door.

"Good morning, Sergeant," Williams replied. "How ya doing today?"

"Fine, sir. Just fine!"

"Glad to hear it."

Williams stepped into his windowless, second-floor office past his secretary's desk, past his exec's office, and then into his own small but comfortable office. As always, his executive officer had already unlocked his office door, had tea steeping, had the mail opened and organized, and was sitting at the small circular table across from Williams' desk organizing the message traffic that had come in the night before. Behind Williams' desk stood his blue flag emblazoned with three large white stars.

"Good morning, Colonel Markham," Williams stated in a friendly tone.

"Good morning, sir," Markham replied.

Williams smiled as he looked down at the various piles of messages sitting on the conference table that had come during the night. Above the table stood the painting of a P-51 fighter in flight, a painting that Markham had selected for Williams' office, primarily because Markham's father had flown a Mustang during World War II. An efficient exec is a dream, thought Williams as he quickly reviewed the messages that had already been organized by priority and subject matter.

Colonel Allison Markham was the best exec officer he had ever had. A daughter of a squadron commander, graduate of the Air Force Academy, F-15 pilot for three years and then flight instructor, Colonel Markham knew exactly where she was heading. Many pilots would decline to take a desk job right in the middle of their peak flying years, but by doing so they lose in the long run. You can't fly forever, Markham knew, and the pilots who failed to see that did not deserve to work up the ranks into the higher echelon.

Markham, like any good exec, knew that Williams had been to a play at the Ford Theater the night before. Executive officers were required to know the whereabouts of their bosses at all times, and Markham was no exception.

"Did you enjoy the play last night, sir?" Markham asked.

"The play was excellent, Allison. Thank you for asking. Anything interesting?"

"Yes, sir. You have a message to see the chairman when you arrive."

"Any indication what it's about?"

"No, sir."

"Well, let's go."

General Williams and Colonel Markham walked out of the NMCC onto the Chairman's Corridor and directly into to the chairman's office via a door marked 2E872.

"Good morning, Nancy. How are you today?"

"Just fine, General Williams," the chairman's civilian secretary replied. Everybody who had anything to do with the chairman knew Nancy Hughes, the woman in charge of every aspect of the chairman's schedule. Williams knew that handling the Chairman's schedule is an almost insurmountable task given the fact that the chairman attends over four hundred public events a year, not to mention his other tasks of attending any National Security Council meetings (of which he is an active participant), testifying on the Hill, and generally running the entire United States military apparatus. "The chairman is on the phone," Ms. Hughes continued, "but is expecting you. It should be only a few minutes. The others are already in there waiting for him to finish his call."

"The others?" Williams asked.

"The vice chairman, the J-2, and a few others." Before Ms. Hughes could explain who "the others" were, the door to the chairman's office opened, and Admiral Matthew Hacker, vice chairman of the joint chiefs of staff, stepped out into the anteroom.

"Hi, Matt. What's up?" Williams said. Williams liked Hacker, even if he was still a little parochial when it came to Navy issues.

"Got us a suit, Italian made."

"Oh really!" Williams said laughing. General Williams loved Matthew Hacker's open disdain for the senior CIA officials who like to play soldier without knowing what it was about. Although career "suits" were tolerable, the walk-on "experts" were the worst, many of whom had been nothing more than political hacks who helped get a president or a senator elected. The reference to "Italian" suit meant that the official used to be a lawyer. Lawyer suits were always the greatest pain; they knew how to argue, but not how to listen. Williams was glad for the warning.

"Great. Who's on trial this week?"

"No trial. An assignment, but I'm sure you'll be cross-examined just the same."

Richard Williams muttered "assholes" as Hacker led the way toward the chairman's office and knocked on the door.

"Enter," came General Scott's familiar voice. Scott sat behind his huge oak desk, definitely looking the part of a general: six foot three, sandy gray hair, his left side covered with ribbons, and four stars on each shoulder board. Although first in his class at MIT, he still maintained his down-to-earth qualities and homespun graciousness. "Richard, this is Mr. Jackson, deputy director for intelligence at the agency." Everyone knew *which* agency.

Another warning, thought Williams. Scott rarely left out first names when introducing people. Williams walked over to Jackson, reaching out his hand. "Hello, sir," Williams said. "It's a pleasure to meet you." Jackson looked to be in his early forties; small and wiry. The suit was indeed Italian; gray silk, perfectly cut.

Scott continued with the introductions. "Jackson is here with Ms. Gail Smith, one of the assistant deputies from the National Security Council." There was no need to introduce the joint staff's senior intelligence officer, the J-2.

Once all the introductions were completed, General Scott sat down at his desk. Behind him were many mementos from his thirty-plus years of service to his country. In front of the chairman's desk sat a conference table capable of seating five to six people, and behind the conference table stood two large conformable chairs that faced the couch that sat at the opposite end of the chairman's office. On the wall above the couch stood a large portrait of General Bradley, ever-watching the implementation of history, military justice, and the quest for international stability. "Well," the chairman stated simply after waiting for everyone to get seated at the conference table close to his desk, "let's get to it."

Jackson immediately took the lead. "Thank you, General Scott. Before we begin, I remind you that we're doing this on a need-to-know basis." Jackson paused and looked directly at Colonel Markham, clearly implying that Colonel Markham should be asked to leave.

General Williams leaned forward to defend the right of his assistant to stay, but was silenced before he could speak by a quick glance from General Scott. "That is correct, Mr. Jackson," General Scott began, "and if you are referring to General Williams' assistant, I can assure you that she is part of that need-to-know. General Williams will be in command of this operation and his assistant will need to know as much as he does. Please continue."

"Very well. General Williams, what experience does the Air Force have flying into Russia?"

General Williams looked over to General Scott, who nodded his approval to discuss the issue. "Well, Mr. Jackson, we've had certain experience in flying into Russian territory. Of course, I'm not at liberty to go into detail as to the specifics of those particular missions."

Jackson clearly took umbrage to Williams' comment. "First of all, General, I am sure that I have a higher clearance than even you do, and I have full access to anything that you may know or have access to." Jackson calmed himself, knowing that alienating the military would be counterproductive. He needed them in order to convince the national security advisor to put the issue to the president. Jackson continued his questioning, returning to a friendlier tone. "But it's not the details I'm interested in. What I want to know is whether it can be done."

"Yes," General Williams replied, "it can be done."

"Is it possible for you to get in, say, three hundred miles, and back out safely?"

"Yes it is, although it depends on the area—the defensive installations, number of interceptor squadrons within range of the flight path, type of radar, SAM sites, et cetera."

"What if those things looked good, would you be able to get in, land, pick up someone, and then get out?"

Williams thought for a moment. "It's possible, though tricky. Once again, it depends on the location, the spot where we're going to land, the problems we might have at the landing site."

"But can it be done?"

"It *has* been done, Mr. Jackson." Apparently General Williams had more information about flying into Russia than Jackson after all.

Jackson brushed off the disclosure that this type of mission had been done before; best to make them think he also knew about it. "Excellent," Jackson said, as he pulled out his briefing notes. "We have a double agent inside Russia who needs to be retrieved. The information he has is vital, and it is essential to get him out quietly, without an international incident."

Now it was General Williams' chance to take the lead. "And where is this pick-up point, sir?"

"Inside of Southern Siberia; a city named Chara."

Williams considered the location for a moment. Anyone who had been in SAC knew of Chara; it was one of the targets in the SIOP—Single Integrated Operational Plan, the nuclear battle plan. "Which airport do you plan to use? Chara, or Chara Southwest?"

"The regular Chara runway," replied Jackson, "the civilian one."

"Not much of a runway there," Williams noted. "Only four thousand feet."

"True," Markham added, "but at least it's not part of a military base; except for a single military hangar used to house their Kamov Ka-27C search and rescue helicopter, there's no military hardware to speak of."

Jackson was impressed with Williams and Markham's knowledge of Russian airstrips. "That's right. The Chara airport is basically a civilian airport, if there is such a thing in Russia, although the military owns the Helix, so there are probably two or three technicians there during the day, and maybe a guard or two at night. The agent would take them out before you land."

"Actually," Williams mused out loud, "that's not a bad spot. If we flew in along the division line between the Transbaikal and Far East military districts, we may possibly benefit from the confusion of which district had responsibility. The interceptor squadrons are focused mostly on the eastern seaboard and along the western half of the southern border, plus we'd be able to fly in under the Krasnoyarsk radar."

"If Mathias Rust can do it," Jackson stated, referring to Rust's flight from Germany to Moscow's Red Square in a Piper Cub, "why not us?" Although Smith smiled at Jackson's attempt to make a joke, none of the military officers considered Jackson's flippant attitude at all humorous. Williams thought again of his disdain for the ignorance of civilians who thought modern war as nothing more than some sort of macho high-tech video game.

"The problem wouldn't be getting in, Mr. Jackson," Williams explained slowly, so the point would not be lost. "The problem is getting out. By the time we landed at Chara, there would be a very good chance that we'd be spotted and an alert sounded."

Jackson did not like to hear that his plan might have problems. Once again trying to hold back his temper, Jackson looked directly at General Williams. "But as I understand it, a stealth plane couldn't be detected."

"You're talking dreams, Mr. Jackson," Williams replied. "Like I said, there's a very good chance of being detected. When you're flying several tons of hot metal through the air, it's hard not to be detected, stealth or no stealth."

General Scott interrupted, trying to smooth things over and get the conversation back on track. "All planes can be detected, Mr. Jackson, even those using stealth technology. It's just a question of lowering the chance of detection by applying what we know about radar cross sections and infrared sensors."

"We really don't have to worry that much about the chance of being detected," Williams continued. "That doesn't really matter, as long as we get out; it will be listed as a false sighting. No Russian commander is going to admit that he or his men allowed an unidentified plane to land inside Russia and then escape, especially after the Rust incident."

"Then it can still be done?" Jackson asked General Williams.

"Yes," Williams replied. "It can be done, but only with one of our most advanced stealth planes or a very fast recon plane. The plane would have to get in quietly, and get out very quickly. Also, I doubt we would use a stealth platform; I doubt we would want to take a chance for the Russians to get a piece of our radar absorbent materials from one of our stealth planes. We'd most probably use something else. How much time do I have to prepare?"

"Twenty days," Smith replied. "We need a preliminary briefing on Monday."

Williams thought for a moment. "I can handle that."

"Just one other thing," Jackson commented. "Whoever goes in to get him has to know him personally."

So, Williams thought, they want us to set it up, then the CIA will use one of their own pilots. Second fiddle, again. Williams turned toward Jackson. "Then I suppose that means you'll want to use one of your own people?" Williams stated with but a hint of coldness.

"No," Jackson replied looking at Smith, clearly dissatisfied. "That request has been denied. It has to be one of yours." Jackson reached down to the floor and opened his briefcase. "We've done a computer check. The agent we are withdrawing used to teach at an American college, cover for when he was in charge of operatives over here. One of your F-15 pilots had him as a political science teacher. Here's his file," he said to General Scott, placing the file on Scott's desk.

Training a pilot to do this mission will make it difficult, Williams thought, but he'd be damned if he'd let Jackson know it. That's all Jackson needed was to get further ammunition to use his own man to fly the mission. Besides, Air Force pilots, unlike pilots from other branches of the service, have to be physically capable of flying any Air Force plane in its inventory.

"Monday it is," said Scott with an air of finality. "Where's the briefing?"

"Downtown," Jackson said, referring to the White House.

That figures, Williams thought. He's the only one who can approve flights into unfriendly territory. "Will he be there?" Williams asked.

Jackson stood up, looking back toward Williams. "I guess you'll just have to wait and see," Jackson said as he gathered his papers. Without saying anything more, Jackson walked out of the room, purposely leaving the door open.

Gail Smith could not help but laugh out loud. "Well, gentlemen," she said as she stood up to leave, "you certainly are showing your valor today, assuming discretion is the better part of valor. Sorry he's such a pompous ass."

General Scott laughed, standing up as he followed Smith to the door. As they reached the door, Smith turned toward General Scott, smiling. "Don't worry, General. The president won't be there." General Scott liked her relaxing smile; she clearly felt at home working with the military. Smith reached over and shut the door. "Jackson has to convince my boss before it will be sent to the Security Council." Ms. Smith paused, talking quietly but loud enough for all of the planners to hear. "If it happens, it will happen three weeks from yesterday, 0400 Chara time." She paused, her smile waning as her eyes fixed on General Scott, clearly conveying the national security advisor's specific instruction. "Your people know the implications of a mission like this. If there's any doubt about its feasibility, we want to know. We realize that some risks aren't worth taking even if some of our colleagues in intelligence do not. Don't misunderstand me, we want this man out; but we also want to know if it can be done without undue risk."

General Scott wondered whether she meant undue risk to the pilot, or undue risk of an international incident. It didn't matter. He was being told to be objective, and to be wary of the CIA.

"I understand, Ms. Smith." General Scott smiled at Smith as she opened the door to leave. "Please tell Frank I got his message."

"Gladly. Have a good day, gentlemen."

★      ★      ★      ★

Following a two-hour brainstorming meeting, General Scott made a phone call to the NASA research center located at Edwards Air Force Base, and then gave tentative approval to the plan proposed by General Williams. Within one-half an hour, orders were issued to various operations officers stationed at Kadena Air Base (Okinawa), Beale Air Force Base (Northern California), Hurlburt Field (Florida), Kelly Air Force Base (Texas), Holloman Air Force Base (New Mexico), and Peterson Air Force Base (Colorado).

# CHAPTER 13

## In transit beginning at Yokota Air Base, Japan

Captain Thomas Bennett landed his C-21A, the military version of the Lear Jet 35A, on Runway 1L at Andrews Air Force Base. It had been a long trip. Beginning at Yokota Air Base, Japan, headquarters of the Fifth Air Force (PACAF), Bennett, Allan Erickson, his copilot, and a senior operations specialist flew nine hundred miles southwest to Kadena Air Base, Okinawa. At about midnight Okinawa time, they picked up Major James Hanna from the 353d Special Operations Group, and Major Daniel Maki, Operations Officer of the 18th Wing, also stationed at Kadena.

After picking up Hanna and Maki, Bennett flew the C-21 east to his two trans-Pacific refueling stops, Wake Island and Hickam Air Force Base, Hawaii. Bennett then landed at Beale Air Force Base, California, where he picked up Colonel Richard Dobson, Deputy Operations Officer of the 9th Reconnaissance Wing. Bennett then flew eight hundred miles to the Air Force Academy runway at Colorado Springs, Colorado, and picked up Colonel Vander Parsons of the 50th Space Wing from Peterson Air Force Base. Next Bennett flew the four hundred miles to Holloman Air Force Base to pick up Colonel James Coe, Operations Officer for the 49th Fighter Wing. Another short hour flight at four hundred miles per hour resulted in landing at Kelly Air Force Base to pick up Colonel Jody Harper of the 67th Information Operations Wing. Finally, Bennett aimed his Lear Jet seven hundred miles east to Hurlburt Field, Florida, to pick up his last passenger, Colonel Joseph Sandstrom, Director of Plans, Air Force Special Operations Command. Now that everyone was aboard, Bennett took the entire group eight hundred miles north to Andrews Air Force Base.

Thus, some twenty-three hours after leaving Yokota, Bennett watched his seven passengers exit his plane at Andrews Air Force Base and enter a dark-blue, unmarked Air Force van on its way to the Pentagon.

# CHAPTER 14

## The Pentagon, Washington, D.C.

"Please be seated, gentlemen," General Williams stated as he entered the National Military Command Center's special conference room adjacent to his office. Normally this conference room was used during operational missions, with the chairman at the head of the large U-shaped table that seemed strangely similar to the Star-Trek insignia worn on the left breast of all Star Fleet personnel. The chairman, when he used this operational conference room, would be flanked by his senior staff, with his director of staff on his right, the assistant director to his left, and all his other joint officers assigned to the other open chairs on each side of the table. The large wood table opened up and faced three large screens flanked on each side by two podiums used by the briefers.

Colonel Markham sat behind General Williams, seating herself in one of the dozen or so chairs behind her boss while Williams stood behind his chair at the end of the conference table. Williams looked around at the group he had assembled for the mission. Seated at the large, oak table were Colonels Dobson, Harper, Sandstrom, Coe and Parsons, and Majors Hanna and Maki.

"I assume everyone has received the security clearance briefing from intel and have signed the special clearance agreement for this compartmentalized mission." Everyone around the table nodded affirmatively.

"Good. Then we can begin. We have received a priority callback from one of our agents inside Russia. The CIA tell us that this agent is extremely valuable. Our own J-2 didn't know about him until this morning, that's how closely held his existence has been. According to his message, he is under surveillance and unable to get near a friend-ly border or to the sea for a more traditional pick-up. There are con-cerns that if he attempted to leave the country, even for some normal event, he would be arrested, just like we did with Ames right before he was scheduled to go to Moscow to meet with the Russians. The agent has therefore requested a fly-in pick-up, which in this case would occur at the city of Chara, approximately 350 miles northeast of Lake Baikal." General Williams waited a moment, allowing the officers to consider the goal of the mission.

"Those of you who have worked with the Intelligence Service or other intelligence groups know that only a few agents are allowed to request interior pick-ups, and a pick-up from inside the former Soviet Union is almost unheard of. As you know, normally the agent can get to a friendly border or at least within twenty or twenty-five miles of the border, where special forces can be used to escort him out. But as I mentioned, according to the CIA the agent involved is under suspicion and will probably be arrested if he gets anywhere near a border. Thus, we have to go in and bring him out.

"You all know the problems inherent in such a mission. Your job is to evaluate mission feasibility. The mission has not yet been approved, and may be scrubbed due to the risk of international reper-cussions. We, luckily, do not have to worry about that aspect. Our job is to tell the national security advisor within seventy-two hours whether it can be done, and provide him with an objective likelihood of success. While we're doing that, the intelligence community will try to determine if other alternatives will work."

Williams once again looked around the table at the officers, gauging them, reading their reactions. "Those of you who have worked with me before know that I don't like 'yes-men.' Every plan, every comment, is subject to critical analysis. I have no use for timid souls. If you disagree, say so and say why." The general paused for a moment.

"Each of you will be provided with Code 3 authority. Any information you request, except information restricted to the president and the joint chiefs of staff, will be available to you without having to clear channels. You need only keep a record of each person you con-tact and a general description of the information requested. Don't worry about recording the details; there isn't time, and besides, you'll be debriefed later. I've assigned six intel specialists, seated right behind me here, to get you any information you may need during your mission planning.

"Obviously this mission is on a need-to-know basis. Do not discuss it with anyone, even the people you get information from. One of the reasons the mission is being assigned solely to the Air Force is to limit the number of personnel who will have knowledge of the mission." Now that the ground rules are set, Williams thought, we can get to work.

"Due to the lack of time, an initial plan has been devised for your consideration. By the people we have present, you have probably already surmised some aspects of the plan. The mission will be flown out of Okinawa, which is why we have Major James Hanna from the 353d Special Operations Group and Major Dan Maki of the 18th Wing, both from Kadena Air Base. We also have Colonel Joe Sandstrom from Air Force Special Ops, Hurlburt Field. Colonel Vander Parsons is the operations officer for 50th Space Wing at Peterson Air Force Base, Colorado, and is the operational liaison between Space Command and the National Reconnaissance Office and NIMA, the National Imagery and Mapping Agency. He will be working with the NRO, NIMA, and Colonel Jody Harper from the 67th Information Operations Wing, Kelly Air Force Base, in providing us the intelligence and other details relating to the landing site. Colonel Jim Coe is the operations officer for the 49th Fighter Wing where, as you all know, the stealth fighter is presently assigned. And last, but not least, is Colonel Richard Dobson from the 9th Reconnaissance Wing out of Beale and, it turns out, Edwards Air Force Base.

"As you can imagine, our primary decision has to be what type of plane to use for the pick-up. With that, the floor's open. Any suggestions?"

The five other members of the team looked over to the two special operations guru's sitting next to each other at the end of the table. The members of the team who had been flown in all assumed that special ops would be assigned the mission and everyone else was there for support. "Well, sir," Colonel Sandstrom began, "it seems to me that this is just the type of mission special ops was designed for, that is deep penetration over enemy territory and extraction."

Colonel Sandstrom paused to see if he should continue; Williams gave him a nod of approval. Sandstrom continued. "There are a couple of ways we could get a single person out. If he has special ops training all we need to do is drop him an extraction pack from the plane, confirm it's him by the scrambled radio inside the pack, then have him inflate the extraction balloon, put the pack back on and wait for us to extract him using the Fulton "whiskers" to snatch him up and out of there. Although we're in the process of retiring the Fulton whiskers, we have a few 130s still equipped with them."

"Fulton 'whiskers'?" Peterson asked.

"A kind of 'Y' shaped prong we have in front of one of our MC-130E's; it grabs the wire being held up by the balloon. Works great, and it's one hell of a ride." Sandstrom stopped speaking, thinking he might have been too flippant for the general. General Williams didn't seem to mind at all.

"And if our fellow doesn't have ops training?" Williams asked.

"Well, sir, then we go in with one of our helicopters following a HC-130P refueler, land, pick him up, and head back."

"How many people would be at risk behind enemy lines with that type of mission?" Williams asked.

"Twenty or so," Sandstrom continued. "Depends on whether we use a MH-60G Pave Hawk, or the larger MH-53J Pave Low. If we need to get just one person we could use two MH-60G Pave Hawks, one for cover the other for extraction, accompanied by a HC-130P refueler. The Pave Hawks' range isn't that great, but they could make it."

"What about the radar sites?" Maki asked. "Wouldn't it be better to use the Pave Low since it has terrain following and terrain avoidance radar?"

"Perhaps," Harper stated while thinking about the matter. "The Pave Low is obviously the better choice if we have any significant radar concerns. Also, at three hundred miles in, the longer range of the Pave Low is a definite plus. They could fly out of Kadena a little before sunset, refuel both on the northern part of the Sea of Japan, and then head in north of Korea."

"I didn't think you had any Pave Hawks assigned to Kadena, just the Enhanced Pave Low III's?" Colonel Coe mentioned.

"Actually, the MH-53J Pave Low's assigned to the 31st SOS are stationed at Osan Air Base, South Korea. All we'd have do is fly them to Kadena. And even if they aren't there right now or aren't the ones we want to use, we can load up two of them in a C-5 Galaxy and have them there in a flash."

"Or use the Material Command's special C-141 Starlifter to take the two we need over," Major Hanna added. "But if we use the C-5 we might as well also send an Airborne Battlefield Command and Control pod over to insert inside one of our EC-130Es, and keep the entire mission compartmentalized to special ops."

Colonel Harper of the 67th Information Operations Wing didn't like the sound of Korea as the entrance point, particularly given all of the radar focused at the nexus between North Korea and Russia. "That's a pretty heavily monitored area to get in at, sir," Harper interjected.

Sandstrom looked over at Harper and smiled slightly. "We know a few good spots that will work. The way I see it, we'd be out by the morning light, just in time for breakfast."

"Going in with a full special ops team is of course the first choice," General Williams began. "As a matter of fact we have some of your people at Kadena planning a special ops only mission, if that should be selected by the higher-ups. However, I doubt highly that that mission will be a go. The State Department and the White House have serious concerns about sending that many people into Russia. Although I know it's possible and has been done before, based on what I've been told about the feelings of the higher-ups, it is very unlikely that a traditional special ops mission will be approved. They want less personnel inside, and less chance, if something does go wrong, to have egg on their face. Especially with the present relatively good relations with the Russians now that Putin has pardoned Pope. That is why all of you are here: to find a less risky way to get the agent out, and just as importantly, with the least amount of people at risk."

Major Maki from the 18th Wing out of Kadena spoke up next. "It seems to me, sir, if we can't use traditional special ops and the number one priority is to get in and out without being seen, then we should be talking stealth aircraft."

Colonel Coe was glad to hear this; always nice to have another fighter jock in the room. "Obviously for this type of mission," Colonel Coe said, "the plane must have some stealth characteristics and electronic countermeasures capability. Sounds like a 117 to me." Colonel Coe considered the stealth fighter the obvious choice, especially since it now had now been unveiled to the public. He knew that the F-117, the first generation of these stealth fighters, could get in and out with little chance of detection. The 117 had already flown several missions near the Russian border and had not even been detected by Russian radar.

Colonel Parsons from the 50th Space Wing spoke up for the first time. "But the 117 is a one-seater; rather hard to extract someone in that."

Colonel Coe replied in a friendly manner; Coe had known Parson for years, ever since they had their joint assignment together at SHAPE. "Actually, Vander, we would be able to get him out. Instead of carrying bombs in the bomb-bay we'd put in one of our special human carrier packages designed to transport an individual. Not real roomy, but it works like a charm." Coe turned back toward General Williams. "That still leaves the refueling problem. I assume the reason our friends from special ops are here is to pass the gas." Coe enjoyed giving a slight zing to the special ops boys since usually they're are the ones with the high-risk mission and the 117s, when used, just fly cover. What a nice switch, Coe thought to himself.

Not to be outdone, Sandstrom threw in his own friendly jibe: "Yeah, but where could we find a 117 pilot who is good enough to handle a low-level, low speed refueling from one of our 130s?"

General Williams liked the friendly ribbing—obviously these guys will work well as a team—but he still wanted to get the discussion more on focus. "Nice idea but that still leaves too many people over Russian territory, at least more than the big boys want."

"Couldn't we fill the bomb-bay with fuel tanks?" Colonel Dobson asked.

"But then how do we extract the agent?" Coe countered.

"Eject the tanks before landing," Dobson said, "and then put him in the bomb bay. Put some 'Holy Jesus' straps in there, shut the doors, and have him hang on for the ride. It'll all be low level so we wouldn't have an oxygen problem, or a temperature problem."

"Not exactly first-class accommodations," Coe said.

"Beats a gulag in Siberia any day!" Dobson replied.

"Do we have any 117 'B' models with two seats?" Colonel Parsons asked.

"Only in the movies," Coe replied, laughing at the constant inaccuracies of modern movies. Everyone thought automatically of a recent movie that had six or seven people inside a stealth fighter, even though the plane could only hold one person: the pilot. There was a slight pause as everyone considered the problem at hand.

"The 117 could probably get in and out without being detected," General Williams stated, "but another reason we've discounted using the 117 is that if it were seen it would have a hard time getting out of there fast enough, limited as it is to subsonic speeds."

"There's not a Russian fighter that could find it," Coe contended.

"Perhaps, assuming it could avoid a convergence of Russian MiGs," Colonel Harper commented, "but it would certainly have a hard time outrunning an 'Archer'," referring to the Russian R-73, known as the AA-11 "Archer" by its NATO designation.

"Good point," Major Maki added. Maki was well aware of the capabilities of the "Archer" air-to-air infrared missile since those were the missiles that would most likely be aimed at his F-15C as he flew support out of Kadena in the event of any "problems" with Russia.

Colonel Sandstrom spoke up next. "Wouldn't the cool-down of the exhaust by the auxiliary air inlets prevent the 'Archer' from being able to lock-on?" he asked Colonel Coe.

"We assume the cool down to be sufficient to prevent a lock-on," Harper replied for him, "but there's no guarantee."

Colonel Coe considered what other planes could be used on the mission. As the former exec officer for the commander of Air Force Material Command, he had numerous opportunities to hear about the Air Force's newest planes, including all of the aircraft covered with radar absorbent materials. "What's the most recent estimates of the cruising speed of the 'Archer'?" Coe asked.

"Mach 2.5," Harper replied. Re-thinking what General Williams mentioned about unlimited security clearance and the desire to discuss all options, Harper turned to General Williams. "Sir, am I authorized to discuss other types of aircraft, including proto-types?" Everyone in the room knew that the designation of "proto-types" was a less-than-veiled reference to classified aircraft.

"That's not a problem," the general replied. "Go ahead."

"Well, sir," continued Harper, "our stealth Harrier has some possibilities. As you probably know, we applied radar absorbent materials to one of the TAV-8B's with substantial success, at least given the air intakes we have to deal with. And since it is a trainer, it's a two-seater."

"That's certainly a possibility," Colonel Dobson from Beale said. "But we still have the range problem. Even with all the composites reducing the weight, I doubt it would have the range."

"What if we launched it out of a C-5 in flight over the Sea of Japan?" Major Maki asked. "Maybe that would give us enough distance. As I recall the Brits used a skyhook device on a frigate and it worked out just fine. I imagine we could set up something like that pretty quickly."

"I still don't think the Harrier would have enough legs," Colonel Dobson said. "And I have to assume that the Air Staff doesn't want to use any of the third or fourth generation stealth platforms for this type of mission."

"That's correct," confirmed General Williams. "They're not too thrilled about letting the Russians get a glance at that technology if there should be a malfunction or an accident."

"Or," Harper added, "if it's a trap."

"It would be difficult to justify the use of any of the advanced stealth fighters for the in-country landing," Williams continued. "Besides, we can't take the chance of the Russians obtaining any of our radar absorbent materials. What they have suggested is something that can get out fast if it has to, and won't cause huge international repercussions if it is seen getting the hell out of there."

"If speed is the issue," Coe thought out loud, "that also counts out the the second generation stealth fighter. It has a higher maximum cruise speed than the F-117, but it still couldn't outrun the newer Russian heat-seeking missiles. Nor does it sound like the advanced tactical fighter, the F-22A Raptor, is an option, that is if they're that concerned about the chance of giving up technology." Coe reached the conclusion for everyone: "That means stealth planes are out."

General Williams had expected the team to reject the use of stealth planes for the landing, given the political and tactical constraints

"What do you plan to use, then?" Colonel Coe asked.

General Williams smiled slightly, looking around the table. "We were thinking of using a Blackbird, low-level entry, full afterburner exit." Williams watched the team's reaction. It was not good. Nonetheless, he continued. "With its stealth design and its sophisticated navigation system, we think it has a good chance of getting in undetected. Although difficult to fly at low altitudes, our previous flight tests show that it can be done, at least for a short while. And if it is detected by ground radar, we'll abort and get the hell out of there fast, before they have time to get their alert planes up."

Colonel Parsons was the first to speak up. "But I thought the Blackbird was being retired? At least that's what the newspapers said."

"Well," General Williams explained, "it did retire for a while, but we still have access to it via our contract with NASA. In other words, we kept ownership and had the right to ask for the two Blackbirds and the B-model any time. However, Congress re-activated it a few years ago. It was operational for two years, and now it's 'retired' again. NASA owns it, but is willing, under the circumstances, to loan it to us, not that they'd have any choice on the matter. We also have two more birds in storage, but it may be better to use one of the NASA birds given the time-lines and the additional cover it would gives us. And, of course, the CIA has kept several YF-12A's and a couple of Blackbirds for contingency matters so we could use them too, although they'd bitch like hell if it wasn't their mission. Besides, the powers that be also asked us to keep this an Air Force only mission."

Somebody muttered "Thank God" as Williams said this, though he couldn't tell who.

"Apparently the trenchcoats are not in great favor at the moment," Williams mentioned. No wonder, everyone thought to themselves, given the Ames' spy scandal, the recent China incident, and the numerous other botched-up internal investigations of late.

General Williams continued. "Things would have been a lot easier if the Russians had agreed to an open-skies policy, but that hasn't happened."

"Begging your pardon, sir," Colonel Dobson broke in, "but I can't imagine flying between mountains in a fully-fueled Blackbird. Going that slow it would be very sluggish, and it's not exactly designed for low-level penetration. It's maximum speed at low level is only about point nine Mach. It's more stable at that speed, but it would be difficult for the pilot to react fast enough through the mountains." Dobson had flown the SR for years out of Beale until the Air Force retired them.

General Williams knew that this would be a concern, and replied immediately. "The pilot won't be flying it in, Richard. NASA is adding an enhanced autopilot that can handle the parameters of this mission. We would use autopilot almost entirely; preplanned flight, computer-programmed mapping, flying passive. The only way the pilot would fly the entire mission would be if there were a system failure. The way we have this figured, the pilot would only need to take the controls during the approach, and then fly the last ten miles or so, land the plane, turn it around, pick up the package, and takeoff. As soon as he clears the mountains he'd get it up to an optimum cruising speed and then put it back on autopilot and head home."

Dobson knew that the SR's original computer did not have the capability of flying the plane at low altitude, so he was not in a position to question the newer NASA modification. Nonetheless, he knew that a computer flying the plane on a landing pattern at a commercial airport was one thing, but through mountainous terrain and then landing at a potentially hostile, unknown airport was another thing entirely. Dobson knew that even the most sophisticated unmanned aerial vehicles had crashed recently, and usually as a result of faulty maps or faulty computer programming. How can we be sure the damn thing works, he thought to himself.

"How can we be sure the input on the landscape is accurate?" Colonel Dobson asked. Dobson did not like the idea of possibly sending one of his Beale pilots—many of whom had flown the SR-71 before moving over to the U-2 when the SR went away—into the face of a Russian mountain. And, of course, the active duty pilots who had been flying the SR out of Edwards the last two years were also under his command.

"That's where Space Command and the NRO comes in," Williams explained, referring to the previously super-secret National Reconnaissance Office that receives all of the photographic intel from satellites, airplanes, and other assets, and synthesizes that information into operational products such as maps and very precise target points. "They'll chart every inch of the landing site with their newest Lacrosse satellite, and we'll feed it all into the SR's computer along with the digital mapping already done by the NRO that follows along the flight path."

"What about the SA-10s?" Colonel Coe asked. Coe remembered vividly from his Vietnam days the effectiveness of the older Soviet surface-to-air missiles. He, like all of the others, knew that the more advanced SA-10 "Grumbles" were capable of reaching a maximum speed of Mach 6—deadly to even the most modern jet aircraft, not to mention a low-flying Blackbird.

General Williams nodded to Major Markham, who immediately pulled out a map of southeastern Russia and placed it on the table facing the group. Everybody noted that the point of ingress into Russia was deep inland over China. "As you can see, gentlemen," General Williams continued, "the route we intend to fly, as shown here, won't be within the sixty-two-mile range of any of the SA-10s. Our real problem will be the slower-moving SA-12 'Giants' which, as many of you know, the SR-71 has been able to defeat on several occasions, both by speed and electronic countermeasures."

The room fell to complete silence once everyone had seen enough of the map to determine the flight plan. "Begging your pardon, sir," Harper said, "but you've got the plane flying directly over Bejing and deep into the interior of China."

"Yes," General Williams replied. "Don't you love power politics and the ever-shifting sands of international relations? The secretary of state had a little talk with his Chinese counterpart yesterday about why this mission is so important, and this here's the result. They've authorized the flight over their territory, and will even allow us minor staging rights at a small airport just south of the border called Gen He."

Colonel Coe was still uncomfortable with the thought of using a plane that could be seen by Russian radar. "We still have to worry about the mobile launched SAMs that are all along the Chinese-Russian border," he stated.

General Williams looked over at Colonel Dobson. Dobson was one of the Air Force's most experienced SR-71 pilots, having flown more than forty combat missions over Vietnam in an SR-71. "We've been able to outrun the mobile surface-to-air missiles in the Blackbird, such as the SA-13s and the SA-X-15s, due to their relatively slow speeds. But you're right, there's still a risk if the plane flies directly over a mobile launcher right after an alert is sounded."

As operations group commander at Beale for the 9th Reconnaissance Wing, Colonel Dobson assumed that he would be the logical choice to fly the mission. Would he have any back-up? "Will the SR be provided cover?" he asked.

"That's where Colonel Coe comes in," the general replied. "Cover will be with two of his F-117s. We have been able to get authorization to use them for cover, but not to land. If the Blackbird has to bolt, every sensor for three hundred miles will be tracking it as it heads out at full afterburner. While they're trying to take aim on the Blackbird, the 117s will simply ease out of Russia at low altitude and low speed, making them almost impossible to track."

"Why have them for cover, then?" Colonel Parsons asked.

"In case of interception by a stray MiG," Coe answered.

Parsons thought for a moment about the scenario of an American pilot shooting down a Russian plane within its own borders. "Wouldn't shooting down a MiG be considered a rather hostile act?"

"We don't plan on leaving any evidence of the shoot-down," Williams replied. "In addition to traditional air-to-air missiles, the fighters will be equipped with engine plungers and lightning bolts." Several of the pilots grimaced slightly at the reference to "lightning bolts."

"What are they?" Parsons asked.

"Well," Major Maki explained, "engine plungers are modified Sidewinder missiles. The warhead is removed and replaced with additional infrared detection electronics and some other things, like titanium strips, that reek havoc on jet engines; the missile is accurate enough to literally fly into the exhaust of a jet engine, ripping into the jet's fan drive turbine. The engine is entirely disabled, just as if it had a catastrophic malfunction. Because of the lack of an explosion, there is no evidence of a missile shoot-down. The plane either limps back to base or crashes, with no one the wiser.

"The lightning bolt, on the other hand, is designed to fly over and just slightly in front of the target; just as the missile flies ahead of the plane, it explodes, releasing an intense pulse of radio energy, an electro-magnetic pulse so powerful that it destroys all the electrical systems in the plane, especially the non-hardened, solid-state electronics used by the older Russian planes. Even if enough of the electronics remain operative to continue flight, the pilot is left without radar or radio, and, incidentally, is usually blinded—sometimes permanently—by the flash. His only option is to punch out. The only trouble with lightning bolts is that they can be seen for miles around; but by the time the air defenses react, we're long gone."

"How about the runway?" Colonel Sandstrom asked. Most SR-71 pilots were used to landing at twelve thousand foot runways, such as the one at Beale. "Is it long enough?"

"Yes," General Williams answered, "but barely. We'll have to use computer assisted landing, with reverse thrusters."

Major Dobson cringed. He hated the idea of having a computer land him, especially without the aid of a ground-based instrument landing system. Although he trusted the SR-71's sophisticated inertial guidance system to land him literally on a dime, that was not the problem. In order for the system to work accurately, it was necessary to feed into the computer every detail of the landing site—the surrounding terrain, the height of the landing approach lights, even the placement of the telephone poles and wires. If one bit of information was incorrect, the pilot could be flying right into the ground and never know it.

Colonel Coe shook his head. "Computer assisted landing at an unknown Russian airport? I'm sorry, sir, but that sounds crazy.

There's no way we could obtain all the information we need, even with our best photo recon intelligence."

General Williams smiled mischievously. "I thought you might say that, Colonel." General Williams walked over to the side of the room and picked up several poster boards that were facing against the wall. "This is what we have so far on the runway and the surrounding area. This is as of yesterday at 0500 Zulu. As you can see, this side-angle chart shows every detail—not only the height of the surrounding trees, but even the placement of power and phone lines, and the height of those lines. Here we have the top-side view. We believe this L-shaped object next to this truck is a tire-iron; the small dots are probably lug nuts. Because the right side of the vehicle is eight inches higher than the left, and the front of the vehicle is two inches higher than the back, we assume that the vehicle is jacked up and awaiting repair of the right front tire."

No wonder there was such a rush to get the Lacrosse radar imaging satellite into space Coe thought to himself. With this type of info, he thought to himself, he could fly to hell and back.

Colonel Sandstrom looked over the charts, trying to find a reference to guard posts. "How about military emplacements? As I recall, there are no military planes stationed at the Chara civilian airport."

"That's correct," Colonel Harper replied. "According to our intelligence, it is used only by civilian planes, and one helicopter, apparently used for search and rescue operations, though that's unclear as of yet."

"Any military or police detachment?" Sandstrom asked.

General Williams pointed to a small building near the entrance to the airport. "We understand that there are six military police stationed at Chara. Normally there are only two on duty, and they are both positioned here at the entrance. It will be the responsibility of the individual being picked up to take care of them, and then signal our pilot. The all-clear will be shown by three flares at the end of the runway, in the shape of a perfect triangle; any other combination will signal the pilot to abort the mission."

General Williams paused. "Any more questions?" There was no response. "Then let's start working on the details to find out if it can be done."

# CHAPTER 15

## Commander's Office, 5th Bomb Wing, Minot Air Force Base

Jack Phinney stuck his head into the commander's door. "You asked for me to drop by, sir?"

Colonel Linhard, the commander of the 5th Bomb Wing, looked up from his desk. "Yes, Jack. Come on in. Have a seat. I'll be right with you."

Jack Phinney seated himself at a chair across from the Linhard's desk and waited for the wing commander to finish reviewing the file before him. The new commander was known to almost everyone; everyone, that is, but Phinney. Previously Linhard had been assigned to Minot as the Ops Group Commander, and then had been assigned to the Joint Staff working special issues for the Air Force Chief of Staff.

To say that he was "on his way up," Phinney thought to himself, would be an understatement, given the fact that he still looked thirty-years-old and was already a full colonel. Everyone knew he was six years below the zone—the date upon which promotion to colonel was expected. And, of course, everybody also knew the stories of his unbelievable accomplishments intellectually, like his master's and doctorate degrees from MIT in electrical engineering. If this fellow didn't make general, no one would. Phinney, like everyone else, had heard the rumor that he needed only four hours of sleep a night, just like Napoleon, and that he virtually remembered everything he read. But since Phinney was stationed at Barksdale when Linhard was the ops group commander, he had only observed him at group settings, commander's calls, and the like. On the other hand, he had observed enough to decide that he was, in addition to a fine commander, a decent fellow who deserved not only the position he was in but also Phinney's respect. A few minutes later the colonel finished going through the file and looked up at Jack Phinney.

"I've been looking over your file, Jack. As you know I've only been here a month or so and I haven't had a chance to review everybody's file, nor would I do so normally. I'd rather watch you in action and see how you do, and from what I've seen so far, you're doing quite well as the safety officer."

"Thank you, sir."

"Because you weren't stationed here when I was here last time I haven't had the chance to know you ahead of time. Your OPRs are consistently superb. We have had an unblemished safety record since you've been here, what's that now, ten months?"

"Yes, sir." Phinney assumed Colonel Linhard was considering him for some other position, perhaps a promotion to be a commander of one of the 5th Bomb Wing squadrons. That'd be just fine with him.

"How have you enjoyed flying the BUFF?"

"Just great, sir."

"Quite a difference from a fighter, isn't it?"

"Yes, sir. Frankly, it's a lot more to remember, much more stamina required, more people to be responsible for. I've really enjoyed it, not to mention the camaraderie."

"I see in the file you flew F-15s and then worked for the ACC commander."

"Yes, sir. That's correct."

"How is it that you switched to B-52s?"

"I got a DUI in Langley, sir. I got out of it on a technicality, but received a letter of reprimand, as I should have."

"So then you were sent to Barksdale."

"Yes, sir. I worked for the 8th Air Force commander as his protocol officer, and then after six months he sent me to Castle to get trained on the BUFF. Then back to Barksdale."

"Back to flying."

"Yes, sir. The only thing I ever wanted to do. I know I was very lucky to get to do it again, in any plane."

"You must have impressed quite a few people in Barksdale."

"I tried to do my best. Like they say, the most important job is the one you're doing."

"How about the drinking. Any other problems with that?"

"No, sir. I don't drink anymore." There was a slight pause as the colonel thought to himself.

"Back to the flying," the colonel continued, "have you kept current in the ACE program?"

"Yes, sir. I've got over two hundred hours this year in T-38s."

"That many?"

"Yes, sir. I know the program is primarily for the co-pilots to get command experience, but under ACC directive I'm also supposed to be actively engaged in those training hops, kind of quality check each of the co-pilots before they move into the left seat of the BUFF."

"And you feel comfortable doing high speed landings in the T-38?" Linhard knew that the T-38 and the SR-71 had similar landing characteristics, particularly the high landing speeds of 165 and 155 knots respectively.

"Yes, sir. Very comfortable."

"OK. Another thing I need to check on. In the last ten months while you've been here have you attended any of the senior SIOP briefings?" SIOP: Single Integrated Operation Plan. In other words, the briefing on the present full-scale nuclear plans.

"No, sir. I was off-station for the last one."

"Glad to hear it." Phinney wasn't sure why his attendance—indeed, his *lack* of attendance at such a briefing, would be a good thing.

Linhard continued without explanation: "One last thing. I understand you are divorced."

Phinney's mind once again began racing. Was he being considered as a commander? Everyone knew that very few people received command spots who weren't married. "Yes, sir. Six years now."

"How long were you married?"

"Twelve years, sir."

"Any regrets?"

Phinney wasn't sure what the colonel was trying to get at. "Regrets, sir? Well, I guess I regret that it didn't work out, but in the long run I think it was right for both of us. She wasn't happy and went her own way. Just one of those things, I guess."

"And what did you learn from it."

"Sir?"

"What did you learn from it? A good pilot, a good aeronautical engineer, always reviews the situation, learns from it, and applies what he learns."

"Yes, sir. I understand, sir. Well, I guess I learned that I could have been a better husband, and I guess she could have been a better wife. Any way, as a result I later taught myself how to cook, developed a green thumb. And got over the guilt."

"Guilt?"

"Yes, sir. I finally decided that guilt is intended to be a rudder, not an anchor."

"That's not bad, Phinney. Not bad at all. Who said that?"

"I did, sir."

"Thus your call sign, 'English.'"

"Yes, sir. Everybody used to razz me because I'd quote Shakespeare, that type of thing, or I'd be reading something they thought was a little weird, or at least pedantic."

"Nothing wrong with being well-read, Phinney. Nothing at all. Back to the women thing. Are you dating anyone now?"

Phinney thought it strange to be asked, but felt comfortable in answering. "Well, sir, I guess you could say I'm between girlfriends at the moment. No one serious right now, no one on the line."

"I'll put it to you this way: If you were to leave tomorrow and be gone for say three or four weeks, would someone be wondering where you were?"

"Other than my staff and the pilots?"

"Yes."

"No, sir. That wouldn't be a problem."

"That's what I needed to know. All right, here's the deal. I've been asked to see if you'd be available for a special assignment, off base. It would involve flying, and some risk. Any problem with that?"

"No, sir."

"I want you to understand, Jack, that this is not a normal special assignment. You would be working with special ops. You could never talk to anyone about what you did or anything you learned. And you may not even be used, even after all the training is completed. And except for three of four people, no one will know anything about it. No special awards. No citation. No credit. That's what special ops is about. Do you think you could handle that?"

"Yes, sir. Not a problem."

The colonel was pleased. Everything that had to be said was said. Phinney had responded just as he—and they—had hoped.

"What we'll do, Jack, is list you as gone on an accident investigation board. Those are always short-notice assignments, and in your position as safety officer no one would think anything of it."

"That would make sense, sir."

The colonel handed Phinney an envelope. "Here are your orders and your ticket for the 5:10 flight tomorrow morning. There's also a NASA badge in there to use to get onto the base. Wear civilian clothes in transit; take your flight suits and one class A uniform."

"Yes, sir." Phinney picked up the envelope off the desk. "Where am I heading?"

"To Edwards Air Force Base. Your Northwest flight arrives at Minneapolis at 0636, then you transfer to a direct flight to Ontario; it leaves at 0910 and you arrive at Ontario at 1049. Chris has already booked you a rental car, unlimited mileage. Head to Edwards; they want you there at the main gate at 1600, civilian clothing. Any questions?"

"No, sir. I've got it. Any idea what type of mission it is, sir?"

"Yes, as a matter of fact some of my old cronies at the Joint Staff filled me in; unfortunately, you aren't going to be briefed until you're fully trained and they know the mission is a go."

Makes sense, Phinney thought. Need-to-know basis. "Anything else, sir?"

"Yes. Two things you need to know. First, these special ops people, they're a different breed. They never say it can't be done unless it really can't be done. Under normal flying operations up here in Minot or anywhere in ACC, it's safety first. If a generator goes, we scrub the mission. With these guys, everything that goes wrong is just a challenge; in their environment things are supposed to go wrong, or at least things are supposed to change on a moment-by-moment basis.

Don't do anything stupid, but throw the standard book out the window. Everything can be done; it's just a matter of how to do it."

"Yes, sir."

"That's the first thing. The second relates to perceptions and motives. Around here, 90 percent of what is said you can take at face value; 10 percent you have to ask yourself what the underlying motive is, who is giving you the information and what that person's agenda is. When I worked inside the loop in D.C., I figure the percentages dropped to fifty-fifty. Sometimes it's a hard to know whether what you are being told is true, or if you are just being used."

"'Men should be what they seem . . .'" Phinney stated simply.

"And 'those that be not, would they might seem none!' Bet you didn't know I knew Shakespeare, did you?"

"No, sir. I hadn't heard that about you."

"Now some of these intel people have got the mind set that when it comes to international politics, it's 90 percent questionable motives, and only 10 percent can be taken at face value. Pretty soon they're chasing their own tails and missing the forest for the trees. What I'm trying to say is in most situations, even in the special ops world, you can take 75 percent of what you see and hear at face value. Use your gut, your instincts. They won't fail you; overthinking possibilities and permutations is one of the quickest ways to get yourself all screwed up. Understand?"

"Yes, sir."

"You said you didn't drink?"

"Yes, sir."

"Well, you'll fit right in with these guys. Hardly any of them drink, and they tend to be on the religious side so watch your language. They're not prudes, but they're a bit more conservative than probably either one of us."

"Yes, sir. I'll keep that in mind."

"Good luck, Jack," the colonel stated as he reached out to shake Phinney's hand.

"Thank you, sir," Phinney stated as they shook hands. A few minutes later Linhard called General Williams on his STU-III secure telephone and briefed the J-3 on his conversation with Phinney.

# CHAPTER 16

## Moscow, Russia

Dave Mobbs looked over the edge of his book at the young man seated on a small couch next to the window overlooking Lenin's tomb. He, along with all of the CIA agents assigned to Moscow, had been trying to locate Pavel Kerlov for three years. They of course knew of his military connection with his uncle and his previous unimpressive career as a scientist. But then, allegedly after a visit from his powerful uncle, he essentially disappeared. Perhaps he had visited Moscow on occasion, but if he did no one had noticed him. The so-called disappearance caused no great concern at the Embassy or at the CIA until the rumors began to surface six months later that Pavel had hired a dozen or so of the most promising young Russian scientists, particularly Russian nuclear scientists and engineers. So the word went out to Mobbs and others to watch for Kerlov and, if possible, follow him to find out where he now worked. But for two years he was not observed by any of the American or British operatives, which, of course, caused even greater concern since such a fact meant that his assignment was outside of Moscow, and therefore was probably not a theoretical project. Thus, when Dave Mobbs was called an hour earlier and told that Pavel was sighted in a bar inside the G.U.M., Mobbs rushed immediately to the place, taking the time only to call Riana and grab his cassette player.

So where is she? Mobbs thought to himself as he watched Kerlov nearing the end of his glass of beer. She should be here by now. Mobbs' nervousness increased exponentially as he watched from the other side of the small bar as Pavel drank the last of his beer. A woman glided past him without a sound.

"May I sit here?" she asked Pavel as she began to take off her beautiful fur coat. Pavel looked up at the woman and was struck by her simple beauty; the woman's medium-length brown hair curled inward slightly, her eyes and disarming smile immediately conveyed to Pavel an exquisite woman of simple warmth and kindness.

"Certainly. There is plenty of room," Pavel replied. As the woman folded her coat over the small couch Pavel observed her small-ish size and pleasant figure. At about the same time a waiter walked over to the table.

"May I get you something?" the waiter asked.

"Yes," the woman replied, "a glass of wine please. White." Pavel looked over at the woman, once again impressed with her beauty and her wonderful smile. His thoughts, however, were interrupted by the waiter.

"Sir? Sir, would you like another, also?"

"Yes, another please."

The waiter nodded and walked the fifteen or so steps back to get the wine and another beer. In all, the cafe was no more than twenty feet by forty feet and was capable of seating only twenty or so patrons. But the location was unmatched, overlooking Red Square as it did. The woman looked out the window at Lenin's Tomb until her wine was served.

"Thank you," she stated to the waiter as he brought her the glass of wine. As she began to reach inside her purse Pavel interrupted.

"Please, allow me. Take it out of here," he said pointing to the one hundred thousand ruble note sitting on his table.

The woman nodded to Pavel. "Thank you." She sat back on the couch and sipped on the wine. "I love this view."

Each of them looked out the window across Red Square at Lenin's Tomb. The fresh snow, just a few inches high, made everything look clean and pure, a rarity for Moscow. They each fell silent for a few moments as they absorbed the view.

"I am amazed the tomb is still here given all of the changes during the last few years," Pavel stated.

"Yes," the woman replied, "I suppose. But I am not one for politics. Everything comes and goes. And I suppose some things that go, come back."

"Indeed. I take it you are from Moscow."

"Yes."

"If I may ask, what do you do?"

"I work for a German company, a trade company."

"So you must get to travel a lot."

"Sometimes, though most of the time I stay here. I prefer it here . . . ." The woman paused for a moment, seemingly trying to decide whether to divulge anything of substance to the man. "I need to be here, to take care of my mother."

"Is she not well?"

"No, she is not very well. She is old, and always in bed." She again paused for a moment, looking down.

"Tell me, what did she do in the old days?"

"She worked at the radio station. Sometimes as a journalist. Sometimes as a reader. Later as a producer. All sorts of things."

"I'm sure she was wonderful, especially if she looked anything like you."

The woman blushed slightly at Pavel's comment. "You are too kind," she stated simply, showing her embarrassment by again looking downward. Pavel once again looked carefully at her ring finger to make sure she was not married, and was pleased to see that she apparently was not.

"And your father. What does he do?"

"He also was a journalist, and still does a little of it. But he is much older than me. As is my mother."

The two stirred their drinks. Pavel's mind stumbled, not sure what to say next, or how to say it. He hated himself, his nervousness, his awkwardness at these type of things. He looked out the window again as he searched for something to say.

"Perhaps they should re-name it White Square," he said nervously.

The woman looked back outside at the snow and laughed pleasantly. "Yes," she stated smiling at Pavel, "perhaps they should!"

"I am Pavel Kerlov," he said as he reached out his hand.

"Hello," the woman replied while shaking his hand. "I am Riana Kovapiova."

"May I get you another drink?"

"Yes, thank you. That would be fine. And what do you do, Pavel, now that you know all about *me*?"

"I am a scientist."

"Really!"

"Yes, actually a director of a project."

"That sounds wonderful."

"Yes, I like it."

"But you are so young to be a director. You must be very good at what you do."

"I hope so," Pavel stated with more pride than modesty.

"Do you work in town?"

"No. Out in the country." Pavel paused knowing that he should not reveal much more to his new acquaintance. "Some ways from here. I usually take the train. But it has been very busy, so I have not been back here for a long time. Almost six months."

"Well perhaps I can convince you to come back more often."

"Yes," Pavel said now only slightly embarrassed, "I'm sure you could." So, Pavel thought, at least she is interested. "Say," he stated with more volume than he intended, as though he had just thought of something, "how about if we'd go to dinner? I know a nice cafe. I know you would like it."

"Well, I don't know . . ."

"Really, it is very nice. I know the owners, and it is close. A short drive."

Riana again stammered slightly. "I really should go home."

"But it is Friday afternoon, and with the holiday next week you will have plenty of time to see your mother. And I am such a nice fellow, one you can trust. Really."

Riana looked up at Pavel, ostensibly trying to judge him, to decide if he could be trusted. "Yes, you do seem very nice." She paused thinking for just a moment. "Yes, I will go with you to dinner, but tomorrow night. If I were to go with you now you would think me too forward, true? Here is my telephone number," she said as she wrote the numbers on the napkin.

"All right," Pavel said happily. "And here is my number."

"Shall we take the Metro tomorrow, or should we drive?" Riana asked.

"Let's take my car. The cafe is close to here, though not that close to a Metro station."

"Fine," Riana said a little bit formally, as if she were making a business appointment, "we'll meet outside the north door, at six?"

"Certainly," Pavel replied. "I look forward to it!"

Riana finished her wine and reached back along the small couch for her coat. "I must be going." Pavel immediately reached for Riana's coat and lifted it for her.

"Please, allow me," he said in his most gentlemanly manner.

"Thank you, Pavel. I will see you tomorrow at six, no?"

"Yes. Definitely. The north door, on this side. At six."

"Good," she said reaching out her hand and shaking Pavel's. "See you then." And with that the beautiful Riana left.

Soon thereafter Pavel finished his beer and left the bar, thinking only of Riana and his date with her the next evening. Pavel was so deep in thought that he did not notice Dave Mobbs following him as he exited on the south side of the G.U.M. and down the escalator to the Metro station that took him home to his rarely-used Moscow apartment.

# CHAPTER 17

## Moscow, Russia

Pavel pulled his car toward an empty spot across the street from the café, boldly marked in Western tradition with a brightly colored neon light. "I went to grade school over there," Riana stated pointing to her right as the vehicle slowed down. Pavel looked over at the small playground as the car stopped.

"It looks wonderful," Pavel replied. "Very small, close-knit. I'll bet you enjoyed it." They both got out of the car; Pavel reached forward and took off both windshield wipers and the side mirror and placed them on the floor in front of his seat. "I hate that it is no longer safe, that there are those who dare to steal now."

"Yes," Riana agreed. "It is terrible. How can so much change so quickly?"

Pavel and Riana walked across the street, Riana's arm softly resting inside Pavel's. Such a wonderful custom, Pavel thought; perhaps it is European, though he was not sure, but in Russia, the women everywhere walk with an arm inside their companions' arm, even if the companion is another woman. Of course nowadays in Moscow such customs are essential, especially in the winter when one is likely to fall on occasion on the inch or two-inch thick ice left on the sidewalk.

"You would think that people would clean the ice and snow off the sidewalks," Pavel asked, "especially in front of businesses."

"It is terrible. They should mandate such a change. The old dare not walk the streets anymore."

Pavel and Riana entered the café and walked up the one-half flight of stairs and checked their coats. The restaurant was small, but modern, perhaps able to seat twenty or so patrons. "A perfect size for a café," Riana thought out loud.

"Indeed," Pavel replied as they were taken to their table. "This is my favorite place. When I am in Moscow I come here on Saturdays and play chess for hours on end. They have some very good players."

"And I bet you are the best," Riana said as she was being seated.

"I seem to be able to win a few," Pavel replied with more bravado than modesty. Soon the waiter brought ice water and heavy, dark Russian bread broken upon a plate with salt on the side.

"So," Pavel began, "you grew up around here. You are a true Muscovite."

"Yes," Riana replied as she whimsically thought back to those early years. "Things were simple, and safe. Did you grow up here as well?"

"Yes. My father was in the military. I was somewhat stubborn, though, and refused to follow in his footsteps. My father was not very happy with my choice, but he later forgave my decision in his own way. And your father? What does he do?"

"He is much older than me. He turns seventy-two this year. For the most part he is retired. But he is still a journalist. He served all over the world after the War."

Pavel took note of this fact, realizing that most journalists sent out after World War II were KGB spies. Riana immediately surmised what Pavel was probably thinking. "No, he was not a spy. The others who were sent with him were KGB; they had to have at least one journalist to perform the job, while the others did what they did. Unfortunately for my father that meant he had to do the journalistic work of three men, since the other two knew nothing of reporting, or, at least, they said they did not. But I did not know my father at all until recently. I was raised by my mother."

"Why is that? Were they divorced when you were young?"

"No. It was not until I was a young woman that I ever met my father. My father was in the War, and when he came back in the 1940s there were, as you know, very few men. My father is Armenian, and very handsome. The times warranted different morals, different concerns; there were few men, and many women who wanted children."

The waiter showed Pavel a bottle of wine, his favorite.

"Thank you, Gregory," Pavel stated with a slight air of self-importance. "That will be fine. So how is it that you met him, then?" The waiter began opening the wine.

"My mother told him right away about my coming. My father, however, was not convinced that I was his child and therefore was not around when I was born. Later mutual friends would see me when I was young and would tell him that I did not look anything like him. He therefore took their word and assumed that I was not his daughter, and life went on." Riana paused to drink a sip of wine as the waiter looked on. "Yes, it is very nice. Thank you." The waiter completed filling the glasses.

"Let's see. Where was I?"

"Your father did not think it was you because you did not look like him."

"Yes, of course. So every couple of years this friend or that friend of his would see me, and they would once again report to my father that I looked nothing like him. Soon I was all but forgotten, until I reached the age where I naturally wondered about who my father was and began asking questions. Eventually, at my mother's insistence, my father agreed to meet me at a café. I was seventeen. When I walked into the café my father immediately rushed up to me, tears flowing from his eyes, begging my forgiveness."

"Why?" Pavel asked. "What happened?"

"The moment he saw me he immediately recognized in me the perfect image of his grandmother, shown in the family pictures, when she was a young woman, and he knew without a doubt that I was his child, the quintessential reflection of his grandmother long since dead. He has been a part of my life ever since."

As Riana told Pavel about her father he began to feel sorry for him, sorry that the father had not been able to see such an exquisite creature grow into womanhood. Her every word exuded warmth and kindness; her eyes seemed to him like dark coals leading directly to her soul. Within an hour he knew he would marry her, if given the chance, and Pavel decided at that point that every waking breath would be directed to that end.

# CHAPTER 18

## Alta Loma, California

Jack Phinney sat parked at the north end of the street, looking southward toward the house where his niece—his first niece, that is—now lived. Years ago Jack's oldest sister lived in the same house, and before that Jack and his family had lived a mere four blocks away, along a row of eucalyptus trees. Jack hadn't seen his sister in over ten years. She had became a Mormon when she married her first husband, but years later they were divorced, and she had to raise the kids by herself. Jack couldn't remember if she had raised seven or eight children in that house, including Jack's niece, Christina. The trouble with military life, Jack thought to himself, is you move around so much you tend to lose track of your relatives. It's not that you don't care about them, or don't remember them often. It's just that after awhile you don't feel like you know them anymore—they become blood strangers, people you continue to love based on shared parents and old, fading memories. But who they are now, you really don't know.

But the memories were grand to Jack, and came back to him as he drove over the mile or so east to the Interstate that would take him north over and through the San Bernardino Mountains. Several visions flashed before him as he drove towards the high desert: seeing his father in the backyard wearing his bright-orange jump suit, his flight helmet in his hand; watching his two older sisters being picked up by boyfriends for dates; the sounds of the Hells Angels riding along the highway towards their home just north of Chaffee College; jumping off the Chaffee College high dive feet first, feeling like the water was one hundred feet below.

Looking to his left as he drove north on Interstate 15, Jack could see the foothills which perched along the beginning of the San

Bernardino Mountains that arched up into the sky in front of him. Taking a deep breath, he smelled the eucalyptus trees, and recalled climbing them in his youth, their sticky sap clinging to his hands and smearing his clothes. Jack smiled as he thought about the time he had been knocked unconscious while riding his blue, Schwinn Stringray bike in front of the house. Jack had heard a jet plane in the sky; he looked up, watching as the plane passed overhead. The next thing he remembered was being attended to by his mother, who was rightfully chastising Jack for not watching where he was going. He had ridden his bike right into a curb, flipping forward over the bike's handle-bars and landing on his head, knocking himself unconscious. His brother, Don, who was also outside, had carried him into the house, undoubtedly shocking his mother considerably.

Of all his family, he felt closest to his brother. Only a few years apart, they had experienced much of the same things: the constant moves, the need to make new friends quickly, the subtle realization that nothing was permanent—that which may be considered important one day would be insignificant the next.

Phinney eventually exited the Interstate some twenty-three miles later and headed northwesterly on Highway 138 the fifty miles or so to Palmdale, the home of the famous Skunkworks and the location where the last fully-modified Block 30 B-2 would soon be coming off the production line.

Turning north on Highway 14, Phinney drove approximately twenty miles to Rosamond and then turned right and headed east towards Edwards Air Force Base. It was three in the afternoon, and it was hot, over one hundred degrees Phinney guessed. Phinney recalled being at Edwards Air Force Base for an air show many years ago when he was a young boy. Perhaps it was when he was in third grade, or even the fourth. It was quite an air show! He remembered seeing the XB-70 up close, the immense delta-wing bomber designed specifically to bomb Russia from eighty thousand to one hundred thousand feet in the air; seeing a small flying wing sitting underneath a B-52B, its research instrumental to the modern-day shuttle; and remembering that next to the flying wing sat the famous X-15, the rocket plane that broke every speed and height record possible for a non-orbital vehicle. He remembered seemingly hundreds of other planes that day in the

125 degree heat. He was just eight or nine years old at the time. It seemed so long ago now, as if it weren't really his own memories, but something he had read or seen in a book.

Phinney drove the twenty or so miles east on Rosamond Boulevard, passing the introductory sign showing where the base began, seeing the black metal "shark's fin" on the right jutting out five or six feet into the air from the flat lake bed. Every spring, when there was an inch or so of rain on the Rosamond Lake, the students at the Air Force test pilot school would perform the ritual of wading out into the now mushy lake and place the heavy metal plate shaped like a "shark's fin" into the mud. That way, the unknowing would drive by and look out onto the Rosamond Lake and "see" a shark's fin and perhaps be tricked into believing that the lake is shark infested!

Phinney slowed down as he approached the West Gate.

"Can I help you, sir?" the guard asked.

Phinney showed him his NASA badge and Air Force ID as a group of vans filled with tired-looking "civilians" exited, their workday over. Blackworld, Phinney though to himself, just like when the F-117 was still secret.

"Do you know where the Dryden facility is, sir?"

Phinney nodded "yes."

"Very good," the airman stated formally as he stepped back and saluted Phinney through.

Everyone in the military was aware of the Hugh L. Dryden Flight Research Center. Situated on the Mojave Desert northeast of Los Angeles, the desert community transformed itself from a population of less than four thousand in the 1950s to over thirty thousand in just ten years, primarily due to the development of the United States' first jet, the Bell XP-59A, and the subsequent Bell XS-1. High above Rogers Dry Lake, the largest dry lake in the world, the XS-1 broke the sound barrier for the first time in October of 1947. But other "barriers" were left to be broken, and six years after Chuck Yeager's daring flight, A. Scott Crossfield, sick with the flu, carefully flew past Mach 2 in a follow-on to the XS-1 known as the Skyrocket.

The first flight beyond Mach 3 belonged to Mel Apt in his ill-fated flight in September of 1956. After flying over Mach 3 for at least ten seconds, Apt lost control of his X-2 plane as he turned back towards the lake; the plane began a series of rapid rolls and began to disintegrate. Apt jettisoned the nose section in preparation to bail out, but it was too late; the capsule and what was left of the X-2 crashed separately onto the desert floor, killing Apt instantly. But the race for speed and the desire for knowledge about hypersonic flight continued on, and a few years later the North American X-15 flew past Mach 6.

Six miles after passing the West Gate Phinney entered the main area. Phinney passed the billeting on the left, drove past as he passed the rows of hangars on his right, and eventually reached the last set of hangars directly on the flight line. "Turn at the flying wing," the Bomb Wing's exec had told him. "You can't miss it." He was right.

Phinney parked next to the supercritical wing plane and walked toward the main entrance, showing his NASA badge to the guard before entering the main building.

As he entered the main building a woman in a green flight suit approached him. She was at best five foot five, had short hair and a pleasant smile.

"You must be Mr. Phinney."

Mister Phinney, Jack thought. Does she think I'm a civilian? "Yes, ma'am. That's correct."

"Welcome to NASA. My name's Marta Whisenand. I'll be helping with the training. As a matter of fact, I'm in charge of your training for the next couple of weeks."

Phinney looked somewhat confused; he was going to be trained by a NASA civilian for an Air Force mission? Marta observed the confusion.

"I take it that you haven't been briefed yet on the mission."

Jack wanted to blurt out, Hell, I don't even know what type of plane they plan on using, but he instead merely stated, "That's correct, ma'am."

"Then you're in for a surprise, and a real treat. Come on, let's head to the briefing room. I'll introduce you to the project director on the way. I'll warn you though, he's a little miffed about your flying this mission with one of our birds; Lord knows the Air Force had every right to re-activate the bird under our old contract, but after the final retirement the planes were transferred over to us. Now that we own them, we're not real pleased to have to loan it back. Over the years we've thought of the plane as if it was our own personal property."

So what the hell do they have me flying? Phinney asked himself as he followed the woman down the corridors. If it was a black-world plane I'd be at Palmdale, unless they were doing the testing stage here for some reason. And why would they have these guys do the flight testing for a new plane? And a woman? How many female test pilots could there be since it's only been a few years that women were allowed to fly combat jets? Although it didn't make any sense, Phinney kept his mouth shut and went with the flow. He'd learn soon enough, he supposed.

Marta stopped in front of a door marked "Project Director" and signalled with her hand for Jack to go in ahead of her. As Jack entered the room he was surprised how small it was, especially for such a large man. Behind the desk sat a large balding man in his forties looking over papers. His name-plate said David Heckman. The man looked up.

"So you're the son-of-a-bitch who's takin' one of my planes for a joy ride!" Dave Heckman said smiling. Jack felt a little more comfortable when he realized by the man's tone that the anger was feigned, at least for the most part.

Marta spoke up before Jack had a chance to say anything. "He hasn't been briefed yet. He doesn't even know what he's going to be flying."

"No shit! What a laugh. These spooks never cease to amaze me. Well, let's let him take a look. Follow me, Colonel."

Well, Jack thought as he followed the man into the hallway, at least he knows my rank. The three of them walked quickly down the stairs and into an unguarded hangar, the high desert heat hitting Jack once again as he entered the hangar. Before him were two planes he had seen thousands of times in photos but never personally: two SR-71A Blackbirds. He was surprised at their great length.

"Beauties, aren't they," the project director commented as they walked below one of the wings. "These are the two 'A' models given to us by the Air Force. The 'B' model is out there sitting on the flight line. So what do you think? How'd you like to fly the fastest plane in the world?"

Jack was in shock. Why an SR? Why him? "This isn't exactly what I expected."

"I bet not. Come on. Let's go inside and visit, somewhere we
can talk in private." Jack followed the project director back into the
building, with Marta following close behind. Heckman walked up to
a door, pressed several digits on the security box next to it, and opened
the door marked "Simulator." Jack continued to follow the project
director as he stepped into the room and up the few metal stairs onto
the simulator platform for the SR-71.

"This room is a secure area. We can talk here. We've been
asked, actually ordered, to train you to fly a Blackbird. If you develop
sufficient proficiency in the plane, you will be assigned to fly into hostile territory to pick up someone of great importance to our government. The mission will be entirely black. You'll go in, pick up your
passenger, and get out. No one will ever know about it."

"Why do you know about it then; you're civilians."

"Yes, we are. But given the training parameters and the fact
that you are using one of our birds, we were fully briefed on the mission. Each of us, and Marta's husband, have been given SCI clearance
to assist on this mission. And by the way, it's not the first time we've
assisted in this type of thing. The loan agreement between NASA and
the Air Force was in place from July of 1990 until just recently.
Paragraph X allowed the Air Force to have full use of the SR upon sixty
days notice, though of course we never hold them to the sixty days. As
soon as we had it ready for them, it was theirs. They re-activated it for
about two years, and then cut the funding again. It costs a lot to fly
the 'Habu'," Heckman said, referring to the Blackbird's nickname that
had originated in Kadena when the native people likened the long, fast
black plane to a similar-looking snake indigenous to Okinawa named
habu. "I guess they thought the satellites and UAVs could do the trick.
This time when they retired the Blackbirds they switched ownership
to us. But that really doesn't matter that much. We all work for the
government, and when one department asks another one for a particular asset, the powers that be make it happen. And it's not like we're
not used to dealing with classified missions or assets, so they know they
can trust us. And in this case, they know our bird is the best one for
this particular mission."

"And the mission is flying into where?" Jack asked.

The project director paused, looking evenly at Jack. "That's all we need to tell you at this point," referring implicitly not only to the need-to-know rule but also to the possibility that Jack might wash out. "Are you still interested?"

"You bet. Very interested."

"All right." Heckman looked over at Marta. "Marta here will be in charge of your training. She will make the final recommendation whether to use you. In other words, if you can't convince her you can fly this baby and use all of its special equipment, you're screwed. Any questions?"

"Only one, sir. Why me? You obviously have SR-71 pilots already trained to fly these types of missions."

Maybe this young man will work out, the project director thought to himself; at least he has the astuteness to ask perhaps the most relevant question to the success of the mission—and the guts to ask it, especially when it may work directly to his disadvantage.

"I am told there are several good reasons," the director stated, "all of which you'll find out later if you succeed in convincing Marta that you're capable of flying the mission. But I can tell you this: If you can't be used, the mission becomes very difficult, and maybe impossible."

"I'll do my best, sir."

"I'm sure you will. I'll leave you two to begin your work. You've only got two weeks to become fully proficient in this plane and all its various systems. I'd suggest that the two of you get right at it."

"Yes, sir," Phinney stated simply as the project director walked down the steps and toward the door. Jack turned to Marta. "I'm all yours."

"You bet your ass, you are!" she said smiling. "I hope to hell you can fly like a son of a bitch or we're both screwed."

"Ma'am, I can fly to hell and back and send you a postcard signed by the devil himself."

"Glad to hear it, since that's pretty damn close to what you're going to be doin'. Now let's see if you can fly as well as you can bull-shit!"

Marta pointed over to the simulator's pilot seat. "Have a seat."

# CHAPTER 19

## Moscow

Raina and Pavel walked slowly past Lenin's Tomb upon the bricks of Red Square, her arm fit snugly inside his as they walked. The weather was clear, the day exceedingly warm for the season. It was, in short, a beautiful day for a walk in Alexandrovsky Garden along the northwest wall of the Kremlin.

They were not the only couple who decided the day was a good one for a walk. It had been days since the weather had been good, days well spent, Riana surmised, in getting to know Pavel. Following their diner a few weeks ago, Pavel had to return for a week or so to his position outside of Moscow to entertain, he said, a very important visitor. But as he promised, he returned as soon as he could. Raina had a few days of leave coming from her work and took them. This was there third day straight together, and frankly they were both ready to get outdoors.

After walking past Nikolskaya Tower, the couple turned left past the northwest corner of the Kremlin at Sobakina Tower, standing 180 feet high, its base over twelve feet thick and containing a secret well (ever so important if under siege) and an outlet to the Neglinnaya River, which had been covered up by bricks and still flows beneath. The couple walked past the famous tower and found themselves standing at the Tomb of the Unknown Soldier. The large red and black marble structure was itself imposing, and all who approached it approached with reverence. Even the babbling tourist knew well enough to not chatter loudly. Death, it seems, has a way of quieting the living as well as the dead, Riana thought.

Riana and Pavel stood for a few minutes as they watched the new wedding couples leave flowers at the Tomb of the Unknown Soldier. Raina watched one young couple, the bride wearing her traditional white wedding dress, as they followed the tradition of placing flowers on the tomb next to the sculptured helmet and having their photograph taken by relatives and friends. Built in 1967 to honor the over two million dead from the Great War (1941-1945), the tomb contained the remains of an unknown soldier who died defending Moscow itself in 1941. Next to the raised granite slab where the flowers were laid stood a lower slab, this one black granite instead of red granite, upon which an eternal flame burned, and to the other side stood six urns holding soil from the six "heroic" cities that resisted the Germans at such a great cost.

As Riana watched the flame flicker, she could see out of her peripheral vision the couples come and go. She allowed her mind to wander. How could these couples marry and have children at such a time? Everything is so uncertain. There may be no jobs tomorrow. New and old diseases are springing forth from the unsanitary prisons and from foreigners from distant lands. Alcoholism and crime are rampant, and the government—the new government—is just now starting to attempt to create something out of this chaos that was Russia. Everything is so uncertain. And frightening. And her life, she thought, is passing her by. Soon it will be too late to marry. I am already an old maid. I am thirty, and shall never live the life I had dreamed.

"You look so serious, my love," Pavel said after staring at her for the last minute or two.

"Oh, I am sorry, Pavel," Raina replied, startled that she had lost her focus for even a moment. "I do not mean to be. But here, it is hard not to be."

"Yes," Pavel said, "it is hard not to be serious here. As I've told you, my father died in a war, one which we lost and would not have lost had we done what should have been done. At least here the men did not die for nothing."

"At least they are happy," Riana said, referring to the newly-weds and trying to change the tone.

"Perhaps someday we can be so happy," Pavel said smiling.

"Perhaps," Riana said, returning the smile. "Perhaps."

The two spent the next hour walking in the garden, slowly circling back towards Red Square, and then along the northeast wall, looking at the names of the dead so honored to be buried at the Kremlin itself. All Russians knew many of the names—such as Stalin, Andropov, Chernenko, and cosmonaut Yuri Gagarin—although some were less famous than others. And of course, not all of the names were Russian, such as Communists from Germany, Britain, and the United States. Raina stopped in front of the tomb of John Reed, the American journalist.

"I wonder what he would think of our country now?" Riana said to Pavel.

"He would say he was right all along. That pure economic freedom is just as dangerous as no freedom at all. The few in power based on ideology have been replaced by the rich oligarchs that have no ideology at all, except to stay rich. At least the State attempted to create equality, or at least general equality. He would say he was right, that inequalities of wealth are just as dangerous as placing ultimate power in the hands of the few for the many."

"But at least now the many have the power to change things," Riana responded.

"It is but an illusion of power, just like democracy is nothing more than an illusion of justice. Only the powerful, backed by money or others with money, can reach those positions of power. It is a sham, and everyone knows it."

Riana thought for a moment as they once again began walking along Red Square and back towards the Metro. She agreed that extreme inequality is itself an injustice. Such a view is rightly held by almost all Russians, even following the collapse of the Soviet Union. Soviet doctrine could not help but teach the masses the pre-Marxist theories relating to property rights, such as the writings of Locke and Hobbes who used their radical concept of individual property rights to steal away the absolute powers of kings and queens. And following the collapse of the Soviet Union, the evils associated with unfettered property rights and capitalism run amuck were especially pronounced. And given the advent of inalienable property rights "discovered" by the likes of Hobbes and Locke—not to mention the practical inability to lessen the power of the wealthy—Riana also realized that abuses based on economic status rarely go unchallenged. Money, she concluded, is power. Money is freedom. And in Russia, money is just one more way for the few to assert their will and injustice upon the masses.

But Riana also knew democracy was not a sham. She understood that the adoption of a democratic framework at least *in theory* made it possible to correct an abuse of power by taking away that person's power by the vote. It had potential, even in her country. But the chaos created by the shock of unfettered capitalism had indeed brought about a poverty that equaled the poverty of ideas and freedom under the old system. And she also knew that their economic situation, as some Westerns incorrectly thought, was not that the Russian people were ingrained with the old Soviet system and were too lazy or bureaucratic to work or dig themselves out of their hole. The Russians were no more lazy than the Americans were in the 1930s. The vast majority of the Russians would be glad to work any job that paid, if such a job existed.

So, Riana had to ask herself, why am I doing this? When I started to spy for the Americans, there was freedom to be won. I did it for principle, to lessen such injustices. But now, the economic system foisted upon us by the West and particularly the Americans, has caused perhaps even more harm. Before there were jobs, and at least some food and affordable items for sale. Now there are few jobs, and nothing is affordable. Our population is actually shrinking! No other modern industrialized country is losing its population. And it will only get worse, she realized.

Why do I continue to do this? At first it was to undo the Soviet system. And when it collapsed, then the excitement kept me in it, I suppose. And I always dreamed of getting to go to America, to see what true freedom is, what it is like to live in such a rich and prosperous country. Perhaps it's just the commitment to a job, if not the cause. But I must have a cause, I must have a reason to continue. Something more than just because it's what I do, what I enjoy doing.

But at least here, walking with this man, there is no dilemma, patriotic or otherwise. If Pavel is indeed the head of a secret military base unknown to our civilian leaders, then the issue is an easy one. Democracy does have a value. There is at least the chance for some semblance of justice and equality, both political and economic. And civilian leadership over the military has to be one of the most important aspects of democracy. Indeed, it is probably the first step towards any true democracy, Riana thought. Hadn't Professor Ivanian at the Institute of US and Canadian Studies written a book describing all of the American presidents, and in that book he mentioned that a few years before the famous constitutional convention the military who had served under George Washington had asked him to take over the country in a military coup since they had not been paid by the Revolutionary Congress, and when Washington went to speak with his former soldiers about their repeated requests for payment he scolded them for even suggesting a coup? And Washington did so knowing full-well that given the weak state of the colonies under the Articles of Confederation and his great popularity that the people would have gladly accepted him over a fragile and so far unworkable democracy that had barely started in the States!

Yes, Riana thought, we are no longer run by the KGB. We alone are in charge of our destiny. The Americans have failed in their attempt to help us out of this morass. I will complete this mission, but it will be my last for the Americans. My country is free—indeed, too free—and the enemy is no longer the State or the Communist Party. The enemy, Riana decided, is now ourselves and our shameful economy, and I must decide how to fight that instead of spying for a country that deserves at least some of the blame for this mess that I see all around me.

# CHAPTER 20

## The Pentagon

"That, sir," Colonel Sandstrom stated to the chairman of the joint chiefs of staff, "concludes the briefing on Operation Quick Style. I would be happy to take any questions."

General Scott looked pleased, but also contemplative. He paused for a few moments thinking. "Gentlemen, and, I should add for Colonel Markham's benefit, lady, you should be commended for a job well done. Given the parameters that may be necessary to this mission, I think you have developed a very feasible and safe plan. I am glad you added the SAR component to it just in case we need to go in and do a search and rescue operation away from the landing site, presumably not in-country, or, at the most, within a few miles of the border. Colonel Sandstrom, I understand from General Williams that you were asked to do the briefing because you are the individual most opposed to the framework of the mission."

"Well, sir, . . ." Sandstrom began, his uneasiness obvious.

"That's OK, soldier. I would just as soon hear the bad news here, before the mission is given a go, then after it goes all to hell. I assume your biggest beef is with not using our normal special ops people and platforms."

"Yes, sir. That is correct."

"All right. For what it's worth I have read the special ops mission plan and I can tell you I like it better, too. And I intend to present both plans to the NSC and will be recommending the special ops plan. But if political reality, and those State Department naysayers, reduce our options to using this plan, with all its weaknesses, or not going at all, what would your answer be then?"

"Sir, I cannot answer that without knowing the exact importance of the information being retrieved. Operation Quick Style has more risk than the special ops plan, but it is do-able, sir."

"Do you believe you have adequately covered all of Quick Style's weaknesses?"

"Yes, sir. Perhaps too well, which is the way I prefer special ops briefings. Everyone might as well know all the risks, at least that's my view, sir."

"And mine too, Colonel, which is probably why General Williams insisted on you giving us the briefing. All right. Does any one else have any input? I'd rather hear it now."

The room was silent. The planning team all looked around at each other. Majors Hanna and Maki felt way too low on the pay scale to say a word; but at the same time, they certainly would if they had grave concerns. Colonels Dobson, Parsons, Coe, and Harper said nothing; they too were satisfied. Each of them believed Sandstrom had done a superb job in outlining the details of the plan, being careful to note how it should go, describing each of the elements of the plan where a breakdown could occur, and all of the usual risks of such a mission.

"All right. I've got one more question. Well, actually, two general concerns that I want to address, and which I will pose to Colonel Harper. Colonel, the two of us are the only people in this room who know exactly what information it is we are trying to get out of Russia; and neither of us know the identity of the person, but we know the importance of the information that he has supplied over the years. You and I are also privy to what special steps the CIA and the DIA, as well as the 70th Intelligence Wing at Fort Meade, have taken to confirm the value of the information and the veracity of the contact being rescued, if you will."

The chairman paused a moment, thinking. "My first concern relates to whether the intel we have on the landing site justifies the mission? Specifically, do you believe that the steps we have taken to confirm the intel have been sufficient? Will our real-time survey of the site while the mission is being flown, combined with our communications suite, be capable of giving us adequate warning to abort? Are the steps we are taking to ensure the accuracy of the information sufficient?"

"Yes, sir," Harper answered, "I believe the steps we have taken will give us adequate notice if there is something wrong with the site. We will have triple-redundant coverage, each of which has several optical and other receivers that will be on or over site observing and sending back real-time imagery."

"All right. The next question is, given the planning you participated in, the intel you have access to relating to the landing site, and the value of the information that will be obtained by the successful completion of this mission, would you fly it? Would you approve it?"

Colonel Harper had considered nothing else since he had been assigned as the intelligence officer of this mission. He had no doubt and answered almost immediately. "Sir, I would approve this mission even if the risks were five times more than we anticipate. And yes, sir, if I was qualified to perform the mission I would gladly do it myself. Like any special ops mission, it has its risks; but in my opinion, sir, the value of the information far outweighs those risks."

General Scott had been told what he wanted to hear, and what he expected to hear. And, in the event the president opted for Operation Quick Style, he would tell him the same thing.

# CHAPTER 21

## Whiteman AFB, Missouri

Alexander Konesky, the senior Russian START compliance officer from Moscow, looked up at the massive B-2 Stealth Bomber as he observed his inspectors completing the START treaty on-site inspection. Everything had gone perfectly. During the hangar inspections his ten inspectors made all of the necessary measurements of the B-2 Stealth Bomber's bomb-bay, and had demanded access to any container large enough to hold a listed nuclear bomb or cruise missile. If only they were allowed real access to the most sophisticated plane in the world! But of course the treaty focused only on the platforms, either the planes, missiles, or submarines, or a simple verification of the number of warheads. From an intel stand-point the inspection had little value. You could read in the Kansas City paper how many B-2s have arrived yet at Whiteman, and of course everyone involved with the inspection process knew the exact dimensions of the bomb-bay. But from a "trust-but-verify" perspective, the inspection had immense value.

Colonel Randy Broughton, Air Attache assigned to the American Embassy at Moscow and START verification liaison officer, was also pleased at how well the inspection had gone. "Well Alex," Broughton stated to Konesky, "I believe that concludes the inspection. I assume you will want to write the report here."

"Yes, that would be my preference."

"As the inspected party, we hereby authorize you to complete your inspection report at this facility. We have of course prepared a room for your use. The escorts are prepared to take your people to that location."

"Very good," Konesky replied. "I assume they are to board that bus?" Konesky knew the drill, as well as the treaty, as well as Broughton. He had assumed that they would allow the Russians to complete the post-inspection report here, but of course that was up to the Americans since they were the party being inspected.

"Yes, that is correct. However, since the inspection is over and your people will need some time to begin the report, General Robertson would be honored to give you his regards and present you with a mission brief of the 509th."

Konesky almost flinched at the thought of a boring mission briefing—my God, the Russians knew the mission of the 509th and its organizational structure probably as well as the Americans did—but he had been trained well in diplomacy and kept his thoughts from his facial expressions.

"I would of course be honored," Konesky replied.

"Would any of your staff like to join us?"

Konesky looked over at the officers standing next to him. He was not surprised when they clearly indicated a preference to get to the report; the report rarely took long, but they had had enough of briefings, thank you kindly. "No," Konesky replied, "it seems that they have other work to do."

Good, thought Broughton, we don't have to worry about the GRU. "Why don't we take my staff car, then, Alexander?"

"As you wish."

The two officers got into the staff car and watched as the bus containing the nine other inspectors and their escorts left the hangar area. After the bus pulled away Randy looked over at Konesky. "As it turns out, Alexander, we have decided to show you a few other things which you might find of interest. Does that sound all right to you?"

"Certainly," Konesky replied, his interest being piqued.

"Also, at some point during the tour I would like to discuss something with you, away from the others; just the two of us."

Konesky realized the strangeness of such a request. "Relating to the treaty?"

"Perhaps," Broughton replied obliquely, "or at least its inter-pretation under, shall we say, unusual circumstances. So that you would feel more comfortable, you may choose where and when we will talk."

Konesky quickly understood that Broughton was allowing Konesky to select the place for the discussion so that he would be comfortable knowing that he was not being overheard by an electronic device. Obviously this was not going to be some simple treaty issue.

"I accept," Konesky said simply.

During the next one-half hour Konesky received the traditional mission briefing from the wing commander himself, Brigadier General Thomas Robertson. Robertson, a former B-52 bomber pilot, had previously flown the F-117 Stealth Fighter before it had been declassified. Konesky knew his biography well, though he always wondered how someone who appeared so exuberant—if not crazy—could be such a teetotaler. And although there were rumors of wilder days, those were obviously over, despite his penchant for wolfing down a raw egg or two, shell and all, as part of a crud bet.

General Robertson quickly went through the mission briefing, discussing first the history of Whiteman, which had initially been Sedalia Army Air Field beginning in 1942 where glider pilots were trained for the war. Although deactivated in 1947, the base became one of the early Strategic Air Command bases in 1951, hosting B-47 bombers and KC-97 refueling tankers. General Robertson noted that the base was renamed Whiteman Air Force Base in 1955 in memory of Lt George A. Whiteman, a fighter pilot from the local area who died trying to takeoff in his P-40 fighter during the attack on Pearl Harbor. General Robertson went on to inform Konesky that the base was also assigned Minuteman missiles in the 1960s until the deactivation of the 351st Missile Wing in 1995 as part of the START treaty.

"That concludes the briefing, Colonel Konesky. Did you have any questions?"

"No, General," Konesky replied, "I do not. Thank you very much for the excellent briefing." Konesky realized that a wing commander has better things to do than give briefings; what he couldn't figure out is why he was being given such royal treatment.

"It was our pleasure, sir. I understand that we have a tour set up for you. My public affairs officer, Captain Ward Swigler, will serve as your tour guide. I'm afraid I have some other things which I must attend to."

"Of course, sir. Thank you once again for all of your kindness."

"No problem at all," Robertson replied as he shook Konesky's hand. "I'll see you in a few hours at the out-brief."

"If you'll follow me, sir," the public affairs officer stated, "we'll begin the tour."

Although the briefing was standard, what followed was not. Following the public affairs officer, Konesky and Broughton left the headquarters building and walked the fifty yards or so past the statue commemorating the dropping of the two nuclear bombs on Japan by the 509th. After reviewing the statue, the group walked the twenty or so yards to the operations building.

"This, sir," the public affairs officer explained to Konesky, "is where we do most of our maintenance training." Konesky looked around the medium-size room filled with only ten large screen monitors and a central console. "If you'd step over here, sir, we have prepared a demonstration for you. You can see on this monitor a photograph of a wheel of the B-2. As an example, we have already programed in the changing of a tire. The student is asked which tool he wants; he inputs the tool, like this on the keyboard, and the video-slide program moves him through the changing of the tire step-by-step. Thus, the next slide shows the first lug nut removed."

"Do you still use the traditional tech manuals?" Konesky asked.

"Yes, sir. All of those items are available both in here, in those cabinets over there, as well as in each hangar. And of course our students are required to know them like the back of their hands as well, but we find that the visual training has a much higher retention rate. Also, before we send someone out to work a particular maintenance task on the plane, we have the maintenance worker run through the task here. He literally walks through the entire task, visually, so the technician is reminded of each step along the way."

"Amazing technology," Konesky stated.

"Yes, sir. We think so. Now, once the maintenance worker has gone through the task, we download it into this mini-computer." Konesky looked down at a thin folder, no more than one-half an inch thick and the size of a legal pad. "The computer opens up like this, just like a book, and the task we just went through shows up on the screen. The worker can take this to the flight line with him and, while he actually is working on the plane, can double-check every step visually. Throughout the process he is reminded of what the next step is, what tool is needed, and any special precautions that apply."

Konesky merely shook his head in amazement. What technology!

"Now, sir, if you'll follow me we have a few more things to show you." Konesky and Broughton walked with the public affairs officer out of the maintenance training section, through a security check point, and then up a long, narrow flight of stairs. "This area is our operations area. The ops group commander and squadron commander's offices are up here, as well as the briefing rooms. And if you'll step over this way we'll head on into the simulator section. These individuals are our civilian contractors who keep the three simulators up and running. The monitor consoles are what you are looking at now. We have three simulators, one for the Block 10 plane, another for Block 20, and the third for Block 30. As the planes are updated to the higher blocks, the simulators are too. Now if you'll step through here, we'll go inside one of the simulators."

Konesky stepped onto a removable platform toward the simulator. "As you can see, sir, each simulator has full range of motion; the hydraulics allow the platform to move up to twenty degrees at each of the four corners. Watch your head, sir, as we step into the simulator. We don't have the simulator programed for a flight, but we have the visuals on so you can observe this generation of software." Konesky looked at the screen and was once again amazed. The plane was positioned on the Whiteman runway; the hangars in front of the plane were perfectly visible; the clouds were absolutely life-like. "Once we program in a particular mission, we can literally fly the entire mission from take-off to landing visually. We have the entire world mapped out and digitized into this system. Within twenty minutes of receiving a target location we can have the pilots in here running approaches to the target as many times as they want, from any direction."

Konesky would have loved to ask to see a fly-by of Moscow but knew full well that that would not be allowed. Instead, he simply said, "very impressive. The visuals are as real as one could get."

"Thank you, sir. Now if you'll follow me, we'll get you out to the flight line." A few minutes later Konesky and Broughton were escorted into one of the massive hangars. "Inside here, sir," the public affairs officer continued, "we have a training hangar for munitions. Northrop provided us with this bottom section of a B-2. It is accurate in every way. Our munitions people can train all they want with inert bombs. This way we're not using one of the real planes with our students. And over here, sir, we have the GATS/GAMS that we used until the JDAMs, or Joint Directed Attack Munition, became available."

Konesky looked at what first appeared to be the traditional two thousand pound gravity bomb sitting lengthwise on a stand. "As you can see here, sir, we have taken a two thousand pound gravity bomb and added some new equipment. On the top here, at the mid-section of the bomb, we've added a global positioning receiver." Konesky looked at the four-inch circular disc mounted on the top and center of the bomb. "We've also added these directional flaps at the back end, and up here at the front end, we've added this rubber bra, if you will. You can see that the black rubber is about a fourth of an inch thick, and is wrapped around the tip of the bomb. What's unique is this fin coming out on each side about an inch. The fin acts as an air foil, keeping the bomb straight and level as it flies downward. This gives us a pretty decent drop and forget range. Inside we've added an inertial navigation unit that gets constant updates from the global positioning receivers. When the bomb gets to the target," the public affairs officer stated as he walked over to the back end of the bomb, "the computer tells the bomb to fly inverted. It rolls over 180 degrees and dives into the target. And, as you can see here, we've added a second global positioning receiver at the back end so the bomb can make its last-second adjustments while inverted, with the receiver pointed straight up into the air at the global positioning satellites."

Konesky stood back. "I take it, Captain, that everything here are parts you had available beforehand, and you basically, as you would say, took everything 'off the shelf' and turned this dumb gravity bomb into a smart weapon until you get the weapons specifically designed for the B-2?"

"That is absolutely correct, sir. Thus the designation, GATS for GPS aided targeting system, and GAM for GPS aided munition."

"I congratulate you," Colonel Konesky said in all sincerity. "That was a great way solve your problem in getting munitions. Can you tell me the circular error probability for the GATS/GAM?" In other words how close to the mark the bomb can actually get.

"I'm sorry, sir. I am not at liberty to provide you that information. But I can tell you, sir, that it is as accurate as the bombs we dropped in Desert Storm, and without the need for a laser designator."

And these are just the stop-gap bombs until they got the real ones that had been specially designed for the Stealth Bomber, Konesky realized. "Very impressive, Captain."

"Thank you, sir. Now if we head back to the vehicle, sir, I'll take you across the tarmac to one of the other hangars."

As they drove across the taxiway, the captain continued his briefing. "As you can see we are completing the final hangar for the 20th B-2. As of now we have received eighteen planes from the Palmdale plant. Northrop has been consistently on time in the deliveries. The two Block 10 planes just left for Palmdale. The few remaining Block 20 models will go next. They will all come back as Block 30s, fully operational for both conventional and nuclear missions." The captain stopped the vehicle in front of an open hangar. The pilots and crew chiefs stood waiting for the tour.

"Colonel Konesky, this is Captain Keith Payne, one of our instructor pilots."

Captain Payne saluted the colonel. "A pleasure to meet you, sir."

"Thank you, Captain."

"If you'll follow me, sir, I'll be glad to show you the Spirit of New York, sir." Konesky was fascinated by the workmanship of the plane. Obviously there would be no rivets or any of the protrusions that could increase the radar signature. The gray-black skin was absolutely smooth. And, the plane being so new, everything about it was clean; indeed, spotless.

"What's it like to fly this thing?" Konesky asked the captain.

"An absolute dream, sir. She takes off like a U-2 and flies like a fighter. Well, maybe not like a fighter, but damn close. I never would have guessed how maneuverable it was until I flew it myself."

The two gentleman completed the walk around of the plane, with Broughton trailing closely behind. "Would you like to go inside, sir?" the major asked.

"That's allowed?" Konesky stated.

"Yes, sir. We've been authorized to do so."

"You bet!" Konesky replied.

Konesky followed the major up the ladder and into the cockpit. "There's much more room than I thought there'd be."

"That's correct sir. Initially the plane was designed to have a crew of three, with the two pilots up here and a navigator back here. But with cost concerns, and the development of user friendly navigation systems, it was decided to hold off on having a third person. We have the capability to add in the seat and electrical components later, if we want. Go ahead and have a seat, sir." Konesky sat down in the pilot's seat. "As you can see the field of view is quite extensive. It's pretty easy to see all around. As far as the controls, everything is electrical. We don't have the power on so I can't show you the various options, but I can tell you that we can do almost anything with just a touch of a button."

Konesky sat in the seat for a while, wishing the whole time that Russia had had the technology and industrial base to create such a plane.

"I am very impressed, Captain," Konesky stated with all honesty. "Very impressed."

"Thank you, sir. Is there anything else you'd like to see?"

"No, you have been too kind as it is. Thank you very much."

Randy Broughton leaned forward between the two pilot seats. "If you like, Alexander, I have one more place to show you, that is if you have the time."

"I'm all yours."

After exiting the cockpit Konesky thanked the captain and his men for the time. Konesky, Broughton, and the public affairs officer got into the staff car and proceeded off of the flight line to a fenced in area about forty yards square.

"You probably recognize this, Alexander," Colonel Broughton said.

"Yes, of course. Your missile launch facility for the Minuteman IIs when they were here. I understand you've turned this into a museum."

"Yes, that's correct. We'll go down below this way. Ah, Captain," Broughton said looking at the public affairs officer, "would you mind waiting up here? I can handle this part of the tour."

"Yes, sir. No problem, sir."

Broughton and Konesky walked the fifty feet down into the once operational capsule. "Over here to the left," Randy Broughton explained to Konesky, "is the maintenance section of the launch facility, with food storage, generators, et cetera. And over this way is the launch facility itself. This is where one launch officer would sit," he said as he pointed to an empty chair, "and the other over here."

The two soldiers sat down at the seats that, not so many years ago, would have been filled by two officers prepared to turn their keys at the same time and launch hundreds of missiles toward the Soviet Union. And now it was just a museum! Of course both men knew that there were still forty-five such sites in control of the four-hundred-and-fifty to five-hundred Minuteman III missiles, not to mention the Peacekeeper silos.

"Randy, I must thank you. I know that what you showed me is not part of the regular tour. Except for the Chief of Staff of the Russian Air Force, I know of no one else who has been allowed such an honor of being able to get inside your Stealth Bomber. I greatly appreciate your kindness in this regard."

"It was my pleasure, Alexander."

"So, what is it you wanted to talk about? I take it this would be a suitable place for us to visit."

"This would do nicely," Randy stated as he rolled his chair closer to Konesky's chair. "As you know, the purpose of the START treaty is to reduce the number of nuclear weapons and to allow each side to confirm this reduction by inspections of designated sites, platforms, and warheads."

"Of course," Konesky stated.

"And the purpose of the treaty, signed by each of our presidents, is to make this happen, to build that level of trust."

"Yes," Konesky stated, "we both know this very well."

"And we both know that for the most part we can only inspect locations specified in the treaty."

"Unless you have a concern that we have developed a new site, and if so, the treaty allows you to ask the commission to give you access to a suspect site. Article XI, Paragraph 5."

"True," Broughton replied. "But my concern is this. The provision for suspect-site inspections is limited to the covert assembly of ICBMs for mobile launchers. It does not, on its face, allow inspection of other sites that may be suspect and are not part of the joint lists of locations contained in the annexes."

Konesky thought a moment about what Broughton had just said. "I fail to see your concern. If both countries have listed each site in the annexes, there should not be any other suspect sites. So all you would ever have to check are the listed sites—that is, the only sites that would be unlisted are the mobile launcher assembly plants, which the treaty takes care of."

"And if the government in question has not listed every site?"

Konesky pondered the question for a moment. "I would hope that that were not the case. But if such a thing were to happen, I suppose the inspecting party would need to bring the matter to the Joint Compliance and Inspection Commission and demand access to such a site."

Now Broughton paused for a moment. "Alexander, what if the site were unknown to the delegates of the Commission, and even unknown to the president when he signed the treaty, or for that matter, your new president? What then?"

Konesky paused, thinking. "It seems to me the same process should apply. Go to the Commission and ask to see the site."

"And if the site could be moved, or destroyed, or, God forbid, used, before we could get there?" Broughton asked, observing that Konesky was getting frustrated; he obviously could not understand either the logic of or the need for this discussion.

"Enough of this dancing around, Randy! Just tell me what is going on. If there is a specific problem, let's hear about it. We are soldiers. Let's leave the dancing to the ambassadors!"

"I agree, Alexander, but first I must ask a favor. Actually, a proposal, but I would consider the acceptance of my proposal as a favor since the treaty does not authorize either of us to do what I am suggesting. What I need to know is this: Are you willing, for the sake of the treaty, to bend the rules slightly? In other words, if we come across a situation not explicitly covered in the treaty, but the spirit of the treaty would require action, would you be willing to work with me, outside of the treaty but in support of its intent?"

Konesky relaxed and thought for a moment. "That depends. First of all, would you do the same for me?"

"Absolutely."

"And what exactly do you mean by your statement, 'bending of the rules'?"

"You and I are the two contact points for each country. Every inspection on either side goes through the two of us. Perhaps on some occasions it may be necessary and appropriate not to go through the normal notice requirements, or go through the normal process but go to a different site instead of the one announced."

Konesky was confused. In his mind the treaty already took care of this problem. "If you are concerned about a particular site, why not go to the primary site, then immediately request a follow-on site inspection to the one you are concerned with?"

Broughton took a deep breath and looked Konesky directly in the eyes. "Because, Alexander, it may be necessary to go to a location that is not listed in the annexes. That is the problem."

Konesky thought for a moment. He replied calmly, thoughtfully. "You realize that as soon as this were done our superiors would know immediately. Going to some non-listed site would be patently obvious. Our staffs would report us immediately, as they should. We would be fired, perhaps court-martialed. It could become an international incident. It could result even in one or both sides terminating the treaty. You must realize all of this."

"I do. And I would not ask you to do this, and I assume you would not ask me to do this, without a very good reason. But that reason may have to be just between us."

Konesky leaned back in his chair. "I understand the problem, and your proposed solution. I take it, then, that you think that there is a site that we did not disclose to you."

"We do not know. But we think it may be a possibility."

"And you want me to ignore my orders and my superiors by keeping such a possibility to myself."

"Yes," Broughton replied.

"And suppose I wanted to go to Nekoma or Grand Forks to see if you've set up an ABM base that violates the ABM Treaty, or go to White Sands to see if you have completed your StarWars project, would that apply?"

"No," Broughton explained, "I am merely proposing that we bend the rules, if necessary, in reference to START treaty compliance, which means an un-listed ICBM site."

"But what if I had information that one of those alleged ABM or StarWars sites is in reality a non-specified ICBM base; if I were to demand access, would you 'bend the rules' and give me access, to let me and my staff come in and check it out?"

"Yes, if the information you supplied convinced me that your concern was substantiated."

"Interesting." Konesky thought for a moment about what was being asked. True, if he agreed, there could be problems. But at least the new president of Russia would understand such an agreement given his background as a former KGB agent (and then head of the FSB). There are times where deals must be made, times when those at the pointed end of the sword must do what is necessary to implement a broader goal. Yes, Konesky thought to himself, the new president would indeed understand.

"All right, Randy," Konesky said. "I agree with your proposal. You are right. The treaty indeed has a loophole that needs to be closed. And the only way to close it, at least until the treaty can be modified, is for the two of us to trust each other and, if necessary, 'bend the rules,' as you say. But our agreement can only apply to the two of us. If either of us is replaced, the deal is off. This is the type of deal that must be made between only the closest of friends. If your replacement, or my replacement, is worthy of such trust, then the deal can be made anew. Otherwise, we should leave such shenanigans to just ourselves."

Broughton was particularly honored by Konesky referring to him as "the closest of friends." Konesky put out his hand to Randy.

"Agreed?" Konesky asked.

"Agreed, my friend," Randy confirmed as the two soldiers shook hands, each wondering if they could be tried for treason for what they had just done.

# CHAPTER 22

## Northern Russia

General Kalganov stepped out of the somewhat rusty civilian vehicle hardly before it stopped, to the great concern of his bodyguard and driver. Kalganov knew the consternation that would be caused to the two soldiers but he did not care; he had waited five long years to visit this place that first began in his mind so many years ago as he had witnessed the Soviet military disintegrate before his eyes. Besides, there were few more secure places in all of Russia. He briskly walked past the vehicle as the gray of dusk tried to fight back the inevitable night, his eyes trying mightily to take it all in despite the coming darkness. Pavel had argued that only a night visit—at three or four in the morning—would be safe from the prying eyes of spies and satellites, but Kalganov would have none of it. He insisted on at least having a glance at what the "farm site" looked like in the day. So just after sunset Kalganov arrived at the site.

The farm building out front looked old and weakened by the hard, polar winter, even though it had but recently been built. The large building to the south looked like any other massive grain storage facility: a huge, rectangular concrete building with an angled roof coming in from both side walls and meeting at the mid-point. The building was relatively low to the ground, thus lessening any suspicion. The Volga plains had hundreds of such buildings; nondescript, white-concrete buildings. True, few of them were so far north, but the Russian tradition of using one basic design over and over again would bring no question to that type of building five hundred miles further north than any other. Besides, the common analysis would go, the bureaucrats of the northern reaches needed some place to store the grain for the long winter.

After the vehicle had fully stopped, another man stepped out of the opposite side. Pavel stood on the steps in front of the farm house observing his uncle carefully as the older man slowly finished his 360 degree survey of the area until he once again faced his nephew.

"Pavel," Kalganov finally said, "this is Andre Ruschev, the scientist I told you about."

Pavel walked down the steps and over to Ruschev and shook his hand. "Good evening, sir. I am glad to finally meet you." Pavel observed that the scientist was much smaller in stature than even himself and somewhat demure, as he had heard. But Pavel had also heard of this man's great intellectual prowess and his abilities as an administrator in turning weapons grade uranium and plutonium into relatively harmless reactor fuel. True, there were those who say that he is but a pawn of the Americans and their Department of Energy, but those who know him still call him a great patriot, a man doing what he is told to do; in short, a man of honor and a patriot in times when there are few of either. But such is the reality of modern society, where the pleasures and needs of man too often supersede a duty that was once common-place and commonly done.

"I am pleased to meet you as well, Pavel," Dr. Ruschev said. "I was honored to know your father. He did not know me well, for I was much younger and of no consequence. But I had occasion to work with him and try, in a small way, to assist him in his endeavors. He was a good man, and we shared many of the same views." Pavel simply nodded in thanks to the compliment. "Which, by the way, is one of the reasons I am here," he said glancing first at Pavel and then towards General Kalganov.

"Uncle, if you would, I would like to get inside as soon as possible."

Kalganov, however, refused to budge. He looked over at Pavel almost in disgust. "You mean to tell me I paid trillions upon trillions of rubles for *these* buildings?" Kalganov almost yelled, waving his arm at the debilitated farm house behind him and the four simplistic concrete grain storage buildings farther back. The farm house was a mess: one-half of the building was made of logs, the other half cheap sheet metal; even the bricks on the top of the chimney were crooked.

Pavel just smiled up at the general, waiting for him to realize his and their own brilliance. Kalganov saw Pavel's smile; a flash of anger rose, then dropped as quickly. Kalganov paused from his waving and simply stared at his nephew, waiting for his explanation.

"Yes, Uncle, you paid much for these buildings, and they are worth every kopek! What you see here," Pavel stated as he pointed toward the farm house, "is an exact replica of what stood here six years ago, at least as it appeared from the outside. But behind those logs is reinforced concrete encased in a lead shield. The windows are bulletproof glass."

Pavel moved over to the side of the house. "I have placed security sensor devices throughout this area," he said as he raised his arm and pointed outward toward the surrounding fields. "Our every move is being watched from at least two different locations, no matter where we go. Those buildings back there, the grain storage buildings, if anyone could get near one of them they would discover a storage building without a door, but of course no one would be able to get that close. Each building is surrounded by a mine field fifty meters out; the walls themselves are electrified with sufficient amperage to cause immediate death upon just the touch of a finger. You see that wooden fence over there on the outer perimeter? Those rotting wooden posts are actually steel beams set in concrete; they just look like rotted posts. Even a tank couldn't get through it. An army of five hundred could not get to those buildings; and by the time they did, their work would be done. So, as you can see, we need very few guards here."

"Excellent, Pavel, excellent," Kalganov exclaimed. "Now, let me see the rest of it!"

"Certainly," Pavel said, glad to get the general and his guest inside where they would not be seen. Pavel had heard rumors of the newest American reconnaissance satellites that were capable of actually identifying an individual from space, supposedly in real time. The odds were against it, but in this game he preferred not to play the odds. The three men walked up the steps. Pavel stopped at the door, which Kalganov assumed would be opened for him. It was not.

"Why don't you knock?" Pavel spoke while smiling mischievously.

Kalganov laughed and shrugged his shoulders. "Why not?" he said. He knocked, and the door opened. An old woman answered.

"Yes," she said in the bored nuance of a traditional farmer's wife bothered once too often by a lost traveller.

Pavel answered for General Kalganov. "Nina, these are friends of mine. May we come in?"

"Oh, of course my son, I am glad to meet friends of yours. Please, please, come in."

The door—which at first glance appeared to be made of wood—opened with ease and friendliness. General Kalganov could smell the cabbage and chicken stewing upon the stove. The three men automatically took off their shoes upon entering the house.

"Please, put these on my good friends," the woman stated enthusiastically, handing each of them a pair of slippers. "They will keep you warm on the wood floors. May I get you some *chi*?"

"No thank you, Nina," Pavel swooned. General Kalganov was at first confused, and then exhilarated by the fact that Pavel had devised such a superb facade for a security system. Pavel saw Kalganov's look of approval.

"You must watch out, my friend," Pavel said to his uncle. "Nina is the best cook in all of Russia. She will feed you until you burst, and then ask you if you want more. Thank you, Nina, but perhaps we will have some tea afterwards."

"And a full meal too, I hope. You never eat enough. I know you too well, you bachelors. How you can live without a woman I do not understand. You are not complete. A woman for you. I shall find a woman for you, one who will feed you as I do. That is what you need, my sweet Pavel. But where I will find one out here, I do not know. But there will be a farmer's daughter for you yet, my Pavel, and she will make you fat and happy"—she smiled and looked directly at Pavel, with a subtle wink—"very happy." She now looked back at General Kalganov. "That is what he needs. He should not be alone, not alone. He is too handsome, and young." And then looking back at Pavel: "A woman for you I will find. One of these days. One of these days."

"Yes. yes, I know, Nina. You tell me this every time. But you never have a woman for me. But when you do, I will be pleased, and

I will be glad to grow fat and happy. But for now, my Nina, I would like to show my friends your basement."

"Yes, of course. Well, sir," she said to Kalganov, obviously aware that he was the most senior of the group, "it has been good to meet you. And you, too," she said to Dr. Ruschev, even though she had not formally met him.

She then turned her attention back to Kalganov. "Since he calls you 'Uncle,' I hope you have some influence on this young man so he will see that I am right about his needing a woman."

"I will certainly do my best," Kalganov replied. "Thank you for your kindness. I am honored to be in your home."

"And I am honored to have you here," she replied.

Kalganov was impressed; never did she ask his name, or inquire as to where he was from. She was indeed well-trained, he noted to himself. It was almost as if this was her own home, and in many ways it probably was.

"Thank you for everything, Nina," Pavel said. "I will let myself in."

"Certainly, sir," Nina replied, now more as a servant than a doting surrogate mother. "Certainly."

And with nothing more said, Kalganov and Ruschev followed Pavel past the two neatly-kept bedrooms to the back of the house and down the stairs adjacent to what must have been the bathroom. The smell of must was pervasive. How could he get this smell into a new building? Kalganov asked himself in amazement.

Kalganov began walking down the stairs toward a single light bulb that dangled near the bottom of the stairs, its perfect location blinding Kalganov as he half stumbled down the stairs; somehow, the seemingly low-powered light was capable of blinding him as he walked down the stairs, while at the same time he noticed that it projected little light to the surrounding room. He realized that the light must have been designed with a directional, mirrored effect on the inside of the light bulb so that all the light is aimed in one direction upward toward anyone walking down the stairs, thereby allowing the persons in the basement below to see who was coming down while at the same time not blinding them.

A voice permeated the room from behind and to the right of Kalganov, Pavel, and Ruschev.

"Good evening, sir!" the official-sounding voice said to Pavel.

"Good evening," Pavel replied officially as he turned right toward the man in his neatly pressed uniform that showed no rank, name, or, for that matter, any form of identification.

"Do you recognize this man?" Pavel asked.

"Yes, sir!" the soldier replied.

"He is the only one, and I mean the only one, from the south who knows of us and has access to this facility. Do you understand?"

"Yes, sir."

"Here is his photo. Show it to your replacement this evening, and instruct him to do the same. When the picture comes back to you, destroy it. Understood?"

"Yes, sir! Absolutely."

"Very well. I require entrance to this facility," Pavel said to the soldier, beginning the formal entrance procedure.

"I understand, sir. May I see your identification?"

Pavel pulled out the card from under his shirt (leaving it on its chain) and leaned forward to allow the guard to view his photo. No words were on the card, just a colorful drawing of an eagle with six wings surrounded by lightning bolts next to Pavel's photograph.

"And the word, sir?"

"The end is the beginning."

"Thank you, sir. You may enter with your guests."

At the soldier's words "you may enter," the wall behind him split in half, the two sides receding into the wall almost noiselessly. The three gentlemen entered the well-lit stairway and began their descent down steps occasionally alternated with platforms. For once, Pavel noted to himself, Kalganov was silent—and truly impressed.

Once the two men reached the bottom of the stairs, they entered a hallway that slowly turned inward and proceedingly downward as if it were a large circle slowly closing in upon itself, perhaps symbolic of turning inward and reflective as we age and consider what we have done and should have done.

"Excellent defense strategy, Pavel," Kalganov stated simply as he observed the ability of a defender to retreat as much as he wanted, defend at any point, then retreat again. Finally they reached two massive steel doors. Kalganov watched as Pavel once again removed his card from underneath his shirt and placed it into a slot on the wall to his right. Pavel then pushed several buttons on the counsel above the slot, and the door opened.

Pavel stepped into the corridor and began walking up a short flight of steps. "'Come up here, my friends, and I will show you what must take place after this.'" Kalganov was unsure what Pavel meant by these words; it was as if Pavel was quoting something that Kalganov couldn't recognize. Kalganov, with Ruschev right behind him, stepped up into a large ornate conference room.

"Very impressive," Kalganov stated as he looked around the room. Approximately two dozen chairs were positioned along a long arched table, twelve chairs stationed up against the wooden table, and another twelve behind and between the front row of chairs so that each person would have an unobstructed view to the speaker. Kalganov noted that the chairs had white upholstery with gold cloth on the upper third. Seven lamps were affixed to the front of the table. Kalganov walked around the large table and up to the large speaker's chair made of what appeared to be oak.

"This is quite a control room, Pavel," Kalganov said as he sat down on the large wooden chair. "And what is this at my feet?" the general said as he looked downward. "A mosaic! It's quite beautiful. Byzantine, isn't it?" Kalganov looked down at four lightning bolts spreading out from each corner of the chair inlaid and surrounded by many colors of stones—red, brown, yellow, jasper, even carnelian. A circle of gold rocks surrounding the bolts and the other colors. "It is indeed beautiful. You have your father's eye for art, Pavel. Your father's eye. And these creatures, let's see, a lion with wings, an eagle with six wings, that's interesting; an ox with wings, and what is this over here? A man with wings. Well, I'm not sure whether all of this ostentatiousness was necessary, but I'm sure you have your reasons."

"My men may be down here a long time, Uncle," Pavel replied. "I thought I'd give them something to look at. Other than, of course, this." Pavel pointed to the large royal purple curtain behind the speaker's chair some seventy feet long and at least twelve feet high. In the center was a large Persian sword placed on the wall above the large purple curtain. Pavel stepped over to the speaker's chair and pressed a button on one of its arms, and with a quiet buzz the curtain divided in two from the middle, the center opening not unlike a parting of the waters.

"There, dear Uncle, before you is the real art, for which you hired me, for which I have strived all these years. Before you is the praxis of power which we dreamed of and created out of whole cloth. I give you Armageddon. I give you the world, and its future, merged as it must be, with all of its possibilities."

As Pavel spoke these words, the ponderous curtains opened, and the men saw the large metal cylinders before them; Kalganov counted seven cylinders on the right side and seven on the left. Each cylinder was approximately two and one-half meters across, or about eight feet in diameter. Kalganov could not see how high they stood, but he of course already knew that. "Marvelous," was all Kalganov could mutter. He kept repeating that word over and over until he was interrupted a short time later by Pavel.

More to Ruschev than Kalganov, Pavel began speaking. "I have arranged the missile in seven groups of seven. For structural reasons I have placed one missile in the middle and six circling around the center missile in equidistant, each connected by beams to the others. This allowed not only greater structural integrity but also will facilitate a combined firing sequence. We can fire one missile from each batch of seven at a time, in twenty second increments. There are seven batches of seven missiles in front of you in building number one; there are three more identical building behind his one."

By this time Ruschev had moved up to the huge Plexiglas window. "How is the roof extracted?"

Pavel pointed up towards the top of the building on the other side of the glass. "The roof is on rollers; at the time of firing we have charges throughout the highest point of the roof along the center-line where the two sides of the roof come up and meet. The charges will go off, separating the two rectangular masses of concrete, and each side will roll down to the side of the building out of harm's way. As long as the charges go off separating the two roofs, gravity does the rest."

"Is there a system to bring the roof back into place?" Ruschev asked.

"No," Pavel replied. We assumed there would be no need for one. Obviously this complex is designed for a complete launch of all of the rockets at basically the same time, so we do not have any retraction device."

"I assume you do not have the option of firing them all at the same time," Ruschev stated.

"That is correct," Pavel answered. "The missiles would most probably run into each other since they are in such close proximity. However, as I mentioned, I have been able to design it so one missile from each group can be fired at the same time without any interference to the other missiles. By putting the individual tubes together as I have done in groups of seven missiles, there is enough stability to fire off a missile from each set at the same time. That is why we can fire twenty-eight missiles at a time."

"When did you say you can you fire again?" Ruschev asked.

"Approximately every twenty seconds. Same as the Typhoon can, but of course the Typhoon can only fire one at a time. Here, I simply use a rotation firing method. Missile one, three, five, two, four, six, and, after a slightly longer delay because it is in the center of the matrix, missile seven."

"So how long does it take to fire them all off?" Ruschev asked.

"If we use the under-attack mode, two minutes. Normal firing would be three to five. But the odds are we would always use the fastest method so we could take out the American Inter-Continental Ballistic Missiles and the American submarines before they would have a chance to react."

Kalganov and Pavel could tell that Ruschev was impressed, as well as pleased.

"Amazing," Ruschev said simply. "So, if I understand you, you are able to fire all 196 missiles within two minutes. From one site! Amazing. And the status of the warheads?" he asked Pavel.

"That is of course where you come in, my friend. As you know, we have had difficulty getting so many warheads. This first building is fully armed—ten warheads per missile. We are slowly filling up the other missiles as the SS-25s are being deactivated pursuant to the START treaty. The new facility that I understand that you will be in charge of will now be getting the majority of the warheads as they are taken off of the missiles. Instead of dismantling the warheads, as I'm sure my uncle has already explained to you, we want you to give them to us to keep here on top of one of our missiles, as they should be."

General Kalganov now jumped into the discussion. "You see, Andre, we have been doing this for years now. Approximately one-half of the missiles are armed and ready to go. We just need to obtain the other nine hundred or so warheads and our task will be complete."

Kalganov paused for a moment. "I brought you here to see first hand what we are doing with the warheads. It would have been easy for you to imagine that we wanted them for sale to some foreign country, but we are not black marketeers, we are patriots, like you, who consider the dismantling of our most destructive weapons as foolhardy. The weapons will be here, ready for our use, if necessary, ready at a moment's notice to defend our land and our people."

"How about the records on the destruction of the warheads and fissionable material at the other plant?" Ruschev asked. "Hasn't something of this magnitude been discovered?"

"No. It has gone very well. The warheads will be picked up by your own team, as it normally would be done, or are delivered to your plant. You sign for them. The records show them turned over for destruction. You store them for a short time until our people come to deliver the spent reactor grade material. You box it up as if the material came from the disassembled warheads and send it out for storage, just like normal. As we unload the spent fuel we load up the waiting warheads! We bring them here and place them on the missile."

"And if my plant is inspected?" Kalganov asked.

"There is no weapon there, as there it be. According to your records each one has been functionally destroyed by turning it into non-weapons grade material. How can they prove a negative?"

"And once the material arrives at the weapons grade storage facility, how does that work?"

"Just fine. Our friends in Arzamas-16, or should I now say Sarov, record the receipt of the material and the destruction of the weapon. The containers are marked and sealed properly; the only way they would be able to determine that the material is actually spent reactor rods instead of former weapons grade plutonium or uranium is to open up the container and test it, which of course is very unlikely. And, if that happens, what could the authorities do? Tell the world that several tons of weapons grade material is missing? I doubt it! They would say nothing, and nothing would be done."

Ruschev began to smile and look much more at ease. "So, General, do you think we have enough warheads to do the job?"

Kalganov smiled openly knowing that he had won Ruschev over. "I can guarantee you, Andre, that 196 missiles will be more than enough. Each missile carries ten warheads, each of which can be assigned a different target. This means that when we are finished, with your kind assistance, we will have nineteen-hundred-and-sixty warheads sitting here on the ready. Each warhead has a yield of one hundred kilotons, if needed. Of course we can adjust the yield as desired for precision targeting. But if we were to use full yield, that means each warhead is over seven times more powerful than the bomb dropped on Hiroshima, and almost five times more powerful than the bomb dropped on Nagasaki. And once we have all of the warheads, thanks to you, we will have the equivalent of over fifteen hundred Hiroshima's, or eighty-nine hundred Nagaski's."

"And do you feel there are enough bombs for each target?" Ruschev asked as he looked more intently at the cylinders before him.

"Yes, once you have supplied us with the rest of the warheads, especially when you consider it will be a 'shot out of the blue' as the Americans say. We will have enough firepower to hit every American ICBM site—which is now coming down to five hundred—with two warheads per site, every American air base in the world, and every command and control facility left in the United States, and still have more than enough warheads left for their industrial base and any other country that concerns us."

"What about the submarines?" Ruschev asked.

"That of course has always been the tricky part," General Kalganov replied. "As you know, our government monitors the United States' submarines at all times. Thanks to certain friends, we are privy to that information as well. Only one-third of their submarines are out to sea at one time, and we usually know where at least five of those seven are."

Ruschev looked concerned. "Two American submarines have quite a few warheads, as I recall."

This time Pavel answered. "Yes, but if we wait until we know where each sub is for the strike, then there is no concern. Besides, we usually know where they all are at. If we are forced to fire without perfect knowledge, we will still prevail. And as soon as one of the submarines fires its first missile our own traditional rocket forces will have no choice but to react."

Ruschev seemed totally satisfied with the answers. The seriousness of his face that witnessed the beginning of the tour had slowly yielded to a relaxed smile, so Pavel continued with the rest of the tour. "Come this way, Andre, and we'll step into the missile area itself." The three men stepped through an oblong pressure door not unlike a door from a submarine. "Each missile stands fifteen meters or approximately forty-nine feet tall. As of right now we are approximately twelve meters underground. The missiles themselves have a diameter of 2.2 meters or approximately seven feet. As you can see, each missile is surrounded by its own launch tube, as it would be in the Typhoon submarine, so one launch does not interfere with the other missiles."

"Are they hot or cold launched?" Ruschev asked.

"They are cold launched," Pavel answered. "Same as if they were launched from a Typhoon submarine."

"But don't these missiles need to be submerged when launched?"

Obviously not, Pavel thought to himself, but he ignored the occasional ignorance of his fellow scientist. "The R-52s are also capable of being launched while the Typhoon is in dock. Once the roof is clear the rocket is catapulted into the air over one hundred feet, at which time it ignites."

"What, Pavel, do you use to catapult it into the air?" Ruschev asked.

"The rocket stands on a flat piston. Below the piston is an explosive charge sufficient to force the missile well into the air."

"And if the missile doesn't ignite?"

"Then we have a problem," Pavel answered simply. "It falls back to the ground and probably takes out four or five other missiles.

However, in tests where there was no ignition the solid propellent did not ignite on impact with the ground. Thus, relatively little damage is done. On the other hand, the R-52 is a very good missile. It rarely fails to ignite."

"According to the military tests," General Kalganov added, "we estimate a 95 percent probability of all missiles firing without incident."

Pavel continued. "As you saw above, the missiles are contained in four separate buildings. Each building is color-coded; this is the 'white-room' and therefore the walls are painted accordingly. The other three buildings are coded red, black, and gray, respectively. Each building, as here, has in it seven groupings of missiles, with each group having seven missiles.

"As I mentioned earlier, in order to enhance stability during firing I designed the firing sequence so that each group would have seven tubes connected together; a missile in the middle surrounded by six missiles. Each missile is far enough away to allow a safe launch. You can see the order of firing by the Roman numerals on each missile tube."

"I see, Pavel," General Kalganov interrupted, "that you have continued the artwork in here as well."

"Yes, Uncle, that way if we have a problem with a particular missile it can be quickly and easily identified. Each of the seven sets of missiles is identified by these paintings on the outside of the tube. This set of seven has the depiction of a yellow horse with a black-robed man riding it. Thus, if there is a problem with this missile I simply say 'Missile three, yellow horse, white room' to the technician and he knows right where to go."

The general began walking around looking as proud as a young father observing his first-born. Pavel and Ruschev followed, talking generally about the intricacies of circular error probable and other nuances of nuclear targeting. Almost as an afterthought Ruschev noticed as they walked the different artistic renderings on the missiles contained in each grouping: a man wearing a crown and holding a cross-bow while riding on a white horse; a man on a red horse holding a large sword; a man on a black horse holding a scale; the figure wearing a black robe riding on a pale or yellow horse; a white robe; a black sun next to a red moon; and seven trumpets. Each drawing was beautiful in its own way, blending perfectly into the natural symmetry of the vertical tube.

The general, now done with his tour of all of the missiles in the first building, stopped and looked more carefully at the Roman numerals on each tube, and the artistic drawings. Pavel, not sure what the general was thinking, thought that it was at least possible that the symbolism made General Kalganov nervous, even though it appeared that the general had no idea what the drawings meant.

"Don't worry, General," Pavel said soothingly, "as I said earlier, we get pretty bored around here, and some of us are artistically inclined."

"Oh, no, my dear Pavel, it is fine," Kalganov said as he walked away from the drawing he was studying. "Just fine. I must admit, I did not think this would work so smoothly. You have exceeded all of my expectations!"

"Thank you, Uncle. And just think, Uncle, with Andre's help within two years every missile shall be filled with all ten warheads, and our work will be complete."

# CHAPTER 23

## Edwards AFB, California

Phinney eased himself into the front seat of the SR-71 with the assistance of the two airmen from the Physiological Support Division. He was not yet used to the bulkiness of the David Clark Company S1032 pressurized space suit that were similar to the ones used by the Shuttle astronauts. Sitting himself down into the metal seat, he was surprised how comfortable he felt. By extending his arms above his head, the airman were able to plug Phinney's air hoses into the life support connectors. After making sure everything was operational, the life support crew waited for Phinney's thumb's up, and then cleared the cockpit.

"How's everything feel," Marta asked from the back seat.

"Great," Phinney replied. Since this was Phinney's first training flight Marta had decided to leave the intercom mic open throughout the mission. Although having a "hot mic" was somewhat bothersome since each of them would hear the breathing of the other, both Phinney and Marta preferred to be able to talk throughout Phinney's first check ride.

Unlike the other Blackbirds, the "B" model (like any other trainer) had dual flight controls so that the instructor pilot—who sat in the back seat of the SR-71—could also fly the plane. Of course, from the visual standpoint it was quite easy to tell the "B" model from the "A" model: unlike the sleek fuselage of the "A" model, the "B" model's rear cockpit area was raised several feet higher than the front cockpit, allowing the back-seater the ability to see forward past the front cockpit; of course in the other Blackbirds the reconnaissance systems officer's position, or RSO's station, is not raised. Thus, while flying the "B" model Marta could, if necessary, assume control of the aircraft.

Marta and Phinney spent the next fifteen minutes going through the preflight checklist while continuing to breathe the 100 percent oxygen being supplied through the life support system. The pilots are required to breathe pure oxygen for at least forty-five minutes before takeoff to ensure that in the event of a bailout or equipment failure at altitude they do not get the bends.

After concluding everything was OK, Phinney signaled to the crew chief to start the first engine. Since this particular flight for number 17980 was ending in an odd number, the left or number one engine would be started first. Phinney immediately heard the roar of the Buick V-8's starter cart reverberating through the entire hangar and the Blackbird.

When Phinney could feel the left engine beginning to rotate, he placed the throttle at idle. "One thousand r.p.m.'s. Fuel flow OK." Suddenly there was a bang, and Phinney knew that the chemical ignition system had ignited. "R.p.m.'s rising. Thirty-two hundred r.p.m.'s. Ground starting unit disengaged. Idle speed levelling off at 3975 r.p.m.'s. Exhaust temp normal. Fuel flow at fifty-two hundred. Oil pressure above thirty-five p.s.i. Hydraulics fine. Looks like we're OK on left engine."

"I agree," Marta replied. "Let's light the other one."

"Right engine started. Everything nominal. Generators on line." Phinney signaled the ground crew to disconnect external power. "Fuel system check. Left and right bypass confirmed open. Spikes and brakes OK."

"OK," Marta stated, "that takes care of the flight checks. Let's give the boys the green light and get out of here."

"Sounds fine by me," Phinney replied, wishing he wasn't so nervous. It's just another plane, he kept trying to tell himself. Phinney applied full brakes and gave the go-ahead signal to the crew chief to remove the chocks by flashing the landing lights. In a few moments he saw the signal that the chocks had been removed. Looking forward he followed the signals instructing him to advance out of the hangar.

Once on the tarmac Phinney was given the all clear to apply full brakes and ease the throttle up to military power. The roar of the engines, coupled with the vibrations, did not surprise Phinney; each engine was capable of producing over twenty-six thousand pounds of thrust given the temperature outside. What amazed Phinney was the fact that the amount of thrust produced by each engine would increase exponentially with speed and the lowering of the ambient temperature. Indeed, most of the thrust created by the J-58 engines while at cruising speed came not from the engine combustion process, but from the forward inlets that turned both engines into ramjets; thus, the ramjet effect created more thrust than the burning of the JP-7 fuel itself!

Phinney looked down at the gauges and saw that the engines were both functioning properly and within norms. Phinney eased back the throttle to idle.

"Looks good to me," he stated.

"Same here," Marta replied. "Let's go. I've already obtained permission from the tower for taxi."

"Roger that." Phinney followed the chase vehicle along the taxiway up to the entrance to the active runway, and then obtained clearance to enter the active runway.

Phinney eased the plane onto the end of Edwards' single fifteen-thousand-foot runway and then stopped the SR-71, quickly reviewing all of the instruments. "Looks good to me," he stated to Marta.

"Same here. Let's do it."

"Brakes on hold. Nosewheel steering engaged. Advancing throttle." Phinney watched as the IGV lights for both engines went out at approximately six thousand r.p.m.'s, indicating that the inlet guide vanes system was working. "Brakes off. Throttle at military. Engine check. R.p.m.'s good. Going to minimum afterburner."

Phinney pushed the throttle forward and raised it slightly so it would jump over the lip designed to stop the throttle at full military thrust. A few moments after he had pushed the throttle to minimum afterburner Phinney felt a slight jerk when the left afterburner engaged and then watched as the plane begin to veer quickly to the right; immediately compensating, Phinney then felt another bump indicating that the other afterburner had also engaged. Just as Phinney had been warned, the slight delay in one afterburner igniting before the other and the fact that the afterburners rarely ignited at the same time made takeoff of a Blackbird just a little bit tricky. After both afterburners had ignited, Phinney then pushed the throttle forward to full afterburners.

"Maximum afterburner," Phinney stated as he pushed the throttle forward with his left hand. The acceleration was breathtaking. What power! Phinney thought. Now that both afterburners were creating full thrust, what a rush! Within a second or so the plane was accelerating down the runway at over one hundred knots.

"One-fifty knots," Marta's voice informed Phinney over the open mic. "One-eighty."

"Pulling up nose," Phinney stated out loud. "9 degree attitude."

"Two hundred," Marta continued. "Two-ten."

Realizing that 210 knots provided sufficient speed for lift off, Phinney pulled back slightly on the stick, immediately feeling the termination of the vibrations from the runway. Although it seemed much longer to Phinney, it had taken less than five seconds from the time he had released the brakes to lift off. Phinney took his left hand off the throttle and reached up to the left console and raised the landing gear lever, all the while watching his angle of attack indicator on the upper left side of the instrument panel to make sure he did not exceed a 14 degree upward angle while so close to the runway so as to prevent any damage to the aft fuselage as he took off. He had been told numerous times about the importance of getting the landing gear up immediately after takeoff, not only to lessen the drag but because the gear could not handle the stress imposed at anything over three hundred knots. "Landing gear up." Phinney eased forward on the stick so as to allow for a ten degree climb out as the Blackbird continued to accelerate quickly to four hundred knots. Phinney increased the upper angle of the plane so it would not go supersonic until they had reached at least thirty thousand feet.

"Ten thousand feet," Marta continued stating out loud to Phinney. "Fifteen thousand. Twenty. Twenty-five. Thirty. You're clear for dipsy."

Dipsy, Phinney had thought. What a strange word, but accurate for what he was about to do. Leaving the plane on full afterburner

Phinney angled it downward slightly so that the plane would go past the high-drag Mach barrier easier and without using as much fuel. The plane eased past Mach and continued to accelerate with even more power as its engines started acting as two ramjets.

"KEAS HOLD on," Phinney stated over the mic, referring to the activation of the plane's "cruise control" system. As with all supersonic aircraft, KEAS—pronounced "keys" and standing for knots equivalent airspeed—are used instead of knots to determine the equivalent speed of the plane once supersonic flight is reached.

"Let's head out towards the Pacific Ocean, Jack."

"You've got it."

Phinney steered the plane westward, and within moments they were over the ocean. By now they were going one thousand miles an hour, past Mach 2 and still climbing seemingly without effort. As they approached Mach 3 Phinney brought the throttle back to one-half afterburner. And the plane continued to accelerate! Phinney pulled the throttle back to one-quarter afterburner, and then a little lower so that the plane would stabilize at Mach 3.2. Reaching down to the panel to the right of his seat, Phinney flipped the autopilot "KEAS HOLD" switch off and then began focusing on making sure he levelled off at the planned Mach for the training mission. Phinney then engaged the MACH HOLD and looked down at his altimeter and, below that, the vertical speed indicator.

Amazingly, the plane was still climbing and accelerating! "How do you slow this thing down?" Phinney said out loud to himself. Phinney reached down to the autopilot control panel and slowly rotated the pitch control back, thereby raising the nose of the plane in an attempt to slow it down. At this speed Phinney knew that it would be dangerous to manually fly the plane; pitch and roll corrections were instead made primarily by two control wheels to the pilot's right side. Using his glove, the pilot need only rotate the pitch control wheel back or forward to get the Blackbird to go up or down, and rotate the adjacent control turn wheel left or right for a slow turn. At first Phinney had thought the two control wheels looked more like lids from a peanut butter jar standing on their sides, but he was sure glad to have them. Rotating the pitch wheel back, the plane finally reduced speed to Mach 3.2. Phinney reactivated the Mach hold to maintain that speed, reviewed the other instrument readings, and concluded that the plane was now at a fixed speed and altitude.

"Good job, Jack," Marta said.

"Thanks. Man, what a plane! How far over optimal speed did we end up at?"

"You we're pushing 3.5 for a while," Marta replied, "but you got her back down soon enough. The surface temperatures stayed within parameters, thanks mainly to the heat sink through the fuel tanks. But if you ever do that when you're low on fuel, you'd probably have a hell of a problem."

Phinney breathed a sigh of relief. So far so good. Looking out the window for almost the first time since turning towards the ocean, Phinney noticed how dark the sky had become. Even though it was daylight beneath him, he could see the stars above, as well as the curvature of the earth reaching out in front of him.

"How do you like the view?" Marta asked.

"Gorgeous!" Phinney replied. "Absolutely gorgeous."

# CHAPTER 24

## Northern Russia

Riana watched with no little trepidation as Pavel switched and swerved along the bumpy dirt road. She giggled at each bump and swerve as if she was watching Pavel playing some humorous game, succeeding in her attempt to convince Pavel that she was as drunk as he. Luckily for her, the drugs she had taken to counteract the effects of the alcohol had worked well; so well that she was now able to focus on her surroundings and, for the most part, keep her internal direction. Riana guessed that they had travelled ten or so kilometers to the north-north-east. The wooded valley seemed to follow along an unseen river.

"Here we are!" Pavel shouted as he arched the vehicle into a left-power slide, the outer wheels struggling to maintain their footing on the wet dirt road. Riana searched for any marker or directional sign but could not see any. The vehicle groaned and chugged up the incline, its back tires spinning aimlessly from the left to the right and back again until they reached the beginning of a flatland, sending Riana's head to the roof as the vehicle and its occupants were subjected to negative g's.

A few hundred yards later Pavel allowed the car to slow down to what would be considered by any sane person as a safe and appropriate speed. Riana shook her head vigorously as if to clear her senses, which, as it turned out, was the case. When her eyes focused anew she observed a small farm house on the left side of the road. Everything about the house seemed normal. The wood looked weathered. No lights were on, for it was late. Two or three barrels stood outside for extra water. There was no sign of electrical power. In short, the traditional Russian farm house in the middle of a flatland and, presumably, surrounded by only fields of winter wheat.

Pavel drove past the house another one hundred yards and wedged the car to the right and down a dual, narrow pathway that would not be worthy of being called a road. The trail darted down into a ravine, in which Pavel stopped. Pavel opened the door, laughing as he stumbled onto the ground, and then stood up again, almost losing his balance.

"I told you we would make it! Come on. This way. I have a back entrance I put in just for me." Pavel continued to stumble down the ravine and stepped between two large bushes. Riana followed, finding herself in a small alcove facing a metal door. Pavel, still giggling, reached over to a panel, almost falling over in the process. "Let's see, three, three, three, seven. Damn. Missed it. Three, three, three, seven." Riana heard a click inside the door. "There!" Pavel stated as he opened the door and motioned to Riana to go inside. "Come, my love, let me show you one of my more solid creations!"

★          ★          ★          ★

The guard watched the TV monitor as Pavel entered the rear entrance to the facility. "Look at that idiot," he said to the other guard. "This time he brought someone with him. Doesn't anyone train these damn scientists about security?"

"He *is* in charge," the other replied. "But still, bringing a woman in. We had better report this to the colonel," he said as he picked up the phone.

# CHAPTER 25

## Pentagon, Office of the J-3

General Williams twirled his pencil in his hand, his size 11 shoes sitting on the right side of his desk as his executive officer sat across from him on the other side of the desk. "Everything seems too simple here, Allison," the general mused as he looked over at the painting of a P-51 behind and above his exec. "Too pat. Too easy. I hate a plan that sounds too simple."

Colonel Allison Markham observed her boss as he stared at the painting above her, watching his mind thinking, calculating. She knew to say nothing at this point. Let him think out all the possible permutations, all the possible scenarios of how things could go wrong and cause an international incident. The two flags behind him stood motionless in the windowless room deep inside the National Military Command Center, one flag of the United States and the other flag of a three star. She too glanced up at the P-51 painting, remembering that her father flew the Mustang in World War II.

"I think we should add a fail-safe to the mission," General Williams said more to himself than to Markham. "We've installed a lot of navigational equipment and automated electronic countermeasures that are still classified. I'd rather not have any of that equipment fall into the enemy's hands, particularly the microchip processors on the INS. Has the team discussed a self-destruct package?"

"No, sir," Markham replied simply, contemplating herself what the team would think of potentially blowing up one of their own planes inside Mother Russia with the pilot aboard. Surely General Williams would not approve a suicide mission, or the voluntary suicide of the pilot if things went wrong. We aren't the CIA, for Christ's sake, she thought to herself. "I assume the pilot would be in charge of initiating the self-destruct," she stated simply.

"Or us, from the outside if necessary. He could be captured, or the plane malfunction after he's on the ground. He could be hit and eject, and the plane still be somewhat intact as it fell to the ground. A self-destruct could prevent any essential assets from being obtained by the Russians. But we'd want to equip the pilot with a short-range device so that he could engage the self-destruct after bailing out. And we would be able to activate it via satellite if necessary. I assume the team has taken all the steps to have real-time full-sensor coverage?"

"Yes, sir. Outrider at about five thousand feet AGL" — above ground level — "connected real-time to the mission commander in the field with up-link to us, and Global Hawk at sixty-five thousand feet using UHF/Ku SATCOM link. We'll also use real-time satellite coverage, optical, infrared, and synthetic aperture radar."

"I assume Predator was rejected because it doesn't have the legs to get in that far."

"Yes, sir. Predator has only a four hundred nautical mile range. Global Hawk, on the other hand, has almost a thirty-five hundred nautical mile range, and DarkStar has a range of five-hundred-and-seventy-five miles from base, more than enough to get there and back from the forward-operating point."

"OK. That sounds good. Why don't we check with the Operations Support Directorate at the Information Warfare Center at Kelly to coordinate a non-random, digitized destruct burst signal with a dual-modulated frequency drive. That should prevent any accidental destruction sequence, but still give us the option if we need it."

"Yes, sir," Markham replied as she jotted down what he had instructed word-for-word. "I assume we'll need to set up a quick-access portable device for the pilot."

"Yeah, the CIA has a green no-identification flight suit with an internal right pocket that will do nicely for inserting the activator. Let's just make sure the pilot understands how to use it, and how not to set it off accidentally. God, would that be a great way for this mission to go all to hell!"

"Yes, sir. I'll make sure one of the special ops guys fills him in on the details."

# CHAPTER 26

## Edwards Air Force Base,
## NASA Dryden Research Facility

"This is where the engineering comes in," Marta stated to Phinney as they walked around the SR-71 number 832 as it sat in Hangar 4801 at the NASA Dryden Research Facility. "This baby was built in 1964 at the Lockheed Skunkworks. The Air Force number is 64-17971, but we re-numbered it once it got here. Then the Air Force took it back for two years, so it got back the traditional red tail number. When the program was again deactivated, we got her back and gave her back 832 again." Marta led the way as she and Phinney walked around the front of the Blackbird. "The 'B' model sitting out there on the ramp," Marta continued as she pointed outside into the glaring sun-baked taxiway, "that used to be 17956, the only Blackbird trainer the Air Force built; we numbered it 831."

Phinney looked over at the other SR-71A. "Why isn't that one 833, then, instead of 844?"

Marta looked over at the other Blackbird sitting in the hangar, impressed that Phinney would note the difference in the sequence of the numbers of the planes. "It took us awhile to get 844 in, and by then we already had eleven other NASA planes designated."

Phinney noted that Marta didn't bother to mention what those other planes were. Need to know, he thought to himself.

"We've made quite a few changes on 844," Marta stated as they both walked over to the other Blackbird in the hangar, "which is one of its values. This one was number 17980, the last SR-71A built. When we got it it had a dart board on its tail, with a Blackbird flying out of it and a dart on the double two spot. We never figured out the significance of the dart board, or the double two for that matter. If you look down here, you can see we've already expanded the lower bay area to hold additional fuel instead of the heavy equipment it used to hold." At about the same time that Marta was showing Phinney the internal payload locations a fairly tall man in a green flight suit matching Marta's flight suit walked up to the two of them.

"So this is our boy, uh?" the man stated as he leaned down and gave the woman a quick kiss.

"He sure is," Marta replied. "Colonel Jack Phinney, meet my husband, Bob Holdiman. He also flies back seat in these Birds."

"Glad to meet you," Bob Holdiman stated as he shook Jack's hand. "How far did ya get?" Bob asked his wife.

"Just started. Want to tell some of the fun things we've done to 844 so he gets an idea of how well we know the insides of this beast?"

"Good idea," Bob said as he began the traditional pilot's pre-inspection walk around the plane. "As you probably know, Ed Empey and Rogers Karr do the flying, and Marta and I sit in the back as engineers and run the tests. We like to think of them as our personal designated drivers," Bob said as he smiled mischievously.

Marta immediately picked up on the point. "And we get to be the ultimate backseat driver," she explained. "Pretty much everything but the flying is done from the back, and that makes sense since we are the ones telling the pilot where to go and how to do it."

Phinney was not at all surprised by the gentle ribbing that the backseaters were giving the pilots; it's the same in any plane that seats more than one person: the other guy, truth be known, is just along for the ride; the real important stuff is done here.

"We've done all sorts of experiments with this baby," Bob continued. "We've put the D-21 Drone on top—the drone that used to sit piggyback on a modified A-12 aircraft—and conducted ramjet experiments, launching it at eighty thousand feet. We still have 17 drones in storage at Davis-Monthan in Arizona for whenever we get a good idea for high-altitude experiments. We've already designed a Hypersonic Drone Launch System and would like to use it on 06937, an old A-12 that we now designate as a YF-12C. We figure we can launch a scaled NASA HT-4 fifty-foot long drone at seventy-seven thousand feet at normal cruise, which is between Mach 3.0 to 3.2, let it loose and see what its Pratt and Whitney RL-10 liquid rocket engine could do. At first we thought we would have to ignite it then jettison it upward, but instead we set it up so the drone would have a low angle of attack until launch time, and then the pylon would allow the nose to lift up into a high angle of attack and let the aerodynamic lift launch it up and away from us on its own. At its elevated position we were able to get a positive lift of at least twice its weight. Most of our experiments, however, have related to pushing the envelope for the National Aerospace Plane, the HL-20, and the Hyper-Sonic Transport."

Marta stood by as the two men leaned under the plane to review the open bay doors. "Years ago," Bob continued, "we used a YF-12A to check out the effect of the Reynolds number on aft-facing discontinuities in a thick boundary layer. We've even played around with infusing nitric oxide into the jet engines to increase the r.p.m. at the transonic region, and we've carried a nine foot cylinder underneath the plane to check the validity of certain theories relating to skin friction and heat transfer at high speeds."

"Easy Bob," Marta interrupted. "This guy isn't a NASA engineer."

"Oh, yeah. Sorry about that. Sometimes I get carried away. I'll try to be a little less technical, but I want you to know what we've done and have succeeded in doing so you'll have a comfort level on what we've done to your plane."

"No problem," Phinney replied. "I've had some engineering background, but I have to admit you were way past me there for a bit. So what else have you done?"

"Well, I guess my favorite is the Aerospike Experiment where we put a rocket motor on a pylon assembly right where the D-21 drone used to be carried, right up there on the upper centerline or backbone of the airplane, on top of the fuselage right back there. We attached a triangular mount as the nacelles for the engine itself, inserting the fuel on the leading edge of the mount and an ignition device on the aft portion. We were trying to figure out a way to create a rocket without the weight of a rocket engine. In other words, instead of having a heavy metal 'funnel' to contain the rocket flame, we were hoping to use the supersonic airflow to contain the flame, thus reducing the weight of the engine itself substantially."

"Operating a rocket engine on top of the plane while at normal cruise?" Phinney stated incredulously. "Wouldn't you blow right past the flight parameters?"

"Only long enough to test the concept. Seven seconds or so, but if we were to operate it for a sustained period, yeah, we'd blow past the parameters until the heat on the compressor inlets made us slow down."

"And the increase in speed?"

"If we ran a sustained burn, I figure we'd easily go from Mach 3.2 to over Mach 4 on a sustained power curve. We had Warren Gunderson from Pratt & Whitney help us tweak the engines a bit so they could handle the higher r.p.m.'s and higher exhaust gas temperatures during the testing, but since the test only ran seven seconds we didn't get a chance to see how the modifications worked on sustained high Mach speeds. The changes did, however, allow us to accelerate the transonic regime more rapidly, which saves us quite a bit of fuel. We figure with the mods this 'Bird can give us a little more thrust and would be able to maintain a sustained operating speed of Mach 3.5 or so, but it raises all sorts of havoc on the life of the engines. Basically that type of sustained speed will compromise the six-hundred-hour engine life to about 150 hours, but it'd be a hell of a ride, though!"

Phinney had heard about test pilots' characteristics, had even read several books on what Ben Rich and others had accomplished, and risked, at the famed Skunkworks, but to listen to an engineer describe what sounded like a suicide mission like a little boy planning a sophisticated jump on his skateboard gave Phinney even more respect for these engineers focusing well beyond the next century of flight.

"All right," Bob continued, "let's show you what we've done to the plane in the last few days since we got this mission." Bob, Marta, and Phinney walked back toward the front of the plane. "Marta's in charge of all the SR assets and has a speciality in comm systems."

"Why don't you step over here, Colonel," Holdiman continued, "underneath the plane's nose section. We have four options for the front sections of the plane, that separates right here. We can use the basic nose, a radar nose, a Winkler nose with the window looking down, or a nose we designed ourselves with the window looking up. Makes it real easy to put on, say, from one mission to another. Anyway, we've installed the NASA nose and already have in it our experimental data link that we've been playing with. It's got a phase array antenna for secure, real-time communication, via the TDRS satellites we use for the Shuttle. It also allows for real-time telemetry transfer, and has a camera link in which we relay two cameras, one looking up and the other looking aft, normally at the experiment being conducted. This little window looking forward is where we've installed the third camera, just to see forward and a little bit downward. We've also added a passive warning detector at the very tip of the nose area that gives you a 360 look around to the sides and forward, and a forty-five degree look back capability. We've also added a rear-view passive detector in the tail cone, but it's not nearly as accurate. But it will give you a good 60 degree aft cone and will pick up any threats from your six: planes, air-launched missiles, and SAMs."

Phinney looked at the bottom of the nose cone and saw a glass plate. "For recon?" Phinney asked.

"Oh, heavens no. If we wanted to do recon we'd use one of the Air Force noses. This system was developed so we could get real-time data to feed into the Cray computers while in-flight, and then make adjustments to the experiment while we were doing it."

"And if you went down . . . ?" Phinney asked. Obviously they were dealing with real risks in such experiments, just like combat pilots deal with real risk everyday, even in training missions.

"And if we end up playing lawn darts and auger in, maybe we'd know why," Marta stated simply, just like any combat pilot or test pilot would say. "This back here a little ways," continued Marta without missing a beat, "is where the starter system is located. In case you have to land at an alternative airfield we've placed inside one of the payload bays a turbine probe that is inserted right into the bottom of the engine, right here. All you'd have to do is have someone hook up the turbine probe and start one engine, then do the same on the other side."

Phinney looked up into the bottom portion of the right engine. Marta continued the briefing. "The probe goes in here; the gears connect to the drive-shaft gear-assemblage. Obviously during the mission you should keep both engines going after landing, and then leave as soon as you can. If you do land at an alternative base and have to re-start either of the engines you will need two people to initiate such a start, one on the turbine probe and one in the pilot's seat. The 3AG1100 air turbine should not be used for more than five seconds between 1370 to 1470 r.p.m.'s. Hopefully you get a start before then. Once you have ignition, disconnect at thirty-two hundred, and move on to the second engine using the same procedure. The air hose connects right here."

"Got it," Phinney said.

"The rest of the bays consist of about 120 cubic feet of space, in which we have added additional twenty-two hundred pounds of JP-7 fuel. We've also added two mounts under each wing where we will install one thousand gallon drop tanks, one on each side."

"Won't that kill the air flow and prevent supersonic flight?" Jack asked.

"No," Marta replied, "we can still go supersonic, but we can't reach optimum flight speed while they're attached. But at the beginning of the mission there is no need for sustained supersonic flight, and this will give you the maximum amount of fuel. The drop tanks have no markings and should be jettisoned right before landing. That means you should be landing with a full load, which means the landing will have to be very smooth."

"I bet."

"Now, take a look up here, Jack. Look how wide the gaps are here between the sheets of titanium. When the plane is cold these gaps exist. Once the plane gets airborne the friction heats up the metal and it expands right into place, a perfect fit. The wings literally seal themselves from the leaking. What will happen is you will takeoff at medium to minimum weight, get airborne for a while so the heat seals the wing tanks, and then refuel."

Phinney marvelled at the technology that must have been used, long before the advent of supercomputers, to design such a system. But he also realized what would happen if the plane ever cooled down. "And if I have to slow down and the plane cools?"

"That's what else we've come up with," Bob stepped in. "After you refuel we're going to have you sprayed by a special polymer on both wings that will seal the wings, like a plastic wrap. As long as you remain under supersonic the polymer seal will hold, for up to seven days, it turns out. But as soon as you enter close to Mach speed the polymer will melt away, just at the same time the heat seals the leaks by the expansion of the titanium."

"Doesn't the polymer affect the lift?" Jack asked.

"Only by 10 percent, which isn't a problem as long as you don't come too close to the flight parameters."

"Let's see if I've got this right," Phinney stated to Bob and Marta. "I'm supposed to fly an overweight supersonic plane on a slow approach, gentle landing, and then takeoff at close to maximum weight, with a 10 percent less efficient lift ratio? Does that sound about right?"

"Damn close. The only thing we haven't mentioned is that when you land, if you land hard enough to create, say, anything more than 2 g's, the fuselage may break in half."

"Perfect," Jack replied simply and without anger. Welcome to Special Ops, Jack thought to himself.

# CHAPTER 27

## Vnukovo Airport, Moscow

Tsinev exited the vehicle, was handed his luggage by the driver, and turned toward the terminal building. Unlike Sheremetyevo 2 International Airport thirty kilometers northwest of the center of Moscow—where almost all foreigners enter Russia—Vnukovo Airport serves the Russian people with domestic Aeroflot flights, or what's left of Aeroflot. The difference is immediately apparent. Sheremetyevo 2 is clean, relatively efficient, and provides at least the veneer of organization; Vnukovo, on the other hand, is dirty, generally dishevelled, and the essence of organized chaos.

Into the din of hundreds of voices and bodies scurrying in every direction, Tsinev entered the building. His ticket already purchased at the Aeroflot office on Dobryninskaya Street, Tsinev went directly to the right upon entering the building to Gate 15, checking his luggage at the gate. At Vnukovo one can see the surface of the third-world country that Russia has become: poorly clad baggage clerks place the luggage on beat-up carts that look at least twenty years old, the clerks' pretense of officiousness equaled only by their inefficiency.

One of the clerks looked carefully at Tsinev trying to determine if he was a foreigner despite his presentation of a Russian passport. She apparently had sufficient enough doubt on the matter. "You may wait in there," she stated matter-of-factly as she pointed to the enclosed waiting area. The other passengers began presenting their tickets and passports to the uniformed guards, but were not allowed to enter the waiting area where Tsinev sat alone. The clerk had apparently decided that Tsinev deserved to be treated as a dignitary or a foreigner and therefore was not subjected to the rabble that stood outside the waiting area. Within an hour the female clerk led Tsinev and the entire group downstairs, where they boarded several buses and were taken to the plane some three hundred meters away. The passengers were stopped at the base of the ramp by a stewardess; no explanation was given for the delay. The passengers, not being allowed to ascend the ramp, instead crowded around the plane's deteriorated ramp, a mass of bodies without even the semblance of willingness to create a line. This alone, thought Tsinev as he shivered in the October cold, depicts the end of Russia: a country such as this cannot survive without order, and once order is lost it is rarely reborn without great effort and, usually, great fear. Tsinev could not help but reflect on E. Adamson Hoebel's prophetic words written clear back in 1954 about the relationship between order and society: "Without a sense of community, there can be no law. Without law there cannot be for long a community."

Finally a stewardess allowed the mob to enter the plane, everyone grabbing their seats as a free-for-all. Tsinev had actually witnessed a fistfight on board one Aeroflot plane a few years ago as the plane took off; apparently the stewardess had let more people on than there were seats so two men were fighting over the last one. The loser sat in the bathroom, at least when it wasn't in use, for the rest of the flight.

Tsinev went up to the front section, knowing that most of the rabble would at least have the good sense to leave the front seats to those who were worthy—foreigners and such. As in most Aeroflot flights, the rules relating to carry-on, assuming that there were any, were totally ignored. Almost all of the passengers had massive packages which were unceremoniously piled up in front of the exit door. After sitting down at an open aisle seat Tsinev observed that a rectangular portion of the carpet on the plane's aisle had been removed, obviously the point directly above the nose gear. "Great!" Tsinev muttered out loud, realizing that the carpet had been permanently removed to allow the pilots to put the nose gear down manually, something that apparently had to be done on a regular basis. All around him people were opening their bags and containers filled with food—few dared eat the Aeroflot supplied food, never knowing how long it had been sitting out—as the plane taxied onto the main runway and took off into the eastern darkness.

*Lynn M. Boughey*

# CHAPTER 28

## Moscow

Randy Broughton exited the Arbat Metro stop and stepped into the daylight facing the strange lime-green, garishly adorned French style house. The Muscovites claimed that the building was constructed by a very wealthy Russian aristocrat; legend has it that when his mother first saw the building, she scolded him by saying, "Beforehand we knew you were a fool, but now everybody knows you are one!" Broughton turned left on the street, then walked down into a tunnel shaped like a "Y" with the right-hand fork going towards New Arbat Street, and the left-hand fork going towards the original Arbat Street. Broughton went to the left, and walked up the stairs out of the short tunnel. All around him standing along the cement stairs were women holding puppies or photos of puppies and dogs. Anything for a buck, Broughton thought to himself. The dogs were shivering in the cold, not unlike their temporary masters.

Broughton walked past the women selling the puppies and began walking along Arbat Street, past the caricature and portrait artists, past the old women selling afghans and strands of amber and the young men selling the traditional Russian fur hats and Matryshka dolls to the tourists. Aside from the Kremlin itself, Arbat Street is one of the most popular tourist traps, and therefore a perfect place to plan a meeting with Konesky. A light snow began to fall, and Broughton turned up the collar on his old Russian gray, military-style coat.

About two-thirds down Arbat Street Broughton reached No. 53, where Pushkin lived for three months after he was married. He paid the twelve hundred ruble tour fee, noting the sign above the cashier stating that it would cost one thousand rubles for each picture

that is taken. Having no bags or cameras to check, Broughton merely continued down the stairs into the basement where he was instructed by a not-so-friendly tour guide to put on the light-blue, paper slippers over his shoes. Broughton was then led upstairs with the small
group of tourists who were already waiting in the basement. He always
marvelled at the upper two stories of Pushkin's house, filled with wonderful art, including portraits of Pushkin's friends, beautiful drawings
of Moscow at the time when Pushkin lived there, and of course portraits of Pushkin and his wife.

While Broughton looked at some of the antique furniture
located in one of the corners of the house facing Arbat Street, he heard
the sound of a group of five or six Hari Krishna's outside chanting,
with the added effect of a microphone and several large drums.
Within a few moments a woman obviously in charge of the museum—and more obviously furious at such an intrusion—put on loud
classical music that easily drowned out the chanting. Broughton
glanced out the window and watched as the Krishna were pelted by
snowballs from some of the younger onlookers. The Hari Krishna do
not seem to have any more popularity here than in the United States,
Broughton thought to himself, and then continued going from room-
to-room waiting for Konesky to arrive.

"Rather exquisite, wasn't she," Konesky stated to Broughton in
Russian as he peered over Broughton's shoulder, also looking at one of
the portraits of Pushkin's wife, Natalya Nikolayevna Goncharova.

"Indeed," Broughton replied also in Russian. "Very beautiful!
And how are you, my friend?" Broughton asked as he shook Konesky's
hand.

"Quite well, thank you," Konesky replied switching to
English. "I see you were in a romantic mood today," Konesky continued, referring of course to Pushkin's introduction to the Russian people of Byron's works and style.

"As a matter of fact, I am. That, or I was just looking for an
excuse to be near a MacDonald's so I could get rid of that urge for a
Big Mac."

"I've often wondered, Randy, is your love for such unhealthy
food an acquired taste, or just a matter of being politically correct?"

Broughton realized that Konesky was now poking fun at a former American president's alleged penchant for fast food.

"When in Rome . . ." Broughton retorted.

"Is that where we are today. I keep losing track."

The two men walked over to the other side of the room and looked at the next set of portraits hanging from the wall. "It is not very crowded here today," Konesky mentioned as he looked around to see who was near. As he did so he observed some people in the adjacent room to their left, and no one in the room to their right. "How nice. Perhaps we should review the portraits in this room over here?" Broughton nodded affirmatively and followed Konesky as he moved to the adjacent room in which there were no tourists.

"So, how can I help you, my friend," Konesky said to Broughton in a somewhat muted voice as the two men appeared to be studying the portraits.

"We have received confirmation that one of your scientists is in charge of a secret nuclear weapons facility that is not listed in the annexes or appendices, and that the facility may be operational or is soon to be operational."

"I take it that since you are talking to me here, as opposed to talking directly to my seniors, that you have decided to use the alternative method of checking."

"We believe that would be best for both countries."

"The reason for not going through normal procedures?" Konesky asked.

"As we discussed, the treaty is vague on how to inspect non-listed sites. We also have concerns about the man in charge of the possible site."

"What type of concerns?"

"Psychological." Upon saying this, Broughton observed several tourists walking by the open door, and switched to speaking in French. "What do you think of this painting?" Broughton asked Konesky. The two men examined the portrait of Pushkin while in Mikhaylovskoye in the 1820s, where he sat exiled for two years and arguably produced his best works, including his masterpiece Boris Godunov.

"Perhaps we should use the power of exile more often," Konesky replied also in French as the tourists walked by behind him and Broughton. "Look what great works it produces!"

"Too bad about those in-laws, though," Broughton joked, referring to the fact that Pushkin died in a duel with his bother-in-law.

"Yes," Konesky replied laughing as he looked around and saw that the tourists had gone into the next room, "it must have made the remaining Christmas dinners rather uncomfortable for Natalya." Now that the room was once again clear of the other tourists, Konesky reverted back to English. "And, my friend, I assume you will provide me some positive basis to justify ignoring the treaty and putting my career in such peril."

"Of course," Broughton stated as he handed Konesky a manila envelope about one-half inch in thickness. "You have everything that I have, and, of course, must keep it between us only."

"I understand, as agreed. From one soldier to another, as long as it is in both our countries' best interest."

"I believe you will find that it is."

"And what is it that I now have?"

"We do not know the location of the site. We received one short signal from a locator last week in Northern Russia. The signal meant that our contact had seen the site and was going to place the locator at or near it. So far we have not received the final signal."

"And you want me to help look for the site."

"Yes. The packet tells you what we know so far. We know where the missiles came from, we know they were transported outside military channels somewhere near Plesetsk, and we know who the scientist is who designed the facility. But we can't find it."

"I will call you tonight at the *shalman* and tell you 'yes' or 'no.' If it is 'no' we will never speak of it again. Agreed?"

"Agreed," Broughton stated.

Both men knew which *shalman* or, in Russian slang, dive, to which Konesky had referred. The run-down cafe was close to the American Embassy building and easy to get to for Broughton. The two men shook hands, and Konesky turned and left, with Broughton looking at the envelope in Konesky's hand as he walked away. Broughton knew full well that he had just given Konesky more classified and top secret information than had ever been provided to a Russian. I bet the CIA had a fit over this one, Broughton thought to himself as he watched Konesky walk down the stairs toward the exit.

# CHAPTER 29

## Omsk, Russia

Tsinev looked out the window of the Aeroflot plane as it taxied toward the Omsk airport, noting the numerous missing taxi lights as the plane left the bumpy runway and entered the even bumpier taxiway. The plane stopped one hundred meters away from the terminal and, as usual, all of the passengers exited the plane so it could be refueled. Tsinev watched as most of the passengers entered the small bus on the right. It was cold and late at night; not everyone could fit into the regular bus, so once the three foreigners and Tsinev had seated themselves in the newer bus on the left, the remaining passengers filled up the VIP bus.

Tsinev was of course very familiar with Omsk, and had travelled here regularly on his way to other points eastward. The city of Omsk, situated three hundred miles east of the Ural Mountains, is the second largest city in Siberia. Positioned at the confluence of the Om and Irtysh rivers, Omsk was understandably founded by a military expedition in the early 1700s. The famous writer Dostoyevsky unfortunately found himself a "guest" of the Tsar at the prison in Omsk, where he served four years hard labor and received an occasional flogging, all of which served as a basis for several descriptions contained in his novel *The House of the Dead*.

Tsinev always thought it strange that Dostoyevsky—unlike Pomyalovsky and others who had lived through such horrors in exile—did not lose his faith in humanity and the Russian people. Indeed, Dostoyevsky continued not only to hold on to these convictions, but also his strong faith in humanity, thus strengthening his ability to put forth his optimistic views within the context of his writings. Thus, as is often the case when an oppressor tries to destroy a thoughtful and artistic opponent, the opposite of what was intended occurred: Instead of destroying Dostoyevsky or his idealism, the experience of being imprisoned here had the opposite effect from that which the Tsar had hoped, and many years later Dostoyevsky wrote that his four years in Siberia actually caused the regeneration of his convictions. Knowledge, thought Tsinev, can indeed come from the coexistence of suffering and sufficient time to reflect upon one's situation and the human condition.

Soon the driver of the airport bus began the short drive toward the terminal, slipping in a cassette tape into the portable cassette player sitting to his left. An amazed Tsinev listened to the words that blared out of the speakers from Pink Floyd's *The Wall* as the bus travelled from the flight line to the terminal:

Daddy's flown 'cross the ocean
Leaving just a memory
A snapshot in the family album
Daddy what else did you leave for me?
Daddy what did you leave behind for me?
All in all it was just another brick in the wall.
All in all it was all just bricks in the wall.

"It is complete," Tsinev whispered aloud to himself, the music drowning out his words; the Americans have won. The assimilation has begun, and the powerful forces of culture and desire and greed will do the rest. Unbelievable. How can so much happen in ten years?

"We don't need no education, we don't need no thought control," the music blared. The bus stopped and the regular passengers, *en mass*, surged for the terminal door. "This way please," the stewardess told the foreigners and Tsinev. The four VIPs followed the stewardess as she walked to the left of the main terminal door and up the broken concrete stairs alongside the building, the entire group having to step over boards and debris from the construction on the concrete slab that was presumably being done immediately outside the building.

What a mess! Tsinev thought. Tsinev could not help but wonder how many days or months it had been like this. Maybe years! Everyone knew that once the Soviet Union collapsed, buildings half-built remained exactly as they were, either because there was no more money to pay the workers, or no ability to get the necessary supplies to the location. The economy, and in many regards the entire country, simply shut down.

The VIPs entered the small lounge and ordered a beer. Tsinev ordered a Lonestar. A Lonestar beer in the middle of Siberia! Tsinev thought to himself. Amazing.

Tsinev seated himself at one of the folding tables overlooking the other passengers downstairs, undoubtedly putting a major dent in the vodka supply. About twenty minutes later the stewardess came to get the VIPs and escorted them back by themselves on the newer bus. The passengers began boarding the plane. Tsinev stopped at the top of the ramp momentarily and looked around, considering to himself how desolate Omsk was. Here he was at night, within miles of one of the largest cities in Russia, and he could see no city lights around him; just the cold reaches of Siberia preluded by broken taxi lights and half-completed construction gone awry. A short time later the plane lifted off the decrepit runway and headed east for Bratsk, leaving behind the darkness of a dying city.

# CHAPTER 30

## Northern Russia

"Hello, Pavel," the colonel stated as Pavel Kerlov and one of the colonel's guards entered the security chief's office adjacent to the control room at the launch facility. The colonel noted that his guards had not exaggerated Pavel's worsening condition. He looked like he had not slept in a week: his eyes were bloodshot, his clothes disheveled, and his hair greasy and uncombed. "How are you doing?" the colonel asked trying not to sound too patronizing.

"Why the hell should you care?" Pavel responded, making no attempt to hide his distain for this man. His uncle had insisted on his selection as Chief of Security of the facility. But as they came closer and closer to completion of the project Pavel watched as this man tried to usurp more and more of his power. "What do you want?" Pavel continued brusquely. "I am not a school boy you can summon like your lackey dogs," he said quickly so that the guard who had brought him in would hear the insult before he had left.

"I need to talk to you about a security matter, Pavel," the colonel continued in a placating tone. Kerlov noted that the colonel seemed almost kind to him and was not responding to his feigned out-rage. This more than anything made Pavel begin to worry.

"Please, Pavel, have a seat. This won't take long."

Pavel did so, all the while wondering why the colonel was being so professional, almost friendly.

"I am afraid we had a security breach, but you need not worry, it has been corrected." The colonel reached across his desk and hand-ed Pavel a black and white photograph. "Do you recognize this woman?" the colonel asked.

Pavel looked at the picture and saw it was Riana. He swallowed hard; he had forgotten how beautiful she was. "Yes, I know her. She was a guest of mine a few days ago. What about her?"

"She is a spy. She works for the CIA, and was obviously assigned to you."

Pavel grew weak. He felt queasy as his mind rushed along a thousand ideas, and another thousand possibilities.

"Impossible," Pavel finally blurted out. "I met her by chance. She is a Russian! She is no spy."

"Then perhaps you can explain this," the colonel stated as he handed Pavel a small box. "It is a locator devise that we found on her when she tried to find her way back here after your little unauthorized tour of the facility."

Pavel noted the emphasis the colonel placed on the word "unauthorized." Pavel looked up at the colonel almost in a daze. The room seemed to pulsate from darker to lighter. His elbow slipped off the wooden arm rest, almost sending Pavel onto the floor.

"Don't worry, Pavel," the colonel said without emotion or concern for Pavel almost falling to the ground, "it had not been activated yet, and I have made sure it is now inoperable. It is a locator, like the ones used to find a missing plane. Her intent was to find the site in the daylight, and then activate the device so the Americans would know where the site is located."

"How do you know this?" Pavel demanded, coming out of his daze slightly.

"She told me herself," the colonel replied, "though I must admit it took a little prodding on my part."

Pavel understood immediately what the colonel meant by "prodding," and also realized right then that she was dead. Pavel tried to get up, but his legs buckled and he landed back on the chair, almost tipping himself over backwards, his head turning to one side as he threw up on the floor.

The colonel waited for the heaving to subside. "You really must take better care of yourself, Pavel," the colonel continued in his most professional and concerned voice. He had the upper hand and decided he need not be petty or vindictive. "Besides, we need you to finish your uncle's great project, even though I am sure your assistants could complete the task, if necessary."

The colonel looked over at the guard, speaking forcefully as a man in full authority and now in full control. "Take him back to his apartment and his friends. Tell them to feed him and get him back to health. And give him this, when you get there. It is his grandmother's ring. The dumb *svoloch* had given it to the *shkura*. What an idiot! And send someone in here to clean up this mess."

# CHAPTER 31

## Bratsk Airport, Russia

The plane landed on time onto an icy runway and an icy land. Tsinev had no doubt he was now deep into the reaches of Siberia. As he exited the plane around five in the morning he could see the dawn approaching from the east. The hundred or so passengers slid and slipped their way across the icy tarmac to the airport building. How the plane was allowed to land in such conditions was beyond Tsinev's imagination.

Although originally founded in 1631 as a Cossack fort, the city of Bratsk did not really begin until the 1960s when hydro-electric power transformed the sleepy town into a huge city, its new massiveness equaled only by the extensive harm done to the environment in the process. Not even the devastation surrounding the Tungus meteorite at Varnavara 350 miles north of Bratsk, the location of the largest meteorite to hit the Earth, came close to the damage that humans had inflicted upon their own land and water supply.

Inside the Bratsk airport building the passengers, including Tsinev, waited for their bags. The baggage area was not heated, and the wait long. Finally a truck pulled up and the bags, most of them wrapped in brown paper and tied with string, were thrown unceremoniously onto the metal ramp, gravity and the forty-five degree angle of the ramp taking care of the rest. Tsinev was glad he had used hard-sided luggage. Soon the truck pulled away, and the passengers dissipated with their luggage. Only Tsinev and a Vietnamese family remained.

"Where is our luggage?" one of the Vietnamese asked the officious women clerks in charge of making sure each person's luggage was checked to see if the baggage claim ticket matched.

"Your luggage was placed up front in a heated compartment, but the door is frozen shut. They will get it here soon."

The officious woman looked over to Tsinev. "Your luggage, too." Tsinev nodded his understanding. Ten minutes later the luggage arrived, and Tsinev entered the slightly warmer airport building. The building looked like it was built in 1950. The waiting area was only a hundred meters by twenty meters.

Tsinev walked to the opposite side and outside looking for a taxi. Most of the passengers had already left, presumably with people waiting for them. By now it was light out, and exceedingly cold. "Where do I get a taxi?" Tsinev asked the old man guarding the bathroom. The cardboard sign posted on the door leading into the bathroom proclaimed the prices for the privilege of using the hole in the floor: One hundred rubles if you stay standing, three hundred rubles if you squat.

"You are not in Moscow anymore," the man said abruptly.

Apparently not, Tsinev thought to himself.

"There will be a bus soon," the man said as Tsinev began to walk away.

"Thank you." Tsinev walked outside. The bus arrived sometime later, and ten or so passengers boarded the bus with Tsinev, the strong smell of diesel wafting itself into the bus as everyone boarded. The woman driver finished collecting the fare and began the drive into Bratsk. Tsinev looked out the window amazed, as he always was, at the stark beauty of the Siberian forest surrounding the road. No wonder the runway was icy, Tsinev thought to himself as he looked at the trees and electrical lines all covered with ice.

"This stop for the train station," the woman bus driver announced after the bus had travelled approximately three miles slipping and sliding along the snow-covered road. Tsinev stood up, grabbed his suitcase, and exited the bus, now reeking of diesel exhaust. Obviously no one had checked, or cared to fix even if they had checked, the exhaust system. Tsinev sat his luggage down for a moment as the bus noisily pulled away, putting on his thick gloves for the three hundred meter walk down a slippery, muddy trail that led to the train station.

# CHAPTER 32

## Edwards Air Force Base, California

"NASA Control, Blackbird Eight Four Four ready for takeoff, Runway 22," Phinney stated into the microphone.

"Roger, Blackbird Eight Four Four, cleared for takeoff."

"Blackbird Eight Four Four, Roger."

Phinney looked down for a final time at the numerous gauges and dials. Everything looked good. He pressed his left hand forward pushing the throttle past idle, up to military thrust as he eased off the brakes, once again reviewed the instruments, and then pushed the throttle into afterburners. Keeping his eye on the end of the runway, Phinney once again felt the rush of power from the two J-58 engines that pushed him forcefully back into his seat. Because the SR-71 was filled with fuel and the specially installed drop tanks, Phinney used almost twice as much runway as normally necessary for takeoff.

"NASA Control, Blackbird Eight Four Four, off at 0640, VFR Flight to Nellis, negative radio contact requested, over."

"Blackbird Eight Four Four, we acknowledge VFR to Nellis, negative radio contact authorized. NASA Control out."

Phinney allowed the Blackbird to climb relatively slowly until he reached Mach .95; to his right he observed Fremont Peak, to his left Red Mountain and beyond it China Lake. He pushed the stick forward momentarily, allowing the plane to glide into Mach plus flight. The slow climb then continued until the plane reached a lazy cruise speed of only Mach 2.2, or fifteen hundred miles per hour. In the process Phinney angled the plane slightly to the right, bearing northeasterly towards Las Vegas. Phinney knew he had to be careful to maintain a relatively slow speed and had to handle the over-weight plane delicately, at least until he got rid of the drop tanks, realizing that any sudden moves or faster speed would tear off the drop tanks, causing who knew what damage to the Blackbird. Despite taking it easy on the speed, the 165 mile trip to Nellis took only a few minutes, with Phinney spending most of the time deaccelerating and descending toward the 3.5 million acres of air space used by Nellis Air Force Base for war games and training.

Phinney was glad to be out of the David Clark pressure suit which he had used so far in his training as he got accustomed to the Blackbird, including the high altitude regime where the space suit was, for safety reasons, a must. Today, however, Phinney had donned a partial pressure suit, known as the "jerkins" suit because its appearance is similar to the attire worn clear back in the sixteenth century by British men known as a jerkin. Also made by the David Clark Company, the two-piece suit, consisting of a pair of G pants and an upper half pressure suit, looked more like a sophisticated set of green chaps and a vest. Phinney particularly liked the fact that his arms were relatively free to move normally, that he was able to use thinner and more comfortable gloves, and that the helmet was more like the traditional pilot's helmet. All of these factors made it much easier for Phinney to maneuver about the cockpit while he was flying the Blackbird.

At exactly 0700, Phinney entered the northwest corner of the massive Nellis range at five hundred feet above the desert floor. Travelling at approximately four hundred knots the plane felt heavy and labored to Phinney. If it was a nice day out, Phinney didn't know; his eyes never veered from the two full-color cathode ray tube (CRT) multi-functional displays (MFDs) in the center of the main instrument panel. The top display provided a TV (or infrared, if needed) view ahead of him, superimposed upon it the traditional altitude director indicator with the aim points for flying as well as a bar scale on the side showing exact altitude and another aim point for altitude desired given the upcoming terrain and mission parameters. The other side of the screen showed the plane's current speed, and when adjustments needed to be made an arrow aiming upward or downward appeared on the screen so the pilot could respond accordingly. This screen, basically a souped-up version of what he used everyday flying B-52s, provided Phinney with everything he needed to fly the bird on time and on target. And, thanks to the multi-functional capability of the display, Phinney merely had to push one of the five buttons on the bottom of the glare shield to select the configuration necessary for takeoff, insertion, mission, extraction, and approach and landing.

The lower screen, however, was something different entirely. Prior to this mission, Phinney was not at all familiar with the lower display; the only thing he saw close to it was the electronic warfare officer's display used in the B-52 to thwart interception and missile attacks. Derived from the B-2 bomber, the lower screen provided the defensive management sub-system, or DMS. Designed by Lockheed Martin, the APR-50 provided Phinney with real-time detection, classification, identification and location of all hostile systems that emit radio-frequency energy. This system clearly and quickly told Phinney if he was being tracked by radar from the ground or the air, if the radar had a lock on him, if a missile had been fired at him, and what defensive maneuvers he was required to take. Phinney knew that the APR-50 was capable, when operating at cruising altitude, of locating and identifying all aircraft within three hundred miles, all the while acting as a completely passive system! And, God forbid, if a missile was fired at the plane, the APR-50 automatically turned active and sent out the most appropriate electronic countermeasures needed to defeat the threat, at the same time telling the pilot what to do to maximize the effect of those countermeasures.

It was this system that Phinney was testing today, as well as Phinney's ability to single-handedly fly the over-weight SR-71 through twenty miles of mountainous terrain at low level, and then attempt to land at one of the two ten-thousand-foot runways at Nellis, all without radio contact. Phinney had already been advised that Nellis had just begun a Green Flag exercise in which approximately nine hundred Air Force, Navy, and Marine fliers gathered to participate in the most sophisticated electronic combat in the world. Stationed on the ground were dozens of Russian built radar sites, such as the SA-11 "Gadfly" and the SA-13 "Gopher," and over one hundred other radar tracking devices (including hand-held SA-14 "Gremlins" and the SA-16 "Gimlets"), all used to target and "destroy" the incoming mission aircraft with electronic missiles. Above the ground, sometimes as many as one hundred planes would participate in both defensive and offensive operations, with the scores being tallied electronically, every move and jot recorded and observed real-time in the Air Operations Center. Today's tasking order was simple, however: Radar ground sites were instructed to identify and electronically destroy any hostile or unknown aircraft; and the aircraft in the air at this early portion of the day-long mission had been instructed to fly the normal perimeter watches and defend the home base, Nellis.

As Phinney flew over Groom Lake, some eighty miles north of Nellis, he began his run. Marta, seated in the RSO's back-seat, would remain silent throughout the mission, her function to evaluate Phinney as if this were his solo flight, but also to speak up if absolutely necessary to warn him if he were going to run into a mountain or into another aircraft. Phinney eased the plane up and over and mostly between the mountains, edging his way south towards Nellis. At first he had problems getting the heavier-than-normal plane to react, but once he thought of the SR as the flight equivalent of an empty B-52, his task became exceedingly easier. It was just a matter of finding the right comparison, he realized, and therefore the right comfort level. Within thirty minutes Phinney had tossed and turned the plane to within ten miles of the base, carefully following the pre-planned detailed route. He had only one more group of mountains to circumnavigate, and then he would ease the plane into his approach at Nellis.

As Phinney began the slow turn around a mountain and aimed the plane toward the lowest point between the next pair of jutting rocks, he heard the familiar sound of beeping that told him that a radar site had acquired him and was trying to lock on. Phinney quickly looked down at the lower ECM screen that showed a large red arrow pointing to the right with the number "25" next to it. Phinney tried to "delicately" jerk the plane to the right 25 degrees, never taking his eyes off the screen. The arrow, now green in color, flashed downward, with "5K" appearing boldly within the arrow. Phinney, realizing that he must have already gone between the two mountain peaks that he had previously seen, pushed the stick forward and headed for the flat desert, leveling out at five thousand feet. Looking up slightly at the upper screen Phinney was relieved to see a clear screen with just the map display showing the runway immediately in front of him.

Just as Phinney began to relax and aim the Blackbird toward the runway for his wheels up fly-by approach, a different sound, this time a beeping sound instead of a tone, emanated from his 360 degree stereophonic speaker system inside his helmet, adjusting the location of the sound based on the direction of the pilot's head so the pilot would be able to hear exactly from where any threat emanated. One beeping sound came from behind his right side, a little low; another came from his left almost straight across from him. Phinney looked down at the lower screen, already realizing that he had a hostile aircraft at his 5 o'clock position, and another one at his 10 o'clock position. The lower screen, however, showed a solid green arrow facing straight ahead. Phinney looked down at all of the various smaller signals at the bottom of the screen describing which countermeasures were being used, all of which must have been working Phinney realized or the computer would have instructed him to veer off. As Phinney began the straight-in approach to the runway the two beeping sounds diminished to hardly a noise, and Phinney leveled the plane off at five hundred feet as he flew directly over the runway.

Nice, Phinney thought to himself. Real nice. His self-aggrandizement did not last long, however. As he passed the end of the runway a loud beeping sound emitted from the surround speaker system immediately behind him. Obviously one of the planes must have gone passive and then came in for the kill from behind. Phinney pushed the throttle forward as much as he dared given the added weight and drag of the drop tanks and watched as the Blackbird accelerated and climbed away from the shimmering desert below him. As he began his shallow climb away from the Nellis runway Phinney heard the obvious sound of a missile lock on from his 6 o'clock position.

"You are authorized to drop the tanks," Marta stated over the internal intercom system.

Phinney didn't need any further encouragement in that regard. He reached down and jettisoned the now empty drop tanks, and then immediately rammed the throttle forward into full afterburners. At the same time he jerked the plane upward and to the right, putting as much distance as possible between the hostile plane or SAM site and himself. As the plane streaked away from Nellis and back west toward California, Phinney heard first the missile lock tone disappear, and then smiled as the enemy plane's radar signal grew quieter and quieter until, within ten seconds or so the cockpit fell silent. A few minutes later Phinney once again began the slow process of deceleration as he prepared to land at Edwards Air Force Base, continuing his radio silence.

# CHAPTER 33

## Bratsk Train Station

At five thirty in the morning the train station was empty, and cold. Several windows were broken out letting in the cold air. The next train was scheduled for eight fifty-five. Tsinev sat down on a plastic chair and closed his eyes, resting. It had been a long night, but there would be more than enough time to sleep on the thirty-six hour train ride before him.

Around six thirty the train station began to fill with at least a few people. Everyone knew the Trans-Siberian Railway ran exactly on time and therefore all steps were made to arrive at the train station well before the scheduled departure. Tsinev watched as two young soldiers ate their breakfast of sausage, bread, and several shots of vodka. One must only be awake in Russia to drink vodka.

At eight forty-five the train arrived, Number 7 Tsinev noted, and was boarded within five minutes. Tsinev had been assigned a sleeping berth with a couple and a child who were also going to Chara. Once again Russian efficiency; one was assigned to a berth with others who are going to the same place, not so you can potentially visit with friends or acquaintances from the same place but so the car, upon arriving at that final destination, can be cleaned by the *provodnitsa*.

As always, the train departed on schedule. At least something still runs right in this damn country, Tsinev thought to himself. Sometimes confused with the Trans-Siberian Railway, Tsinev realized that he was actually riding on the Baikal Amur Mainline, or BAM, a northern branch of the original Trans-Siberian Railway beginning at Tayshet and going all the way to the Pacific Ocean ending at Imperatorskaya Gavan. Originally conceived in the 1920s, initial work on the line was stopped during World War II and not begun again until the 1960s as part of Brezhnev's 1976-1990 Fifteen-Year Plan. Following ten years of work at the cost of over $60 billion, the line reached completion in 1984 and spanned over three thousand kilometers, or almost two thousand miles. As the train began to pick up speed an officious-looking woman wearing a bright-blue coat with gold epaulettes demanded to see passports and tickets. She was of course the conductor and not to be fooled with by the looks of her, Tsinev thought; she appeared quite large, determined, and without a sense of humor. Many a person had probably been thrown off this train by such a woman if one's credentials and ticket were not absolutely in order.

After the conductor left Tsinev introduced himself to his new travelling companions. "I am Sergie," the young man stated as he shook Tsinev's hand. "This is my wife, Helen, and our baby daughter, Natalie, though we call her Natasha."

"Hello," Tsinev replied. "I am Dmitri." Tsinev nodded at the women, who smiled nervously and nodded back as she held her sleeping baby daughter. "Did I hear you tell the conductor you are going to Chara?"

"Yes," the young man replied. "We are from there. We were visiting her family," Sergie stated, glancing at Helen.

"Would you like some sausage?" Helen asked as she pulled out some bread and sausage from her bag under the seat.

"Yes," Tsinev replied. "Thank you."

"And how is your family?" Tsinev asked Helen, trying to draw her into the conversation as he took a bite of salt and then began eating a slice of sausage. She merely smiled slightly, and shrugged her shoulders.

"They are not well," Sergie answered for her. "They used to live in a village near Cherynobyl. The cloud of radioactivity went to her village. Her family now lives in a special city, which they can never leave."

"I am sorry," Tsinev stated.

"Yes, it is sad," Sergie continued. "Helen's younger sister was only a year old when it happened. She died three years later. Her parents and other family members have never felt well since."

Tsinev thought for a moment as he ate some more sausage. "Can they not go to Moscow to get treated?" he asked.

"They have been told that all the treatment available is brought to them. They can never leave. It is a closed city."

Tsinev shook his head in understanding. "And what do you do, Sergie?"

"I am a train engineer. That is how we can go on such a trip. I get one pass every year for myself and my family. This year we visited her family; next year mine at Vladivostok."

"How do you like living in Chara?" Tsinev asked.

"It is fine," Sergie answered without any enthusiasm. "We live in a wood house, like most of the others. Only a few lucky ones got the new apartments that were built when the railroad came through."

Tsinev understood. He had been in many small villages in Siberia that had old wood houses that barely kept out the cold in the winter. Often the water left out in a pail would be frozen solid the next morning and had to be thawed by the heat of the stove. "At least we have electricity," Sergie stated somewhat happier.

Over the next few days Tsinev found out as much as he could about Chara from Sergie, and at times even Helen would add a fact or two or gently correct her husband when he seemed inaccurate or mistaken. Sergie explained that Chara has two airports, one civilian and one military. "No one is allowed on the military airport," Sergie stated simply. Sergie also described the difference between Old Chara and New Chara. "New Chara was built some ten years ago along the railroad track as a workers' village for those who were building the railroad. New Chara even has a few apartment buildings, though most of New Chara consists of the traditional wooden houses. There is also a bus to Old Chara, but it takes about an hour to get from New Chara to Old Chara on the bus."

"What is the history of Chara?" Tsinev asked Sergie.

Sergie thought for a moment. "Chara, or Tchara in the native language, means The Valley of Death. The native people's name was Avanki. The people named the area The Valley of Death because of the great cold, and the two mountain ranges on each side of the valley. The native people lived somewhere else prior to the Revolution, I think in Chita. After the Revolution there were a lot of *shayka* in

Russia and one group of *shayka* was in the Chita Region. The government relocated the group to Chara, where they began to build Old Chara. This happened in about 1930. The boss was Simemenov. He moved them there without shelter, so that is why so many people died the first year. When the people first moved to Chara they lived in tents. Many people who had been relocated to Chara died before housing could be built. They later developed buildings made of wood from the trees they cut down themselves, and there is a little village with some of the native people still living there. Some of the original native people are still in Chara. That is, their relatives are."

Tsinev understood Sergie's term *shayka*, translated as hooligans or criminal gangs, for what the term really meant: anyone who objected to the Communists or their policies. "When did the railroad come through?" Tsinev asked.

"The Baikal Amur Mainline began in 1974. It took over fourteen years to complete. New Chara was built in 1982. As you probably know, the Baikal Amur Mainline was built by people from many different cities, including Moscow." Sergie did not have to mention that the workers included many "volunteers"—consisting of refuseniks, political prisoners, and petty criminals—from throughout Russia.

"The Trans-Siberian Railway," Sergie continued, "was built from two directions, one from east and the other from west. There was one boss from the west, Bondar, and another boss from the east, Varshaveskeoiy. The railway went from Tayshet to Lena. Then World War II began, and production on it was stopped. It was started up again by Brezhnev in the 1970s. That is when this portion of the railway was built," Sergie noted, pointing his hand downward toward the tracks below them. "The two sides met at Kuanda, where there was a great party. Three thousand rivers were crossed, over twenty-four hundred bridges were built, and seven huge tunnels had to be dug directly through the mountains. It is said that on the day of completion the workers drank champagne out of their metal construction hats! It was quite a party, for everyone thought they were done and would be free to go home. But a few weeks later they were told to go to another place to work. Some of them, though, stayed in Chara."

"What is the weather like in Chara?" Tsinev asked.

"It can snow in Chara sometimes in June or July," Sergie stated as he played with Natalie. "In the winter time it usually is forty-five degrees below zero, but once a few years ago it got sixty degrees below zero."

Tsinev enjoyed observing Sergie as he related to Natalie. As a father, Sergie was loving and caring, like most Russian fathers. Tsinev watched as Sergie walked the child along the bed, kissed the child and then walked her again, excitement in her laugh and joy in her heart.

"Are there many visitors in Chara?" Tsinev asked, concerned whether his presence would cause concern.

"Numerous visitors come to Chara," Sergie replied, "including Japanese, Canadian, Indian, and Americans. The geology is very unique. The area surrounding Chara is a desert three miles wide and twelve miles long. Underneath it is an underground spring. Many scientists come to Chara. There are many plants and rocks that can only be found near Chara, or in the valley surrounding Chara. And, there are two volcanoes near Chara. There is a museum in New Chara where you will be able to find out lots of information on the town."

"The tourists stay in the hotel in New Chara right across from the train station," Helen added as she changed Natalie with an old-style cloth diaper. "It is nothing like Moscow, but it is good. Some of the rooms have a shower, and one room even has its own television."

"The old hotel had burned down," Sergie stated as he got up to take the soiled diaper out to be washed in hot water, "and so they built a new one."

"And there used to be a movie house in Chara," Helen continued, "but it burned down too. Now people simply stay home and watch TV," she explained.

Soon traces of snow begin to appear in the air and along the side of the tracks. Helen picked up the little girl and held her up to the window. "Look!" she said excitedly. "That is snow, Natasha. You're first snow!" Sergie leaned up close to his wife and daughter, repeating again the word "snow" to Natasha, the child most probably not having any idea of what she was supposed to be seeing but becoming excited merely by the tone of her parents' excited voices.

Tsinev could not help but laugh to himself as he observed Sergie and Helen's excitement when they pointed out the first snow to

Natalie. If only the Americans could see this everyday aspect of Russia and Russian humanity, Tsinev thought to himself, perhaps if they could see this we would not be pointing missiles at each other and rattling sabers like little boys in a playground seeing who is really king of the hill. But power politics is never so simple as that, Tsinev realized, although maybe it should be.

A little while later Sergie pointed out the window as the train continued eastward. "Look at that," he said to Tsinev. "What a terrible thing."

Tsinev looked out and saw hundreds of yards, perhaps even a miles' worth, of stacked logs along the railroad tracks, stacked many meters higher than the train itself. "All that work done, and then the end of communism. They just sat there until they rotted, now no good to anyone. The Japanese wanted to buy the lumber, but the Siberian provincial governor refused to sell it to them and allowed it to spoil instead. We would rather have it spoil than allow foreigners to have use of it," Sergie stated matter-of-factly. "But of course," Sergie added, "this was some years ago." Neither Tsinev nor Sergie were sure whether the same would still be true today.

# CHAPTER 34

## Twenty Miles North of Edwards Air Force Base

Phinney deaccelerated to 550 knots as he aimed the Blackbird southwest toward Rogers Dry Lake that served as the emergency landing area at Edwards Air Force Base. Marta spoke over the intercom.

"You did good," she said matter-of-factly referring to the Green Flag run. "Can you handle a few more hours of flying?"

"Sure," Jack replied, "but we're low on fuel."

"No problem," came Marta's reply. Phinney then heard the familiar click activating the squadron-common frequency and listened as Marta contacted the tower. "Edwards, this is NASA Blackbird 831 Trainer approaching, request green-light clearance for straight-in landing Main Runway Two Two."

Phinney immediately realized that the information being conveyed was intentionally inaccurate: Marta and he were not flying in the Blackbird trainer; they were flying in the "A" model, NASA number 844. In addition, use of the phrase "green light" normally involved a silent launch in which the air controller is merely given the time of take-off and required to make sure the runway and air space is clear and then the pilot visually given a green light at the time of take-off.

"Roger NASA Eight Three One, you have the green light. The space is clear. Landing approved runway Two Two, VFR rules."

"Edwards this is NASA Eight Three One, Roger that. See you in a minute. Eight Three One clear." Marta re-activated the internal microphone. "As I'm sure you've already guessed, we're not landing. Leave the wheels up, proceed normal approach, level off at Zero Five Zero, bank right at end of runway, maintain altitude during slow right turn 100 degrees, obtain heading Zero One Zero, then ease us over the mountains. We'll refuel at the northern refueling track. Understood?"

"Gotcha," Phinney replied. Piece of cake! he thought as he lowered the aircraft down towards the main runway, heading almost southeast at Two Two Zero, leveling off at five hundred feet along the length of the runway. Phinney then turned right in a slow turn until he reached the required heading of ten degrees, or north northeast. After doing so, he slowly increased his speed and began to gain altitude, easing the plane over the mountains to the north for refueling.

"I assume we will maintain radio silence from here on out."

"That's affirmative," Marta replied.

Phinney reached down to activate the map projector, pressing the CRS control button for refueling. The screen immediately showed not only Phinney's location, but also the KC-10 tanker thirty-five miles ahead of him going the same direction.

As Phinney approached the tanker and positioned himself for refueling, he reached up on the upper portion of the forward instrument panel and pushed the air refuel switch to the up position, thereby opening the refueling door approximately six feet behind Marta's cockpit. Phinney watched as the green READY light on the air refuel reset switch illuminated. He then eased the plane forward and upward, feeling the plane entering the huge KC-10's slip-stream, the slight buffeting immediately ceasing. Watching the indicator lights on the belly of the refueler, Phinney positioned himself until the lights on the bottom of the plane showed green on both the left and the right rows of lights. His job now was to hold this position while the boom operator lowered the refueling boom into the refueling receptacle.

A few moments later Phinney heard and felt the boom as it connected and latched into the receptacle, and then looked down momentarily at the refueling indicator light to make sure the READY light had gone out, showing that the boom was seated and latched; the light was out, which meant that everything was fine.

Phinney was used to refueling the lumbering B-52 in which refueling was considered akin to wrestling a bear. The Blackbird was no easier, particularly when it approached maximum fuel. As the KC-10 carefully pushed six thousand pounds a minute of JP-7 into the fuel tanks at sixty-five to seventy p.s.i., the handling of the Blackbird became increasingly more difficult. The plane was not designed for sub-sonic flight. To make matters worse, as the refueling neared completion it almost always became necessary for the pilot to light one afterburner so that the Blackbird would not fall away from the tanker. This meant that Phinney would have to control the heavily-burdened plane as one burner kicked in—albeit at minimum afterburner—and the plane concomitantly yawed to the side given the asymmetrical thrust.

Phinney was able to do all of this, all the while watching the tanker's indicator lights and occasionally looking slightly downward to the left portion of the main instrument panel to check how much fuel the Blackbird presently had in its tanks. It normally took twelve to fifteen minutes for the fuel quantity indicator gauge to approach and then exceed 80,280 pounds, the Blackbird's normal total fuel capacity. It would take even longer in this Blackbird, however, since many of the bays or compartments had been specially modified by NASA to hold an additional five thousand pounds of fuel. The time it took to refuel seemed like an eternity to Phinney, but at least he was somewhat used to it given his B-52 experience in refueling.

Phinney particularly liked refueling from the KC-10 because the KC-10's refueling system—unlike the KC-135's system—was able to automatically reduce the flow of fuel and maintain normal refuelling pressure. Rarely would there be a disconnect during the refueling with a KC-10; Phinney knew the same could not be said for the KC-135. Once the Blackbird was filled with fuel, the boom operator pulled the boom back toward the KC-10; as he did so Phinney observed the illumination of the disconnect light. Phinney immediately reached up and pushed the air refueling switch downward to the center position, disengaging the refueling system. Phinney then heard and felt the refueling door close.

The Blackbird now fully fueled, Phinney eased back on the throttle slightly so that both afterburners were now disengaged and the Blackbird eased away from the tanker. Keeping his eye at all times on the KC-10, Phinney veered left and downward away from the tanker, and then, once he knew he was clear of the tanker, Phinney pressed forward on the throttle so that both afterburners lit, the plane accelerating to a speed that allowed the controls to be much more responsive. As his speed increased Phinney noted that his ability to control the plane also substantially increased.

"Where to now?" Phinney asked Marta.

"West, young man, go west, via the Aleutian Islands. Heading Three One Five. Normal cruise altitude, normal cruise speed."

Phinney pressed forward on the throttle, performed the "dipsy" to ease the plane past Mach, and then slowly angled the plane upward as it steadily increased speed. Within seven minutes the sleek plane went from thirty thousand feet to eighty-four thousand feet and increased in speed from Mach 1.25 to over Mach 3.

"Press in Target One-One-One-Four," Marta stated over the microphone.

Phinney reached down to the side of the CRT display and inputted the target number. "Target One-One-One-Four entered," Phinney stated into the microphone.

The map display immediately reverted from a detailed map of California to a long-range mission planning map that showed the Blackbird on the far right and a bright-yellow line from the plane's position to the Island of Okinawa, marked as "KADENA." The curved line curved northward along Alaska's Aleutian Islands and then back downward along the eastern coast of Japan. Printed at the top of the map were the following words blinking on and off every few seconds: "Is this your requested destination?"

"I show Kadena Air Base as our target. Do you want me to confirm and engage navigation autopilot?"

"Absolutely," Marta replied.

# PHOTOGRAPHS

*AWACS (Photo USAF)*

*5th Fighter Interceptor Squadron F-15s (Photo property of Jim Lynn)*

*5th Fighter Interceptor Squadron Patch (Photo LMB)*

*Russian Tu-142 "Bear" Bomber being intercepted by F-15 (USAF)*

*Inside Kremlin, Spassky Tower (Photo LMB)*

*Statue of Lenin, inside the Kremlin (Photo LMB)*

*World's largest bell, inside the Kremlin (Photo LMB)*

*Gold domes, inside the Kremlin (Photo LMB)*

*World's largest cannon, inside the Kremlin (Photo LMB)*

*Red Square, outside Spassky Tower (Photo LMB)*

*Martos statue, Cathedral of St. Basil, Red Square (Photo Greg Stites)*

*Kuibishevskiy Street bar/cafe entrance (Photo LMB)*

*Inside Kuibishevskiy Street bar/cafe (Photo LMB)*

*Outside Kurchatov Institute, Moscow (Photo LMB)*

*Marble plaque outside Kurchatov reactor (Photo Greg Stites)*

*Control room of the Kurchatov reactor (Photo LMB)*

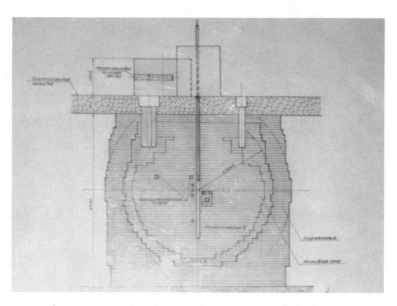

*Diagram of Russian F-1 Reactor, Kurchatov Institute (Photo LMB)*

*Kurchatov's home inside the Kurchatov Institute (Photo LMB)*

*Marina's statuettes inside Kurchatov's home (Photo Greg Stites)*

*The Moscow Conservatory (Photo LMB)*

*The G.U.M., Moscow (Photo Greg Stites)*

*View of Red Square and Lenin's Tomb from inside G.U.M. bar
(Photo LMB)*

*Edward's AFB, Rosamond Lake "shark's fin" (Photo LMB)*

*NASA Dryden Flight Research Center, Flying Wing (Photo LMB)*

*NASA Dryden Flight Research Center entrance, X-1B (Photo LMB)*

*NASA X-15 (Photo LMB)*

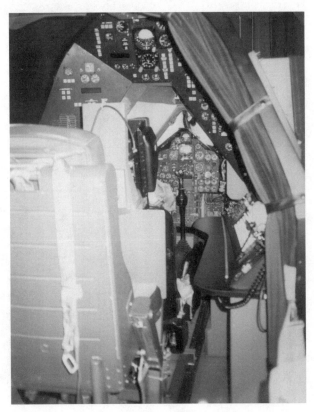

*NASA SR-71 Blackbird simulator (Photo LMB)*

*SR-71A Blackbird cockpit (Photo LMB)*

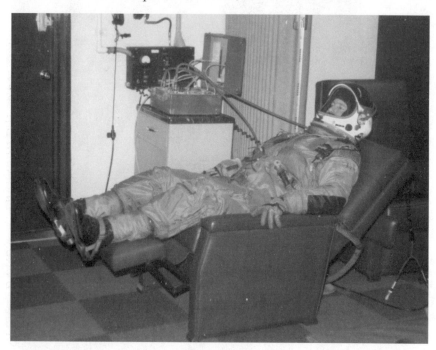

*David Clark Company S1032 pressurized space suit (Photo LMB)*

*NASA SR-71B taking off, Edwards AFB (Photo NASA)*

*NASA SR-71A Blackbird 832, refueling boom receptacle (Photo LMB)*

*NASA Blackbird 844 in NASA hangar (Photo LMB)*

*Front of NASA SR-71A Blackbird 844 with nose removed (Photo LMB)*

*SR-71 payload bay (Photo LMB)*

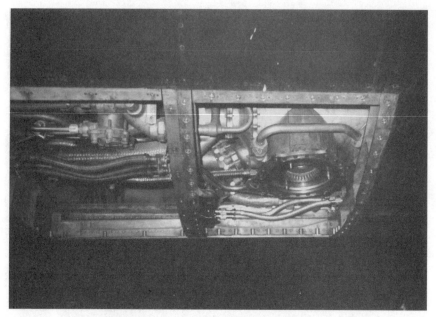

*SR-71 air turbine probe insert point (Photo LMB)*

*Muscovites selling dogs on Arbat Street (Photo LMB)*

*Artist at work on Arbat Street (Photo LMB)*

*Dog begging for money on Arbat Street (Photo LMB)*

*In front of Pushkin's house, 53 Arbat Street (Photo LMB)*

*B-2 (Photo USAF)*

*Poster of Lenin, Bratsk
(Photo Mariya Kovapiova)*

*Unfinished building,
Bratsk (Photo LMB)*

*NASA SR-71A Blackbird 844 taking off, Edwards AFB (Photo NASA)*

*NASA SR-71A Blackbird 844 after refueling (Photo NASA)*

*David Clark Company
"jerkins" partial pressure suit
(Photo USAF)*

*NASA SR-71A Blackbird 844 landing, Edwards AFB (Photo USAF)*

*Aboard the Baikal Amur Mainline: Bratsk (Photo LMB)*

*Monument of BAM East-West meeting point, Kuanda, Siberia (Photo LMB)*

*Photo of native woman of Chara at Chara Museum, New Chara
(Photo LMB)*

*Train station, New Chara, Siberia (Photo LMB)*

*Apartment buildings, New Chara (Photo LMB)*

*Lenin portrait, Old Chara (Photo LMB)*

*Wood building, Old Chara (Photo LMB)*

*Wood home and log garage, Old Chara (Photo LMB)*

*Airport fence line bordering Old Chara (Photo LMB)*

*Airport Building, Old Chara (Photo LMB)*

*MC-130H Combat Talon II over water (Photo USAF)*

*Cockpit, MC-130E Combat Talon II, Hurlburt Field, Florida
(Photo LMB)*

*Navigator's counsel, MC-130E Combat Talon II (Photo LMB)*

*Cargo bay, MC-130E Combat Talon II (Photo LMB)*

*MH-53J Pave Low III over water (USAF Photo)*

*MH-53J Pave Low III over land (Photo USAF)*

*Cockpit, MH-53J Pave Low III (Photo LMB)*

*MH-53J Pave Low III Helicopter after inserting Special Oprations Forces (USAF Photo)*

*Russian major entering office, Old Chara (Photo LMB)*

*Russian SAM-5 (foreground) and SAM-3, Nellis AFB, Nevada
(Photo LMB)*

*Chara runway, Old Chara, Siberia (Photo LMB)*

*RQ-4A Global Hawk at Edwards AFB (Photo USAF)*

*Lynn M. Boughey*

*Chara runway, Old Chara, Siberia (Photo LMB continued)*

*Dark Star takes off at Edwards (Photo USAF)*

*Tunnel entrance to Cheyenne Mountain, Colorado (Photo LMB)*

*AIM-9M Sidewinder being loaded onto F-16, Fargo, ND (Photo LMB)*

*AIM-120A being loaded onto F-16, Fargo, ND (Photo LMB)*

*AIM-120A being loaded onto F-16, Fargo, ND (Photo LMB)*

*B-52 "Balls 23" on ramp, Minot AFB (Photo LMB)*

*B-52 in flight near Minot AFB, ND (Photo USAF)*

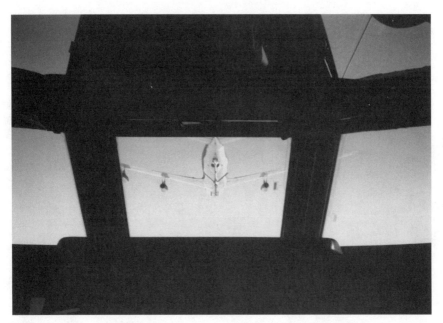

*B-52 lining up for refueling from a KC-135 (Photo LMB)*

*B-52 low level over Montana (Photo LMB)*

*Newly married couple in front of tomb of The Unknown Soldier, Moscow (Photo Greg Stites)*

*Author in right seat of B-52 in flight somewhere over North Dakota (Photo Randy Spetman)*

# CHAPTER 35

## On the Baikal Amur Mainline, East of Lake Baikal

The next day, as the train came within a few hundred miles of Chara, Sergie pointed out to Tsinev the many dead trees standing interspersed with the live coniferous trees along the railroad tracks. "See how dry this summer was?" he stated to Tsinev. "It was so dry that there were many fires, and the animals had little to eat. The bears in the mountains came down scavenging for food, which rarely happens. Two people were killed this summer by bears near Chara. One man, the only thing left of him was his gun, and one leg still in his boot."

Later that evening Sergie asked Tsinev whether he liked living in Moscow. "Yes," Tsinev replied, "but it is now so much more dangerous. The crime even scares me."

Sergie, however, was undeterred by such comments. "Moscow is the center of all time," he stated with conviction. "We invested our money in Moscow," Sergie said proudly, referring to the 1993 stipend of ten thousand rubles given to each Russian family in the form of an investment voucher that could be given to any business or investment company the family chose. "Only in Moscow is there hope. North America will someday be underground, swallowed up by the sea. This will happen because they have not given their lives to God. I know some people who have mystic powers," Sergie continued, "and they tell me this. They can also see on each credit card the number 666. The ocean will swallow them up, the Americans. Swallow them up." Sergie said this without anger or spite, merely stating a fact of what he knew to be true.

Because the train was approaching Chara, Helen and Sergie got dressed in their good clothes. By now the three of them—and of course Natalie—had been travelling together for over thirty-six hours and had crossed perhaps only one-fifth of the length of Siberia. Helen had changed into a beautiful yellow dress and had put on her makeup. She was indeed beautiful, Tsinev thought as he watched Helen tickling the baby with her hair.

As the train slowed down to stop at Chara a miniature production of preparations began in the berth. Everybody was organized and assigned what items to grab and take off. Tsinev offered to help and was assigned to carry the baby seat. The moment the train stopped, everyone scrambled to get themselves and their belongings off the train quickly. One never knew if the train was behind schedule, and the normal five minute stop could, without warning, become a thirty-second stop.

After the hurried unloading onto the train platform, Sergie breathed a sigh of relief and pointed out the hotel to Tsinev. "It is right over there. That building there," he said as he pointed to a three-story building approximately one hundred meters away. The two men shook hands, and Tsinev began walking toward the hotel, suitcase in hand. "Goodbye, Helen," he said as he turned around slightly waving with his free hand. "Goodbye, Natalie!" May you be luckier than your parents, Tsinev thought to himself.

# CHAPTER 36

## Kadena Air Base, Okinawa

Phinney jumped up out of his seat and brought himself to attention as soon as he saw the three-star general walk into the conference room. The general went to the head of the table and sat down, his various aides and others filing in behind him and taking their seats around the perimeter of the conference room.

"Lt. Col. Phinney, my name is Lt. General Spetman, Commander of the 5th Air Force. Do you recognize me?"

"Yes, sir."

"Good. That was the point, or at least part of the point of my being here. Please be seated. The people seated over there against the wall have spent several weeks setting up a mission for you. I have been instructed to brief you on the mission, or at least the basics of it, and, if you decide to accept it, these other gentlemen will fill you in on the details. This briefing is Top Secret and compartmentalized. If you choose to reject the mission you can do so without prejudice. Do you understand the clearance?"

"Yes, sir. No problem, sir."

Deaton could tell Phinney was nervous. Who wouldn't be? Deaton thought to himself. "Look, Colonel Phinney. You can relax a little. You've already qualified for the mission. You passed every test that we gave you. We are convinced you can fly the SR-71 where we want you to go. The hard part's over, at least as far as the training goes. So relax, listen to what these guys have to tell you, and then make your decision on whether you're willing to accept the mission. OK?"

"Yes, sir. I understand. That would be fine."

"Now. I understand you just landed here about an hour ago. Three hours ago you left the California coast to fly here. You just completed a Green Flag mission, a refueling, and then a Trans-Pacific flight. I'd understand if you'd prefer to talk about this after you had some shut-eye. Would you prefer that, son?"

"No, sir. I'm OK. I'd just as soon to find out now what this is all about."

"All right. That's understandable. Here's the short version. We want you to fly into Russia and pick up someone at the Chara civilian airfield in the SR-71. You would fly alone, no RSO. You'd be on the ground for only a few minutes, just long enough to pick up the passenger and get the hell out of there. China has approved our flying over its airspace. You would refuel once over China and then enter low-level into Russia and proceed the three hundred miles or so to Chara. Obviously that entails a fair amount of risk. You land, pick up the passenger, and fly back at maximum speed. We believe you will be able to get in without being detected and without too much risk, but once you land the odds are that the alarm would be sounded and your egress will have to be done quickly. Very quickly. That is one of the main reasons we are using the Blackbird. The other reason is if you are spotted we can at least claim that you were on a non-military mission. That's the short version. Any questions or concerns thus far?"

"Yes, sir. Only one. Why me? Obviously there are better qualified pilots, people who have time flying the Blackbird."

"Good question, and one that we were going to get to. But first I need to know if you are you willing to accept the mission, at least based on what we've told you thus far."

"Yes, sir. I accept the mission."

"I thought you might. The person you're going to pick up is Dmitri Tsinev, your old political science professor at Grinnell College. He has been back in Russia for almost ten years. When he was in the United States he worked for the KGB. He also worked for us, and has done so for forty-some years. He is one of our most important agents. He has signaled that it is necessary for him to get out, and we have reason to believe that the information he has is worth the inherent risks of this mission, including the chance of causing an international incident. The president has already approved the mission and signed the necessary executive order authorizing it. Your professor friend apparently was unable to get out any other way but this way, something that we designed many years ago before he went back in to Russia."

The general paused for a moment while Phinney digested the information.

"The reason we need to send you is because he has to be picked up by someone who can recognize him. And you are the only pilot in the Air Force, or for that matter in any of the armed services, who knows him personally, who could confirm it is he. We don't want to bring out the wrong man, and he won't come out unless he knows the person who is bringing him out. Still interested?"

"Yes, sir. Very much so."

"Good, then these chaps here will give you the details. Are you sure you've gotten enough sleep?"

"Yes, sir. I'm still on CONUS time, but I think I'm acclimated, if that's what you mean, sir."

"That's indeed what I mean. The flight is the day after tomorrow, at night like most special ops flights. That also means that you will retain your state-side sleep schedule, which takes care of the jetlag issue. Thus, we have two days to get you up to speed, get you rested up a bit, and then send you on your way. Can you handle that?"

"Yes, sir. No problem, sir."

"Good," the general said, and then looked over at the training team. "He's all yours, boys."

# CHAPTER 37

## Northern Russia

Gregory opened the window and yelled down toward the end of the street. "You! Yes, you, old woman! Do you still tell fortunes?" She nodded yes. "Come on up," he yelled back. "We will pay you well."

"Is she coming?" someone asked from inside the room.

"Yes. She's on her way up. What a stroke of good fortune. We shall have fun with this!"

"Why waste our money on the likes of her," one of the young scientists moaned. "First she sells her body, and when there is nothing left she sells her soul."

"So what? It will be fun. Just what Pavel needs to cheer him up. Here she is. Yes, yes. Please come in. Welcome. Let me take your coat. Tell me, what is your name? I have seen you often along the streets and I have heard that you read Tarot cards."

"I am Madam Zosima. Yes, I do read the cards."

"We would be very honored if you would read for us. How much will it cost."

Madam Zosima looked around the room trying to gauge the right price, one that they could afford, one that would make the reading seem valuable, yet not too expensive. The furniture was good, sturdy wood. The walls had pictures and some paintings. They could afford much, she decided.

"Thirty thousand rubles," she stated forcefully so as to lessen the chance of any negotiations on the matter. She looked around at the group of late-night partiers. "Per reading," she said.

"Twenty thousand," Gregory replied.

"Twenty-five thousand," she countered.

"Fine," Gregory said, closing the deal.

"For you I shall use my best cards!" she said enthusiastically. She pulled out a box tied in burgundy-red felt. "Do you know the artist, Salvador Dalí'?" she asked. "These are his cards. They are most beautiful, don't you think?" The old woman sat down at the kitchen table and looked up at Gregory. "So! Whose fortune should I tell? Who should have his life revealed by the cards?"

"Pavel!" several people shouted. "Yes, yes! The quiet thinker!" others shouted. Clearly, Madam Zosima thought, the vodka had been flowing some time here. She looked around to see who this quiet one was. All eyes looked to the corner of the room to the young man who had been slouched down in a chair saying nothing. Madam Zosima carefully observed the man. He sat up somewhat slowly as if it took great effort, his arms now resting on his knees, his deep black hair disheveled, a two-day beard looking scratchy, his clothes crumpled. Zosima watched the young man as he reviewed his friends with his eyes. He appeared to be sober, though this could just be the mood derived from too much alcohol; his dark eyes did not waiver as he looked up at his mob of friends shouting his name. Madam Zosima noticed that throughout all of this the young man did not blink or show any real emotion.

Pavel Kerlov looked directly at the woman. "Do your cards tell what is? Or what will be?"

"They tell what is, which will lead to what will be."

"Your answer tells nothing," Pavel replied. "I hope you are better at cards."

Pavel stood up and approached the woman at the table.

"Shuffle the cards seven times," Madam Zosima instructed Pavel, "and then hand them back to me."

The other young scientists gathered around the table as Pavel shuffled the cards. He handed the cards back. Madam Zosima began placing the cards on the table.

"You are a powerful man. We already have three cards from the major arcana. And now a fourth, and a fifth. A few more from the minor. Now a sixth. And the last one, another major arcana. Seven in all. This will be a very significant reading. Rarely does the major arcana speak so much at one time." Madam Zosima studied the cards in the order that she had placed them on the table.

"Now, let us see. You are a scientist, no?"

"Of course I am," Pavel stated with distain. "Most everybody here is, and everyone in this town knows that."

"Yes. Yes. But so do the cards. Look. The first card is the High Priestess, which shows that science should follow will. And next to it we have the Empress, which shows the union of will and science. But it is upside down." Zosima paused, allowing this fact to sink in. "The next major card, the card of Strength, shows courage, energy, challenge and action. This card, the World, shows evolutionary development of man, but . . ."

Madam Zosima stopped. She looked directly at Pavel, as if pronouncing sentence. "It is followed by the Tower and the Hanged Man." Madam Zosima looked back down at the cards while shaking her head.

"So? What does that mean?" Pavel asked.

She answered, almost at the level of a whisper, all the while looking down at the cards. "The tower represents catastrophe that follows evil; the Hanged Man foretells violent death."

For a few seconds there was silence, and then Pavel suddenly leaped up and threw himself over and across the table, his hands outstretched towards Madam Zosima. Before the others could react Pavel had his hands encircled around the old woman's neck, choking her and beating her head against the wall immediately behind her.

Shouts were heard—bedlam ensued. Gregory tried his best to wrench Pavel's hands away from the woman's neck; cards flew everywhere as the table crashed down from the weight of Pavel and those trying to restrain him, sending both Pavel and Madam Zosima rolling onto the floor. Pavel, upon hitting the floor, lost his grip on the woman's neck. Now being held back by others, Pavel's arms flailed at her, his hands grabbing at the air, reaching again toward the old woman. The men pulled Pavel back against the wall and forced him away from the woman. Once pinned to the wall, Pavel's rage quit as suddenly as it had begun.

Still being held against the wall by his friends, Pavel stared without emotion at the old woman as she struggled to her feet and slowly began gathering her cards. She said nothing, and nothing was said by the others. Gregory began to say her name, perhaps to apologize to the woman, but she cut him off with but a slight movement of her hand. She finished gathering her cards and calmly walked over to Pavel—still being held against the wall by his friends—as if to study him. She looked into his eyes for a few seconds, seeming more curious than fearful. And then suddenly—without any explanation—she fell onto her knees, and bowed slowly, almost reverently, toward Pavel, her forehead actually touching the floor in the process. As Madam Zosima arose from the floor, she smiled faintly, like a person who knew something that she was not supposed to know.

"Forgive me," she said several times, first to Pavel and then to each of the others, slightly bowing her head each time she said it. "Forgive me, all of you." She backed out of the room, her requests for forgiveness slowing becoming a soft mantra, barely audible. Silovoy opened the door for her, and she began down the stairs, looking back once more at Pavel, still trapped by his friends. Silovoy shut the door, and the others finally released their hold on Pavel. He stayed where he was and simply leaned up against the wall, his thoughts to himself. No one dared ask him why he did what he did, or what it was that made him so angry. The party was clearly over, and everyone went their own way.

# CHAPTER 38

## Vnukovo Airport, Ten Miles Southwest of Moscow

The C-141B pulled into the previously assigned hangar at the far end of the Vnukovo Airport just outside Moscow. Alexander Konesky watched as the transport plane completed parking in the hangar and the pilot shut down all four engines. The hangar doors were immediately closed, shielding the plane from view by the outside world. Although Konesky had seen many C-141As over the years, this was the first "B" model he had had the opportunity to see close up. Over twenty-three feet longer than the previous model, the C-141B had been upgraded to realize the plane's full payload potential, including structural upgrades, state-of-the-art autopilot, and an all-weather landing system.

As Konesky looked over the plane he realized that this model of the C-141B somehow looked different than the pictures of the standard C-141Bs that Konesky had reviewed; there were more antennas along the top and bottom of the fuselage, and there were bulges in the front of the plane that looked decidedly similar to the bulges located at the front of a B-52 bomber for its television and infrared systems. Looking back at the tail Konesky observed the normal Air Material Command markings used on all US military transport planes; however, at the front portion of the fuselage Konesky saw the markings "305th AMW" and "514th AMW" printed in black letters. Upon seeing the reference to the active and reserve wings at McGuire AFB, New Jersey, Konesky immediately understood why this plane was different from the other C-141Bs he had read about. This is one of the new special ops versions of the Starlifter, known as SOLL II (Special Operations Low Level), that had been modified even more so to enhance its special operations low-level capability and survivability.

A ladder was placed on the port side of the plane. The transport's door opened and Konesky looked up and saw Randy Broughton looking down at him.

"Hello, Alexander! Would you like to come up for a tour?"

"Certainly," Konesky yelled back up as he started up the ladder by himself. The others had not been invited; rank, they probably thought to themselves, has its privileges.

"Welcome to Moscow," Konesky said to Broughton as he shook Randy's hand. "I take it by your means of transportation this isn't the normal START inspection that we're used to."

"Not in the least," Randy replied as they both entered into the cabin area of the plane.

"May I review your flight manifest?" Konesky asked, both men knowing that such a review constitutes the beginning of the formal inspection process.

"I think we should wait on that, Alexander, if you don't mind."

Konesky considered this, and decided to say nothing at this point. Concede nothing, agree to nothing. The bulwark of the inspection process. Konesky realized that this must be one of those times that Randy and he had talked about at Whiteman Air Force Base while visiting in the old Minuteman II silo.

"Shall we sit down?" Randy asked as he gestured toward one of the tables.

The two men sat down across from one another in the seating area immediately behind the cockpit.

"Have you had a chance to look into the people I asked about?" Randy asked in a relaxed manner.

"I have," Konesky replied formally.

He's in formal negotiation mode, Randy thought to himself. Fine. At least I know where he's coming from.

"Are you willing to discuss it?" Randy asked.

Konesky smiled slightly at Randy. "If given sufficient basis for the inquiry."

"Isn't the information contained in the package I gave you at the Pushkin Museum sufficient enough?" Randy asked.

"Let us say that it has piqued my interest, and as a result I have made certain discreet inquiries." Konesky paused for a moment.

"Very discreet inquiries. However, before we actually depart for a site I would prefer more, at least under the circumstances."

"Fair enough," Randy said as he pulled out a map of northern Russia. "We believe that you have an operational site not listed in the annexes of the START treaty. We have reason to believe that it is located somewhere around here, near the Plesetsk Rocket Base. One of our operatives found it, but was killed before she could give us the exact location."

Randy had noticed that Konesky's eyes had widened when he referred to the site being operational, and also when he mentioned that one of the American agents had been killed. These two facts clearly had an impact on Konesky.

"And you hope that I know the exact location," Konesky surmised.

"That is correct."

"Then we are both in trouble," Konesky said dejectedly, dropping the formality altogether.

Broughton looked up at Konesky questioningly.

Konesky sighed and then reached over to pull the map towards him. "You have better information than I do regarding the possible location of the site. I did check on the individuals you asked about. I am ready to discuss the information, but on my terms. Can we agree to share the information just between ourselves and that it goes no further without our mutual agreement?"

Broughton thought about this for a moment. If he didn't agree, he would get no further information. If he agreed he may have to keep something important from his own government. Of course, that was exactly the same position in which Broughton had placed Konesky. Fair is fair, Broughton realized.

"As long as I can do so in good conscience," Randy replied, parroting Konesky's own response some weeks ago when Randy had asked him to do the same thing.

"With you, Randy, I can agree to that. Here is what I found out. By the way, you should know that I obtained the information very quietly and through certain sources that will not relay my inquiries further up the chain of command. Obviously if this is indeed an operational site we must take serious precautions that the word does not get out."

Konesky paused for a moment, took out his small notebook, and continued as he occasionally looked down at his notes.

"You asked me about the present whereabouts and activities of General Aleksei Kalganov, Ivan Flerov, and Pavel Kerlov." Konesky looked down at his notes and continued.

"It appears that General Kalganov, commander-in-chief of the Russian Air Forces and deputy minister of defense, and Ivan Flerov, Deputy Minister of Russian Military Science, have set up a military within the military. Flerov is one of the few ministers who is still allowed a relatively secret budget. As best as I can tell General Kalganov convinced Flerov and others that the Russian military needed to develop a military within the military that would maintain the former Soviet Union's military strength, especially in regards to nuclear weapons. Kalganov apparently recruited several hundred military officers and several Soviet scientist, and placed Pavel Kerlov in charge. Flerov provided the cover and the money."

Konesky looked up at Broughton for a moment. "I have talked with several officers who did not accept Kalganov's generous offer, at least those who are still alive."

"I guess that's one way to keep your security closely held," Randy commented.

"No shit," Konesky stated, rather proud of his use of American slang that he picked up from spending years around Broughton. "Initially the personnel were assigned to Flerov's branch, but after a few years he arranged to have the records show the disbanding of what was designated 'Special Operations Group Zulu.' The personnel were initially paid by the proceeds of the military black market, and eventually paid perhaps by the sale of nuclear weapons or weapons grade uranium. We don't know for sure, but the money had to come from somewhere, and that is the most likely source given the resources they have at their disposal."

Konesky paused for a moment to see if Randy had any questions, particularly since he had just admitted for the first time that it was possible that Russian nuclear assets were sold and exported out of Russia. Broughton smartly made no response, and Konesky continued.

"I have checked certain records at the plant at Biysk Rocket Facility, as well as numerous transportation records soon after the fire at the plant. If the fire was indeed a set up, it appears that Flerov and Kalganov were quite possibly able to procure approximately two hundred SS-N-20s, as you call them, sea-launched ballistic missiles, each capable of being armed with ten nuclear warheads. The records of these missiles were destroyed, but my people have been able to reconstruct transportation sheets to determine the general area where the missiles were taken which, coincidentally, is around the area you have mentioned."

"Unfortunately," Konesky said as he looked up at Broughton, "they are unable to determine the exact location of the base. Worse yet, my sources do not dare inform our civilian leaders or arrest those suspected in the plot for fear of triggering the launch of the missiles, assuming the site is operational."

Konesky paused for a moment. "And that, my friend, is all I know. So it does not look like we have a site to inspect after all."

Broughton looked over at Konesky and put his feet up on the table. "Then perhaps we should wait here until we do."

"Interesting," Konesky said, clearly perceiving Broughton's not so subtle indication that he may soon have the site's location. "Will it be a long wait?"

"If everything goes well," Broughton replied, "no."

"Well, if that's the case, perhaps now I can get that tour you so graciously offered me a while ago?"

"With pleasure, Alexander," Broughton said as the two men stood up from the table and Konesky followed Broughton towards the back of the plane. Broughton opened the door and walked into the cargo hold of the C-141B, followed by Konesky.

"Gentlemen, meet our official Russian tour guide, Alexander Konesky."

Konesky looked over the forty or so special ops men in full gear sitting along the sides of the cargo hold. These men were clearly not the usual START inspection team. These men were obviously the best of the best of special ops, probably from the secret nuclear-threat-interdiction group. Behind them were three Russian military trucks—or at least trucks built to look exactly like Russian military trucks—undoubtedly filled with equipment, explosives, and special monitoring equipment for the detection of nuclear weapons and materials.

"You're not planning to invade us, are you, Randy?"

"Oh no, just a few extra people to help us out in our joint mission, which is, of course, under your direct control and authority, as allowed under Special Provision One One Three of the Protocol on Unlisted Site Inspections."

"Indeed," Konesky stated, knowing that there was no such protocol within any of the treaties or agreements between Russia and the United States. "Remind me to bring my copy of that particular protocol next time you're in town."

"No problem," Broughton said smiling. "No problem."

# CHAPTER 39

## Kadena Air Base, Japan

Phinney sat alone at the northeast end of Runway 23 in his Blackbird waiting to see the green-light signal from the opposite end of the runway. Both engines were at idle. A slight dusk could be seen in the sky ahead of him, and nothing else. No planes in the sky ahead of him could be seen. Obviously the air traffic controllers had cleared the airspace; all he could see was the brightest stars beginning to shine through the twilight and the runway lights on dim. The Blackbird's own lights were off and would stay off. Not only would there be no clearance on the radio from the air traffic controller, he would also be taking off without using his own landing lights. A silent launch, they called it. If it got any darker, Phinney thought to himself, he'd have to call it a blind launch, too! His takeoff time was in three minutes and now, for the first time in the weeks of training, he was nervous.

At two minutes to takeoff Phinney suddenly realized why he was nervous: he was sitting on an active runway with no verbal communication with the tower. What if someone hadn't gotten the word? What if a plane landed right on top of him? He knew intellectually that the air controllers probably had everything under control, but his gut told him that mistakes happen, screw-ups occur, planes collide on runways. Especially black planes sitting on ever-increasingly dark runways with no lights!

Now that Phinney knew what was making him nervous, he reached up above his head and pushed the white nylon handle to the left, unlocking the rear-view periscope. Phinney pushed the periscope tube upward. Once extended Phinney could see the fuselage of the plane, the light from the dimmed runway lights glistening over the pitch-black surface of the plane. The surface looked especially smooth, Phinney thought, most probably from the special sealant used over the surface of the plane to prevent leakage of fuel, a common problem with the Blackbirds.

Rotating the periscope horizontally so he could look upward about ten degrees above the center line, Phinney strained to see any lights coming up from behind him. No planes. Lovely. At least he didn't have to worry about that! Phinney retracted the periscope and waited.

The last forty hours had been a blur. He had spent most of his time with Sandstrom and Hanna learning the basics of special ops, and Maki and Coe going over the details of the operational plan. At first Phinney couldn't understand why Coe was even there: Sandstrom and Hanna were special ops from Hurlburt and Kadena, and Maki was ops from Kadena who had experience with SR-71 missions into China and the Soviet Union. But Coe, he was from Holloman, the home of the F-117 stealth fighters. Everything made sense, however, when Coe told Phinney that at least for the first part of the mission—from the refueling point right before entering Russia until he approached within one hundred miles or so of Chara—he would be escorted by two stealth fighters. At that point the slower moving, subsonic fighters would head back across the Chinese border. The fighters would then refuel and hold a pattern low along the Russian-Chinese border waiting to see if any Russian planes pursued Phinney as he escaped out of Russia at full-speed across the Chinese border. If they did, they would be in for one hell of a surprise!

The wait on the runway for the green light seemed to take hours to Phinney, but finally the green light came—right on schedule—and Phinney pressed the throttles forward to minimum afterburner, felt both afterburners light, then pushed the throttles forward to full afterburner, feeling the rush of speed as the plane flashed down the runway and into the air. At thirty thousand feet Phinney executed the dipsy and felt the plane almost jump forward into Mach plus flight. Phinney then began his slow turn to the right, thereby angling the plane away from Okinawa and towards China.

Within minutes Phinney crossed over the Japan Outer ADIZ, air defense zone, and into international airspace, and flew parallel along the Asian Coastal Buffer Zone approximately thirty miles off the coast of China. Phinney smiled slightly as he read the warning on his ONC G-10 Defense Agency Map:

> WARNING: Aircraft infringing upon Non-Free Flying Territory may be fired upon without warning. Consult NOTAMS and Flight Information Publications for the latest air information.

As the map projector showed his plane crossing the 35th parallel and entering into the Asian Coastal Buffer Zone aimed between Shijiusuo and Wanggezhuang, Phinney hoped that the approval by China of his flight over the mainland had reached all of those concerned, particularly the Chinese Air Defense squadrons. A few moments later the Blackbird was "feet dry" over Chinese soil, flying northwest first over Zhucheng, then just to the west of Weifang, and next over Binzhou, approximately 175 miles southeast of Bejing.

Phinney then felt the plane's automatic pilot system angle the Blackbird slightly to the right. He watched the map projector as the plane veered just to the east of Bejing around the 40th parallel and continued its slow turn until it was headed now toward the northeast deeper yet into Chinese territory. After heading northeast about twenty minutes, the plane covered the 650 miles past the 41st through 46th parallels, and then made a relatively sharp left turn northward at the 47th parallel, following the 123rd longitudinal due north as the plane decelerated and began its quick descent as it headed toward the Da Hinggan Ling mountain range.

As the plane eased below Mach speed, Phinney took the controls and carefully weaved his way in between the larger mountains as he flew past the 49th parallel, then over the Bila He and Nuomin He rivers, and then flying within three miles of the Nuomin Dashan. The next seventy-five miles constituted Phinney's refuelling track; but unlike before, Phinney was not flying at thirty thousand feet. He was flying due north at three thousand feet, a large mountain range to his right and another large mountain range sixty miles to the northwest along the Russian-Chinese border.

The KC-10 appeared ahead of Phinney on schedule. Phinney only needed thirty thousand pounds of JP-7 so the refuelling did not take long.  Once the Blackbird had been refueled, the tanker carefully sprayed the Blackbird with a clear liquid that sealed the wing's so they would not leak any fuel while Phinney flew subsonic.

By the time the KC-10 veered off to the left to return to the Gen He airport, Phinney had already pushed his plane downward on the valley floor, crossed between two mountains and past the 52nd parallel at less than one thousand feet above the ground.  As he crossed the 53rd parallel Phinney angled the Blackbird to the west and then back toward the north.  Reaching downward with his right hand, Phinney activated the automatic pilot and watched as the computer took over the plane and aimed the Blackbird between two mountains ahead.  Phinney ran a final double-check on the automatic pilot and the INS system.  Everything seemed fine.

As the plane cleared the two mountains Phinney looked at the position of the two mountains and personally confirmed that the map projection was accurate and on line.  His comfort level increased substantially, and Phinney began the somewhat boring duty of simply monitoring the autopilot system.  He would rather fly the plane himself, but he knew he would be unable to visually fly as close to the mountains as the computer.  In addition, Phinney knew that by now the two F-117 stealth fighters were behind him by probably no more than three or four hundred yards, following the heat signature of his two J-58 engines as the computer flew along and occasionally over the mountains.  If the stealth fighter pilots thought the computer was malfunctioning in any way, he knew that they would break radio silence and call an abort.

So for now it was sit back and watch as the plane veered back and forth, weaving its way closer and closer to the Russian border.  Phinney watched his screen as he cleared the last two mountains, the plane dipped downward into a slight valley and crossed the bold, double-red boundary line shown on the map screen at 121 West 53 degrees 35 minutes North.

"Welcome to the Soviet Union," Phinney muttered to himself, not even realizing he had used the old nomenclature in referring to present-day Russia.

# CHAPTER 40

## National Reconnaissance Office Headquarters, Langley, Virginia

Richard Defresne, a lowly G-10 civilian photographic interpreter temporarily assigned to the National Reconnaissance Office from STRATCOM for training, looked carefully through 3-D glasses at the photo of a mound of dirt at the end of a runway somewhere in Siberia.

"Two weeks ago," he muttered to himself. He then moved over to the next photograph.

"Ten days ago," he muttered as he looked down at the second photograph. "They look like drainage grates," he said again to himself after studying the photograph for a few minutes.

"Drainage grates on this end . . ."

He moved the 3-D glasses to the other side of the photograph. "But not this end . . ."

Defresne shook his head in wonderment. "Weird," he said to himself, "just plain weird."

"I better report this," he said as he moved over to his computer console and began typing:

<u>*Secret special compartmentalized QS-18*</u>
<u>eyes only</u>

> TO: JACKSON, CIA DO—EYES ONLY
> FROM: STRATCOM ANALYST 735
> RE: OPERATION QUICK STYLE—
> ANOMALIES AT TARGET POINT

*Lynn M. Boughey*

# CHAPTER 41

## Trans Baikal Military District,
## Headquarters Unit, Irkutsk

It was late. The young captain was tired and bored. He sat at the command counsel, his knife open as he pared a slice of sausage from the loaf.

Once a part of the Troops of the Air Defense (IA-PVO), an independent arm of the Russian military, the once proud PVO had recently been absorbed into the Voyenno-Vozdushnyye Sily (VVS), the Russian Air Forces. Just months ago the captain would have reported any possible attack from the air to the Air Defense Corps headquartered at Novosibirsk. But now that the PVO had, for the most part, been incorporated into the Russian Air Forces via the traditional military districts, he would report any unusual activity directly to the 23rd Air Army headquartered at Chita.

Not only had the officers of the former PVO taken a downward step in prestige, none of the officers believed the new system could respond quickly enough to any major attack from the air. At least the former Air Defense officers had the solace, however slight it may be, that what was left of the PVO was now commanded by one of their own, Colonel General Anatoly Mikhailovich Kornukov, the former commander of the Moscow Air Defense Military District. Not that this change of command did anything to fix the major problems that the reorganization had caused in what used to be simple communications from one Air Defense area to another. Communicating quickly from one military district to another had become almost an impossibility. But at this moment it was not the captain's problem, or even his concern. It was time to eat, and he did so.

"Sir," an even younger man called over to the command counsel from a few desks away.

"Yes, Lieutenant?"

"Takhtamygda Air Control reports an intermittent radar signal at low attitude, no flight plan filed, no known military aircraft in that area."

"How many times did it show up on the screen?"

"Just once, sir, 'in and out for a few seconds' is what he said."

"With the lousy equipment he has, he's lucky to pick up one of our Ilyushin-22s! Any report from Svobodnyy/Belogorsk sites?" Both officers knew that the radar sites at the various airports and runways around Svobodnyy and Belogorsk were much more sophisticated, as they should be given the fact that there were SS-11 intercontinental ballistic missiles bases stationed near Svobodnyy.

"No reports from any of those bases, sir."

"How about on the western side? Anything from Nerchinskiy Zavad, Novo Tsurukhaytuy, Olovyannaya, or Drovyanaya?" All SS-11 bases stationed along the western side of China's northern border.

"No, sir. Nothing there, either."

"Tell them, 'Thank you for the information. It's nothing to worry about.'"

"Yes, sir."

The captain reached into his knap-sack and pulled out a loaf of bread, breaking off a piece to go with his sausage. Stupid civilian controllers, he thought to himself as he brought the bread to his mouth, they see ghosts every time the moon is full.

# CHAPTER 42

## Old Chara, Siberia

Tsinev took his time as he walked around Old Chara. Unlike New Chara—where most of the housing was new and had running water—entering Old Chara was like entering into the early 1920s and 1930s, the time in which the city, if you could call it that, was built. All of the buildings were made of wood, and there was no running water in the homes. Twice a week the water trucks would drive through the town and fill each of the two barrels in front of the house with water. Most of the year, of course, it would freeze in less than an hour. Thus, most of the time it was necessary to chip off a chunk of ice and bring it inside to melt it for cooking or drinking. None of this surprised Tsinev since he was well aware of these types of conditions throughout Siberia.

The village was small; only two or three thousand people at most. Tsinev walked with a young Muscovite he had met at the hotel named Marsha. Marsha was twenty-five, single, and a graduate of the University in Moscow. But she, like so many others in Russia, was no longer employed, and so to make money she hired herself out as a tour guide in Moscow, primarily catering to Americans. She was in Chara doing just that, bringing an American geologist to Chara to see the unique rocks and land formations indigenous only to Chara.

Marsha's goal was a simple one: To find the artisan named Sasha, an artisan who specialized in making jewelry and small jewelry boxes out of charoite. Tsinev had seen the purple rock known as charoite for sale on the streets of Moscow, and was aware that the rock was found only here in the mountains surrounding Chara. And according to all of the people Marsha had talked to in New Chara,

Sasha was the best craftsman in all of Chara. So Marsha found someone willing to drive them to Old Chara who knew where Sasha lived, and they were off. Unfortunately Sasha was not home when they first got there so Marsha, Tsinev, and their driver drove around Old Chara to look around.

Tsinev was pleased to have the opportunity to tour Old Chara. Although he had studied the satellite photos carefully he still needed to get his bearings. Tsinev was fascinated by the beauty of the town, despite its evident poverty. How difficult it must have been for these "old worlders" to watch a new city spring up around the Baikal Amur Mainline just ten miles to the south; just as in the Old West in the United States, Tsinev thought to himself, survival of a town was dependent mostly on where the railroad was placed.

As Marsha and Tsinev were driven around Old Chara they observed the slowly flowing Chara River, some one-hundred to two-hundred feet wide, already sprinkled with slivers of ice even though it was early in October. At one bend of the river was a large campsite. "Many people come here to camp and fish in the summer," Marsha explained. "It is very beautiful."

"Indeed it is," Tsinev answered honestly. Once again they drove to Sasha's house but he still was not home.

"I don't know where he could be," the driver apologized. "He is almost always here."

Tsinev had been waiting for this chance. "Perhaps," he told Marsha, "this would be a good time to look at their airport." Marsha asked the driver if he had the time to show them the airport; he did; he had nothing but time, he told them. So the three of them drove northeast toward the airport. Turning into the entrance road Tsinev observed the fencing, only eight feet high and no barbed wire on top. Easily surmountable, Tsinev thought to himself. As they approached a wood building Tsinev realized that the building was the airport terminal itself. Tsinev and the others departed from the vehicle and walked up one set of the dual stairs into the building. Several people were still working in the kitchen at the rear of the building. Walking past the two scales set out to weigh luggage Tsinev walked outside onto the wood deck overlooking the east-west runway. An orange helicopter sat motionless to the right, or east side, of the terminal. Several hangars paralleled the terminal, while another lone hangar sat quiet on the other side of the runway. Tsinev observed the straightness of the two mountain ranges that ran parallel to each side of the runway. He tried to remember the names of the mountain ranges, but could only remember one: Kodor. Geography had never been his strong suit.

"Come," Marsha spoke from behind Tsinev, "he should be back now."

The short drive back to Sasha's house took little time, although Tsinev became somewhat concerned at one point that another car was following them. There were, of course, very few cars in Old Chara, perhaps ten at the most driving around at one time. Thus, when Tsinev noticed the same vehicle behind them for the third time he asked Marsha to ask the driver to stop for a moment. The driver did so, and Tsinev proceeded to open his door, stand up next to the car and look back at the other vehicle. The vehicle stopped, backed up, and proceeded down a different dirt street.

"*Spaseba*," Tsinev told the driver as he got back into the car. If the driver had noticed the other vehicle, he made no mention of it and continued to drive on to Sasha's home.

Sasha, like everyone else in Old Chara, lived in a small wood hut approximately ten feet by twenty feet. This time he was home. He was understandably glad to see two travelers from Moscow who, by definition, would have more money than those left unemployed in Siberia. Sasha considered all Muscovites to be rich, and certainly those who could afford to travel into the depths of Siberia had to be especially wealthy.

Tsinev noted as he entered Sasha's home that he had turned the building into a workplace with a kiln, artisan tools, and hand-made work benches. Little room, it appeared, was left for sleeping or cooking. But at least Sasha had a trade, and one that kept him alive and well fed. Sasha signaled with his hand for Marsha and Tsinev to come over to one of the tables. At the table Sasha pulled out a box filled with beautiful light-purple rocks, already polished and made into various shapes.

"They are quite beautiful," Tsinev commented as he looked at the charoite and other colorful rocks. Marsha herself then selected several pieces of charoite.

"For my mother," she said.

"And what would you like?" Sasha asked Tsinev.

Never in the streets of Moscow had Tsinev seen such beautiful charoite, devoid of the dark purple spots which are slightly radioactive. Tsinev studied the rocks and picked out five or six. "These, and one of the jewelry boxes." Sasha was clearly happy. Tsinev realized that Sasha had probably made more in this single transaction than he had made in the last two months. Tsinev paid the price requested by Sasha without even dickering; he is an artist, Tsinev decided, not some lackey selling souvenirs and bobbles to the rich foreign tourists on Arbat Street. He deserved to pick his price.

"Would you like to stay for dinner?" Sasha asked Marsha, motioning his hands to show that Tsinev and the driver were included in the invitation. They all agreed. "Good! We will go next door to eat, then we will come back here. There is something special that will occur when we return. All of the children who live near here are coming over tonight to hear me tell a story. I am, as you would say, the village storyteller. It is quite fun for everyone."

"That sounds wonderful," Tsinev replied.

After dinner Sasha led Marsha, Tsinev, and their driver back to his workshop. Even from the outside Tsinev could hear the cacophony of tiny voices inside. As the four of them stepped in the twenty or thirty children shouted with glee at Sasha'a appearance. Several other adults were also inside, apparently to watch over the children and to build a fire in the wood-burning stove, the only source of heat in the small building. The room was very warm, and Tsinev felt immediately relaxed. The sound of children, he thought to himself, how much I miss this sound, their exuberance, their purity.

Sasha told the children hello, introduced his new friends, and sat down in the only open chair left in the room, the one right next to the stove and the one clearly assigned to Sasha. The children also sat down, fidgeting and talking all the while.

"Children," Sasha began. "Children, quiet down and we will start." Sasha sat forward, his forearms on his crossed legs, and stared intently at the children stretched out before him. As he situated himself upon the wooden chair, its creaks and groans paralleled the sound of winter outside the only door. Sasha and the wood burning stove next to him naturally created the focal point to the children's warmth and attention.

All of the children stared back at him. The children obviously loved how Sasha's eyes would sparkle as he talked, how his deep black eyebrows would move and express things that words did not, how the wrinkles around his wise smile created a full circle around his moustache. And of course, all the children envied Sasha's beautiful sable hat which he wore throughout the fall and the dark Siberian winter.

"You all know two great mountain ranges that create our peaceful valley," Sasha began. "To this side is the Udeken Mountain Range, and to the other side the Kodor Mountain Range. And you all know of the River Chara that flows throughout this valley, sometimes calm, sometimes fast; sometimes warm, but usually cold." Sasha paused for a moment for effect. "But do you know the story behind Udeken and Kodor and Chara?" he asked.

Sasha paused again for a bit longer to let the children settle down. Once it was relatively quiet, he began the tale thusly:

"Long, long time ago, everything was able to turn into stone. There was on this land a king named Udeken. King Udeken had many deer, and much land filled with gold, silver, and copper, and all of the goods from the lands and the beasts throughout his realm, such as furs, leather, and carpets. The major business in this land was deer trading, for the deer were plentiful and could be found throughout the hills. However, King Udeken claimed that all deer belonged to him, and that anyone who would trade a deer would have to give another deer to him. But this was not enough for King Udeken, for he insisted on choosing which deer was to be his deer, and always took away the strongest one and the bigger one and the most beautiful one, and left the weaker and less valuable deer to those who actually went out to find them. And the King would do this on all things in his realm. He would take away the best of the furs, the best of the berries, and the best of the food that was to be found in his realm. And so soon it came to be that the people were poor, for the best was always given to the King, and the worst left to the people who toiled the soil, and found the deer, and picked the berries.

"King Udeken would enforce these unjust laws by his servants, or policemen, who were very large and very violent. And at these people's hands the people suffered greatly, and those who refused the King's will were sent to Lepriedo, the fortress that served as the King's prison at the edge of his realm. And all the people knew that once you were sent to Lepriedo, you would never be seen again, for no one came back from that cold and evil place.

"Now the King, it should come as no surprise, was not very well-liked by the people. But when he became the age of 40, his aunts told him that he had to get married. So King Udeken sent his servants to Demisty Leprindikan to search for a woman to be his wife. And soon the servants returned with Kaunda, the woman who would be the King's wife. Kaunda was not very beautiful, but King Udeken decided to marry her because she was the only woman who could look him in the eye without flinching or looking away because of fear.

"Kaunda did not want to marry King Udeken, but was nonetheless forced to do so. She cried for three years without stopping, and five times she tried to run away. But the King's servants would always find her and drag her back to the King. When she could no longer escape, she tried to commit suicide, but the King's two aunts watched her at all times, and she could not even take her own life.

"For fifteen years she lived this way, trapped, alone, and always under the watchful eye of the two aunts. And for fifteen years she had no child, but on the sixteenth year a girl was born, and she was named Chara. And for the first time in a long time Kuanda smiled. And it was her last smile, for soon thereafter she died.

"So without Kuanda to raise Chara, she was educated by others. But Chara was a different child, not interested in toys. And her eyes were deep and dark and wise, even at a young age. And Chara loved to run along the mountains around the King's castle, darting in and out between trees, across small streams, and up and down hills without any cause or care. And all the people agreed that Chara looked like a young deer, her head popping up and glancing around, then quickly darting from tree to tree as she ran into the forest into the happiness that she found there.

"And as she grew, her hair became black as charcoal, matching her deep and swift eyes. And Chara ran and ran throughout the area of the King's realm, even up into the high mountains called Taiga.

"Now, despite Chara's rank and status as the King's daughter, she played with the poor children wherever she would go, and talked with the poor people as if they were equals and friends and worthy of her attention. And she would ask the people and the dealers who sold deer why they were so poor, but they would never reply for they were afraid to tell her the truth. And this confused her, the fact that these people were so poor when her father was so rich, and the fact that these people would not say why they were poor, despite her asking in every way she could think of. And finally, one day, one of the brave ones told her that her father took away everything they owned, and that is why they were so poor.

"Now it should be said that when Chara found this out, she was of the mature and ripe age of twelve years. And although she was not yet a woman in full bloom, she looked with all of her twelve years distinguished, indeed beautiful. And her beauty was so striking and so pure and so calm in nature that the people called her Krasavitsa, which means pure beauty. And Chara was liked by all the people. And the people sang songs about her, and wrote poems about her, and tried to be with her as much as they could.

"Now Chara, knowing the great wrath of her father the King, did not confront him at this time as to what the brave person had told her about why they were poor. But from that time forward

Chara looked at the people and looked about the realm with different eyes, for her eyes now showed sadness and guilt for what she knew must be true. And one day as she walked along the trails contemplating what she should do, she came upon the King's servants who had just returned from a tribe that had refused to do the King's bidding. And upon the cart led by an ox was that tribe's leader, tied to the wagon, on his way to Lepriedo Fortress. And Chara, as quick on her feet as a deer, jumped up upon the wagon and cut the ropes with a knife and freed the leader of the tribe. And soon word spread throughout the realm that Chara had saved him, and the people wrote more songs and more poems and spoke more of the beautiful Chara with the coal-black hair. But this did not make Chara happy, because although she felt she had done a good deed, she did not feel that she had done enough. So, now at the age of fifteen, Chara approached her father, King Udeken, and said, 'We are so rich, we drown in prosperity, but all around us is poverty. Let's just take what we need and give the rest to the people.'

"And the King, upon hearing Chara's words, was so furious that he shook with anger and could not speak for some time. But when he did speak, his words were shouts of anger as he ordered his servants to take Chara to the Lepriedo Fortress.

"And so the servants followed the King's orders, and took Chara to Lepriedo Prison. And the people, and the winds, and the water, and all of nature decried the injustice that had become of Chara. And so nature, which is all-powerful, came to aid Chara, and used its frost, wind, rain, and water to destroy the walls of Lepriedo Prison. In three years time, there was a break in the wall, and Chara ran out of the prison and escaped into the forest. And when King Udeken was told by his servants that Chara had escaped, his fury and madness and anger was so great that before he uttered another word he turned into stone, the huge mountain range which we now call Udeken. And to this day in that mountain range, is the gold and the silver and the copper that the King had kept from all the people of all the land.

"And when Chara came out of the forest and saw what had happened, she became the queen of this same land. And as her first act, she gave all of the land to the people keeping only enough for her castle, and the people rejoiced and were happy. And they gladly brought her food and berries and deer and furs to thank her for her kindness and wisdom.

"And as a few years went by, Chara became even more beautiful and more womanly. Her cheeks were red as if they had natural rouge, and her black eyes—once sad—now shined with warmness. And wherever she went it was a holiday, and everyone thought her beautiful and kind.

"Now in a neighboring kingdom there was a *bogatyr*, or warrior, named Kodor. And as with all *bogatyr*, Kodor was as large as two men, and as strong as five men, and had a great opinion of his physical abilities and of himself. And as Kodor looked upon Chara's kingdom from on top of a close mountain, he saw Chara and fell immediately in love with her. And as he stood on the border of his country looking down on the kingdom that Chara ruled, he watched her every move, constantly on guard at his station but not on guard of his heart. And finally Kodor could stand it no more, and yelled down to Chara, 'Hey, Krasavitsa, look at me!' But Chara was so busy running her country and making things good for her people, that she did not pay attention to his words. By now Kodor had fell so deeply in love with Chara that he quit talking, and he followed her and ran after her and gave her a powerful hug. But Kodor, with his strength of five men, had too much feeling, and like King Udeken, he too turned into stone as he hugged Chara, and became the mountain range Kodor. And Chara, now trapped in the mountain range, realized that the only way she could get free was for her to turn into water. And so Chara turned herself into water, but the water that flowed from Kodor came out hot, the same temperature as her heart. And as we know, people still come to this place, for the warm water treats them and cures them of their ills.

"And everywhere else Chara had been, her water flowed out upon the land. Even the Lepriedo Fortress, its walls ruined and broken upon the ground, turned into many lakes of crystal clear water, and this water ran through the hills and followed the trails where Chara the child and woman had once walked. And wherever she had been in her calm happiness the river goes slowly, always calm, always with a sense of peacefulness, with one exception, for when the waters reach the place where Kodor gave Chara a hug and he turned into stone, the water roars around the rocks that are Kodor himself, and become rapids. And the water that is Chara beats down upon the rocks that are Kodor, for Chara is to this day still mad at Kodor because he stopped her life so early.

"And so it was, in olden times, where everything could turn into stone."

Sasha waited a few moments, reviewing the room to see how many of the children were still awake. Almost all of them, he noted. Good, he thought to himself, I must have kept them interested.

"Another one, another one!" one of the children yelled. The others joined in. "Yes! Yes! Please, please," they pleaded.

"All right," Sasha replied. "But just one more, for I have work to do tomorrow." Sasha sat back into his chair undoubtedly contemplating which story to tell.

At the same time Tsinev, sitting in the back of the room next to Marsha, whispered into her ear, "I am going outside. If I do not come back in a few minutes don't worry, I'll meet you back at the hotel."

"How will you get back?" Marsha asked.

"I know the way. There will be a ride, or if not I will come right back. See you back at the hotel."

"All right," Marsha replied.

Tsinev left Sasha's warm home and began his two-mile walk to the airport.

# CHAPTER 43

## Above Southern Siberia

Phinney continued to watch as the Blackbird flew itself along the pre-planned flight path, knowing full well that there were several occasions where it was necessary—indeed, unavoidable—to rise above certain mountain ranges and risk being spotted by a Russian radar site. Each time the plane ascended over a mountain range the map display would superimpose a marker showing the direction of any radar signals that could be a threat and indicating the level of each threat by a separate yellow, orange, or red arrow.

Luckily, so far Phinney observed only yellow arrows showing the existence of radar sites; if the arrow was orange it would mean a very close radar site or a site that was attempting to acquire the Blackbird; and of course, a red arrow would mean that the radar had acquired the plane. In the event of a radar lock by a SAM or a hostile plane, the red arrow would begin flashing and an alarm buzzer would sound, telling the computer to take immediate electronic countermeasures and allowing the pilot to disengage the autopilot and take evasive maneuvers.

For the most part the Blackbird flew northward along the river valleys, winding in between the various mountain ranges, first along the Asmazar River, over the Amazarkij range, dangerously close to the town of Amazar, back into a valley, over another range, then once again into a valley following along the Tungir River until it flowed into the Olekma River, where the Blackbird now turned up stream for a short time along the Olekma River, and then almost due north along one of its branches, the Mokia River.

Phinney watched the map display as the plane flew over map coordinates 120 West 56 North, now only 160 kilometers or approximately one hundred miles southeast of Chara. The plane continued to fly itself almost due north, easing over the tail end of the Jankan mountain range, then downward slightly, then steeply upward into the Kalarskij range, flying itself in between the mountains on each side of the Blackbird as its automatic pilot followed the pre-planned flight along the river valley created tens of thousands of years ago by the Kalar River. Several times Phinney noted both yellow and orange arrows coming at him from the southeast, most probably from Tynda or Nerjungri. When the Kalar River turned west, the plane turned first eastward along the Udokan Range, then aimed northward over the Udokan Range and then downward into the Chara Valley. As he did so he noticed several orange arrows from the southeast apparently trying to acquire him, but as the plane lowered itself into the Chara Valley and turned left going due west, the arrows disappeared.

Time to land, Phinney thought to himself as he pulled the throttle back close to idle and allowed the Blackbird to slow to a tolerable landing speed.

After making sure the Blackbird was lined up for landing, Phinney reached down and pressed a button on the CRS; the screen flickered and switched over to a forward-infrared view. The green colored screen showed the landing strip clearly as a bright light green strip directly ahead; the screen provided Phinney with an internal head-up-display monitor that showed him where to aim the plane, with a bar on the right side showing present altitude and a mark along the bar graph showing the desired altitude; next to the bar the plane's speed was shown in knots as well as an arrow showing up, down, or flat telling Phinney if he had to make any adjustments for the landing.

The autopilot was doing its job, so Phinney continued to monitor the instruments, all the while checking and double-checking the area at the end of the runway for any flares. Phinney levelled the plane off at five hundred feet just one thousand yards in front of the runway and pulled the nose upward preparing for the high-angle-of-attack landing, continuing to watch the infrared screen for any hot points.

By now Tsinev should have given him the signal. Seeing none, Phinney put his left hand on the throttle and prepared to disengage the autopilot and push the throttle forward to afterburners and abort the landing.

# CHAPTER 44

## Forward Operating Point Fengming, Gen He Airport, Northern China

Colonel Harper sat inside the MC-130H Combat Talon II which had been positioned next to the only hangar that existed on this God-forsaken Chinese runway in the middle of nowhere. Two MH-53 special ops Pave Low helicopters sat along side the special ops 130, all four pilots at the controls ready to start up the General Electric T64-GE-100 turboshaft engines if necessary. The rest of the mission crew had spread out in a standard hostile environment perimeter awaiting further orders from Harper.

Harper sat at the navigator's counsel directly behind the pilots' station watching the four CRS screens. Next to him sat the UAV mission specialist. The top left screen showed a map display similar to the one used by Phinney in the SR-71 Blackbird. The screen showed Phinney flying almost due west at ten miles out and decelerating for landing. The upper right screen showed an infrared view of the Chara landing strip; the view was from a very high altitude looking south and showed the heat signature of the Blackbird on the far left, and the landing site on the far right, a bright light-green sliver of a line. At the top of the screen were the words "DarkStar" and various numbers and letters showing that the Tier III Minus unmanned aerial vehicle was at sixty-five thousand feet flying westward at 345 miles an hour forty-four miles north of the landing site. The fact that the national security advisor had authorized the use of the second prototype for this operation demonstrated to Harper how important this mission was, particularly since DarkStar 1, the first prototype, had crashed on its second test flight at Edwards Air Force Base. As Harper watched the real-time infrared image coming from DarkStar 2, he was glad that the powers that be opted to expand the UAV's sensor suite to include real-time infrared and visual imagery instead of the near-real-time-fixed-frame images that had initially been part of the original DarkStar.

Harper looked at the bottom two screens. The one on the left showed a television-like view of the west end of the runway at Chara from the opposite side; in other words, looking northward. The screen on the right showed the entire runway, also from the south of the runway. Above both screens were the words "Global Hawk" and the same type of numbers shown on the upper-right screen except that these numbers showed that the Tier II Plus unmanned aerial vehicle was flying at about two hundred knots eastward just a few miles south of the Chara runway at about two thousand feet.

"Colonel Harper," the mission specialist said, "we have someone approaching the west end of the perimeter. I can see him on the infrared."

"Can you get it closer?" Harper asked.

"Yes, sir." The mission specialist reached up and touched the upper-right screen at the point on the far right where a small green light could be seen moving slowing towards the fence at the end of the runway, and then touched a CRS button below the screen marked "10x" several times as the screen increased magnification by powers of ten until the small figure basically filled up the screen. Harper noticed that the camera, after the mission specialist touched the target, continued to follow the target as it moved closer and closer to the fence.

"Here you go, sir."

Harper watched the figure, its face and hands brighter than his clothing, as he apparently cut through the fence from the bottom upward to about the half-way point, and then slipped inside the perimeter and walked quickly toward the runway. As he got close to the runway his right hand disappeared into his coat pocket, and then came out, apparently holding something. Both hands met then separated, then met again, causing a bright flash of infrared heat shooting forward about eight to ten inches.

"There's flare number one, sir. Number two lit. Number three. In the shape of a triangle, sir, as planned. We have a go."

Harper continued to watch the man's every move. "Is he armed?" he asked the specialist.

"None visible, sir. No rifle. No hand-held SAM. He's clean as far as that goes."

Harper continued watching as the SR-71 began its descent onto the Siberian runway.

# CHAPTER 45

## National Military Command Center's Conference Room, The Pentagon

Allison Markham picked up the phone at the far left end of the U-shaped briefing table. "This is Colonel Markham."

"Yes, ma'am. This is Mr. Defresne at the NRO. I understand you're the point of contact for Operation Quick Style."

Markham looked down at the STU-III secured phone to make sure they were both talking on a secure line. One would think that any phone call coming from the super-secret National Reconnaissance Office would automatically be a secure line, but Markham looked down at the phone's display to make sure anyway. The line was secure.

"That's correct. How can I help you, Mr. Defresne?"

"Well, ma'am, I was assigned to review the long-term data on the site and I came across a few things that I thought you should know."

Markham could tell Defresne was nervous. "What type of things, Defresne?"

"Activities on site that would make me think that maybe the mission is compromised, ma'am."

"Did you relay these up the chain?"

"Yes, ma'am. That's the problem. They didn't seem to care, so I thought I'd go directly to you."

"Who'd you talk to?"

"Mr. Jackson, ma'am."

That explained why he was nervous.

"What did Jackson have to say about it?"

"Well, ma'am, I didn't actually talk to him, but I sent him the priority message two days ago. The mail bag shows he received it and opened it, but I didn't get any response back from him. I assumed that he would have talked to you about it, but it sounds like he didn't. And when I came in today and saw the mission was in progress, I thought, you know, that maybe I should check with you."

"OK, Defresne, you did the right thing. Can you display the info directly to the Command Center?"

"Yes, ma'am. I'm at my station. I have the info up and running. All you have to do is give me access and a screen number."

"All right. Access number 3XY20, screen number 8."

"Yes, ma'am. I've got it. Do you show my screen intro."

Markham looked up at screen number 8 and saw the words "Reconnaissance Services Organization."

"We've got you, Defresne. Go ahead."

"The first satellite photo shows the west end of the runway as it has appeared for several years. The second shot shows it two weeks ago. Note the piles of dirt along the west end of the runway that show digging along the parallel of the end of the runway about ten meters from the end of the runway. The third shot is ten days ago; the ditch that was dug has grates on it now."

"Could those be used for normal water flow."

"That what everybody thought. But I wasn't convinced. So this morning I directed an infrared shot at the grates. If it was water drainage it would be cooler than the ground temperature. Instead, this is what I got."

Markham watched as the next photo showed up on the screen. The ditch was a substantially brighter light green.

"It looks hot to me, ma'am. Like the temperature that it would be if there were five or six bodies sittin' down there waiting, ma'am."

Markham looked over at the big screen as she watched the SR-71 landing on the runway in Chara. "Shit," she said, and then immediately turned toward General Williams at the head of the conference table. "General Williams," she said loudly, "I have an NRO analyst on line that thinks it may be a trap. Visual at Screen 8. May I put him on speaker, sir?"

General Williams spoke up immediately. "Absolutely!"

"Mr. Defresne," Markham said quickly into the phone, "I'm putting you on speaker.  Tell General Williams what you just told me, and make it quick."

*Lynn M. Boughey*

# CHAPTER 46

## Forward Operating Point Fengming, Gen He Airport, Northern China

Colonel Harper watched on the screen as the SR-71's back wheels touched down on the runway at Chara, the TV screen showing smoke and the infrared screen showing first two bright spots under the rear tires and then the tires themselves becoming a light green as they heated up from the friction of touching down and then, after the rear chute was deployed and the front wheel touched down, the added heat from Phinney beginning to apply the brakes. At the same time Harper could see the reverse thruster panels that had been installed just for this mission moving upward from below the afterburners, then locking in place. Suddenly the infrared screen showed two large plumes of heat emanating from the back of the plane forward as Phinney put the Blackbird throttles at full afterburner. Within seconds the plane was slowed down to a normal taxi speed and the two plumes disappeared from the screen. The plane continued travelling to the west end of the runway, stopped, and then another plume shot out of the right engine and immediately angled forward thanks to the right-reverse thruster, thereby pushing the right side of the plane backwards and turning the plane to the right until the plane had performed a perfect 180 degree turn facing eastward, ready for takeoff.

Once the plane had been turned around Harper observed the reverse thrusters being disengaged and then the drag chute being released. Harper watched the drag chute fly backwards away from the plane from the push of the two idling engines. Harper next observed four bright flashes emanating from the back of the engines. Phinney had obviously activated the the four explosive bolts at the fulcrum of both reverse thrusters, thereby dropping the reverse thrusters unceremoniously to the ground.

"Here comes the package, sir," the mission specialist stated to Harper. Harper watched as the man who had lit the flares approached the cockpit of the plane, and the pilot and RSO canopies rose upward.

# CHAPTER 47

## Chara runway, Siberia

Phinney took off his flight helmet as the canopy lifted upward, leaving the brakes on and both engines at idle. Phinney leaned over the left side of the cockpit and looked down at Professor Tsinev.

"Good morning, Professor. Do you remember me?"

"Mr. Phinney. How nice to see you."

"Thank you, Professor. I'd love to sit here and chat, but frankly I'd really like to get the hell out of here. Here's the rope to climb up. The plane isn't too hot because I wasn't flying above Mach, so it's OK to touch the fuselage as you climb up. Get in and put on the gear on the seat, a pair of pants and a vest. Do you know how to hook up the oxygen mask?"

"You bet," Tsinev said as he reached up for the rope.

Tsinev paused for a moment as he looked to the rear of the plane, and then began climbing up the rope with Phinney holding onto the rope and reaching out his hand to help Tsinev swing into the back RSO seat. Almost half way up, Tsinev slipped and lost his grip on the rope, falling downward about three or four feet and landing with a thump.

"Shit!" Phinney said. "Are you all right?"

"I don't know. I hurt my ankle pretty badly."

Christ! Phinney thought to himself. That's all we need. "Can you make it up on your own?" he asked as he looked down at the man.

"I don't think so," Tsinev said as he sat on the tarmac rubbing his left ankle. "It's twisted pretty good."

"Damn," Phinney said, thinking quickly. "OK. Give me a second to get undone here and I'll be right down."

Phinney detached his shoulder harness and set his flight helmet on the control panel to his right. "I can't believe this!" Phinney muttered to himself as he began pulling himself out of the cockpit, despite the fact that he had been told time and time again that he was not to leave the cockpit under any circumstances.

"I'll be damned if I'm coming all this way for nothin'!" Phinney muttered to himself as he crawled out of the cockpit.

# CHAPTER 48

## Forward Operating Point Fengming, Gen He Airport, Northern China

Harper watched with trepidation as he observed the package sitting on the tarmac and then Phinney getting out of the plane and easing himself downward to the ground, apparently to assist the man in getting into the plane. At the same moment all of the screens suddenly showed everything in a red tint, the signal to abort obviously sent directly from the Pentagon. Phinney's screen was doing the same, Harper realized, but Phinney was now out of the cockpit and wouldn't see it.

"Shit!" Harper yelled more to himself than to anyone else. "Show me a larger area," he said to the UAV technician. "Get the whole plane in there at about 50 percent."

The mission specialist reached up to one of the screens and pressed "-2x" several times until the plane showed up in the center of the screen at about one-half the size of the screen. What Harper saw sent chills up and down his back: Five troops in standard SWAT gear, night-vision goggles and all, were approaching from the back of the plane, closing in on Phinney as he lowered himself from the cockpit. By the time he reached the ground he was surrounded.

# CHAPTER 49

## Chara runway, Siberia

Phinney released himself from the rope and fell the foot or so onto the runway. As he reached his hand down to Tsinev to help him up off the ground he observed that Tsinev was holding a Makarov pistol and aiming it directly at him.

"I'm sorry, Jack," he said to Phinney, "but you are under arrest."

Phinney immediately moved his left hand toward his right shoulder to grab the plastic self-destruct cylinder clipped to his right shoulder harness, but as he did so someone from his left grabbed his arm from behind him, jerking it back so quickly that Phinney thought his arm certainly would be broken, or at least pulled out of its socket. Phinney watched the plastic cylinder bounce across the tarmac as another man grabbed Phinney from his right side.

"I would suggest," Tsinev said as he got up off the ground, "that you not move another muscle, that is if you want to live for more than the next two seconds."

At that point Phinney felt the two men shove both of his arms backwards while a third man put on handcuffs. A man dressed in SWAT gear walked over to the plastic cylinder, picked it up, and brought it over to an older man wearing civilian clothes.

"A signalling device?" the SWAT member said to the older man.

"Or a destruct signal," Tsinev interjected forcefully. "Either way, let's get the plane out of here!"

The guards paused for a moment, looking first at the younger civilian that had was part of their team, and then at the older man who had captured the American pilot. "I'm in charge here, you idiots," Tsinev said forcefully. "This man," he said as he pointed at Phinney, "is my prisoner. Take him to the jail in the hangar," Tsinev barked. "And get that plane in the hangar quickly. The signal won't be able to penetrate the hangar. Until it gets in there, the signal could be received off-station! I would suggest not wasting any time!"

The men needed no further encouragement. Within minutes the plane had been moved into the hangar on the north side of the runway. The men rushed to close the large metal hangar doors before a self-destruct signal was received.

# CHAPTER 50

## National Military Command Center's Conference Room, The Pentagon

Markham looked over at General Williams questioningly. Williams immediately considered the situation, and then slowly shook his head "no" while looking at Markham. It would be one thing to blow up the plane after it had been hit by enemy fire and Phinney had already ejected, or if the plane had had a severe malfunction and was headed into a populated area of China. But there would be little value to blow it up on the runway except to provide confirmation not only that the United States had violated Russian airspace, but also that as a result of some malfunction, or worse yet perhaps intentionally, an American military plane had exploded while on the ground, killing six or more Russians in the process. No, they had to wait to see if there were any other options, or, if necessary, take the heat. Williams realized that it would take several days for the news to reach the true decision-makers in Moscow, and they would not act quickly; they too would ponder their options to determine what the best course would be. Either way, it was clearly going to turn into an international incident. Best not to make it worse by killing Russian soldiers on the ground. So, instead of activating the destruct mechanism that Markham and Williams had covertly installed aboard the Blackbird, Williams picked up his phone and asked to speak to the chairman. It was not a conversation he looked forward to.

# CHAPTER 51

## Chara Airport, Siberia

Phinney was led by the guards to the lone hangar on the north side of the runway. He remained silent and observant, trying to remember as many details as possible. While they walked toward the hangar Phinney watched as several other guards attached the SR-71 to a small tractor and moved it into the hangar. Thus far Phinney had noticed a total of only six guards.

"In here," Tsinev told Phinney as they approached an entry door on the east side of the hangar. Phinney stepped into the poorly-lit hangar and climbed the three flights of metal steps onto a narrow hallway that appeared to house offices. The guards led Phinney to the end of the hallway and unlocked a door at the farthest northeast corner of the hangar.

"Have a seat on the cot," Tsinev ordered. As Phinney did so, Tsinev spoke to one of the guards in Russian. The guard came over and removed the handcuffs. "You should be more comfortable that way," Tsinev stated simply. Tsinev said something else to the guards, and they left the room, shutting the door behind them.

Tsinev pulled up a chair and faced Phinney. "I'm sorry things did not work out as planned."

Phinney said nothing. He was a prisoner. There was nothing to say.

"It has been many years since I taught you political science and foreign affairs. I understand you have done well in the military, except perhaps for that DUI some years ago. And of course there was the divorce, but those things happen."

"Go to hell," Phinney replied.

"Oh, so I hit a nerve, did I?" Tsinev was thoughtful for a moment. "I too have had losses. For most of us, we do no more than survive the work and worry of life. That is what life is. If possible, we try to do so with graciousness and perhaps a little honor. Dignity and hope is but a dream." He paused, closely observing his former student. "Continuing on one's chosen path has become the mantra of the walking dead, don't you think? Rarely are we given a chance to impact society, to make a real difference. But here we sit, you and I, at such a point. Whatever we do from this point will have meaning. Whatever we do here will have substance. And whatever becomes of us will be decided by the two of us and no others. That, my friend, is decidedly rare. This is our destiny, and ours alone."

Tsinev sat back in his chair, relaxing. "We can ask nothing more of life, and normally expect even less. So, my friend, at some point soon you will have to decide whether to trust me. If you make the right decision, we will survive this and some day drink a quiet toast to ourselves, we alone knowing what transpired."

"And if I don't trust you?" Phinney asked.

"Then we are both doomed. But that too is part of the deal. That is something I accepted long ago and you, I would guess, accepted the same possibility as part of this mission. It is just that the card to be played is to be played now. And, my friend, you have more control over the situation than you may think."

Phinney considered what Tsinev had just said, what he had meant. A riddle wrapped inside an enigma, Phinney thought to himself, knowingly condensing the famous Winston Churchill comment about trying to understand Russia, just as he was trying to understand what Tsinev was trying to say.

"Talk what you will about life," Phinney said simply, "my duty is clear: To escape. I am your prisoner. There is nothing further to be decided, and nothing else I need to know."

Tsinev sighed. He seemed tired to Phinney. And old. Older than he really was. "There is much I can do to help you, Jack," Tsinev said quietly. "You must consider me as your friend."

"You are very kind, but it is my duty to thwart you in every way that I can, to escape. You know that as well as I do."

"Kindness and duty," Tsinev said aloud as he looked up at the ceiling in contemplation, his arms behind his head. "Everything I have ever done in my life has been based on kindness or duty. It is all I have left. Kindness and duty. It is through kindness and duty that I have served both God and man. I have often thought that kindness comes from God Himself, something Valjean discovered and Portia knew."

"And duty?" Phinney asked.

"Duty relates more to man, I think, although of course we also have the duty to do God's will. But for the most part, it is duty to ourselves, duty to our country, duty to our fellowman that determines true virtue among men. To fail to do one's duty is a sin, as worse a sin as any other, I suppose. This and kindness have been my creed my whole life."

"Then be so kind as to let me leave," Phinney said almost jokingly.

"I am kinder than you think, my young friend." Tsinev's voice became quiet once again. "Are you so sure that I am not a prisoner of the situation as well? Nothing is ever simple in the world of espionage, Jack. Nothing is ever obvious or easy, in life or here. Perhaps we are both prisoners at the moment, each waiting for the chance to escape. Our paths, like the paths of our two countries, have indeed finally converged. Only this time the true focal point of Russia is not communism or international revolution, or the false hope of democracy advanced by the hopeful adherents of the same."

Phinney understood perfectly Tsinev's reference to "convergence" as it related to the paths of the United States and the Soviet Union, and particularly to the Wilsonian view of the Soviet Union that Roosevelt had so naively adopted throughout the 1930s and even into the depths of World War II. Shunning the opinion of the experts in the State Department and every Ambassador (save one) sent to Moscow from 1933 to 1946, Roosevelt repeatedly and consistently gave Stalin whatever he wanted. He did so based on the misguided notion that Stalin was at heart not a revolutionary but a man of the people who would, eventually, create a just and democratic society in Russia. According to this view the destiny of the Soviet Union and the United States were inextricably on a path of mutual convergence, all based on the naive belief that the Soviet Union was heading away from totalitarianism and was instead moving toward democracy, while at the same time the United States was supposedly moving away from traditional capitalism and becoming a modern socialistic-welfare state.

But those who had been stationed at Moscow and refused to ignore Stalin's atrocities and ruthlessness—except for Davies, that congenital sycophant—knew all too well who and what Stalin was. Ambassador Bullitt tried to explain this simple reality to Roosevelt in a one-on-one, three-hour discussion with the president in June of 1943, but to no avail. Interestingly, President Roosevelt acknowledged the accuracy of Bullitt's facts and even the logic of his reasoning, but he nonetheless preferred to go with his "hunch" that Stalin was "not that kind of man" and "will work with me for a world of democracy and peace." And history changed accordingly, with the United States acquiescing to the Russian expansion of influence in Europe, acquiescing to the genocide of millions of Ukrainians, and eventually acquiescing to all of the other atrocities which received tacit approval by Roosevelt's almost unbelievable unwillingness to take a stand. All of this Phinney knew very well thanks to his old professor who sat across from him in this make-shift jail as if they they were back at college sitting in the Burling Library or in the Student Union discussing foreign affairs without a care in the world, as they once did so many years ago.

Phinney could not help but wonder whether Tsinev was just making conversation to bide the time, or was he waiting for some opportunity of some sort? Phinney decided that he needed more time to try to figure out what was really going on.

"So has your Russia changed so much?" Phinney asked.

"Even I no longer recognize it, and I lived here through it all, all that has occurred in the last fifteen years. The people truly prefer democracy. The problem though is that there are those in power who would prefer to go back to a totalitarian state, and if the Russian economy continues to go badly, those people may yet gain power, either through the ballot or otherwise. But for now, right now, there is great possibilities. Russia is indeed at a crossroads. And once again the military is the key, as it always has been. The military commanders' decision not to intervene in the coup against Gorbachev kept him in power, just as the military kept Yeltsin in power in 1993."

"Perhaps," Phinney replied, "but the Russian people's interest in democracy also existed when the Bolshevek's took over, but that didn't stop Lenin from becoming a totalitarian dictator. Who cares what the people want? It doesn't matter one iota whether they want democracy, and you and I know it. What matters is if they are capable and willing to thwart a transition back to an authoritarian state, and frankly given their economic woes and their desire to put a stop to the rampant crime, I wouldn't put money on anything right now, including democracy, whether the people seem to want it or not. Especially when buildings are being blown up in Moscow, Chechnya is filled with religious terrorists, and Degestan is trying to break away."

"Perhaps," Tsinev replied. "But the fact that they are trying democracy and seem to want it at least gives us reason to support them and try to help them stay that course, don't you think?"

"Maybe. But maybe Russia is nothing more than a microcosm of a human big bang, repeatedly moving from anarchy to totalitarianism, and back again, with democracy and the rights of the people existing briefly as it moves from one extreme to the other. Your Russia may mouth the words of democracy, but all it wants right now above all things is stability, at whatever cost. And frankly, I don't blame them."

Phinney was beginning to tire of this discussion. If Tsinev had intended to relay any important information Phinney failed to catch it. Phinney decided it was time to force the issue. "Listen," Phinney stated forcefully, "I'm done talking politics. To tell you the truth, at this moment I don't give one damn about Russia or where the hell it's going! I'd much rather you tell me why I'm here, and why you betrayed me?"

"All will become clear enough later, Jack. But not yet. Here," Tsinev said as he got up from the chair, "have my pack of cigarettes. You may be here awhile."

"No thanks," Phinney stated as he handed the pack of cigarettes back to Tsinev, "I don't smoke." As Tsinev took the pack of cigarettes back Phinney felt a piece of paper remaining in his hand. Phinney immediately closed his hand into a fist, making sure the paper didn't fall onto the floor.

"I will be back tomorrow. Perhaps you will be more easily persuaded that I am right once you have time to fully understand your predicament. If you chose to admit that you were on a spy mission, things will be easier for both of us."

Tsinev rapped on the door, and the guard let him out. The door was then shut and locked from the outside, and the lights turned off.

★       ★       ★       ★

Tsinev left the guard at the door and stepped into the next office. A Russian officer sat on a chair leaning backwards, his feet on a desk. In his hand was the remote control device that had been taken from Phinney when he was captured. The officer nonchalantly inspected the device, twisting it slowly and continuously in his hands as he examined it.

"So how's your friend?" he asked Tsinev.

"He's fine, no thanks to you. I had this operation under control. I sure as hell didn't need you or your soldiers getting in the way!"

"Perhaps not. But I noticed that you would have had difficulty moving the plane by yourself."

"I would have managed." Tsinev said as he walked past the officer and over to the room's only window.

"I also noticed that you did not have the prisoner's quarters prepared. Perhaps our concern about you was justified?"

Tsinev turned quickly and in one simple motion put his foot under the leg of the chair and sent the Russian officer backwards onto the floor; by the time he hit the ground Tsinev had a knife at his throat.

"The next time you question my loyalty I will kill you! Do you understand?"

"Just like you killed the man I sent to follow you in Plesetsk."

"You mean the idiot who tried to apprehend me at the airport? You would think with all your years of experience spying on your own people you could find someone who knew how to make an arrest."

"He was young. He was supposed to just follow you, but he got excited, greedy."

Tsinev pulled back the knife and stood away from the officer.

"I swear to God, Zaykov, if you get in my way one more time during this operation I will kill you."

The officer got up, picked up the chair, and sat back down. "And until I know whether this operation is truly authorized, I will continue to watch you; and, if it turns out the operation is not authorized, it will be me killing you, my dear friend."

"Fine. But don't get in my way again. I will spend a few days trying to get him to admit his role as a foreign spy. Then we will send him to Moscow for a very public trial."

"And if he doesn't turn?"

"Then we will still have the grand prize; an American spy and the plane that he rode in on."

★     ★     ★     ★

Phinney sat in the dark considering what lay in his hand. Crawling over to the sliver of light emanating from the slit at the bottom of the door, Phinney read the note. It said, "Escape is still possible for both of us. Be prepared." Phinney put the small piece of paper in his mouth and chewed on it as he crawled back to his cot, swallowing the paper on the way. He spent the next few hours reviewing in his mind every word that Tsinev had spoken, trying to relive every nuance, every gesture made. "Are you so sure that I am not a prisoner as well?" Tsinev had asked. Even if Phinney didn't trust him, he had to consider every possibility, and he did so the rest of the night.

# CHAPTER 52

## Forward Operating Point Fengming, Gen He Airport, Northern China

Harper looked out at the rugged terrain encircling the small Chinese-built runway. He had been told by his Chinese liaison officer that forty years ago a mountain existed where the northern half of the runway presently sat. When the runway was first built in 1956 its only function was to allow small propeller driven planes to land supplies to the province. However, with the advent and expansion of jet transports, the runway needed to be lengthened to eight thousand feet. Thus the mountain had to be moved, at the cost of tons of dynamite and hundreds of lives in the process. But China, of course, had many lives to spare, and in ten years the project was completed.

Looking around at the mountainous landscape through his night-vision goggles, Harper considered this the last place in the world where he could envision waiting for a mission to be completed: somewhere in the middle of nowhere on a mission into Russia at a FAARP located at the northern-most portion of Communist China. Ops people, that is Air Force ops people, hate FAARPs: Forward Area Arming and Refueling Points. If you want things to go wrong, put a FAARP in your scenario, Harper had stated to his staff at least a hundred times. Unfortunately the special ops planners in the other services, especially in the Army, repeatedly include FAARPs in their planning. Oh, well.

So here Harper sat, at a forward operating point watching a mission go bad. Undermanned and running out of supplies. At least this time it wasn't the FAARP that was the problem. The plan had been the problem, or at least the implementation of that plan.

Phinney was now in enemy hands, and Harper's hands were, for all intents and purposes, tied. Harper understood completely that this mission was designed around the proposition that only one man would be at risk, and if he was captured, so be it. There had been no thought of the possibility of rescue, even though Harper had requested permission to bring in a full contingency of special ops personnel ready to do so if necessary. Harper realized that he had not even been assigned a combat rescue team led by a 13DXA combat rescue officer, a team specifically trained to conduct rescue operations behind enemy lines. But that too, like so many other suggestions, had been nixed topside by the powers that be. International repercussions. Too much risk. All that jazz. And of course the Chinese had veto power over how many people would be allowed in at the FAARP, and what type of people. So here Harper sat, in the middle of Northern China with a skeleton crew of pilots, navigators, one MH-130P refueler, and two MH-53J Pave Lows.

Harper knew he didn't have enough men to mount a rescue, at least not a hostage rescue. Had the plane gone down in egress close to the Russian-Chinese border, or if the pilot and his package had bailed out near Chinese territory, he had been authorized to go in to get them. But pulling out a captured pilot, undoubtedly under guard and three hundred miles into Russia, with a crew of only eight, was impossible, especially since only four of the eight were tactics qualified. "Shit," Harper kept saying out loud to himself. "We're screwed."

Harper had been repeating this mantra for the last twenty hours. The one thing he couldn't figure out is why he had not yet been ordered back to Kadena. By now the F-117s would have made it back to Kadena, so their remaining on site for a search and rescue tasking was no longer necessary. And normally once a mission goes bad you return to base immediately, at least if there was nothing that could be done. But no further orders had been received so Harper and his men stayed where they were, taking turns standing guard outside the hangar which contained their MC-130 and the two MH-53Js.

"Ace, this is T-2," came over Harper's headset as he stood outside the hangar. "Ace" was the verbalization of the initials "AC" or aircraft commander, referring to Harper's role in the mission.

"Go," Harper replied, looking up at T-2's position on the roof of the hangar, his sniper rifle with its huge night-vision scope reaching over the edge of the southwest corner of the hangar.

"I've got a single approaching. Civilian clothes. Single brief-case. Appears unarmed. Approaching T-1 at one hundred yards, south southwest."

"Roger T-2, this is T-1. I've got him in sight."

Harper lifted up his night-vision binoculars to his eyes and looked to the south southwest and observed the man approaching. "Standard procedure," Harper stated into the voice-activated mic. In other words, assume hostile intentions, consider mark unfriendly and the package potentially threatening. Stop the bogey at least one hundred yards from assets, in this case the hangar.

Harper watched through his night-vision binoculars as the man approached T-1's position. He appeared to be oriental to Harper, probably five foot flat, short hair, leather jacket, standard-size briefcase in hand. Harper listened as T-1 told the man to halt in fluent Chinese. He did so. Harper continued to listen in and watch T-1 deal with the man.

"Sir," T-1 stated in Chinese as he continued to hold his M-16 at waist level pointing directly at the man, "you are not allowed here."

"I have been ordered to be here," the man stated in English. "I am an American officer assigned to this mission. May I see your mission commander?"

"Identify yourself."

"My name is Pry Sing. You must be the navigator. I am an American officer assigned to this mission. May I speak to Colonel Harper?"

"Request the code word," Harper stated into his mic. "If correct, clean him and bring him. If not correct, secure him, hold for Sierra."

"Understood," T-1 replied. "Sir, I need you to set down the briefcase, step away from it, and lay face down on the ground."

"Is that really necessary?" Pry Sing asked.

"If you are who you say you are, you know it is. I would suggest that you comply immediately, sir, and without any more conversation. Understood?"

Pry Sing nodded affirmative, set down the briefcase and began to get down on the pavement of the taxi-way.

"Away from the briefcase, sir," T-1 stated somewhat forcefully.

"The briefcase is my asset, Sergeant. I have to maintain control over it."

"Not at the moment, sir. I'm the one in control of this situation, and don't forget it. Now, get down over there like I told you or you'll be ordering your next set of knee caps from a mail-order catalog," T-1 stated, pointing his rifle at the man's knees. "If you want to, face in a way that you can keep an eye on the briefcase, but don't screw with me anymore. If you question any more of my orders you will be shot. Do you understand, sir."

"Yes, Sergeant, I do." Pry Sing moved away from the briefcase and got down on the pavement face-down.

"Spread eagle, sir, then hands slowly behind your head to the back of your neck, one at a time, then clasped tightly. Understand?"

"You bet."

"Then do it!"

As Pry Sing complied with the instructions N-1 approached Pry Sing from behind and aimed his M-16 at him.

"N-1 in position," he stated loud enough for Pry Sing to realize he was there.

T-2 spoke next: "Bead on subject."

"All right, mister. I'm going to pat you down. You might be interested in knowing that in addition to my friend here with the rifle on your head there is a sniper with a bead on your ass who really loves target practice. I would suggest that you lie perfectly still as I check you over. Any problem with that?"

"No problem, Sarge. I just love being groped by a manly man such as you."

"Shut up, asshole," N-1 stated firmly as T-1 swung his M-16 behind his back and pulled out his 9 mm pistol. T-1 walked over to Pry Sing lying on the ground.

"Sir, I would advise you not to move. Do you understand?"

"Understood."

T-1 reached down placing his 9 mm against the back of Pry Sing's head, and then patted down Pry Sing's left side with his other hand.

"I won't tell if you won't tell," Pry Sing stated as T-1 checked his waist and belt for a weapon.

"You're just a barrel of laughs, aren't you, asshole?" T-1 then checked Pry Sing's other side and along his back and belt line. "I would suggest that you hold very still, asshole," T-1 continued, placing his pistol on Pry Sing's thigh while he checked his legs for weapons, all the while aiming at a location that would easily make him a soprano if he moved.

"That's *Mister* Asshole to you, Sergeant. By the way, you're not one of those nervous types, are you?" Pry Sing asked knowing exactly where the gun was aimed.

"Only when the subject talks to me when I'm doing my job," T-1 replied.

T-1 stood up and away from Pry Sing. "This is T-1," he stated into the mic, "mark secured. He's clean. No ID or weapon." T-1 noted to himself that Pry Sing had indeed kept his suitcase in view throughout the process.

"Bring him on in," Harper ordered.

"You can stand up, sir," T-1 told Pry Sing.

Pry Sing stood up, brushing himself off. "Was it good for you?" he asked T-1.

"Yeah, right. A smart ass in every crowd. I hope you're just here to deliver a message and get the hell out. I'm already tired of your shit. I'll get your briefcase."

Pry Sing stopped him. "I can't let you do that, Sergeant."

"Screw you, sir," T-1 said forcefully. "I'm in charge of this situation until someone tells me otherwise. And, in case you've forgotten, I'm the one with the gun on your ass. Cappeché?"

"Cappeché. Just handle it gently, will you, Sergeant. Not like your girlfriend."

"Gez you've got a mouth. Try shutting it, will you, sir, or I may shoot you just on principle. Got it?"

"Got it."

"Now, until we get where we are goin' there's only one thing I want to hear from your lips, asshole, and that's the code word." T-1 turned off his mic.

"Flashlight," Pry Sing stated.

T-1 turned his mic back on. "We're coming in. Walk, ass-hole."

Pry began walking slowly toward the hangar, with N-1 behind and to the right, and T-1, after picking up the briefcase, behind and to the left. As the group approached the hangar Pry noticed T-2 on the roof of the hangar, continuing to aim his sniper rifle at him. Well, Pry thought to himself, at least these guys know what they're doing. Not bad for just cab drivers.

As the men came within a few yards of the hangar Harper stepped up to the triad of men and Pry stopped; he did not salute, which of course was correct procedure behind enemy lines: by saluting he would be indicating to any potential sniper which person was in command, and therefore who to hit.

"Good morning, sir," Pry stated to Harper.

"Identify yourself, soldier."

"Pry Sing, sir."

"What the hell are you doing here?"

"I have orders to assist you, sir. Believe it or not I was your advance party. I've been here about ten days."

"Who's your CO?"

"I work for the 67th Information Operations Wing, sir. Otherwise, I'm here by myself."

Harper looked over to T-1. "Did he know the password?"

"Yes, sir."

"What's your rank, soldier?"

"I can't say." Just like the OSI, Harper thought to himself.

"All right. Do you outrank me?"

"No, sir."

"Good, because even if you did I'm still in charge. Understand?"

"Yes, sir."

"All right. You know the drill. Prove yourself."

"You are Colonel Harper. You graduated 23 out of 202 from law school. You served as a JAG for four years, then went to the Special Ops world. You're married to the former Ellen Dalley, a Russian linguist. Two kids, Miranda Louise and Ariel Louise."

"Enough with the dossier. Anyone could get that off my bio, or for that matter off the internet. Tell me something only I would know or you'll be crawling out of here with metal in your legs."

"Your mother's maiden name is West. Your CO's middle name is Eldon. Your wife has a small rose tattoo." Pry looked around at the other members of Harper's team. "Would you like me to tell you where, sir?"

Harper finally smiled and reached out to shake Pry's hand. "I think not, Mr. Sing. May I call you Pry?"

"Certainly, sir."

"OK, what's the deal?"

Pry glanced over to T-1 and looked at his briefcase. "May I?"

Harper nodded to T-1, and T-1 began to hand the briefcase to Pry. "Sir," T-1 stated, "I wouldn't recommend allowing him to open it."

Harper looked at Pry.

"If I don't open it myself, sir, the contents will be useless to all of us."

Harper considered the proposition.

"What's my favorite team?"

"The Green Bay Packers."

"Since when?"

"Since 1970, in the fifth grade, when they were in the toilet. During half time you'd go outside and play catch with Tim Waswick. You're not a late comer. You were there when they sucked."

"Thanks for reminding me. OK. Go ahead and open it." Harper knew that N-1, T-1, and T-2 would continue to keep Pry Sing under guard until told otherwise.

Pry set the briefcase down on the ground, clicked the combination, then moved back a one-inch square next to one of the combination locks. He then placed his thumb onto the square that appeared to be glass. A light blue glow emanated from the square for a fraction of a second, then a quiet beep sounded. Pry then turned the briefcase upside down, clicked down both levers, and opened it up. Harper looked down at the case at a keyboard and number pad, as well as a nine-inch slit that served, Harper assumed, as either a fax entry point or a shredder. Perhaps both.

"Give me a moment, sir. I have to sign on within a few seconds."

Pry reached over to the number pad and entered several numbers. Harper heard another beep, and then watched as the screen on the upper portion of the opened briefcase flickered on. A regular-sized paper exited from the slit, which Pry pulled out and handed to Harper. "Here are my orders, sir." Harper looked at the orders; they certainly looked legitimate. "I'd like to go over some things with you, sir. But I'd like to do it inside, if we could. Also, I'd like to have the chance to recharge my system with your APU if I that's OK with you."

"No problem," Harper stated. "Follow me. Assume perimeter," he said to everyone else on the open mic. "Ace's mic is closed."

Pry and Harper walked into the hangar via an entry door. The inside of the hangar was fairly dark with only a few lights marking the exits, obviously to allow the team to become quickly accustomed to the night vision equipment upon leaving the hangar and going outside.

Pry looked around to see if they were alone. "Is the Chinese air attache here now, sir?"

"No. He's in one of the offices sleeping. I take it you're here to tell us what the next step is."

"No, sir. I'm here to update you and give you information. You will decide, as the action officer on site, 'what the next step is,' as you put it."

"Go on in," Harper told Pry, pointing at the left entrance door of the Combat Talon. Pry stepped into the plane and climbed the short cockpit ladder and set his briefcase down at the engineers' desk.

"Is it OK if I plug into the APU outlet?" referring to the Auxiliary Power Unit plug-in to the right of the engineers' station.

"Be my guest."

Pry pulled out an electrical cord from the briefcase and attached it into the APU connector, then reopened the case. "Here's the deal." Pry typed a command into the keyboard. "This is a video of Phinney's capture at Chara from one of our UAVs."

"Yeah, I know," Harper said as they watched the capture. "I already saw it real time."

"After the capture, he was taken into the hangar across from the public airport building, the hangar over here on the north side of the runway sitting by itself. The Blackbird was then rolled into the same hangar, and the doors shut. We've continued monitoring the site. As of yet, Phinney and the plane remain there."

Pry paused as he waited for the video to finish. He then pulled out a small antenna and placed it on the desk, and pressed a few more keys. "This is the scene right now, real time. The guards used in the capture have left, except for the two standing guard around the hangar, who you can see from the infrared lay over." Pry pressed several more keys on the keyboard. "And that, my friend, is Colonel Phinney." Harper looked carefully at the red flashing signal at the northeast corner of the hangar.

"How do we know that?" Harper asked.

"He has a secure radio device on him."

"How do we know he still has it on him?"

"The devise is still on him, or should I say in him. That's where he is."

"Is he alive?"

"Yes. The signal is blinking, showing that he's alive. If his body temperature drops too much, it becomes a solid red light. He's been there from the start. We assume it's a make-shift jail. We don't know why they haven't moved him. As best as we can tell, there appears to be only two guards inside, unless someone was already in there two weeks ago." In other words the Intelligence Wing or the Information Operations Wing have been monitoring the site for at least two weeks.

So, Harper thought, we know where he is. We know the number of guards. Yet Pry has not brought him orders, and none have been sent. "You realize that at present I have no orders?" Harper stated.

"Yes, sir, I understand that. And," he said evenly, "you won't be getting any."

Harper thought about this. He had not been ordered back to base. That in itself was strange. He had not been sent reinforcements for a rescue mission. Wasn't even provided new supplies. He and his men had just been left there. Why? He hasn't been ordered in, or ordered out. Only one thing made sense to Harper.

"Pry, I take it you used to do special ops.  Correct?"

"Yes, sir."

"In a Pave Low?"

"And 130s."

"And you and I both know that the commander on the scene does not have the authority to initiate a new mission on his own into hostile territory, against a country we are not at war with, without an executive order from the president, correct?"

"Yes, sir."

"And we haven't been re-supplied for an alternative mission, most probably because our host country either is unwilling to approve such a mission, or we haven't asked because we already know the answer given the military parameters set up prior to our gaining access to this airfield."

"I believe that would be a logical conclusion, sir."

Harper leaned back against the back side of one of the pilot's seats, now well aware of what was going on, and what he was supposed to do, even if he hadn't been instructed to do so.  "Whatever happened to the concept of going in with overwhelming force?" he asked more to himself than to Pry Sing.

"Great concept for the regular Army, sir," Pry stated, "but I'm not sure it applies to us."

"Yeah, no shit!  Well, Pry, with you that makes nine.  I imagine that right before we enter Russian airspace I need to send a data burst message via SATCOM explaining that I, as the commander on the scene, have determined that one of our planes is down and have initiated a standard search and rescue mission, obviously without reference to where we're headed or the fact that in reality it is a mission to extract a hostage."

"I believe, sir, that Executive Order 24609 allows you the authority to implement a SAR when appropriate, such as now."

"And can you be the ninth man?"

"That's why I'm here."

"And, pray tell, what exactly is your mission, just so I know it's compatible with our mission."

"My mission doesn't concern you, sir."

"The hell it doesn't. If you won't tell me, I'll leave you here and we'll do it ourselves!"

Pry could tell that Harper was not bluffing. "My mission is to obtain certain coordinates from the person Phinney was picking up, and forward those coordinates immediately back to the command center. My secondary mission is to assist you in getting the package out."

"I don't get it. It was a trap. That means the agent was bad. The last thing we want to do is go in and give them more hostages."

"We don't think it was a trap."

"How the hell do you figure it that way? He was captured, wasn't he?"

"Yes. But perhaps others found it out. We think we've got a solid agent who needs out. Something went wrong. So be it. But we still need him out, whether he's with us or agin' us."

"And if he's against us?"

"Don't worry, either way we'll get the information he has from him. I'm sure he will be a wealth of information for us, if you know what I mean."

"I'd rather not know what the hell you mean. And if he's dead? What then?"

"He may still have the information on him. There may be a map or a diagram, which is why I have this specialized fax machine. I can digitize the information, encrypt it, then send it via SATCOM data burst back home. The map or the coordinates is all that matters. Everything else is secondary."

"In other words we're all expendable."

Pry said nothing.

"All right. So you intel people have placed me in a no-win situation. According to federal law I cannot, except in times of war, enter a hostile country without the appropriate executive order. The only exception is the continuing executive order that allows me to enter a foreign country as part of a search and rescue mission to retrieve a downed pilot. Under the guise of a search and rescue mission we're going in, undermanned and maybe outgunned, to effectuate a hostage rescue." Harper paused. Pry Sing said nothing. "I sure hope the info you want so damn badly is worth it."

"It's worth it, sir. That I can guarantee you."

"Yeah. Right. When do you want to go in."

"Tonight, if possible. We know where he is now. That could change any time."

"The sun rises in about two hours. That gives us about nine or ten hours to mission plan, and hopefully catch up on some crew rest. How am I going to do that when just about everybody is doing guard duty?"

"Let me do guard duty from right here." Pry set up an antenna and pushed a few more buttons on keyboard. "This is our hangar. It's a little grainy because we're having to receive the real time signal through the hangar. The screen on the left is infrared. Your men are stationed here, here, and here. The right screen is a large field of view, with motion detection and alarm inputted. Now, when I press your people on the screen, the target turns to green, showing friendlies. I'll leave this guy here as red. Why don't you ask him to move five paces or so."

Harper keyed his mic. "T-1, this is Ace. Move five paces left."

"Yes, sir."

The red dot on the screen moved to the north five steps. When it did so a beeping noise emitted from the briefcase.

"Now come toward the hangar."

"Yes, sir."

The blip moved toward the hangar, but this time the briefcase emitted a solid tone.

"Anyone comes near us not listed as a friendly," Pry said as he turned T-1's mark to a friendly, "we'll hear it."

"I'd love to have about twenty of these in the 20th."

"Wouldn't we all."

"Team, this is Papa," Harper said into the mic providing the special call-back command, designation "Papa." "Meet at Alpha."

"Everyone, sir?"

"Everyone." Harper heard numerous clicks from his earpiece indicating "understood."

Approximately twelve hours later a single MH-53J Pave Low, serial number 73-1649, lifted off the grounds from Gen He Airport,

China, and headed southward, away from Russia. Forty minutes later a Combat Talon MC-130P took off from the same airport, also seemingly headed southward and home. At approximately midnight local time, the Combat Talon sent the following message by data burst to Hurlburt Field:

> On-site commander has determined that a downed pilot requires SAR. Have initiated SAR blackout. Unable to transmit henceforth. Out.

# CHAPTER 53

## Chara Airport, Siberia

Phinney looked up from his bunk as he heard the keys jingling against the door and then the click of the lock being opened. He had been in the locked room for a little over twenty-four hours. He had had plenty of time to consider his situation, and what exactly Tsinev had said. Tsinev stepped in, saying something to the guard as he did so. He then turned to Phinney.

"How are you doing?" Tsinev asked as the door shut behind him.

"How do you think?" replied Phinney without emotion. Phinney knew to be careful in what he said; if Tsinev was indeed also a prisoner and had taken the precaution to pass the note secretly to Phinney, he had to assume they were being watched, or at the very least overheard.

"So," Tsinev said as he sat down on the chair across from Phinney, "why don't you help us? Admit to the world that you were sent here to spy on us. We would get what we want, convict you of spying, and then in a moment of pure graciousness that will be applauded throughout the world, we will release you back to your own country, none the worse for wear. It's the least we could do for one of our greatest allies."

"I didn't know you were an ally?" Phinney replied, continuing to remain cold and unemotional.

"Of course we are. We are the best of friends."

"Then why am I here?" Phinney asked.

"A good question. Why are you here?"

"I must have read the instruments wrong and accidentally ended up here."

"Interesting argument," Tsinev replied. "But why land? Why not just turn around?"

"I thought I recognized the runway. Or maybe I wanted to ask for directions."

"Come now, Jack," Tsinev said as he sat down and propped up his feet on a table. "Why not admit the truth and help us all out?"

"Why should I help you?"

"Because it's in our best interests. Both our best interests. Because your country will want this whole thing resolved as quickly as possible. Because your country, even though it occasionally does stupid things like send you here, still wants to be friends."

"Why should we be your friends? You are the only country in the world that has the capability to destroy us."

"Jack, we both know that will never happen. Not any more. We are becoming democratic."

"You call electing a leader who has almost absolute power democratic?" Phinney countered.

"Yes, it is democratic. We vote don't we. We chose who that leader is."

"And your Duma, with almost no powers. You are a democracy in name only. You have no real separation of powers. You have no rule of law," Phinney stated, finally letting his temper flare slightly. "My God, you are closer to anarchy than to democracy!"

"I can't believe you, Jack. Did you learn nothing in my classes! You Americans are so self-centered and egotistical about your beloved democracy. You would rather support a fascist regime that pretends to be a democracy rather than an enlightened non-democratic government. And the hypocrisy of it all! It makes me sick. Think about it. You have had over two hundred years to become a true democracy. When you started with your so-called democracy only white men with property could vote. Poor people had no vote. Women had no vote. And the blacks, we don't even need to describe their situation! And look at your most brilliant man of the time, the man who wrote 'all men are created equal,' the same man who sired a black child at the same time he wrote diatribes against the blacks that even make me shudder. Your country is filled with hypocrisy and you know it!"

"Maybe so. But it's a true democracy now."

"Sure it is! But you keep forgetting that it took two hundred years for it to reach that point! And that's the whole point. You cannot superimpose your particular form of democracy on our country. We will have to ease our way into it in whatever way we can. And frankly we went too far too fast. Someone has to put the brakes on it. Stability, my friend, is more important than your beloved democracy."

"According to whom?"

"The people of Moscow who get mugged everyday, who live in constant fear of violence and crime. The unemployed masses of our country. The unemployed scientists. You extoll democracy without thought. Look at China. They are doing it right. They are slowly moving towards a capitalistic country, but placing stability as the overriding factor. And it is working."

"Not according to the dissidents in jail and labor camps."

"Screw the dissidents!" Tsinev stated forcefully. "They don't see the big picture. They ought to spend a week in Moscow, or here in Siberia, and they'd know the truth!"

"And so in your mind rights and freedom don't count?"

"Sure they count," Tsinev replied. "But only in moderation, and as much as the society can handle at that time. Foreign policy should be based on reality and probabilities, not merely on ideology. Rights and freedom have little value in a society where rights cannot be enforced and freedom has no limits."

"Look at terrorism," Tsinev continued. "We in Russia had no terrorism when the Communists were in control. No one dared! It is the permissiveness of your American society that breeds these types of people, a permissiveness that we unfortunately adopted. Don't you remember reading Walter Laqueur and Paul Wilkerson? It is the very freedom you extoll that allows these social misfits to become martyrs. It is the freedom inherent in democracy itself that allows these ruffians and social-misfits the opportunity to maneuver. Your so-called war against terrorism is really a war against your own sick society that you created by allowing everyone to do whatever the hell they wanted!"

"If that's so true, then how is it that some of the most permissive countries in the world, like Sweden and Denmark, have no terrorism?"

"Maybe so. But your freedom-loving society is allowing these terrorists to prosper, to have the opportunity to do these things."

Phinney thought for a moment. "Did you read that Amartya Sen got the Nobel prize on his study on the real causes of famines?"

"Yes," Tsinev replied, "I'm aware of that."

"And what did he conclude the real cause of famines is? It isn't the shortage of food or inadequate distribution systems. He proved that the common factor in famines, or the lack of famines, is the type of government that exists in the particular country. If it is a democratic country, the government historically responds to the situation and prevents the famine, in part, supposedly, because they need to appease the masses so they can stay in power. But in other countries that have totalitarian or dictatorial governments, that is where they had the famines and little if anything was done! Why? Because they didn't need the people to stay in power. They just needed the power."

"So then we agree," Tsinev said happily.

"How so?" Phinney asked, somewhat confused.

"Neither extreme will work, and every country is different."

"I doubt we agree on anything!" Phinney stated in almost disgust. He was tired of his professor's ramblings. This was not college, and this sure as hell wasn't a classroom!

"I bet we agree more than you think," Tsinev replied simply. "Perhaps you need more time to think. I will be back later. But remember this: The time for thinking will be over soon. Soon the matter will be out of my hands."

Tsinev got up and knocked on the door, and was let out, leaving Phinney once again to his thoughts.

★        ★        ★        ★

"I told you he would not turn," Zaykov stated to Tsinev as he Tsinev entered the room adjacent to Phinney's room. Tsinev set down the earphones and shut off the reel-to-reel tape machine sitting by itself on a table next to the wall adjacent to Phinney's room.

"There is still time," Tsinev stated as he too sat down. "I know him well. The intellectual approach will work. It is just a matter of time. I doubt he wants to be in a Gulag the rest of his life. He knows what he has to do, he just needs time to come to terms with it."

"I have contacted the Second Directorate. They know nothing of your mission. They are waiting for Pavlovich to get back from holidays to find out if he had been told. If not, I will have the pleasure of arresting you and dragging you back to Moscow as my prisoner. I will enjoy that immensely."

"I approve my own operations. The Second Directorate has no control over me. You know that."

"Yes, but an operation of this magnitude? Not being approved by the Second Directorate? That would be most dangerous."

"The operation has been approved. By whom is my business."

"Maybe. Maybe not. But not for long. Soon it will be my business."

Tsinev said nothing, and left the room. Zaykov smiled at how much fun he was having and turned back toward the tape machine to listen again to every word that had been said by Phinney and Tsinev, looking for any indication of a hidden meaning.

# CHAPTER 54

## Near Chara Airport, Siberia

It was 4:00 am, Chara time. The MC-130P—lights out, landing gear up, engines at minimum cruise and sound suppression on—flew over the Chara runway at 350 knots and at an altitude of one thousand feet. The back door had been lowered several minutes earlier.

The two special ops soldiers laid on their backs on the plane's floor, their feet aimed toward the front of the plane and each man attached to a separate cargo rail that went the length of the cargo area. The men wore strange-looking back packs that appeared to have wheels on the bottom similar to the carts used to roll in and out from under cars being worked on. Each man laid directly over a long rail that went the entire length of the floor of the plane; one on the port side of the plane, the other on the starboard side. A rope exited from each man's back pack extending straight out into the darkness of night. At the end of the rope exiting from the back pack was a small drogue chute, only a foot or so across, which held the line taught between the man and the tiny parachute.

The plane had been at minimum cruise speed for several minutes, its four engines baffled—running as noiselessly as possible. A yellow light positioned on the ceiling of the plane came on. Both men crossed their arms over theirs chests and waited. They were dressed completely in black and wore dark-black helmets that had heavy looking goggles protruding from the glass shield in front of their faces. Another rope exited from the side of the back pack and was attached to the inside wall of the plane. The two men did not have to wait long after the yellow light had shone down at them. Only seconds later the light above them turned green.

As soon as the light turned green there was a sound of a click releasing the lock on the rail directly under the man on the starboard side. The man on the starboard side flew down the rail from the pull of the small parachute and out of the plane, followed by the next man about two seconds later. The plane continued at minimum cruise as it slowly executed a 90 degree turn left and to the south. The pilot switched off the baffling devices so he could, as quietly as possible, ease up on the power and angle the plane upward toward the Kolar mountain range, carefully flying to the east of the 2467 meter peak of Skalistyj Golec.

★          ★          ★          ★

The two men floated slowly to the ground, their pre-chutes having pulled out their main chutes as soon as they cleared the plane. The second jumper followed the first as they headed toward the north side of the hangar. With their special night vision goggles they were able to see the ground clearly. They were also able to see the two guards on the south side of the hangar looking up toward the slight sound of a four-engine plane headed west and then south over the mountains.

The two jumpers flared their parachutes at about the same time, each landing silently on the ground, both still standing upright. With several quick motions the chutes were rolled up into a ball, one man packing the used chute into the other man's back pack, and then the same being done by the other man. Reaching into the front of their belts, the men pulled out their pistols and began circling the hangar, one going clockwise and the other counter clockwise.

The two guards remained talking to each other facing the runway, their backs to the hangar and the two approaching men. The last thing the guard closest to the hangar felt was a gloved right hand covering his mouth, a left arm coming up from under his own left arm and firmly circling his chest from left to right, and then his head being pushed quickly upward and then downward upon the left arm that was pushing against his throat. There was a popping sound, and then the smell of human feces releasing itself downward from the now non-functioning bowels. At almost the exact same time the very same sensations were being felt by the second guard, the one farthest from the hangar. The cracking sound originating from the base of the neck was undoubtedly the last thing either of the two guards heard.

The two jumpers carefully lifted and pulled the two guards to the side of the hangar and laid them both on the ground. One jumper brought his right sleeve close to his mouth and said, "T-1 to base, all clear."

A few moments later the Pave Low helicopter landed on the grass near the far eastern end of the runway, some three hundred yards from the hangar. Four more men dressed completely in black and wearing night-vision goggles and armed with automatic rifles ran quietly toward the other two men waiting at the hangar, one at the small hangar door and the other at the electrical power box on the side of the hangar. Once the other four men reached the door, the jumper stationed at the power box severed the power cable going into the electrical box. The door was opened by the jumper stationed at the door, and the five men entered the building, soon followed by the sixth.

# CHAPTER 55

## Vnukovo Airport, Southwest of Moscow

"Sir," the C-141B's senior communication officer said again, trying to wake Broughton up.

"Yeah," Broughton said groggily. "What is it?"

"We have an incoming, your eyes only. Priority one."

"Okay," Broughton said as he crawled out of the cargo cot directly behind the rows of seats between him and the cockpit of the C-141. "I'll be right there." Broughton dragged himself out of bed, wondering if he had slept an hour or twenty. God he hated these time changes!

Walking into the communications suite next to the navigator's position, Broughton shook his head one more time and then looked down at the screen showing his call sign. Broughton punched in several letters and numbers and then pressed "enter" on the typewriter display on the console in front of him.

The screen flickered, showing once again that the message was for Broughton and for his eyes only. Broughton hit "enter" again and waited for the message to appear on the screen. The communications officer, knowing that his task was now complete, discreetly moved away from the screen. Broughton read the message, hit clear, then walked back into the seating area just to the aft of the cockpit.

"Time to load 'em up," he stated simply.

Konesky pulled the curtain back from the other cot next to where Broughton had been sleeping not so long ago. Broughton went over to the cot and leaned against the metal frame as he spoke to Konesky.

"We've got a message that we might as well head to the general area. We expect to know within hours the exact location."

"So, north on M8, I suppose?" Konesky asked, already knowing the answer. Both men knew that M8, one of the main highways out of Moscow, headed north and slightly east near Plesetsk and beyond to the Barents Sea.

"Yeah, north on M8. We haven't got the exact spot, but based on what we know, we'll be damned close to it. How fast do we dare drive on M8?"

"If we go any faster than 120 kilometers per hour we'll start drawing attention. I would suggest one hundred kilometers per hour to be safe. How many hours from here, approximately?"

"At that rate, I'd say nine to ten hours." Broughton pulled out a map of northern Russia. "Our contact sent a message from somewhere near Rovdino or Senkursk, about 120 kilometers southeast of Plesetsk. Hopefully on the way we will be provided more specific coordinates."

"Then let's go!" Konesky stated with some enthusiasm; he was obviously tired of sitting around. "Let's have the men load up and head out," Konesky said in his best imitation of an American western. "Americans on the left of the trucks, Russians on the right."

As planned, each American driver was accompanied in the front by a Russian officer; and in the back, one-half of the soldiers were Russian, the other half Americans. That way, Broughton and Konesky had decided, the men would have a chance to get to know each other better before being in a position to work as a joint strike force. And even though the two teams had been practicing indoor attack procedures for several days inside the hangar, often a real bond develops from soldiers having to sit side-by-side, bored out of their minds, waiting for the order that often never comes.

Within fifteen minutes five Russian military trucks drove southwest out of Vnukovo Airport the five to six kilometers to the *Moskovskaya Koltsevaya Avtombilnaya Doroga*, or Moscow's Outer Ring Road that circles the city approximately fifteen kilometers around the center of Moscow. The trucks turned left onto the Outer Ring Road and made their way the forty-five kilometers to the northeast side of the one hundred kilometer loop, and then turned right going northeast on M8.

# CHAPTER 56

## Chara Airport, Siberia

T-1 and T-2 entered the hangar first, with Harper and Pry following closely. As the four men carefully and quietly bounded up the stairs, the second helicopter pilot, H-1, held his position at the bottom of the stairs with N-1. As soon as T-1 and T-2 reached the top of the stairs, they observed another guard at the end of the hallway standing up, his weapon in hand, looking over the railing. With one muffled shot from T-1's specially modified M-16 aimed at the guards left chest area, the guard fell to the floor. T-2 ran over to the guard, secured his weapon and made sure he was dead. He was.

T-1 and T-2 stood guard as Harper and Pry ran up to the door at the end of the hallway. Pry placed a glob of plastique on door's lock and readied the charge while Harper searched the guard for a key to the door. Having found the key, Harper tapped Pry and signalled thumbs up. Pry removed the charge from the door and placed it back in his front pocket as Harper unlocked the door.

As planned, T-2 entered first, weapon at the ready.

★      ★      ★      ★

Phinney had heard the slight sound of a commotion outside his door; he had heard what he thought was a muffled shot and somebody fall to the ground outside his door, correctly surmising that a rescue operation might be in progress. He knew that if that were the case, the worst thing he could do was make a quick movement of any type that would be perceived as hostile; so he merely sat up on the cot, both hands placed in the open on his knees. A few second later he heard the key being turned on the door and heard it open. Although it was too dark to see much, he could make out at the door a silhouette entering the room, and then two other forms doing the same. He then felt two people, one on each side, grab his arms.

"Are you Lieutenant Colonel Phinney?" the man on the right whispered out loud.

"I am."

"What's your call sign for this mission?"

"I can't tell you that."

"All right, what's your call sign back home?"

"English."

Both men released Phinney's arms and began to help him up. At the same moment the hangar's emergency lights came on, temporarily blinding everyone wearing night-vision goggles, their view turning momentarily into all light-green.

T-1, by this time immediately outside Phinney's door, pulled his goggles upward and waited for his eyes to adjust to the new light. As he did so he felt a pistol being placed on the right side of his neck. The man behind him spoke loud enough for everyone to hear.

"I would suggest that everyone freeze."

Phinney looked up as he observed a Russian man in civilian clothes moving into the room, his back to the wall and a gun to the American soldier's neck.

"Now," the man continued, "if you gentlemen would be so kind as to set down your weapons, slowly please. Thank you. Now, why don't you all move over there against that wall. Very good."

Zaykov relaxed for a moment, surveying the situation. As he did so another man came into the room, a 9 mm Makarov pistol drawn.

"I see we have company," Tsinev stated as he entered the room. "Anyone I know?"

Zaykov looked over at Tsinev and then back to his prisoners. "Looks like a search and rescue operation. Start tying them up."

"I don't think so," Tsinev stated simply, his pistol now aimed at Zaykov. "Drop the gun."

Zaykov paused for a moment, then began to aim his pistol toward Tsinev. He didn't move far, for as soon as he began to move the pistol towards Tsinev, Tsinev fired at Zaykov's arm, hitting Zaykov near his wrist. Zaykov's gun went flying to the ground.

"I told you to drop it," Tsinev said mainly in disgust. "Phinney," he ordered, "grab something and tie this son of a bitch up, and gag him too, will ya'. I'm sick of listening to him." Phinney grabbed his sheet from the cot and tore it into several strips. He then tied Zaykov's hands behind his back, and then took another strip and gagged him.

Tsinev looked around at the men and then focused on Harper. "Okay," he said to Harper, "you look like the oldest. I take it you're the guy in charge."

"That's right. I take it you're Tsinev."

"At your service," Tsinev replied as he put his pistol back inside its shoulder holster. "So, what's the plan?"

# CHAPTER 57

## Chara Airport, Siberia

Harper considered the situation quickly. Tsinev had just shot the man holding the gun on him and his men; Tsinev had disabled him and gave every indication of wanting to leave; and he did so without any knowledge that N-1 had a bead on the man holding them hostage the whole time, ready to take him out whenever Harper gave the verbal or physical signal. Odds are, Harper realized, Tsinev had actually walked in between N-1's aiming pattern, something that undoubtedly pissed him off considerably. Plus, his gut told him Tsinev was for real.

"The plan, sir," Harper responded to Tsinev's question, "is to get you out of here as soon as possible. Are there any more guards?"

"Did you take care of the two guards outside?" Tsinev asked.

"Yes," Harper replied.

"Then that should be it. Zaykov here brought six guards with him. Damn near screwed up my plan. After the plane landed I saw them coming out of the grate at the end of the runway. I considered taking them out, but I had no way of knowing for sure if there were others. And if I let them try to capture Phinney they may have killed him, or he may have hit a self-destruct. So I decided on the capture. I figured that once they were here I had no choice but to use them and wait and see what happened. For a while there I thought I was going to have to kill them all myself and Phinney and I were going to have to literally walk all the way to China. I don't think I would have enjoyed that much."

"When will the other guards be back?" Harper asked.

"They've been using twelve-hour shifts," Tsinev answered. "The other guards are scheduled to be back at noon, but if they heard your plane and realized that it was a C-130 instead of an Antonov An-12, they may be back sooner."

Tsinev looked around at the other men, then over at T-1 and T-2. "You guys are obviously special ops," he said as he looked at them. Tsinev then looked over Pry more carefully. "You, however, are something else. What do you do?"

"Intelligence."

"That's what I thought. You look the type. Do you have a transponder here with you?"

"Yes, sir," Pry answered.

"Then tell me when you're ready and I'll give you the coordinates."

Pry pulled out a small case that looked like one of the old-style beepers used years ago before advances in technology allowed them to get substantially smaller. Pry opened up the case, pressed several buttons, then told Tsinev he was ready.

"41 degrees, 40 minutes, 23 seconds East, 62 degrees, 21 minutes, 15 seconds North. Before you send it in, repeat it for me. Probably pretty important to get it right, don't you think?"

Pry repeated the numbers back to Tsinev.

"That's it," Tsinev replied. "Send it before anything else happens. Then we can get the hell out of here."

Pry pressed the send button and then shut the case. "It's gone, sir."

"I don't know about you, boys," Tsinev said, "but I'm ready to go home." Home, Tsinev thought to himself, almost laughing out loud. "My *new* home, that is," he said to the others.

"Yes, sir," Harper stated, taking control of the situation. "What do we do with him?" pointing to Zaykov.

"Leave him. He's no value to us, and there's no need to kill him. He will eventually understand why I did what I did, and will tell those who need to know. Those in charge will understand."

"All right, then," Harper said, "let's go."

"Wait," Phinney interjected. "I came here with an asset. If it all possible I'd like to bring it back with me."

"You mean the Blackbird?" Harper asked.

"Yes, sir."

"How can we get it out?" Tsinev asked. "The engines are shut down."

"We brought along the turbine airstart adaptor in one of the bays. The Russians almost always have converters for their planes that will work with Western compressors," Phinney answered, assuming they would need them as they took over NATO bases. "Maybe they have the converse downstairs in the hangar."

"It's possible," Harper said, thinking out loud. "It would also mean that there would be little evidence of our ever being here. Are you sure you want us to leave him here?" Harper asked Tsinev as he pointed his weapon at Zaykov.

"Yeah. I'm sure," Tsinev replied.

"Well," Harper said, not really convinced that leaving Zaykov alive was a good idea, "then let's check it out. If it looks like we can get the Blackbird up and running, let's do it and do it fast. Dawn is approaching and I'd rather not fight the three hundred miles out of here in daylight."

The men, all except Zaykov of course, went downstairs to the hangar. Harper found it first.

"Here it is!" he yelled to the others. Harper picked up two metal converter attachments, put one on each of the two hoses that exited out of the large air compressor, and then he and T-1 dragged the two four-inch hoses over to the plane. Phinney, in the meanwhile, had opened up the door to compartment C, known as the center bay, and pulled out a large piece of metal about eighteen inches long with a bottom cross piece that was also about eighteen inches across. The device looked like an inverted "T" with the bottom of the "T" consisting of two four-inch holes, and the top of the devise displaying a large gear. Phinney took the large piece of metal and walked underneath the left engine. Harper and T-1 dragged the hoses over to where Phinney had walked and watched him insert the forty pound turbine airstart adapter into the left engine and, once it was in place, they hooked up each of two hoses to each end of the bottom of the inverted "T".

"The attachments work," Harper almost yelled to Phinney in his excitement. "Now let's figure out how to activate the compressor!"

"Shit!" Pry said out loud to everyone. "How the hell are we going to get the compressor going without electricity?"

Phinney, who was standing closest to Pry, told him. "Usually they're gas or diesel motors. Let's just hope it still works!"

At about the time Phinney finished his sentence he heard Harper yell, "Bingo," and then the hugely pulsating sound of a diesel engine coming to life.

Phinney ran up to the cockpit and started crawling into the plane as Harper came over to help him up.

"What about the Professor?" Phinney yelled down to Harper as the din grew increasingly louder in the closed hangar. "I can get him back faster my way."

Harper thought for a moment as he looked up at Phinney in the pilot's seat, and then nodded his head in agreement.

"Tsinev, come over here!" Harper yelled over the sound of the diesel engine. Tsinev barely heard him, but could tell Harper was waving at him to come over to the front of the plane. Tsinev ran up to Harper as he finished helping Phinney climb into the cockpit.

Harper had to yell into Tsinev's ear. "Phinney here thinks he can get you out of here faster this way! I agree. Any problem with going for a little ride?"

"None at all," Tsinev yelled back as he began to climb up the rope into the back seat of the SR-71 with Harper's help.

"Strap yourself in," Harper yelled up at him. "It may be a bumpy ride!" Harper then yelled over at the others. "Get the doors open!"

Now the lack of electricity became a problem, until Pry found the emergency release on the cables and pulled it, letting the springs on the sides of the hangar quickly pull the hangar doors open.

Phinney could tell that the diesel was running at full power. He gave the "thumbs up" to Harper and Harper pulled down a lever on the huge diesel machine. The hoses puffed up and stretched into a rigid position as the air seethed towards the Blackbird. The connection held and Phinney could feel the vibration of the left engine beginning to turn, waiting for it to reach start-up speed.

As he watched the engine's r.p.m. speed slowly increase, Phinney activated the generator, turned on the electrical system, set the brakes, and then began flipping switches to allow the fuel to begin entering the engine. Looking down to make sure the r.p.m.'s were sufficient, he held his breath and hit the left ignition switch.

With a muffled whoosh and bang on the left, Phinney saw the left engine gauges jump to life. Harper did not wait for Phinney's signal. He was already under the plane disengaging the compression hose and the metal attachment, and then inserting it into the bottom of the right engine. Phinney once again went through the ignition process, and watched as the second engine engaged. A few seconds later Harper came out from under the plane, the metal converter in his hand. T-1 and the others grabbed the hoses and pulled them out of the way while Pry turned off the diesel engine.

Not surprisingly, it was quieter in the hangar now that the diesel engine had been turned off, even with the Blackbird's engines running at idle. Harper, glad to see the Blackbird could be started, continued to analyze the situation. He walked over to the cockpit and yelled up to Phinney.

"Do you have enough fuel to stand by for about twenty or thirty minutes?" Harper yelled up to Phinney. "That way we could get closer to the border before you light up the radar screens!"

"Makes sense to me!" Phinney yelled back. "How bad are the fuel leaks?"

Harper looked at the floor of the hangar, noting only a drop or two of fuel.

"The sealant is still working fine! Hardly any leakage."

"Then get the hell out of here! We'll give you twenty minutes, then head for the runway. Will that give you enough time?"

"You bet! See you at Kadena!" Harper yelled up at Phinney. Phinney watched Harper and his men leave the hangar and head easterly toward their helicopter. One of the men had grabbed the Blackbird's drag chute, and two other men were carrying the two thrust-reversers. Good idea, Phinney realized. Now there won't be any evidence of us ever being here! At least *physical* evidence directly attributable to Americans. Just three dead guards. Maybe we should have killed Zaykov, Phinney thought.

*Lynn M. Boughey*

# CHAPTER 58

## Trans Baikal Military District, 23rd Air Army Headquarters, Chita

The young Captain once again sat at his desk during the fifth night shift in a row. He was bored. He was hungry. He was hung over. Only two more nights to go and he would have three days off. Perhaps he would go to a certain bar he knew downtown and see if any new women had been sent there from Moscow to teach school. Educated and European. Just what he needed, the young officer thought to himself right before he was interrupted by one of the even younger controllers.

"Sir, Takhtamygda Air Control reports an intermittent radar signal at low attitude, no flight plan filed, no known military aircraft in that area. Appears to be a four-engined craft, low level leaving Chara, headed southbound."

"Any report from Svobodnyy or Belogorsk?"

"Yes, sir. They saw it too, but only for a second, then it flew under the radar parameters."

"How long ago?"

"About an hour or so?"

"An hour? What the hell took them so long?"

"They wanted to check with Svobodnyy and Belogorsk before reporting it. The last few days they noticed some intermittent signals and got chewed out for it since no one else had picked it up."

Another controller interrupted. "Sir, Takhtamygda reports another contact, southbound near the Chinese border! Appears to be a helicopter."

"Damn! Well, sound the alert and send everyone along the Chinese border. It's probably one of our own planes testing us!" We'd

· 333 ·

better find it fast, the young officer thought to himself, or we'll all be headed for a new assignment, at even a worse place, although he couldn't think of any place worse than this one in the middle of Siberia.

"And contact the most senior military person at that runway," he said to the communications officer, realizing he'd better go by the book on this one. "Ask him to go check out the runway and report back to us as fast as possible."

"Yes, sir."

# CHAPTER 59

## Chara Airport, Siberia

Phinney waited the twenty minutes as planned in order to allow the Pave Low helicopter to get relatively close to the border, and then, after taking a quick glance at all the instruments, he hit the switch closing both cockpits and eased off the brakes, allowing the plane to ease forward at idle. Phinney carefully aimed the plane down the taxiway to the end of the runway where he had been captured only a few days ago, turned the plane to the east, pushed down the brakes, eased the throttle forward to military thrust, took off the brakes, and then hit minimum afterburners. After both afterburners had lit, Phinney pushed the throttles forward to full afterburner. The Blackbird literally jumped forward as it accelerated within seconds to takeoff speed. As the plane lifted off the runway, Phinney pushed the landing gear lever up. He could feel the bumps of the gear fitting into place, as well as the plane's speed increasing exponentially as he began to veer right toward the south and home.

As he came over the Kolar range and began picking up speed Phinney's instrument panel and map display went wild. With one glance he could see at least a dozen threats about two hundred miles ahead of him, most of them airborne.

"Shit!" he said more to himself than to the open internal mic. "We can't make it over China, Professor. I'm going to try something else."

Phinney yanked the as of yet slow moving plane hard to the left and aimed it north-northeast. His display showed no threats; just open sky. Watching as the Blackbird approached Mach 0.95, the start of the drag rise region, Phinney pushed the flight control stick downward slightly until the vertical speed indicator showed a twenty-five hundred to three thousand feet-per-minute rate of descent, thereby performing the dipsy maneuver. Phinney relaxed a little as he felt the now familiar sensation of the Blackbird easing itself into Mach flight, and then pulled the throttle back to minimum afterburners. Amazingly, the plane continued to increase speed as it rose closer and closer to its optimum cruise altitude of eighty-five thousand feet!

Looking down at the fuel gauges, Phinney noted that he had just under sixty thousand pounds of fuel at level off. Reaching over to the navigation display, Phinney punched in the only other navigation code he knew: Twelve twenty three, for Minot Air Force Base. The display showed the map over the Arctic Circle, following along north of Alaska, and over Canada to Minot. After confirming to the navigation computer that Minot was the destination he wanted, Phinney pressed a few more buttons on the navigation computer console. "Four thousand nautical miles to go," Phinney said to himself out loud. "At Mach 3.4 we'll burn fifteen hundred pounds per one hundred nautical miles. Forty times fifteen hundred is sixty thousand. That means I can just barely make Minot, and if I keep the speed up to Mach 3.5, there may even be enough fuel left to land!"

The calculations completed, Phinney waited for the Blackbird to reach its normal cruise speed of Mach 3.2 and then reached down and switched the Mach hold switch on; he then allowed the plane to continue to rise slightly above eighty-five thousand feet, and then activated the autopilot to hold altitude. Finally, Phinney switched on the navigation autopilot and felt the plane angle slightly to the correct bearing to Minot Air Force Base. Throughout all of this Phinney kept an eye on the compressor inlet temperature indicator to make sure both engine inlet temperatures stayed below 475 degrees Celsius.

As the sky began to darken due to the increase in altitude Phinney noted at the same time the incongruity of the sun rise approaching from the east. His thoughts of the strangeness of entering darkness at the same time the sun appeared on the horizon was, unfortunately, interrupted thanks to Tsinev finally figuring out how to activate the internal mic.

"I hate to sound like a back seat driver," Tsinev stated over the internal intercom system, "but aren't you going the wrong way?"

"I'm going to try it over the pole. It's our best chance. Most of our fuel is used up in getting to altitude and landing; at cruise we hardly use any fuel, at least comparatively speaking. If we went straight east we'd run into as many planes along the Kamtschatka Peninsula and probably have even less of a chance than going south over China. At cruise altitude and speed, hardly anything up north here can touch us. And when we get low on fuel we can slow down and, if necessary, eject over Canada. It sure beats the Pacific Ocean!"

"You seem to be forgetting something."

"What's that?"

"If we don't make it that far, we get to eject over the North Pole."

"Can't win 'em all," Phinney replied in his best Chuck Yeager bravado.

Great, Tsinev thought to himself, so much for getting back alive.

★        ★        ★        ★

## Near the Chinese-Russian Border

"They're coming from everywhere," the co-pilot/navigator told his pilot, looking down at the console.

The pilot pressed his C-130 even closer to the tree line as the plane continued southerly toward the Chinese border. "Anyone peg us yet?"

"No. They seem to be focusing at higher elevations, at least so far."

"How much farther to the border?" the pilot asked.

"Ten, maybe twelve kilometers."

"Could be a tough ten miles," the pilot said out loud, more to himself than his co-pilot.

★        ★        ★        ★

## Several Hundred Kilometers North
## of the Chinese-Russian Border

"Shit!" Harper said as he looked over the shoulder of his navigator. "There are threats everywhere. Better find a place to set down until it cools off," he said to the pilot of the MH-53J Pave Low.

"Already looking," the pilot replied.

"There's no way Phinney can high-tail it through this shit," Harper said as he looked down at the screen.

★          ★          ★          ★

## Trans Baikal Military District,
## 23rd Air Army Headquarters, Chita

"Sir, Svobodnyy reports another contact, a fast moving jet going north out of Chara. Belogorsk confirms."

"It is a test!" the captain almost shouted to himself, knowing now his gut instinct had been right. "The intermittent signals must have been a ruse. Alert the defense planes to go after the jet and obtain radar lock. Highest priority!"

"Yes, sir."

★          ★          ★          ★

## Several Hundred Kilometers North
## of the Chinese-Russian Border

"Sir," the navigator interrupted Harper as he tried to help find a good spot to land, "the bogeys are all turning north, live music, all aimed north."

"They've spotted Phinney! Damn. Well, there's nothing we can do to help him." Harper stepped forward in the cockpit, tapping the pilot on his left shoulder. "Let's get out of here as fast as we can while we still have the chance!"

"Roger that," the pilot replied as he pushed the throttle forward and watched the map display below him. "Initiating maximum low-level extraction speed," he said as he allowed the helicopter to rise higher above the tree line and pick up speed. Now that the Russians were focused on another point, the risk of a radar detection was substantially less. Phinney had now become the main target, thereby allowing them to complete their escape.

# CHAPTER 60

## Chara Airport, Siberia

The Army major unlocked the access gate to the airport, his hands fumbling with the cold lock, still swearing at the Air Forces captain who had woken him up thirty minutes ago babbling about an unscheduled flight out of the Old Chara Airport, and would he please go check out the airport for anything that seemed unusual? Probably just another PVO drill. What do they care? They sit around all day in a heated room and dream this shit up. In Irkutsk, no less. A real city! God he hated those guys.

The major drove up toward the open hangar in his military vehicle, thinking that it was rather strange for the hangar doors to be left open. His vehicle lights shone on the hangar as he approached from the east. The major thought he saw some garbage bags or old clothes stacked up along the side of the hangar, but he couldn't be sure.

It was starting to get light out, but it was still hard to see, so the major pulled his vehicle around to the side of the hangar and aimed his lights at the lumps he had noticed. What he saw sent a chill up his spine; the mounds appeared to be two Russian soldiers dumped on the side of the hangar. The major got out of his vehicle and walked up to the bodies, leaning down to check both of them for a pulse. Their skin was cold to the touch, their arms already becoming rigid. They had been dead for some time, the major concluded.

Standing back up, the major pulled out his pistol and walked around and into the open hangar. The hangar was quiet, and seemingly empty. The major's mind was racing. Had someone stolen a plane or a helicopter? He saw no one in the hangar area itself, so he carefully began walking up the metal stairs. Although it was getting light out, it was still hard to see. At the top of the stairs he noticed emergency lights were lighted all along the walkway. The lights gave out just enough light to barely see. The major continued walking along the upper hallway, checking the doors that ran the length of the hallway. So far all of them were locked. He tried the next one. It was ajar. The major stepped in and could make out a table with recording equipment, some chairs, and a cot. Empty.

He stepped back out into the hallway and noticed another lump of clothing at the end of the hallway. As he approached the next room he could see that the door was open also. The form at the end of the hallway looked all too much like the forms he had found outside the hangar. The major leaned his shoulder against the outside of the door frame and raised his pistol upward as he got into position to enter the last room. He spun quickly to the right, his pistol coming downward to take aim—on a man bound and gagged, sitting on a cot!

★          ★          ★          ★

## Trans Baikal Military District, 23rd Air Army Headquarters, Chita

"Sir, we've got a report in from the military contact at the Chara Airport. He says there are three soldiers dead, and a FSB officer claiming the bandits are escaping in a fast spy plane."

"Tell our pilots to intercept and destroy it! Alert all northern forces, including the SAM units. Tell them all to shoot it down at any cost! Understood?"

"Yes, sir!" the communications officer replied and reached forward activating his radio microphone.

★          ★          ★          ★

## Chara Airport, Siberia

"Major," Zaykov asked as he finished taking the torn pieces of cloth off of his wrists, "do you have any equipment to analyze frequency matrixes?"

"Yes, sir," the major answered. "We have some pretty standard testing equipment for radar that could do that."

"Then get me to it," Zaykov said as he held up a small device the size of a cigarette lighter. "If we can figure out the signal coming from this device, we'll be able to take down the plane without firing a shot!"

# CHAPTER 61

## Northeastern Siberia

Phinney continued to cruise at Mach 3.25. He once again checked his aim point to the northeast to confirm that the autopilot was functioning properly. He realized that speed and height were his two best weapons in this situation. By the time he had turned the plane around away from the Chinese border, he had already travelled over two hundred kilometers to the west of Chara. Phinney looked down at the map projection that showed him crossing the 122nd longitude. The map showed the Russian city of Aldan 250 kilometers ahead and to his right. Phinney knew that even if the fighters at Aldan had been scrambled they would not be able to reach his height of eighty-seven thousand feet in time. At his present speed Phinney also realized that it took less than three minutes from the time he aimed northeasterly to the time he passed Aldan, not near enough time for a fighter to take-off and obtain the speed and altitude necessary for pursuit. It may not even give the SAM (surface-to-air) sites time to fire up their guidance systems and obtain radar lock. It was the planes stationed along the the arctic circle, however, that worried Phinney. Those planes had plenty of time to get airborne and attempt to intercept him.

A few minutes later Phinney watched his lower threat screen as the radar site at Jakutsk attempted and then obtained a radar lock on him. However, no surface-to-air missile was fired at him, most probably because there had not been enough time for the SAM units to activate the radar acquisition systems on the SAMs. Phinney double-checked his speed and altitude; the Blackbird was travelling at Mach 3.25 at an altitude of eighty-seven thousand feet. He had already travelled six hundred and fifty kilometers, or four hundred miles, from his turn point; and yet it had taken him only fifteen minutes! According to Phinney's calculations, he had approximately fourteen hundred kilometers (or approximately eight hundred and fifty miles) to go before he would reach the Arctic Ocean. Phinney pondered the fact that the same trip would take twelve hours of straight driving on an Interstate; in a commercial airliner it would take well over an hour; but at this speed it would take the Blackbird only twenty-two minutes! And yet Phinney had little sensation of this great speed. At this altitude, and given the plane's constant rate of motion, Phinney could only fathom his speed mentally. Looking out the window, there was no great sense of speed; just the steady progress over a massive, frigid land.

★        ★        ★        ★

## Trans Baikal Military District, 23rd Air Army Headquarters, Chita

"Sir, Jakutsk radar shows the plane headed northeast at twenty-six hundred meters, speed thirty-six hundred kilometers per hour."

"Are you sure?"

"Yes, sir. They double-checked it."

The young captain realized that only one plane could go that fast and reach that sustained height, and that was the American SR-71 Blackbird.

"Have you already issued the alert to the Northern Air Forces?"

"Yes, sir. Based on the planes flight path I have already alerted Verkhoyansk, Batagay, Talgys, Buorsysy, and Khonuu."

"How about above the 68th parallel?"

"We are doing that now, sir. We had no idea it was going that fast, or we would have done it sooner."

"Damn! All right. Who do we have?"

"Above the 68th we have Deputatskiy, Abyy, and Druzhina; just above the 69th we have Ozhogino, and above the 70th we have Chokurdakh. Chokurdakh is directly along the flight path and is the farthest north before the sea."

*Lynn M. Boughey*

"Have we coordinated with the 1st?" the captain asked, referring to the 1st Air Army Regiment headquartered at Habarovsk, three hundred kilometers inland from the Sea of Japan. Both men realized that although the enemy plane's flight had originated in the Trans Baikal Military District's area of responsibility, the plane had already crossed eastward into the Far Eastern Military District.

"Yes, sir," the young soldier replied. "They have signaled the alert throughout the northern sector to all of their interceptor squadrons and SAM units, and have transferred control over to us, sir."

Undoubtedly so they won't bear the responsibility or the wrath from above if the plane escapes, the captain realized. "Good," the captain replied. "Give them all the flight path and tell them to destroy the target."

"Yes, sir."

"Tell me immediately once any of the planes attempt to intercept. And put it on speaker. I want to hear it!"

"Yes, sir."

★          ★          ★          ★

## Two Hundred Kilometers North of Jakutsk.

Phinney looked down at the map projection display showing the Blackbird crossing the 130th longitude. The map showed the town of Siyegen-Kyugel less than one hundred kilometers ahead and slightly to his left. The lower screen showed numerous radar sites to Phinney's far left, all of them ground-based sites positioned generally along the 64th parallel. None of this surprised Phinney since he was well aware of all of the industrial and military complexes that bordered the Vilyuy River, a major branch of the Lena River. What surprised Phinney was what countermeasures the lower screen was instructing Phinney to take: The screen showed a yellow arrow indicating a higher altitude and slightly higher speed. Phinney reviewed the engine temperature gauges, and then looked over the other temperature readings, including the outside skin temperature and the temperature of the fuel contained in the fuel tanks.

None of the temperatures appeared close enough to the red-lines to warrant a concern. The computer should have the outer-aerodynamic parameters inputted, Phinney thought to himself. Speed and height. His two best friends behind enemy lines, he had been told by Harper over and over again. Okay, Phinney decided as he reached down to the pitch control on his right side, let's see what she can do!

Phinney carefully turned the pitch control cylinder toward him, once again thinking that the control looked more like a peanut-butter jar lid turned on its side than anything else. Within seconds the plane angled slightly upward into a slow climb, passing eighty-eight thousand feet and continuing beyond ninety thousand feet. At the same time Phinney pressed the throttle forward and allowed the speed to increase to the optimum speed indicated on the lower threat-warning screen. Once the plane reached that point—that is, the speed of Mach 3.5—Phinney eased back on the throttle and pressed the automatic pilot control that automatically maintained the selected speed. He hoped NASA and Gunderson's modifications on the engines had worked!

Phinney then looked over at his altimeter and noted that he had already passed ninety-two thousand feet! Phinney knew that the real danger at this altitude was insufficient air to maintain the plane's stability. Looking down at the threat avoidance screen, Phinney saw that the indicated altitude was ninety-three thousand feet, so he reached over to this right again and turned the pitch control slightly downward, thereby allowing the plane to level off at ninety-three thousand feet. Phinney then reached over to the automatic pilot controls and pressed the maintain altitude control.

Well, Phinney realized as a former fighter-interceptor pilot, it would be very hard for anyone to intercept him at this altitude and at this speed. But, he also realized, the right pilot flying the right plane could do it.

*Lynn M. Boughey*

# CHAPTER 62

## Five Hundred Kilometers West of Provienija

Captain Artyom Belyakov adjusted in his VKK-6M pressure suit as his MiG-31 continued climbing steadily to its optimal cruise altitude of fifty-five thousand feet. Despite the two underwing fuel tanks holding twenty-five hundred liters each, the MiG-31's two D-30F-6 engines easily maintained the Mach-plus speed for which the Russian interceptor was designed. Belyakov knew that very little drag developed from his four long-range R-33 air-to-air missiles that were attached right along the bottom of the plane's fuselage on their special AKU ejecting pylons. More importantly, the MiG-31, designated "Foxhound" by NATO, was the world's first production aircraft to include a phased-array radar, the famous NO-07 SBI-16 Zaslon radar. Thus, the MiG-31 was one of the first planes in the world capable of shooting down not only high-flying planes, but also terrain-following aircraft.

Belyakov also knew that the MiG-31 was one of the most advanced aircraft ever built by the Soviet Union. Derived from the MiG-25 "Foxbat," the newer MiG retained the primary use of a steel frame that could be easily maintained in even the toughest Siberian outposts. And unlike the early MiG-25P model, which thanks to the defector Victor Belenko who treacherously flew "Red 31" out of Russia to Japan in 1976, the newer MiG-31 had substantially greater performance. Capable of reaching Mach 3 flight, the MiG-31 was designed to intercept not only B-52 bombers flying low-level, but also multiple cruise missiles and high-flying aircraft, such as the Mach 2 B-58s or the planned B-70 Valkyrie delta-wing bombers. And although some sources incorrectly assert that the MiG-25 was designed to thwart the

SR-71 Blackbird spyplane, Belyakov and others knew that the MiG-25 was actually developed four years *before* the A-12 first flew in 1964, and two years before the Russians had even became aware of the American A-12/SR-71 Blackbird program!

Ten minutes ago Belyakov was on alert at the 786th IAP (Far-Eastern PVO Interceptor Regiment) at Provienija, located just below the Bering Strait on the Pacific Ocean, a mere four hundred kilometers from the Alaskan coastline. Given the fact that he was told to fly westward into the heart of Siberia, Belyakov understandably assumed that this was just another exercise checking the readiness of the various interceptor squadrons stationed throughout northern Siberia. Nonetheless, Belyakov had every intention of doing his best, particularly since he was flying what everyone considered to be the premier fighter-interceptor aircraft in the Russian inventory.

Belyakov turned the communication control knob to activate his BAN-75 command link, and then pressed the mic button on the control stick.

"Chita control, this is Blue 30, westbound crossing Arctic Circle at Two-Seven-Six degrees, request intercept information."

"Blue 30, this is Chita control. We have high-flying hostile aircraft flying at thirty thousand meters, Zero Four Five degrees true, speed four thousand. Your intercept heading is Three Three Zero, fifteen minutes."

Belyakov absorbed the information as he angled his plane slightly to the right, assuming a compass heading of 330 or north northwest. Belyakov immediately realized that the plane he was chasing had to be an SR-71 spyplane. But they had been retired, at least that was what intel had told his squadron earlier this year.

"Chita control, this is Blue 30. Intercept instructions confirmed." Belyakov glanced down at his map strapped to the right leg of his flight suit, realizing that the intercept path took him over the Arctic Ocean approximately three hundred kilometers above the Medvez'i Islands, well into international airspace. "Chita control. What action is requested upon intercept? Over."

"You are authorized to destroy the target, Blue 30."

"Blue 30 confirms authorization to destroy the target upon intercept. Blue 30 out."

*Lynn M. Boughey*

★　　　　★　　　　★　　　　★

## Two Hundred Kilometers East of Esé-Khayya

Phinney continued watching his lower threat screen as he passed to the east of the town of Esé-Khayya, located just above the Arctic Circle. The screen showed radar sites in front of him in almost a semi-circle two-to-three hundred kilometers out. Phinney realized that these locations were tracking him for the purpose of aiming their surface-to-air missiles (SAMs) at him, as well as using the information to try to get an air-borne intercept. So far he did not see any air-borne threats on the screen, although if he were the one flying the interceptor he would fly passive and obtain instructions for the intercept from the control center so that the enemy aircraft had less chance to take evasive maneuvers. Undoubtedly, Phinney thought, the Russians were doing the same thing.

★　　　　★　　　　★　　　　★

## East of Batagay, Northern Siberia.

Victor Arkhipov looked down at his altimeter reading as he leveled off at his MiG-23P's service ceiling of 18,500 meters, or 60,680 feet. Arkhipov put his swept-wing fighter into a slow turn as he watched his radar screen for any enemy aircraft flying above him, the swept wing being positioned as far back as it could at its full 72 degree angle, creating the equivalent of a delta-wing fighter.

"Chita control, this is Red Three Two One. I am on the intercept path 140 kilometers east of Batagay, One Three Five longitude, Six Seven degrees Four Zero minutes latitude, at One Eight Five meters. Please advise me of intercept direction and speed."

"Red Three Two One, this is Chita control. Hostile aircraft is 150 kilometers southwest, approaching at thirty-three thousand meters, travelling at four thousand kilometers per hour, bearing Zero Four Five. Intercept bearing Two Two Five." Arkhipov noted that the same information was being relayed to his AFCS navigation computer at the same time, thereby providing him with the best intercept flight path, at which point he should engage the R-35 Khachaturov's afterburners, and when to release any one of his air-to-air missiles. This upgraded version of the MiG-23ML was specially designed for the fighter-intercept mission, which included coupling the data link to the autopilot so that the ground-control stations could guide the plane to the most appropriate intercept point.

"Chita control, this is Red Three Two One. I am assuming heading Two Two Five and accelerating to maximum height." Arkhipov looked down at his turquoise-painted control panel, reading his fuel gauges. "Chita control, be advised that I will be able to hold altitude for only a few minutes before running out of fuel. Five at the most. Is intercept within that time-frame?"

"Affirmative, Red Three Two One. Intercept is within one or two minutes. You will need to acquire the target very quickly given its superior speed."

"Chita control, this is Red Three Two One, I understand. Permission to fire confirmed. Red Three Two One out."

Arkhipov pressed down with his right thumb on the red arming button on his control stick, arming all six air-to-air missiles he was carrying. On each wing sat an R-23 long-range air-to-air missile known by its NATO designation AA-7 "Apex." On the bottom of the plane, attached to the twin missile carrier/launch units, were one pair of R-60 short-range missiles know as AA-8 "Aphids" and a separate pair of R-73 long-range missiles known as AA-11 "Archers." Arkhipov knew that the addition of the "Archer" made the MiG-23 a formidable opponent to any enemy aircraft, with its all-aspect capability allowing the firing of the missile in a head-on situation, as well as its increased agility given its fore and aft control fins and its vectoring rocket motor nozzle. Added to all of this was its five-mile range and its 33 pound warhead that was activated by radar fuse once the missile got close enough to the target, thereby making the "Archer" perhaps a better missile than the American's own AIM-9 Sidewinder!

Arkhipov waited for his S-23D-ch Sapphire pulse-Doppler radar to locate the enemy aircraft. Thanks to the data-link between the plane and Chita control, Arkhipov was able to "see" the hostile plane approaching from ahead of him, clearly travelling much faster and higher than he was. As the blip that represented the enemy plane approached within two hundred kilometers of his own plane, Arkhipov pushed forward his throttles to full afterburner. Within seconds Arkhipov's MiG-23 had accelerated to its maximum speed of twenty-five hundred kilometers per hour, or Mach 2.35. Arkhipov then pulled the control stick back towards him, angling the plane upward beyond the plane's maximum service ceiling of 18,500 meters, or 60,680 feet.

★      ★      ★      ★

## One Hundred Fifteen Kilometers East of Batagay, Northern Siberia.

Phinney almost jumped out of his seat when he heard and then saw on the display an airplane directly ahead of him attempting to obtain a radar lock. The display showed the plane over twenty thousand feet below him and closing very rapidly. Phinney watched the threat screen for his instructions for what countermeasures he needed to take. No instructions were given. Instead, it continued to show just the yellow threat indicator telling Phinney that he had a plane in front of him, and the all-too familiar tone coming from the front of the cockpit telling him that a plane was trying to get a radar lock on him.

A few seconds passed, and still no indication to change course! Phinney wondered if this meant he was in no danger, or if perhaps the computer had concluded that no defensive maneuvers would succeed in getting him out of danger! Being told to do nothing, he did just that, the sweat almost pouring off his forehead as the tone became louder and louder as the intercept became more and more likely.

★      ★      ★      ★

Arkhipov tried in vain to obtain a radar lock on the enemy plane. It was either coming at him too fast, or at too high of an altitude for his air-to-air missiles. Arkhipov knew that if he didn't fire now, the plane would be over him within seconds. There was no way he could hope to turn and pursue the enemy plane; by the time he got turned around it would be two hundred kilometers out of his range. Arkhipov made his decision and pressed down on the fire button on his control stick, firing every one of his missiles as fast as he could.

★          ★          ★          ★

Phinney watched the threat screen as it showed first two AA-7 "Apex" missiles being fired at him, and then a succession of four more missiles being fired one-by-one, consisting of two AA-11 "Archers" and then two AA-8 "Aphids." Phinney realized from the lack of a steady tone that the fighter did not have a radar lock on him and that, in despair, he had fired all of his missiles at him with the hopes that one may hit. Although the threat screen showed the missiles coming at him and listed at the bottom of the screen reference to two AA-7s, two AA-11s, and two AA-8s, the screen did not give Phinney any avoidance instructions; the screen did show, however, numerous letters and numbers apparently showing first the frequency of the various missiles' acquisition radar and then the electronic countermeasures automatically employed by the Blackbird's own ECM suite. Phinney watched the screen as four of the six missiles veered away from his plane, and the other two missiles, he assumed the AA-8s, ran out of fuel and fell harmlessly away from him.

# CHAPTER 63

## Trans Baikal Military District, 23rd Air Army Headquarters, Chita

"What happened?" the captain almost yelled at his communications officer.

"The target is going too fast to engage head-to-head, captain! The missiles can't compensate quickly enough."

The captain slammed his hand on the console. "Then have them engage at an angle, or use a parallel intercept! Whatever will work!" The captain looked up at the map display. "How about the Air Defense Rocket Brigades? What's their status?"

"The brigades at Verkhoyansk and Batagay were not able to set up in time; Talgys, Buorsysy, and Khonuu are out of range; Deputatskiy, Ozhogino, Abyy, and Druzhina have been notified and are attempting to obtain radar lock; and he is not within range of Chokurdakh yet."

★          ★          ★          ★

## One Hundred Kilometers East Southeast of Deputatskiy, Northern Siberia

Phinney looked down first at his map display that showed him crossing the 68th parallel, and then down to the lower threat display. Both displays showed him the town of Deputatskiy sixty miles to the left of his flight path, and the towns of Druzhina, Abyy, and Ozhogino seventy to ninety-five miles on the right of his flight path. The lower screen showed active radar on each of these towns; under Deputatskiy the screen showed "SAM-3/SAM-5," under Druzhina the screen showed "SAM-12B" and under Ozhogino the screen showed "SAM-10D." Obviously the frequency used by these sites had been programed into the threat computer and each specific signal for each type of SAM had been identified. Phinney felt the plane steer itself slightly to the right, heading away from Deputatskiy and closer to Druzhina, Abyy, and Ozhogino. All of this made sense to Phinney. He knew as a B-52 bomber pilot every aspect of each of the SAMs listed on the screen, although not as well, of course, as the EWO (Electronic Warfare Officer) who sat behind the two adjacent B-52 pilots, his or her face glued to the threat screen as the EWO inputted electronic countermeasures to avoid the enemy radar and if necessary defeat the radar being employed by the oncoming enemy SAMs or air-to-air missiles. Looking down at the threat screen, Phinney realized that the automatic pilot had veered the plane away from the site at Deputatskiy because the SAM-5 had an effective range of 150 miles and could reach as high as 114,800 feet; the SAMs on the plane's right side, however, the SAM-10 and SAM-12B, had an effective ceiling altitude of 88,500 and 98,400 respectively. The computer had obviously taken these facts into account; Phinney looked to the middle-left of his instrument panel and was amazed to see that the plane's altitude now showed ninety-nine thousand feet and climbing slightly! The threat computer had obviously increased the Blackbird's altitude on its own. Phinney realized that he was now flying above the two maximum heights of the SAM-10 and SAM-12B, so he wasn't surprised when he felt the plane turn slightly as the Blackbird computer angled him closer to those sites and away from the more deadly SAM-5 sites.

★        ★        ★        ★

## Trans Baikal Military District, 23rd Air Army Headquarters, Chita

"Status," the captain demanded.

"The plane has angled slightly to the east, out of range of Deputatskiy. As the plane began to veer away from Deputatskiy the unit fired an Angara at it. It exploded several thousand feet away from the craft. No damage possible."

"How about the other sites?"

"Druzhina and Ozhogino also fired, but the plane is flying higher than the S-300s can reach. It is very difficult to obtain a radar lock; the plane is going from horizon-to-horizon in less than three minutes! Chokurdakh, however, has had plenty of time to set up and has every type of missile at the ready. They will get him!"

★          ★          ★          ★

## Two Hundred Kilometers South Southwest of Chokurdakh, Northern Siberia

Phinney watched the map display as the Blackbird veered back slightly to the left, once again assuming the original course and aim point given to it over one thousand miles ago when Phinney had decided to turn left away from China and go north over the pole. His projected flight path showed the Blackbird going directly over the city of Chokurdakh some two hundred kilometers ahead of him. The threat screen had already displayed four or five rocket firings from SAM units, and several attempts by MiG-23s and MiG-31s to acquire radar lock. So far, the screen did not even show a red arrow! Phinney was very impressed. He hoped that the systems used in the B-52 were just as effective, although of course the B-52 couldn't travel approaching one hundred thousand feet or go Mach 3.5. Nonetheless, the advances and abilities of the American ECM suite were certainly impressive.

But the hard part, Phinney realized, was the many SAM sites and other air defense forces that lay ahead. Chokurdakh was one of the largest towns in Northern Siberia, a town which the B-52 pilots were instructed regularly to avoid at all costs. Armed with a large squadron of MiG-23s and just about every type of SAM unit, the SIOP (as it related to low-level entry into Russia from the north) particularly avoided Chokurdakh, either because it was too hard to get past, or because an ICBM or sea-launched nuclear cruise missile would have already taken the entire town out.

Phinney watched the threat screen as it began picking up the various radars emanating from Chokurdakh. The screen showed several SAM-3 and SAM-5 units just to the west of Chokurdakh, as well as SAM-12B and SAM-10 units to the east. To Phinney's initial surprise, he watched the Blackbird computer angle the plane just slightly to the left or west of Chokurdakh, directly over the SAM-5 site!

Phinney seriously considered overriding the computer and turning the plane away from Chokurdakh, particularly when he saw the reference to the SA-5 SAM site listed ahead of him. But then it occurred to him, as it would anyone who has been in the fighter-pilot interceptor business, that often the best strategy is to come right at the enemy; a direct target is much harder to shoot at than one at an angle since the target point is smaller on a head-on acquisition as opposed to the larger radar cross section from the side. In addition, the direct approach magnifies the speeds involved since the closing speed for an oncoming aircraft must include not only the speed of the target but also the addition of the speed of the plane, missile, or rocket coming at the target!

Phinney also recalled in some of his briefing for bomber missions veiled references by the briefers of the SA-5 rockets being defeated numerous times by the SR-71 Blackbird. No, Phinney decided, the threat computer has kept him alive so far. He wouldn't start second-guessing it now.

★          ★          ★          ★

## Five Kilometers West of Chokurdakh, Northern Siberia

The captain in charge of the Chokurdakh Air Defense Rocket Brigade had been shouting orders for the last twenty minutes straight. He wished that the colonel had been here to take the responsibility, but the captain was the one on duty at 0500 when the alert had been sounded. At first, when he had been told that the enemy plane was coming at him from the south instead of the north, he thought the whole thing was a joke being played on him from one of his senior controller friends in Habarovsk or Chita. But once he was told the speed and altitude of the plane, he knew exactly what was going on, and what type of plane it was that he was supposed to shoot down!

The captain had already repositioned half of the S-300V/9M82 toward the south, and the other half (known in the West as SA-12B "Giants") toward the north. The S-200 Angaras, however, he aimed straight up, realizing that given its maximum speed of Mach 4 and maximum engagement speed of Mach 3.7 gave him little room for a slant intercept on a SR-71 Blackbird.

★          ★          ★          ★

## Twenty Kilometers South of Chokurdakh, Northern Siberia

Phinney kept his eyes on the threat screen as the Blackbird approached Chokurdakh. A yellow threat arrow appeared first from the east of Chokurdakh, then from the west, almost directly below him. Phinney watched as the lower portion of the screen indicated first what rocket had been fired at him and the type of radar frequency being used. Phinney next saw a blur of letters and numbers flashing along the bottom of the screen, like a high-speed calculator doing math problems in a different language. The threat arrows continued to be yellow, and no evasive maneuvers were given to Phinney. He did notice, however, that as the SAM-12B approached to within five thousand feet of the Blackbird, the plane tilted slightly, and then tilted back on course. Although Phinney heard nothing, the screen showed the SA-12B exploding several thousand feet beneath him, its 330-pound high-explosive focused-fragmentation warhead falling harmlessly away from him. Obviously the controller on the ground set off the in-flight proximity fuse as soon as the rocket had reached maximum altitude, hoping for a lucky hit.

As the Blackbird came within a few miles of Chokurdakh, Phinney saw several SA-10 "Grumbles" coming up at him, but thought nothing of them since he knew that even though the newer installed 48N6 missiles could reach a speed of sixty-two hundred miles an hour, their maximum effective ceiling was only 88,550 feet. As expected the "Grumbles" fell back to the ground after running out of rocket fuel.

As the Blackbird flew directly over Chokurdakh Phinney looked down in horror as the threat screen showed ten separate SA-5 "Gammons" streaking toward him from five different locations. The letters displayed at the bottom of the screen told Phinney that all ten of the rockets were the SA-5C upgraded rockets, each of which, Phinney knew, had an effective ceiling of 114,800 feet. Phinney also knew that each battery below was actively communicating with the rocket, using both the ground-based P-35M Bar Lock B target search and acquisition radar and the Square Pair missile guidance radar to aim the rocket to its target.

As he watched the ten rockets approach him, Phinney assumed that at least one of the rockets would come close enough to activate its own radar terminal homing, detonating its 478 pound high explosive fragmentation device and literally tearing the plane to bits. Either that, or the controllers below would aim the thirty-five foot long missile directly ahead of him and detonate the missile right in front of the planes path, filling the air intakes with pieces of metal and shrapnel, destroying the engines and then the plane in mid-flight.

Perhaps flying north was not so good of an idea after all, Phinney thought to himself. However, to Phinney's great relief the threat screen showed first one and then another missile veering off to either the left or right of his plane; several of the rockets exploded behind him, but so far none in front. Obviously the jamming system was preventing the command from the ground to reach the rocket, or the false images created by the Blackbird's ECM of a larger target to the left or right had been successful. Within a few seconds Phinney had flown past Chokurdakh and the threat screen showed no more ground threats whatsoever. For the first time in twenty minutes Phinney took a deep breath and relaxed. He pressed the internal mic button. "Well, Professor, it looks like we might make it after all. We will be over international airspace in about two minutes!"

"Glad to hear it!" Tsinev replied. He too had been watching on his own threat screen in the RSO's seat; he knew enough, however, to say nothing to Phinney as they flew over the dangerous spots. Phinney had enough to worry about without giving him updates. "How much longer until we get to our own base?" Tsinev asked, not even sure what base that would be.

"An hour, or so," Phinney replied. "A little longer. We still have a long ways to go." Assuming there is enough fuel to get us there, Phinney thought to himself.

# CHAPTER 64

## Three Hundred Kilometers North of the Medvez'i Islands, the Arctic Ocean

Captain Artyom Belyakov continued angling his MiG-31 fighter interceptor northwesterly according to the instructions being sent directly to him from the 23rd Air Army Headquarters, Chita.

"Chita control, this is Blue 30, bearing Three Three Zero, three hundred kilometers north of the Medvez'i Islands, requesting final instructions."

"Blue 30, this is Chita control. We have high-flying hostile aircraft flying at thirty-three thousand meters, heading Zero Four Five, speed four thousand kilometers per hour. Your intercept heading is Three Three Zero, three minutes. Suggest parallel intercept. We will direct you to enemy flight path, await cross over, then engage at full speed and altitude."

Belyakov considered his orders for a moment. By "parallel intercept," the controller was asking Belyakov to come along side the plane by assuming the exact same flight path, and then shoot the plane down from behind using an infrared missile. Normally such an intercept of a plane was standard procedure. However, a parallel intercept presupposes that the interceptor *catches up* to the slower moving target and then engages from behind. In this case, Belyakov was being instructed to place himself *in front* of the enemy plane, wait for it to overtake him, and then get behind it and shoot it down after it passes over him. The problem with such an approach is self-evident: the faster plane is provided the easiest possible target, a slower moving plane directly in front of the enemy plane!

"Chita control, I do not understand. Why not go with a normal angle attack?"

"Blue 30, several planes have tried that already. It was unsuccessful due to enemy plane's speed and altitude."

Belyakov decided to ask the obvious question. "Chita control, does the enemy plane have offensive weapons?" Belyakov asked.

"Blue 30, this is Chita control. Not that we know of. No weapons fired yet."

Great! Belyakov thought. And I get to be the target to find out if he does have weapons!

"Chita control, this is Blue 30 confirming parallel intercept. Please provide turn point. Also, please provide authorization for outer engagement." Outer engagement. In other words, permission to attack the aircraft over international airspace.

"Blue 30, authorization for outer engagement confirmed. Enemy plane escaping from Russian airspace with defector on board. Outer engagement authorized."

Belyakov took in the word "defector." So, he thought to himself, either this plane was indeed an American SR-71, or it was one of our own secret planes with another Victor Belenko on board trying to give the Americans our newest and most secret plane. Now at least Belyakov understood the urgency in shooting down the target, even if it caused international repercussions.

"Chita control, this is Blue 30. I understand. Ready on your mark."

"Blue 30, confirming that you will engage right turn to bearing Zero Four Five on our mark. Then accelerate to full speed and maximum altitude."

"Chita control, Blue 30 confirms instructions. Awaiting your mark."

Belyakov waited for the controller to instruct him to turn right 75 degrees to a heading of Zero Four Five. At his present cruising speed of Mach 2.35, Belyakov knew that he would be pulling anywhere from seven to eight g's during the turn. Belyakov told his backseater to prepare for the high-g turn, and waited for Chita control to tell him to turn.

"Blue 30, this is Chita control. Turn Zero Four Five on our mark. Three. Two. One. Mark."

Belyakov pulled his control stick over to the right as he kept his eye on the head-up-display's compass heading marking as his plane angled sharply to the right, passing compass headings 350, due north, 15, and 30. Once Belyakov saw compass bearing 40 he eased the control stick back to the center, allowing the plane to ease out of its turn at exactly 45 degrees, or exactly northeasterly. Belyakov then pushed the throttles full forward and pulled back slowly on the control stick. The plane pushed itself forward high into the air. Belyakov could feel both D-30-F6 turbofan engines exerting their maximum 34,170 pounds of thrust each. Belyakov watched as the altimeter showed his height changing from his cruising altitude of 20,600 meters (67,570 feet) past twenty-five thousand meters (82,500 feet) and began to level off twenty-eight thousand meters (ninety thousand feet), the most Belyakov dared go given the thinness of the air at this altitude which made it close to impossible to maintain aircraft stability.

"Chita control, this is Blue 30. We're at Two Eight Zero meters, bearing Zero Four Five. Awaiting overflight."

★          ★          ★          ★

Phinney watched as the Blackbird became feet wet over the ocean, knowing full well that he was now flying over international airspace. The computer had allowed the Blackbird to come down to the more stable altitude of ninety-three thousand feet. The threat screen showed all clear except for a lower flying plane that Phinney had noticed about four minutes ago that was flying over the Arctic Ocean below him headed westerly, probably a transport or an Aeroflot plane headed from Provienija to Moscow or St. Petersburg. At least that is what Phinney thought until the lower flying plane turned hard right and matched Phinney's own flight path!

By switching momentarily to the infrared screen, Phinney could clearly see the heat signature of the plane ahead of him. The plane had a dual exhaust, close together. A fighter! Phinney realized. But would it shoot him down over international airspace? he wondered. Phinney switched back to the regular threat screen. The screen now showed the plane below him in yellow, showing potential danger, and identifying the plane as a MiG-31, steadily rising towards his own altitude.

"Hold on to your seat," he told Tsinev. "We're not done yet!"

According to the threat screen Phinney would pass over the MiG in fifty seconds. The MiG was travelling at Mach 3.1, approximately 240 knots slower than he. Phinney tried to decide whether he should veer off to one side or the other. Phinney realized that by turning either direction he would bleed off some speed and altitude, making it easier for the MiG to shoot him down. In addition, since the computer was not taking evasive action Phinney knew that that meant any action he took would be manually inputted. At this altitude and speed, a manual input that went just slightly past the design and performance parameters could send the plane reeling to one side or the other, disintegrating the plane in seconds. No, Phinney decided once again, stick with the computer and hope for the best.

Having decided to continue with the overflight of the MiG, Phinney tried to do the math in his head relating to the intercept. The MiG was approximately two hundred feet below him and going approximately 240 to 250 knots per hour slower. Phinney knew that traditionally the MiG-31 carried four long-range, radar-homing R-33 missiles, known as the the AA-9 "Amos" according to its NATO designation, on its belly. Phinney also knew that the MiG-31 could also be configured to hold, in addition to the standard four "Amos" missiles, either two R-40Ts "Acrids" or up to four R-60Ts "Aphids" (two R-60Ts if he had previously been carrying drop tanks). Since the plane was this far out in the ocean and had therefore probably been carrying drop tanks, Phinney made the calculated guess that the plane had been fitted with four AA-9 "Amos" missiles and only two AA-8 "Aphid" missiles. Although the AA-8 "Aphid" was more accurate and used infrared for acquisition and tracking, Phinney knew it only had a 7.5 mile maximum range. The AA-9 "Amos," on the other hand, had a vastly superior range of sixty-two miles!

A 240 knot-per-hour delta in speed between the two planes, Phinney calculated, was the equivalent of a little less than 5 miles per second. That meant that once he passed over him the MiG pilot had only one or two seconds to release the two shorter-range "Aphid" missiles, but had somewhere between 10 to 12 seconds to obtain a lock, fire the longer-range "Amos" AA-9 missile, and for the long-range missile to catch up to the Blackbird with its Mach 3.5 cruise speed and impact. Not much time, Phinney realized, but time enough.

Realizing what he would do if he were flying the same intercept in a fighter plane, Phinney reached down to the flare release button and waited for the Blackbird to overfly the MiG.

★       ★       ★       ★

"Blue 30, hostile plane will overfly you in approximately thirty seconds. Can you reach intercept altitude?"

"Affirmative," Belyakov answered as he pushed his throttle beyond full afterburner, allowed the plane to increase speed for about ten seconds, and then angled the plane upward. The controls felt weak and nonresponsive, but he knew this was the only way he could obtain such a high altitude.

As he leveled off Belyakov watched for the faster plane to pass over him, trying hard not to make any sudden moves on the control stick. He knew he had approached, if not surpassed, thirty thousand meters and was probably just below the ninety-three thousand foot mark, but he didn't dare look down at his altimeter, keeping his eyes instead peering upward waiting for the enemy plane to pass over him, alternating looking upward right and left.

Belyakov could tell by the way the plane was handling that he was well beyond the design limits, particularly in reference to its aerodynamic stability. Watching upward by leaning five or six inches to his right so he could see around the center cockpit strut bar, Belyakov watched as the huge Blackbird, or at least what he assumed was either a Blackbird or the new Russian copy of it, streaked past him just a few hundred feet above him. Even before he looked forward through the new one-piece forward windshield that had just recently replaced the older three-piece version, Belyakov pressed the red fire control button on his control stick.

★       ★       ★       ★

Phinney watched as the lower screen showed him passing directly over the MiG. Just as he did so he pressed the chaff and flare dispenser buttons as quickly and as often as he could.

• 363 •

★            ★            ★            ★

At about the same moment that Belyakov saw the two R-60T missiles firing past his windshield, one on each side, the sky was filled with first flashes of light then glitter. Both missiles blew up directly in front of Belyakov' plane. He knew instantly that he could not avoid the mess in front of him. Almost out of pure instinct he pressed the firing button two more times, releasing first one pair of the R-33 missiles, and then the second pair. He could feel the missiles releasing and thought he saw the first two streaking from below him as they angled up toward the enemy plane, but he couldn't be sure. All of this happened in less than the two seconds it took for his plane to collide with the bits and pieces of the exploded flare cartridges, the silvery chaff, and what was left of the two R-60 missiles that had detonated right in front of him. The hot metal careened toward his face, the first piece or two bouncing off the now shattered and weakened windshield. The next piece flew through the windshield as if it was going through paper. It was the last thing Belyakov saw.

★            ★            ★            ★

Phinney looked down at the threat screen which showed first the flares and chaff falling off behind him, then two missiles being fired, then exploding, and then the plane behind him disintegrating. A fraction of a second later, however, the screen showed two then four red arrows attempting to acquire him. Phinney knew the other four missiles had to be the four AA-9 "Amos," which meant they each had the maximum intercept speed of Mach 3.5, almost the exact speed he was going. Phinney watched as two of the missiles failed to obtain radar acquisition and fell directionless away from his plane. He watched as the other two missiles continued along his path, and then heard the ominous tone of a radar lock. The screen showed both of the missiles going from two red arrows to two flashing red arrows; at the same time Phinney heard the radar lock tone emanating from behind him in the cockpit.

"Damn!" he said out loud as he watched the two "Amos" missiles slowly closing in on him. Phinney continued watching the bottom of the screen as the computer once again sped through a litany of letters and numbers as it attempted to thwart the missiles' radar guidance system. Phinney watched as one of the missiles veered off to the left, obviously following a radar-created decoy. The other missile, however, continued to creep closer and closer to the Blackbird. It had been almost ten seconds, Phinney realized, which meant he had flown at least sixty miles since the AA-9 "Amos" missiles had been fired at him. The rocket motor should run out of fuel any moment now, Phinney thought. At about the same time Phinney felt a slight movement of the plane, as if they had just flown through turbulence or a very high jet stream. But Phinney knew it was neither of those things. The rocket had exploded, sending its 104 pound blast-fragmentation high explosive upward toward his plane.

# CHAPTER 65

## Chara, Siberia

Zaykov sat in the army major's office in old Chara watching a technician activating the destruct device that they had retrieved from Phinney when they had captured him.

"Six hundred and seven megahertz," the technician said to Zaykov. "Standard pulse, fifty ten-hundredths spacing, ten one-hundredths' intermittent signal."

"And that means?" Zaykov asked totally bewildered.

"We can copy it and send it out without any problem."

"Can one of our fighter planes do it?"

"Sure, if we specially modified it to the right frequency and right signal burst. It'd only take an hour or so to program the radio transponder and install the signal."

"Damn!" Zaykov said. Now the technician looked bewildered.

"Look," Zaykov said to him, "this is a destruct signal for a plane. But the plane has already left and is on its way to the United States."

The technician thought for a moment, then held up the device toward Zaykov. "No problem, then. Have a submarine send it."

Within moments Zaykov was talking to the Chita control center.

"Has the Blackbird been shot down?" Zaykov asked the young captain. By now it was morning, and no doubt the colonel who was in charge of the post had arrived. Zaykov still thought it best to talk to the captain since they had visited earlier on the matter and he would have fewer questions for him.

"We don't know if it was destroyed," the captain answered. "We lost radar contact with both planes, but that may be due to the fact that the Pechora radar site doesn't reach that far over the horizon."

"How about the interceptor?"

"We've lost all contact with the MiG; no report by radio, and no radar contact."

"Then the Blackbird may have escaped."

"Yes, sir," the captain at Chita control said dejectedly, probably realizing that his military career was over and hoping he did not end up in a Russian military prison.

"Look, captain. I may have a way to 'shoot down' the plane while it's in transit. There is a self-destruct on the plane. We have the self-destruct mechanism and have figured out the frequency and the signal. The plane is probably headed back to its home base in southern California. Is it possible for you to get the information to a submarine patrolling off of California and have the sub send out the signal before the plane lands? That will destroy the plane and no one will realize that its destruction came from us."

The captain immediately accepted the plan, and within minutes he had one of his electronic experts talking to Zaykov's own electronics expert in Chara. While the two experts talked Zaykov realized that the finer art of electronic communications was indeed a language unto itself.

★      ★      ★      ★

## Two Hundred Kilometers West of San Diego, California.

The communications officer of the Akula-class attack submarine walked up to the captain in the control room and handed him the message. One hundred and seven meters long, the submarine was Russia's most recent and advanced submarine.

"And you've got the signal information?"

"Yes, sir," the sailor replied.

"All right. Tell me when you're prepared to start signaling and we'll go top side. Full speed ahead, bearing due east," the captain ordered.

"Yes, sir!"

# CHAPTER 66

## Cheyenne Mountain, Colorado

Rear Admiral J. Howard Bryson sat in the command console chair deep inside the carved marble of Cheyenne Mountain, Colorado. His short-cropped hair slightly askew, he looked every bit a sailor. Although his rank was that of an admiral, he wore one-star on each shoulder of his light-gray flight suit indigenous only to NORAD (North American Aerospace Defense Command) officers assigned to Cheyenne Mountain. As command director, he was in charge of the entire Cheyenne Mountain complex, the nerve center that would sound the first alarm of an attack against North America.

To Bryson's left in the small thirty-foot by twenty-foot room sat the mission director; to his right his missile officer. The other six members of Bravo Crew sat on the other side of the console. The glass encased briefing room lay behind the three directors, the eight primary chairs empty, the curtains open overlooking the directors as they reviewed the various screens which they brought up on their monitors. Ironically, this assignment reminded Bryson of serving at sea; instead of being surrounded by water, he was surrounded by rock. Sure, he could go home at night, but in an emergency he could be locked inside the mountain for weeks in a room not much bigger than the command centers he served in as Commanding Officer of VA-93 aboard the USS Midway. After his staff tour—the dreaded flying a desk job—he assumed command of Carrier Air Wing NINE aboard the USS Kitty Hawk, and later as Commander Carrier Air Wing FIFTEEN.

The heart of the mountain, and the heart of NORAD, was this room, the focal point of all the military and civilian assets directed to the detection of an enemy strike from land, sea, air, or space. All the information from these assets, consisting primarily of satellites and

land-based radars, were funnelled into the eighty-seven separate computers, eventually spewing out the already analysed information into
this room. Sensors that detected heat or objects that could be threats
relayed the information immediately through high-speed satellite or
land-routed communication lines in moments.

The speaker at Bryson's desk crackled. "Command center this
is air defense ops center. DSP shows level flight, high-level air-breathing IR signature northeast Russian Quadrant exiting Russian air space
bearing Alaska, screen 37 alpha."

"AD ops command center copies, bringing up 37 alpha. Stand
by." Each of the counsels flickered, showing a digitized map of north-
eastern Russia. Bryson looked down at the screen. On each side of the
map were several rectangular boxes for the command level "votes." A
red bogey symbol designated ACUN1 appeared in the center of the
screen, trailed by an eight-inch red line showing the "trajectory" of the
craft from initial IR observation to the craft's present location. The
basic information on the bogey appeared at the lower right of the red-
symbol.

"Air defense center," the mission director stated matter-of-factly, "I show probable air-breathing bogey at level flight, altitude nine-
three-zero, speed two-one-zero-zero knots, bearing zero-nine-five,
leaving Russian air space at 2133 Zulu, flight trajectory US airspace
entering ADIZ 2200 Zulu at Alpha Charlie Three. Event designated
Air Event 93-73. Initial assessment UI, repeat, under investigation."

"Air defense center concurs."

Admiral Bryson sat back in his chair while at the same time
reaching over to flip on his command control mic button. "This is the
command director. Event 93-73 is noted. Air defense do you have a
probable assessment?"

"Yes, sir. Craft has heat signature similar to a SR-71 Blackbird.
However, we have negative military mission, negative civil flight plan."

"Intel," Bryson stated, "any info on this event?"

"Negative, sir. Intel checking ACC, NASA, and special ops
groups at this time."

"Roger," Bryson responded. "Advise me upon further data."
Bryson turned to the left and looked at his mission director. "I'd like
dual phenomenology from Alaskan regional ops."

The mission director picked up the phone on his counsel and pressed three buttons. "Alaskan NORAD this is command center. Have you been following Screen 37 alpha? Very good. We need dual phenom as soon as possible." The mission director paused for a moment. "Roger, you are authorized to enter event communications directly. Please advise the command director directly upon review of dual check. Mission director out." The director hung up the phone and looked over to Bryson. "Alaskan regional ops on board. Will supervise and confirm dual check."

"Very good," Bryson responded, continuing to look down at the counsel screen. "Now we wait."

Inside the one-hundred-million-year-old-mountain sits fifteen steel buildings upon thirteen hundred steel-formed springs ready to cushion the blow of a direct or near-direct detonation of a nuclear bomb. Beginning the excavation in May of 1961, it took a year and one million pounds of explosives to extract the 693,000 tons of granite. Surrounded by three miles of tunnels, the three main chambers, separated by rock pillars designed to provide support and strength, contain a total of fifteen buildings. The only entrance to the complex is by two thirty-ton blast doors fifty feet apart. This windowless city consists of 4.5 acres and two hundred thousand square feet of floor space. As you walk through the cavern you can look up and see hundreds of the some 110,000 bolts lodged six to thirty-two feet into the granite rock above. The bolts provide support that prevent the rock from crumbling, but also "fool" the mountain into believing that the rock removed so many years ago is still there.

"Intel, what's your assessment so far?" Bryson asked.

"Definite air-breathing, similar speed and IR signature of SR-71 at maximum prolonged cruising altitude and speed. Probable SR on black mission. No knowledge of mission over this air space. NASA provides negative knowledge; special mission groups provide negative knowledge. J-2 referred us to Air Combat Command. ACC has not yet responded to inquiry."

"What's your general assessment, Intel?"

"Unknown Air Force mission, unknown Russian craft testing our sensor ability, hostile Russian craft, or anomaly."

"Roger, Intel. Communications, get me ACC intel."

"Yes, sir." A few seconds passed. "Sir, we have ACC intel on 301 secure line, Major Davis."

"Major Davis, this is Rear Admiral Bryson, NORAD command director at Cheyenne Mountain. We're monitoring an unidentified aircraft entering our air defense identification zone from Russian air space into Alaskan airspace that has a signature similar to one of our SR-71s. Do you have any knowledge of an Air Force mission that would explain what we are seeing."

There was a long pause. "Sir, I am sorry, sir, but I am not authorized to discuss such a mission, if it exists."

"Major, is your commanding officer available?"

"No, sir. He's left for the day. I'm it, sir."

Bryson thought quickly about how to get what he needed immediately. Occasionally in his career Bryson had had to "teach" a young officer the reality of judgment, to explain, sometimes by sheer force of will, that rules sometimes must be "bent" to their ultimate purpose, that there are occasions when the purpose of a rule is thwarted by application of that same rule in unique situations. He decided to start with the firm but friendly approach.

"Major, I hereby authorize you to discuss any information that you may have. If you have none, tell me now so I can quit wasting my time talking with you. If you have the information I need, I order you to tell me now or justify your refusal to do so."

"Sir, I do have information. I cannot relay it to you because it's need-to-know and compartmentalized."

So much for reason and friendliness, Bryson thought.

"Major, I am declaring need-to-know. I have an unidentified aircraft approaching our air space at over Mach three. I am about ten seconds from declaring a potential hostile event and calling up the battle staff network, which will include the national command authority. That means, son, that I'm about to call the president, the SEC DEF, and the chairman of the joint chiefs of staff. We have done so only twice before: once during the Cuban Missile Crisis in 1962 and once during the Yom Kipper War in 1973. I believe that satisfies any need-to-know requirements, wouldn't you, Major?"

"Yes, sir," the subdued and now shaky voice crackled over the speaker. "I still have the problem of clearance, sir."

"Major, my clearance is higher than any you have, and probably higher than you will ever get at this rate. Everyone on this line has sufficient clearance and will be appropriately compartmentalized later. I understand your orders and am countermanding them. Do you understand?"

"Yes, sir. One moment, please."

Bryson looked over at his mission director. "I bet that kid saw his career pass before his eyes about three times."

The speaker once again came back to life. "Sir, I have the file. Three days ago an SR-71 from NASA, tail number Eight Four Four, entered Russian airspace from the south and landed at Chara southwestern airport to pick up bio-package. Aircraft and pilot presumed captured. Foreign office has received no information regarding same, and has not inquired. At 1000 Zulu today radio sensors noted substantial Russian interceptor activity south of Chara, with negative engagement. At 1110 Zulu Russian radar picked up a single craft heading generally east northeast at sixty thousand feet and climbing, speed over twenty-one hundred. A single MiG-31 was ordered to intercept and destroy it. Based on what we heard from the radio traffic, we assumed it had been destroyed. Apparently not. That's a summary of the information I have at this time, sir."

"Very well, Major. I want you to stay on line and visit with my intel people and tell them everything else you know. Command director out; J-2 pick up 301 and keep me advised of anything else I need to know."

"Yes, sir," replied the intelligence director as he picked up the phone.

"Well," Bryson stated out loud, "at least we know it's one of our planes. Now all we have to do is figure out who's flying it, and his intentions." Bryson reached down and pressed another button. "Alaskan regional, are you still on line."

"Yes, sir."

"I take it you don't have any IFF responder."

"Yes, sir. That's affirmative."

"Have you tried radio contact?"

"No, sir. Since it had a probable Blackbird signature, rules of contact prohibit any attempt at radio contact until bogey is in our air space."

"How much longer before it enters our air space?"

"Ten minutes, sir."

"Alaska, I waive rules of contact. Attempt radio contact at this time."

"Yes, sir. Alaska acknowledges permission to contact. Comm officer doing so at this time."

Bryson tapped his fingers on the desk as the screen showed the bogey within an inch of the US air space line. "Alaska, did you already flush the birds?"

"Yes, sir, as soon as it crossed the ADIZ."

"Air defense, put our birds on the screen." Two green aircraft symbols immediately appeared on the screen. "Alaska," Bryson continued, "I assume there's no way the Eagles can get a visual ID."

"That's correct, sir. They'll top out at fifty-five thousand and have an eight hundred knot airspeed delta."

"Any luck with radio contact?"

"No, sir. We've tried discreet SR specific bands, Air Force regular bands, and emergency military and civilian bands, in that order. Contact negative."

"Air defense, what do we have for bearing intersect, military installations or assets?"

"Sir, we show constant bearing since initial contact, intersect over Minot Air Force Base."

"Sir, Intel here. Langley advised us that the pilot is stationed out of Minot. If his radio support is out, he could have simply plugged in the navigation code for Minot."

"Well, at least one thing is making sense. Odds are the pilot is one of ours with his communication out. Alaska, what's the intercept status?"

"Two birds flushed. No visual possible. Twelve to fifteen delta. Fifty-fifty chance of IR hit."

"Understood. Bring back the birds. We'll try for a Canadian visual ID."

"Alaska, out."

Bryson's job was clear: Determine if this is a hostile act. But he needed more information. An SR-71 could easily contain a nuclear weapon. If it was allowed in, it could conceivably take out Minot and

Grand Forks in less than twenty minutes. Or it could start with Grand Forks, hit Minot, Malmstrom, then F. E. Warren. Bryson made his decision.

"This is the command director. If we do not have demonstrative evidence of friendly intentions three hundred miles out of Minot or any other STRATCOM base, we splash the bogey. Final authority to splash is left to me. Air Defense confirm this order and flush the birds. Command director clear."

Bryson listened as air defense acknowledged his orders and ordered the fighters to intercept the SR-71. He hated the idea of killing one of his own pilots and destroying an American plane, but he didn't believe he had any other choice.

# CHAPTER 67

## Above Northwest Canada

Phinney "bumped" the map screen and the threat screen for what had to be the two hundredth time, hoping that somehow the two screens would re-activate, but once again it was to no avail. Damn! he thought to himself. At least the plane kept flying! Who knows how much damage was done by the near-miss of the AA-9 "Amos" missile. At the very least it severed something electrical below the cockpit because as soon as he felt the impact from the missile both screens went pitch-black. Luckily the old 1960s style gauges couldn't be affected by a power outage, and even more luckily the engines continued to run perfectly and the gauges gave no indication of a fuel leak. Phinney therefore surmised that only a fragment or two had hit the plane, and apparently the hits had occurred along the plane's forward compartment that housed the radar dome and the front-cockpit electronics and communications suite.

Looking out of the plane at the land mass below, Phinney knew he had to be somewhere over Canada. But with communications out, there was no way to request a refueling or even attempt to land at a major airport. At least the maintain-heading aspect of the navigation system was still operational! As soon as the screens went dead Phinney intentionally veered the plane slightly to the right and then re-entered the coordinates for Minot Air Force Base to see what the plane would do, and it immediately veered slightly to the left and maintained the previous heading. In addition, Phinney was still able to determine his cruising altitude via the old-style altimeter positioned just below the elapsed time clock near the top, and slightly to the left, of the mid-point of the center instrument panel.

Now the problem was how to tell when to slow down for the descent into Minot. If he did nothing he would simply overfly the base and, somewhere over the mid-west, run out of fuel. Not a pretty thought, Phinney realized, especially at a cruising altitude of eighty-five thousand feet. Phinney had decided somewhere over the Arctic that since he was no longer in danger from Russian interceptors his best bet was to lower the plane down to its optimum cruising altitude in order to preserve as much fuel as possible. He had watched during the last hour or so with increasing trepidation as the fuel gauges on the left side panel showed less and less fuel available for the descent and landing.

The biggest problem now was determining when to begin the descent. After passing over the eastern edge of the Rocky Mountains, the mid-portion of Canada looks pretty much all the same when travelling at eighty-five thousand feet. Finally Phinney came up with an idea; and although it took him about twenty minutes to dislodge the survival pack sitting underneath him and carefully pull out all its contents one-by-one past the control stick without touching it, he finally came across the two items he was looking for: the global positioning device and the short-range survival walkie-talkie.

Phinney pressed the GPS device once every two minutes or so, waiting for it to show 50 degrees north latitude. Phinney of course realized that the Canadian-American border stretched across the 49th parallel, and that Minot Air Force Base was a mere forty miles south of that parallel. He therefore reasoned that all he had to do was begin slowing down and descending around the 50th parallel and level out at about ten thousand feet until he saw the base in front of him!

Piece of cake, he thought to himself. Phinney was definitely in his element. Any pilot who doesn't think he can fly to hell and back and send a postcard while he's there shouldn't be flying, at least not for the Air Force.

Finally the hand-held GPS showed that the plane had crossed the 50th parallel, so Phinney pulled back on the throttle with his left hand and angled the plane slightly downward with his right hand by adjusting the pitch control on his right panel. The plane eased out of Mach 3 and progressed downward at two thousand feet per minute. Phinney alternated looking out the left and then the right window of the cockpit waiting to see a glimpse of Lake Darling as he approached, he hoped, Minot Air Force base from the northwest.

# CHAPTER 68

## 119th Fighter Wing, North Dakota National Guard, Hector Field, Fargo, North Dakota

It was Saturday, the Happy Hooligans' busiest day. Colonel Mike Garland had just taxied his fully-fueled F-16 in front of the command center after an hour jaunt down to Sioux Falls and back. He figured he only had three weeks left as the commander before it was "the next guy's" turn, the phrase he kept using instead of his replacement's real name. To him he was just that: the next guy, the s.o.b. who got the best job in the world until his own "next guy" came along.

Oh well, Garland thought. It was a fun three years! And it sure went fast.

The commander's brick crackled. "Voodoo One, this is control."

"Go ahead, control. This is Voodoo One."

"Sir, we have incoming message from NORAD giving us a scramble, intercept bogey northwest of Minot. Message is not a drill, sir."

Holy shit! Garland thought to himself as he ran back toward his personal plane, number 82-926. "Roger that, control. Scramble everyone we have. And have the loaders meet me at the ramp. The gas passers have already turned me and I can be in the air as soon as they can get me loaded!"

"Yes, sir. We copy. Loaders have already loaded up the trailers at the igloo and are already on their way to the ramp! They'll be there by the time you get there."

By this time Garland was already strapped in and ready to go. An airman came over and grabbed the ladder off the left side of the cockpit as Garland began genning up his single Pratt & Whitney F100-PW-220E afterburning turbofan engine. Within seconds he was taxiing past the hangars across from the command post and headed westerly toward the force generation area of the ramp.

Garland watched as his men and one woman munitions handlers (nicknamed "twixels" by Garland because of their AFSC job designation of 2W1X1) carefully but quickly pulled a MHU-141 weapons trailer over to one side of the plane. While the twixels were working on one side of the plane, another team of munition handlers watched as a team member (nick-named a "twoxel" by Garland because of the person's AFSC code, 2W0X1) drove the MJ-1 lift truck, affectionately known as "the jammer," to the other side of the plane and positioned a Hughes AIM-120A advanced medium-range air-to-air missile (AMRAAM) on the station 3 pylon.

After seeing the AMRAAM safely connected to the center pylon of one wing, Garland looked over to the other side as the three weapons loaders placed a Raytheon AIM-9M-9 Sidewinder infra-red missile on their shoulders and carried the missile over to the wing-tip launch rail fitting, and after connecting it to the tip of the wing went back to the trailer and carried another Sidewinder over to the next inward launch position, the outer-pylon missile rail.

After two Sidewinders had been loaded on one side and the AMRAAM on the other, the two teams then quickly switched sides and performed the same ballet, thereby placing a total of six air-to-air missiles on the commander's plane in less than ten minutes. The team chief waited for the jammer to get clear of the plane and then gave Colonel Garland the thumbs-up for taxiing away from the ramp and towards Three Five active, which had already been cleared of all incoming and out-going traffic. Two munitions specialists armed the missiles at the end of the runway, and gave Garland a thumbs-up.

As soon as Garland took off he angled his plane northwesterly toward Minot, first climbing as fast as he could to a little over thirty-five thousand feet in approximately eight minutes, leveling off, and then dipping the nose of the plane down slightly as he accelerated towards Minot Air Force Base. Garland reviewed his instruments to ensure he was at the proper altitude for the direction he was traveling. A quick glance showed him at thirty-five thousand feet heading north-northwest.

Garland next activated his microphone. "Bigfoot," he said into his mic to the Western Air Defense Sector located at McChord Air Force Base ten miles south of Tacoma, Washington, "this is Voodoo One bearing three one five, angels thirty five, request intercept and instructions." Garland had contacted "Bigfoot" by using his Bendix/King AN/ARC-200 high frequency (HF) single-side band radio, proud of the fact that the Air Defense Fighter version of the F-16 was one of the few planes in the air force equipped with this premiere system.

"Roger, Voodoo One. We show your location. Are you able to use Have Quick?" the controller asked, referring to the special high frequency communication mode that allows secure communication between an air defense controller and the F-16.

"Negative, Bigfoot," Garland replied, "there wasn't enough time to coordinate the timing set up." One of the realities of using Have Quick was the fact that the controller and the pilot had to be synchronized perfectly by each radio being set to the exact time—or at least with a few millionths of a second—for the system to work; however, once synchronized, the system was absolutely secure since the only way to get into the loop would be for both systems to be set up at the same precise time.

"Roger, Voodoo One. We understand. Go to Uniform secure voice, and we'll patch you through to Cheyenne Mountain. Do you copy, Voodoo One."

"Roger that, Bigfoot. Switching to UHF secure voice. Awaiting patch in."

Travelling just below Mach 2, Garland had travelled the 270 miles to the east side of Minot Air Force Base in the few minutes he took setting up the proper radio contact. By the time he passed Minot Air Force Base he had positive radar contact with the bogey thanks to his Westinghouse AN/APG-66(V)1 digital pulse-Doppler radar.

Garland's radio crackled slightly as he heard Cheyenne Mountain come on board. "Voodoo One, this is Cheyenne Mountain. Do you copy?"

"Cheyenne Mountain, this is Voodoo One. I copy."

"Do you have acquisition of the bogey, Voodoo One?"

"Affirmative, I have radar contact with the bogey. It's bearing One Three Zero, fifty-five miles northwest of Minot Air Force Base, descending to Two Zero Zero. Request instructions."

"Voodoo One, Cheyenne Mountain. ID bogey and splash if any hostile action taken. Repeat, authorized to splash bogey if any hostile action taken."

"Roger that, Cheyenne Mountain. Voodoo One confirms authorization to splash if hostile actions taken. Voodoo One out."

Garland allowed the bogey to pass by him on his port side, carefully watching his radar screen to see if the bogey attempted to put a radar lock on him as he flew by. As soon as his plane was directly along-side the bogey, Garland turned hard left 180 degrees—pulling 7 g's in the process—and eased up behind the plane.

"Cheyenne Mountain, Voodoo One. Bogey is an SR-71 Blackbird. Some damage to underside. IFF not operative. Appears to be attempting to enter the landing pattern. Negative hostile action, repeat, negative hostile action. Tail number Eight Four Four, NASA."

"Roger, Voodoo One. You are authorized to attempt visual communications with bogey."

"Roger that, Cheyenne. I'm pulling up next to it. He sees me. Signalling radio out. He's got his SAR radio out. I'm changing frequency to guard. Be right back."

Garland turned a knob on his radio console so he could pick up the military aviation emergency frequency 243.0000 MHz, commonly referred to as "guard" and immediately heard the other pilot's voice.

"NASA Eight Four Four declaring an emergency. Request immediate clearance for landing Runway Two Niner. Do you copy?"

"Roger that, Eight Four Four. What is the nature of your emergency?"

"I have been hit on egress by air-to-air missile. Electronics out. Will need verification of front landing gear down and locked during approach. Do you copy?"

"Roger Eight Four Four, I copy. Stand by."

Garland turned his radio control knob back to his intercept ultra high frequency mode and relayed the information to Cheyenne Mountain. There was a thirty or forty-second pause.

What the hell's taking so long, Garland thought to himself. It shouldn't take this long to tell him what to do. Either it's a bogey or it isn't. "Cheyenne Mountain, this is Voodoo One. Request instructions."

"Voodoo One, Stand by." There was another long pause, then finally Garland heard Cheyenne Mountain come back up.

"Voodoo One, advise the bogey that he is authorized to land and then taxi directly to Dock Seven. Also advise the bogey to be very careful not to veer off course during landing. Understood, Voodoo One?"

"Understood," Garland replied as he evaluated the peculiar fact that the controller had continued to refer to the Blackbird as a "bogey," thereby signalling Garland that the plane was to be presumed an enemy plane with hostile intentions. Garland thought about this for just a moment, and then switched back to the search and rescue frequency and relayed the landing and taxiing information to Blackbird pilot. Garland pulled back and to the upper right of the bogey, and then armed and locked one of his four heat-seeking Sidewinders on the Blackbird. His orders from Cheyenne Mountain were clear. If the Blackbird started to veer even the slightest toward the weapons storage facility on the north side of the runway, he was to shoot it down without a moment's hesitation.

# CHAPTER 69

## Above Minot Air Force Base

Phinney angled the Blackbird to the east side of the base, entering the normal landing pattern as he considered what the F-16 pilot had told him: "Do not veer to the north of the landing strip whatsoever. Do you understand?"

When the F-16 pulled up beside him Phinney had recognized the tell-tale marking of the type of F-16 that had intercepted him. The fighter had special IFF antennas in front of the canopy and below the air intake; the fin, known to non-flyers as the tail, had a horizontal bulging about one foot above the fuselage; and, no doubt, the fighter had a special lamp positioned on the port side below and in front of the cockpit for identification of potentially hostile planes in the night, but the plane had pulled up along Phinney's own port side and he did not actually see the Grimes-built night identification light. Only one type of F-16 had these features, and that was the F-16A/B Block 15 Air Defense Fighter, one of the premier fighter interceptors in the nation.

Phinney noticed two other things about the plane when it pulled up along side him. First, he of course noticed the AIM-9 Sidewinders and the two AIM-120 AMRAAM missiles; however, he also noticed that each missile had a yellow band a little past the center point and a brown band just aft of the center point, signifying to anyone familiar with air-to-air weapons that the missiles were not inert—they were live rounds.

The second thing Phinney noticed about the plane was that it was from Fargo and was the commander's plane. He could tell it was from the Fargo North Dakota Air National Guard because unlike almost all other interceptor planes (and for that matter all US military planes), the tail of the planes from the 119th did not have the usual two-letter tail marking designation showing its base of origin, and instead had the "Happy Hooligans" moniker written on the top of the tail fin. Phinney also knew, having flown against the Happy Hooligans years ago at William Tell competitions, that the commander's plane was the only one that carried a portrait of Theodore Roosevelt—sporting his Roughrider hat and bandana around his neck—on the fuselage immediately behind the cockpit and on one of the fins of the Sidewinder missiles carried on the wingtip of each wing.

The fact that the wingtip Sidewinders carried by the commander did not have Teddy Roosevelt's portrait was just one more indication that the pilot who was now flying somewhere close behind him meant business and probably already had a radar lock on him as he turned southward preparing for one more turn to the right to line up for his final straight-in approach. More than that, the commander had probably spent a tour or two in the later years of Vietnam. He knew how to shoot someone down, and he wouldn't hesitate one second to do so if he had to, Phinney realized.

"Do not veer to the north of the landing strip whatsoever," the F-16 pilot had instructed him, and had asked him if he understood. Of course he understood. The weapons storage facility was on the north side of the runway. Phinney knew exactly what was inside the weapons storage facility. Platforms at Minot, both the B-52H models and the Minuteman IIIs, all carry nuclear weapons. There was no way they were going to let a plane crash into the weapons storage area, period.

Phinney replayed those words in his mind as he watched the F-16 ease back behind him in a standard firing position. Phinney knew that standard procedure for assisting a plane in distress would be to fly alongside the injured plane and provide radio feed back, both pilots always staying in the line of vision of each other. That wasn't what was happening here, Phinney realized.

As Phinney made his final turn for the approach he noted that there were no emergency vehicles along the runway. What the hell was going on? he thought to himself. He had declared an emergency! There should be fire trucks. Lots of them!

Phinney pressed the button on his portable search and rescue radio. "Voodoo One, this is Eight Four Four. I don't see any support vehicles. What the hell is going on?"

"Listen, son. There won't be any support vehicles. You're listed as a bogey, understand? You will be considered a bogey until you have landed, taxied to Dock 7, and have shut everything down. Do you understand?"

"Yes, sir," Phinney replied no longer confused. "I understand." They think I'm an enemy plane, Phinney said out loud to himself. And if the front landing gear is screwed up, Phinney thought to himself, I'm a dead man.

# CHAPTER 70

## 67th Information Operations Wing, Kelly AFB, Texas

The senior controller sat at his desk monitoring this afternoon's numbers of calls received. Probably the most sophisticated internet ever developed, the 67th Information Operations Wing provides the Air Force and all other branches of the service immediate information on just about anything they may need to know, all at a top secret or higher level. Now aligned under the Eighth Air Force as an Air Combat Command subordinate unit, the former members of the Air Intelligence Agency continued to rightfully consider themselves as being the most sophisticated research librarians known to man. A military person can get online at any of the hundreds of SCIFs (Secured Compartmentalized Information Facility) in the country, demonstrate his or her need-to-know, and be provided anything from the proper counterfrequency to defeat an Iraqi Russian-made surface-to-air missile, to finding out every bit of information the military has on any of the ten thousand and more "targets" inventoried and provide a single-number reference. On-site commanders and planners can literally plan their entire campaign on their SCIF computer, determine every target that needs to be hit and what amount of firepower is necessary to obtain effective destruction of the site, input the assets available, and then press a button and about two minutes later the computer will provide the on-site planner a detailed task-listing for each asset, with specific reference to the best weapon to use, the time of take-off, time in transit (with refueling route and details, if necessary), the best route, the best alternative route, the time of weapons release, and the scheduled time for return to base. Planning a war has never been easier, the controller knew.

As the staff sergeant was looking at the numbers for the day for his final report, his phone light blinked up at him. "Senior controller," he answered. "Yes. Yes. That's fine, put him through to me and I'll see what I can do."

The senior controller put the phone down and turned to his assistant, a navy lieutenant on loan to learn how the Air Force information operations system worked. "Listen to this," the senior controller said to the lieutenant as he put the caller on speaker.

"This is the senior controller, sir. How can I help you?"

"Son, this is the captain of the USS Charlotte, Los Angeles-class submarine. We've been playing cat-and-mouse with a Russian AKULA sub for about three days until a few hours ago it went topside and headed for San Diego at top speed. I've talked to San Diego and the land-lubbers tell me that the Ruskie is sending some sort of signal as fast and with as much power as it can, sending it over and over. It's been doing it for a good hour or so. Anyway, we had our people try to figure out what type of signal it is, and they tell me that it's one of ours! Apparently it's a signal that you Air Force guys use sometimes as a quick-fix self-destruct signal. And you're not gonna believe this, but the assholes not only are using our own signal, but they are even using one of our own crypto formats! Does that make any sense to you?"

"One second, sir. Intel!" he yelled across the room. A nerdish fellow lifted his head up from a console and stood up part-ways. "We got anything going on right now relating to a self-destruct mechanism on one of our own planes somewhere over the United States?" With one look at the young man's face he knew that something was happening and happening now! Within minutes the senior controller had Cheyenne Mountain on the line.

# CHAPTER 71

## Minot Air Force Base, North Dakota

Colonel Linhard stood out on Bomber Boulevard next to his staff car between the former alert facility attached to the runway and the weapons storage area (WSA). It was a little chilly and windy, but nothing unusual for Minot.

"Bravo," the wing commander spoke into his brick to his vice commander, "this is Alpha. What's your location?"

"Alpha, this is Bravo. I'm at Dock 7, sir."

"How's it going over there?"

"Almost ready, sir."

"Good. Alpha out."

"Alpha, this is command center. We have a priority one from Cheyenne."

"Command center this is Alpha, patch it through."

"You're on, sir."

"Cheyenne Mountain, this is Colonel Linhard. Go ahead."

"Colonel, we just got word that the Blackbird has a self-destruct device installed in it and that a Russian sub is trying to activate it from the Pacific Ocean. Apparently they think it's going to land at Edwards. Out."

"Shit!" Linhard said out loud, but not into the brick. And if the signal reaches here, he thought to himself, I've got a Class One accident on my hands and a runway full of what's left of that Blackbird!

"Cheyenne, do you have the frequency of the signal, over?"

"That's affirmative, over."

"Command center, you still on line?"

"Yes, sir."

"Who we got over there shoved out of the pattern, towards the northwest?" Linhard asked as he looked up at the lumbering B-52H about four miles out, wondering who the aircraft commander is who is in charge of the plane.

"Balls Two Three, sir."

"Patch him in to this line, will ya'."

"Yes, sir! Done, sir."

"Balls Two Three, this is Alpha. Who's the AC up there?"

"Alpha, this is Baron. I'm AC and at the controls."

"Good. We got Cheyenne Mountain on line. We need you guys to block a signal coming from somewhere around San Diego or LA and make sure it doesn't get through to the bird on approach to landing. Can you get your EWO on line, Doug?"

There was a very slight pause. "He's on, sir."

"Cheyenne, tell my EWO the location of the signal, the strength, the frequency and if you got it the matrix being used." That triple-E degree paid off after all, Linhard realized. Someone at Cheyenne Mountain relayed all the necessary information to the electronic warfare officer.

"Balls Two Three, this is Alpha. You got all that?"

"Yes, sir," the lieutenant colonel answered, "we got it."

"OK, keep it up until I tell you otherwise. Control tower, this is Alpha. You've been following this?"

"Alpha, this is control tower, yes, sir, we have."

"Direct Balls Two Three between the bogey coming in and southern California. Can you handle that?"

"Yes, sir. We got it."

I guess we'll find out how good the new system is, Linhard thought to himself, referring to the Northrop Grumman system upgrade for the B-52's AN/ALQ-55 countermeasures system which supposedly is able to deliver five times the jamming power of the old one.

"Colonel Linhard, this is Cheyenne Mountain. Intel advises us that it is possible that even if the bird is being flown by one of ours, it was under the control of others before takeoff. Do you understand, sir?"

"Cheyenne, this is Alpha. I understand. We already went to threatcon Alpha twenty minutes ago. The base is secure. Necessary precautions have been taken."

"We appreciate your pre-planning, Alpha. We'll leave you alone now. Cheyenne out, but remaining on line."

"Roger that, Cheyenne. We'll keep you patched in and up to speed. Alpha out."

Linhard looked up to the southeast as the Blackbird lined up for its landing.

★      ★      ★      ★

Colonel Mike Garland watched the landing gear go down on the Blackbird, and then pressed his mic down. "NASA Eight Four Four, this is Voodoo One. Your wheels are down and appear locked."

"Thank you, Voodoo One."

Colonel Garland went back to his position a half-mile behind and to the right of the Blackbird, his thumb ready to press down on the red fire button if the plane moved even the slightest bit toward the WSA. Garland alternated between looking at the angle of the plane and then looking at the position of the WSA. As he approached the runway he noticed something that really scared him: Three Martin-Marietta Blazer Heavies, a two-person light-armored vehicle that combined the Blazer turret system with a Bradley chassis. Equipped with a forward-looking infra-red (FLIR) television tracking system and a laser range-finder, these U.S. marine air-defense vehicles could use not only their 25 mm, five-barrel GAU-12 Gatling cannon to tear a plane to shreds from as far as two kilometers away, it was also equipped with eight Stinger missiles, each one of which has fire-and-forget capabilities.

One of the Bradley vehicles had been placed inside the WSA perimeter, another next to what looked like a blue command vehicle on the road normally used for the south entrance of the base, and a third vehicle stationed at the east edge of the former alert facility. Garland had no idea that the Air Force had acquired any of these potent vehicles, nonetheless providing a base *three* of them. Garland now hoped even more that the pilot did not veer to the right even the slightest, for if he did the Bradley vehicles would probably take both planes out, whether they meant to or not!

Garland watched as the Blackbird passed by the WSA and came down on the runway perfectly. The plane continued gliding nose-up for a few more hundred feet until the nose came gently down. The pilot either didn't have a chute to deploy, or he had decided to save it for the next landing and instead used the entire twelve thousand foot runway. Garland eventually veered away to the south as the Blackbird reached the end of the runway and began taxiing toward the huge hangar closest to that end of the runway.

"Cheyenne Mountain and Bigfoot, this is Voodoo One. The bogey has landed without incident. Voodoo One heading back to base if that's OK."

"Affirmative, Voodoo One," the Bigfoot controller replied. "Thanks for the assistance. Your mission is RTB." Return to base. "Contact Minneapolis center."

"Roger, Bigfoot, switching Minneapolis center," Garland replied as he angled his plane southeast back to Fargo.

# CHAPTER 72

## Minot Air Force Base

Colonel Linhard sped through the former alert facility in his staff car and onto the three-mile taxiway that paralleled the main runway, approaching one hundred miles-an-hour, his red police lights activated. He already knew that by declaring a Threatcon Alpha the taxiway would be cleared of all planes and people. He did not begin to slow down until he got past the eighteen or so B-52s parked on the ramp to his right, and then only enough so he could negotiate the turn onto the taxiway that led to Dock 7. He pulled up to the west side of the hangar just as the huge hangar doors on the opposite side were being closed. The hangar was thoroughly surrounded by security guards carrying M-16s and wearing camouflage uniforms. The security guard at the southwest door opened the door for his commander, and Linhard ran into the hangar as fast as he could.

Running up to the front cockpit, Linhard observed that the plane itself was also surrounded by guards aiming their M-16s at the two cockpit doors as they both opened upwards.

"Phinney!" Linhard yelled up to the front cockpit.

"Yes, sir!" he yelled back.

"The Russians are trying to set off the self-destruct from off-station! Do you know how to deactivate it?"

"Yes, sir," Phinney replied as he pulled himself out of the cockpit and slid off and down the side of the plane not even waiting for a ladder. Linhard did his best to catch him, but all he ended up doing was breaking his fall, both of them ending up sprawled on the ground. Phinney jumped up and went toward the back of the plane and reached up along the left landing gear assemblage. In a few seconds he stuck his head back out and began walking away back towards Linhard.

"It's disconnected, sir," Phinney said simply.

"Cheyenne Mountain, this is Alpha. The self-destruct has been deactivated. Repeat, everything is secure."

"Roger that, Alpha. Good work!"

"Thank you, sir. Balls Two Three you can wrap it up. Come on in. Sierra One, resume normal threatcon. Alpha out."

Linhard looked over at Phinney. "Sounds like you had a little fun, Jack."

"You could say that, sir."

"Did your package make it?" Linhard asked.

"I don't know," Phinney said as he looked up toward the open back cockpit. "Professor, you OK up there?"

"Yeah, no problem," Tsinev replied. "I just thought it best to keep my head down until you told your boys here that I wasn't this week's target practice."

"Is he OK?" Linhard asked, wanting to know whether it was safe to tell the guards to let up.

"Who knows?" Phinney answered honestly. "I guess so."

"Let's get a platform ladder over here," Linhard ordered. Two of the guards wheeled one over to the plane, and then resumed keeping their weapons aimed at the Russian man as he climbed out of the plane.

"Not exactly the Statue-of-Liberty welcome I had thought I'd get!" he muttered as he set his feet down on the ladder and began using the handrail to walk down to the cement floor. "I don't suppose you have a slip of paper, Colonel, and maybe a pen or pencil. It occurs to me that a diagram of the site may help out our friends if they decide a full frontal attack. If that would be all right with you?"

Linhard looked over at Phinney, who nodded his head affirmatively.

"Sounds like a good idea to me," Phinney said thinking out loud. "But how do we get it to them? It will have to be a very secure system, and by satellite."

Linhard brought his brick up to his mouth. "Cheyenne, this is Alpha. We got a passenger here who wants to send a map back home

to our friends.  Any problem with letting me use the SCIF and sending it to 67th Information Operations Wing, and then letting them
forward it on?"

There was a slight pause, then a fairly quick response.

"No problem, Colonel, but I'd make it fast."  In other words
they are about ready to begin their assault on the facility.

"They need this map," Tsinev said forcefully.  "Without it they
don't have a chance.  I didn't think they would be ready this fast!  They
have no idea what they're walking into, and it takes only seconds for
someone to launch the whole works while they're trying to get in."

Linhard immediately led the way to his staff car, with Phinney
and Tsinev in tow.

"Cheyenne, this is Alpha.  You better tell our boys to hold off
until they get this.  Understood?"

"Understood.  We'll relay your message.  Cheyenne out."

# CHAPTER 73

## Two Kilometers North of Rakovskaja, Northern Russia
## One hour later

Broughton and Konesky approached the "farm house" accompanied by their four "military escorts." Broughton, wearing the civilian clothes he was in when he arrived (it was supposed to be a START inspection, after all!), followed Konesky up the stairs then to the side of the door. Konesky waited a moment at the door to make sure everyone was ready, and then knocked on the door. It was four in the morning.

The door opened just a crack. "Who is it?" a woman's voice asked.

"A friend of General Kalganov," Konesky said officially. "We are here for the inspection."

"We were not notified of any inspection," the woman said more firmly, no longer acting like the scared farm wife but more like an obstinate bureaucrat.

"Of course not, you fool. Otherwise it wouldn't be an inspection!"

"But we have never been inspected before," the woman said almost pleadingly.

"Yes, yes, we know that too! Why do you think we're here? Listen, old woman, General Kalganov himself ordered the inspection of this building to make sure the security was adequate. I am tired of talking and I am tired of standing out here in the cold. Now open the door and let me in so I can present you my orders, finish the inspection, and then leave this Godforsaken place and get back into my bed where I belong!"

The woman opened the door further and looked out at the single Russian military truck, deciding indeed Kalganov must have ordered an inspection. But why? Wasn't she doing exactly as he asked? She opened the door.

"Come on in, gentlemen." Konesky, Broughton, and two of their escorts began entering the house.

"You other two wait out here," Konesky barked at the two men who had stayed farthest back on the porch, their long military over-coats keeping the cold out. Konesky began pulling out several sheets of paper folded in half, fumbling through them as if he was looking for the exact right one to give to the woman. "Let's see," he said as he fumbled, "which one of these is yours?" Finally they heard the voice of whom he assumed to be the woman's husband coming from one of the back bedrooms.

"It's some sort of inspection, dear," the woman said to him.

Konesky waited for the man to enter from the bedroom. Broughton, after hearing what room the voice came from, positioned himself toward that hallway and waited. As the man walked by Broughton and his escort, the escort reached out and grabbed the man, his gloved hand covering his mouth; at the same time the other escort did the same to the old woman. Both people were quietly and quick-ly carried into an adjacent room, and then bound and gagged. While the escorts were tying up the couple Broughton went back to the front door and let in the other two guards, one Russian, the other American.

The two guards opened their heavy wool coats and raised their M-16 automatic weapons as they entered. Without saying a word Konesky lead the two men who had just come in to the door leading downstairs. Thank God they sent us the diagram, Konesky thought. All a normal full-force attack would have done was gotten everybody killed, and the missiles launched, he bet!

Konesky carefully opened the door to the basement, noting the single light bulb positioned about three-quarters the way down the stairs. He diagramed to the others the location of the light bulb. The two soldiers who had just come in pulled down their night-vision gog-gles; the other two soldiers positioned the piece of wood covered on one side with Velcro and the other side with rubber rollers on the top of the stairs. One of the men wearing night vision-goggles laid down face up on the board as the other man with night vision-goggles positioned himself low enough to take out the single light bulb below him. The other two guards lifted the man with the board on his back over to the stairs, his feet up in the air, his head resting on the board now attached firmly to his back, his M-16 resting comfortably at an angle toward his left boot.

Konesky gave the count, showing first a thumb's up, then in a cadence of one finger, two fingers, and then the third. On the third mark the soldier crouching low with the M-16 took out the light. At the same time the other two soldiers released the fourth man wearing the night vision goggles, allowing him to slide quickly but quietly down the stairs. By the time he reached the bottom of the stairs he had shot and killed both guards sitting unconcerned at a table behind and to the right of the stairs. The other guard with the night-vision goggles saw the signal that the coast was clear and entered into the basement, followed by the others.

The two guards who had tied up the man and the woman went directly over to the cipher box next to a door, carefully opening the box and then attaching to it several wires. One of the men held a small box in his hand that displayed hundreds of numbers flashing past the small screen. Finally there was a "click" and Konesky, Broughton, and the others walked into the facility.

★     ★     ★     ★

"Hey, Pavel!" one of the scientists yelled into Pavel's bedroom. "One of the nosey neighbors just called. There is military truck at the site. She says it looks like an inspection!"

Pavel jumped out of bed, threw on his clothes, and ran out to his vehicle as fast as he could, knowing all the while that there could be no "inspection" of this facility. Within minutes he was travelling along the bumpy road that he had used to take Riana to the site not so long ago.

★     ★     ★     ★

Konesky and Broughton glanced only momentarily at the ornate control room and went directly over to the launch board, both of the men holding M-16s at their sides. The guards had already secured the facility, finding no one else around.

"What's in there?" Broughton asked one of the guards after he looked inside a small cherry-wood door.

"Just a closet, sir. Nothin' in it."

Two of the guards had gone back to keep the house secure, and the other two continued looking around at the ornate room.

"Sir," one of the guards said, "I think I found the switch for the curtains."

"Fine," Broughton said, "go ahead."

The guard flipped a switch on the center chair and the curtains slowly opened, showing the row upon row of missiles. "I'd say we found the right place," Broughton said softly, almost in awe of the number of missiles and warheads in front of him.

"My God," Konesky said to Broughton as he put the stock of his M-16 on the ground and used the barrel to lean down and study the controls. "These missiles are all on firing mode. There are no safeties, and no two-man rule. Apparently all that has to be done is push this switch over here and they all go up!"

Broughton looked over at the button built into the console, covered only by a plastic or glass covering that just had to be lifted up.

Broughton came over to the console and tried to help Konesky figure out how to deactivate the system. As he did so he heard a voice behind him coming from the direction of the closet that the guard had just checked a few minutes ago: "And you can all go to hell!"

Pavel Kerlov rushed from his secret entrance toward the launch console.

Konesky turned to his right and pushed Broughton backward out of the way. As Broughton stumbled backwards he saw a young Russian man leaping toward the activation button, his right hand lifting the glass case up and then coming down hard with the palm of his hand toward the activation switch. Konesky had already acted, the butt of his rifle coming up as fast and as forcefully as he could manage. The stock hit the man's arm with enough force to send his arm flying upward, bones cracking in the process. As the man tried to reach over with his other hand Broughton fired, aiming at the man's midsection. In a fraction of a second the M-16 emptied a short burst of five slugs into the man, "drawing" a perfectly straight red line from his belt line on his left side to top of his right shoulder. The man gave Broughton a dumb-founded look, and then collapsed face-first onto the floor. Broughton walked over to the man he had just killed and turned him over so they could see who he was.

"Kerlov?" he asked Konesky.

"Kerlov," Konesky answered.

*Lynn M. Boughey*

# CHAPTER 74

**Director's Conference Room,
Defense Threat Reduction Agency
Dulles International Airport**

**Three weeks later**

The three men looked uncomfortable to Lieutenant Commander Ike Watson, public affairs officer for the newly formed Defense Threat Reduction Agency (DTRA), pronounced as "Ditra." On three different occasions he had told the men to feel free to eat any of the lovely pastries sitting on the conference table or help themselves to the coffee contained in the silver serving set. But the men knew instinctively that the food and setting was not for them but for the higher-ups who were coming over here after the formal ceremony, so they sat uncomfortably in the otherwise comfortable blue conference chairs and watched on the large screen on the south wall of the conference room the preparations being made for the official signing ceremony taking place at the German-owned hangar some five hundred yards away, just across the street. Officially know as "The German Armed Forces Command, United States and Canada" which serves as the focal point for all military sales and training of German military in the United States or Canada, the hangar is more informally known as the "GMR" hangar, which stands for the German Military Representative hangar.

"Are you sure you gentlemen wouldn't like something to eat, or some coffee?" Ike Watson asked now for the fourth time.

"No thanks," Broughton replied.

"Thank you very much," Konesky said, following Broughton's lead, "but I'm doing fine also." When in Rome . . . , he thought to himself. The two men continued sitting next to each other quietly, occasionally watching the screen to see if the program had begun.

"How about you, sir?" Ike asked the other man sitting on the other side of the room by himself, who seemed even more nervous to Commander Watson than the other two.

He too followed the other gentlemen's lead. "No thank you," Phinney replied. "I'm fine."

Ike noted that Phinney seemed almost in pain that he was wearing his Class As or service dress instead of a flight suit. This is obviously a man who would just like to be left alone to fly his big ol' lumbering bomber and go back to his former life of quiet anonymity. Ike shrugged his shoulders and went back to the director's waiting room.

"How are our guys doing?" Allison Markham asked.

"Nervous," Ike replied.

"Who'd blame them? I'd be nervous too if all I had been told is the secretary of state and the Russian foreign minister wanted to give me their thanks."

Ike looked down at his watch for probably the three hundredth time so far this morning. "Two minutes to go," he said. So they waited, and relaxed. Watson had worked this assignment for two years, and thoroughly loved it. A conglomeration of what used to be several disparate organizations, the Defense Threat Reduction Agency now handled everything from scientific research for the identification and prevention of the use of chemical or biological weapons, to preventing the proliferation of nuclear weapons. But that is just about all the public knew about "Ditra." The agency attempted, at least in theory, to bring together all of the people dealing with all aspects of weapons of mass destruction into one agency. Some of the people are linguists, others nuclear scientists, and others treaty inspectors. The public normally would only hear of the On-Site Inspection Directorate of the agency, the group that went into Russia and the other former members of the Soviet Union to check sites and arrange for the Russians to come into this country to check our own sites for compliance with the various treaties that had been signed, even if some of them were not fully implemented officially due to the lack of ratification by some of the signatories. So, Ike realized, some days he would be talking with a nuclear physicist who was trying to explain to him a new technology for locating nuclear materials encased in lead briefcases, and other days he would be hosting ten or so Russian soldiers at a team chief's home trying to figure out where that vodka had come from that they were now gladly using for toasts! Every day was different, he decided. He liked that.

"Shall we head in?" Ike asked Markham as he saw from his watch that it was almost time for the helicopter to land.

"Sure," Markham said, leading the way from the anteroom through the double-glass doors and into the Director's Conference Room. The two remained standing just inside the door leading into the conference room and watched the live feed in front of them. The three men had still not touched any of the amenities. Oh well. Something to eat after everyone's gone, she thought.

The five soldiers watched the secretary of state's Black Hawk helicopter land adjacent to the Dulles north-south runway, and then, after the blades had slowed down considerably, they watched as "The War Wagon"—a black Suburban van specially modified by armor plating and very dark, bullet-proof glass—and the other escort vehicles pulled up to the helicopter and picked up the secretary of state and the Russian foreign minister. As soon as the dignitaries had entered the van they were driven quickly to the German hangar for the ceremony.

Markham, Watson, and the others watched on the screen as the entire room full of dignitaries and DTRA employees stood up at attention when the secretary of state and the foreign minister walked into the hangar and up to the stage to their pre-designated spots to the right and behind the podium. Everyone remained at attention as first the Russian anthem was played, and then the American National Anthem.

As the music played the television camera panned the audience, beginning with the first row immediately in front of the stage, showing several of the members of the DTRA advisory committee. As the screen panned past the front row Phinney recognized General Larry Welch, the chairman of the advisory committee, as well as Ashton Carter, William Perry, and James Schlesinger. Quite a group, Phinney realized.

"Eliker must be in heaven!" Markham whispered into Ike Watson's ear.

"No shit!" he whispered back, recognizing the fact that the chief of public affairs, David J. Eliker, loved this stuff. Live CNN coverage, world-wide; everybody who is anybody in attendance, including members of Congress and the Russian Duma. Ike Watson smiled as the camera next showed the members of Congress and then the members of the Russian Duma, seated side-by-side. The camera, Watson noted, focused for a few seconds on one particular Duma member, Vasiliy Vlasihin.

I bet Eliker's in the control room directing the whole thing himself! Ike thought to himself. Ike Watson knew that it was not so many years ago that one of the predecessors of the DTRA, the On-Site Inspection Agency, had brought a group of Russians to the United States for a demonstration flight of the Open Skies plane, a Boeing OC-135B. Eliker was the public affairs officer in charge and made sure the Russians were treated like gold, provided special receptions, special unclassified briefings, and then access to reporters as they and the reporters were flown over the United States in the specially modified C-135 (previously a WC-135) designed specifically to overfly our most sensitive sites and take pictures of those sites so that all sides could access not only that country's present abilities, but also gauge their present intentions! Indeed, the flight went so well, and the attendant publicity was so favorable, that the Russians reciprocated with inviting the Open Skies people to actually land their OC-135B at a previously closed base, Kubinka Air Base seventy miles west of Moscow, and then do a reciprocal demonstration flight in one of the Russian An-30 transport planes. Perhaps stranger yet, Ike Watson knew, the Russians themselves asked Eliker—the *American* public affairs officer—to serve as the *Russian* press affairs officer for the trip since he did such a great job obtaining world-wide press when the Russians came over to the United States! They were not disappointed. And who met them at the Kubinka Air Base with hugs and greetings? Vasiliy Vlasihin, the member of the Duma who had been initially skeptical of the treaty and had, as a result of the demonstration flight, become one of the strongest proponents of the Open Skies Treaty, eventually convincing the Duma to ratify the treaty. And there Vasiliy sat, waiting to watch history actually happen as the two foreign ministers signed documents officially implementing the treaty.

A young Air Force major stepped up to the podium, his slightly graying hair and graying mustache making him look more English than American. His uniform clearly showed him to be one of the pilots for the On-Site Inspection Directorate.

"Good morning, ladies and gentlemen. My name is Major Brent Franklin. On behalf of all of the twenty-seven signatories of the Open Skies Treaty, we welcome you to a new world of peace, trust, and understanding among all of our countries. Signed at Helsinki, Finland, on March 24, 1992, and just recently ratified by all of the major signatories, the treaty allows all signatory countries the opportunity to overfly the country of its choice so it can personally determine that the rumor of war is just a rumor, so it can personally verify that the whisper of a build-up is false, and so it can maintain peaceful relations with its neighbors and friends without the fear of uncertainty and confusion. This is the laudable goal of the Open Skies Treaty. This is the laudable goal of all nations. This is the laudable goal of mankind. Peace and trust. Common knowledge and friendship."

Major Franklin paused for a moment for effect, probably at Eliker's insistence, Ike thought. Eliker would be one hell of a Hollywood director, or maybe even a first-rate novelist if his clearance didn't prevent it!

"We are pleased to welcome you here today for this auspicious occasion," the major concluded.

The four men and Markham watched the rest of the ceremony on the screen in the conference room, listening politely as the Russian foreign minister thanked his host and extolled the virtues of the Open Skies Treaty, and then similar words were spoken by the secretary of state.

Through it all Broughton and Konesky continued to show signs of nervousness, both men fidgeting in their seats. They watched as the two foreign ministers finished their remarks and were escorted off the stage and out of the building. They were succeeded by Dr. Jay Allen, the director of the Defense Threat Reduction Agency, who asked the audience to stand while he listed the name of each of the twenty-seven countries and a representative from each country stepped onto the stage, the flag of each country simultaneously posted at the back of the stage by the honor guard as that country's name was called.

Phinney watched as the representatives from each country continued past the director. The director's silver hair and matching beard provided the ceremony with added dignity, Phinney thought. Phinney had been given a quick tour of the director's office by Ike Watson when he had arrived. Tastefully decorated and maintaining an organized yet relaxed atmosphere, the director's northeast corner office looked northward toward the small unnamed lake, called "The Duck Pond" by the DTRA employees; to the east the director could observe the construction of the new parking lot that was becoming more and more needed due to the expansion of the various roles and responsibilities of the government's newest agency.

During the tour of the director's office Phinney was pleased to see several beautiful photographs that the director himself had taken and had had framed and placed on the west wall of the fifteen-by-twenty-five-foot office. "Photography is one of the director's hobbies," Watson informed Phinney as he finished the tour. If it had been Watson's purpose to relax him by showing Phinney his surroundings, it hadn't helped. Phinney went back to his chair in the conference room and remained nervous and fidgety. All he wanted at this point was to go home to his house on Sirocco Drive, have a NA beer every now and then at the Blue Rider downtown, and fly the BUFF. He had hoped this would be the last duty required of him so he could get home. Maybe he should get a hobby? Phinney thought to himself thinking of the director's photographs as he sat watching the representatives walk up to the stage one-by-one. Maybe use it to meet some pretty Minot State coed. It was time, he thought. Time to move on.

After informing the representatives and the audience that they may be seated, the director gave his concluding remarks, clearly directing them to the two thousand or so DTRA employees in attendance at the ceremony. "Ladies and gentlemen of DTRA," the director said, "we have again embarked on another awesome responsibility, another of our many duties involved in the promotion of peace in a volatile and uncertain world. To perform this job successfully, we must do many things." Dr. Allen paused for a moment.

"We must have people on the ground who know the truth and understand the reality of both the situation *and* the nuances of that situation. We must have the people back home who can accurately interpret those facts and those realities and create a cohesive and accurate understanding of what it all means. And we must have leaders who understand the system and have the ear and trust of those who make the final decisions. We are the eyes and ears and hopefully the brains behind a safer world." The director paused again and took a deep breath.

"There will necessarily be times when we have to say what has to be said, even if it isn't what people want to hear. There will be times when our warnings may go unheeded and unwanted consequences result. Our job cannot be to prevent every possible misdeed that may occur; but it *is* our job to try. And when we do this job, we do it realizing that we luckily live in a free society, knowing full well that there are scholars who hold the view that it is the freedom of this society that allows such misdeeds to occur.

"This may be true to some extent, but it is also true that by the freedom that this society allows, we are provided discretion and latitude to determine how best to protect and defend our people and our cherished ideals. It is the freedom of this society that allows us to strive to understand other cultures and other peoples. And it is the freedom of this society that allows us to chose what level and types of freedom we can have in a modern society fraught with danger and technological advances that we only yet are beginning to understand. That, my friends, is our mission. It is indeed a worthy mission." The director paused and looked up at the audience, and then continued.

"It is indeed ironic that it has become easier to deal with countries, and that our real difficulty has now become how to deal with small groups of people who may decide to harm us and others. As peace between nations has become our pleasant reality, the threat of other types of harm has unfortunately unfolded before us. It will be our job to come to grips with this new reality and to do our level best to prevent those terrible isolated acts of destruction and inhumanity." Another slight pause as he shifted his glasses.

"As we step back from the brink of human destruction by two massive powers, we find ourselves looking forward not at a precipice but at a quagmire, where social injustice and universal knowledge lead us to a new battle against those who are weak and use the tools of the weak. But it is a battle we can win, by perseverance, by gathering facts accurately, and by steadfast diligence directed at potential risks and cold reality." The director paused and smiled.

"Luckily it is not our responsibility to uproot or excavate or even transform that quagmire that stands before us into something else. We need only build a bridge over that quagmire, a bridge built from mutual understanding and openness. Today, my friends, we have set into place the firm foundations of that bridge. So let us go forward and perform this honorable task 'with charity to all, and malice toward none.' While preventing harm, let us also take the time to understand the root causes of such acts and discern whether other means may prevent them. And if on that rare occasion a weaker adversary succeeds in striking out against us, we will not lose hope, but will re-double our efforts to warn those who need to be warned, make safe those weapons that need to be made safe, and strive to create a world where the specter of terrorism is no more, and our resources are consistently used to help man, not to harm him. This is the world we strive for. And this is the reason we strive. Thank you all very much for being here today."

It was an impressive ceremony, Phinney thought. The band began playing formal but festive music, but Phinney and the others couldn't hear what they were playing since Ike, upon seeing that the ceremony was over and receiving some information on his "brick," turned the volume down on the monitor. Everyone understood what his actions meant.

"Where would you like us?" Broughton asked Watson.

"Nowhere yet. The secretary and foreign minister would prefer to meet you in an informal setting, here." At about the time he said this, Markham and the men observed the State Department diplomatic security officer stationed in the conference room bring his hand up to his ear and speak seemingly into his sleeve, "Confirmed, Eagle in the building." Phinney, Broughton, and Konesky realized that the dignitaries would arrive shortly and got up from their chairs and stood at attention.

The secretary of state entered first, followed by the Russian foreign minister, and then a Russian and an American general. The two generals eased up against the wall, observing.

"Relax, gentlemen," the secretary of state stated as she entered the room, wearing her traditional bright, effervescent clothing. "We're just here to give you our regards. You must be Randy Broughton," she said as she shook his hand. "And you are obviously Alexander Konesky. It is a pleasure to meet you both. You have both done a great service to both our countries."

The foreign minister followed, shaking both men's hands and thanking them.

"And you, young man, must be Jack Phinney."

"That's correct, ma'am. It's a pleasure to meet you."

"I take it you got settled back in after your little trip?"

Broughton and Konesky were initially confused. They had assumed that Phinney was just an escort for one of the dignitaries. "Yes, ma'am," Phinney replied. "I'm ready to go back to work."

"I bet you are. Not much for the limelight, son?"

"No, ma'am. I guess I'll leave that to the people who know what they're doin'." He felt like he was stammering, making no sense.

Broughton and Konesky looked anew at the pilot wings on Phinney's left chest as he spoke with the secretary of state and realized that he must have been the man who flew into Russia to get the coordinates, and the man who got Tsinev back in time to send them the layout of the secret site. They both realized that they owed this man a beer. Lots of beer!

"Well, gentleman. We have a little presentation for you, and then the minister and I have some work to do." The secretary turned back toward the two general officers. "General Williams," she asked pleasantly, "are we ready to go?"

"Yes, ma'am," he replied. "Colonel Broughton and Colonel Phinney, if you'd both stand over here along the wall. That's fine." General Williams opened up a thin leather case and began reading: "'Attention to orders.'" He looked up and saw that both men were standing at attention. "'By order of the President of the United States and by the approval of the United States Congress in special closed session, Colonel Jack Phinney and Colonel Randy Broughton, for unspecified heroic action under fire and at great personal risk, are hereby awarded the Medal of Honor, the highest award given to a member of the armed forces.'"

General Williams closed the leather folder as Allison Markham approached the general and held open in each hand two small felt-covered cases. The general reached into one of the cases and pulled out a pale-blue ribbon with tiny white stars holding a medallion and placed it over Phinney's head, and then did the same for Broughton. After doing so the general stepped back and saluted both men. Phinney and Broughton, both obviously in shock, returned the salute smartly.

"As you can imagine, gentlemen, the details of your missions will remain classified. There will be no need-to-know since there is no need-to-know, for anybody. Is that clear?"

"Yes, sir," both men stated.

"You may wear the ribbons," meaning the small ribbon that is placed on the left breast of the uniform and not the larger ribbon and medallion resting along each man's neck. "That's enough, don't you think, at least until you retire?"

"Yes, sir," both men replied.

As if on cue, the Russian general told Konesky to stand at attention. "Alexander Valinovich," he said looking at Konesky using his first and patronymic name and then looking down as he read from a document placed inside a red-felt case, "by order of the President of the Russian Federation and with the approval of the Duma in closed session, you are hereby awarded the Order of Lenin." The general pulled a red ribbon with a medallion on it and placed it around Konesky's head. The general stepped back and saluted Konesky. Konesky returned the salute. "And by the way," the general said to Konesky with a clear air of impishness, "ditto on the other thing, too."

"Yes, sir," Konesky replied, acknowledging that the general had just ordered him to forget anything that had happened in the last six weeks.

"Well, gentlemen," the Russian foreign minister said, "as our host has mentioned, we have some work to do. I understand the room is ready," the foreign minister stated as he looked inquiringly at the younger officers in the room, Ike Watson and Allison Markham.

"Yes, sir," Watson replied, "if everyone will step into the Flag Room we can begin."

Phinney, Broughton, and Konesky remained standing in the reception room, at least until the secretary of state told them, quite simply, "That includes you too, boys."

The group entered a room adjacent to the director's office. The room was approximately twenty-feet-by-thirty-feet. Along the long wall on the west side were three large black wall boards that out-lined, by white lines that created silhouettes of the various countries of the world, first Europe beginning at Spain and going all the way east-ward to the farthest reaches of eastern Russia; the next map provided a more detailed map of Europe; and the third map displayed the United States. Throughout all of the maps were lighted dots showing every site that could be monitored or inspected by the various treaties in force and implemented by DTRA. The ones blinking, Watson knew, were where an inspection or special monitoring was presently being conducted.

On the shorter north wall hung royal-blue curtains, in front of which stood an American and a Russian flag. In front of the flags stood a small table with two formal documents sitting on the table, and two ornate pens.

"Please, Madam Secretary," the Russian foreign minister stat-ed, "after you!"

The secretary of state smiled graciously and said, jokingly to her good friend, "by all means." She reached down to the table and signed one and then the other document with one of the pens. Her counterpart did the same with the other pen, and then the two foreign ministers shook hands.

"To world peace," the secretary of state said.

"To world peace," the foreign minister replied.

"Shall we have something to eat, Victor?" knowing how much the foreign minister liked to snack at this type of occasion.

"But of course," the foreign minister stated. "It would be a crime to waste such wonderful food!"

The two foreign ministers stepped back into the conference room, followed, after a discreet signal from Watson, by the others.

The work done, the entire room became almost light-hearted. Broughton and Konesky went over to thank Phinney while the generals and the foreign ministers began filling up their small plates with food.

As the Russian foreign minister completed his task of filling his plate with food and went over to sit down, he walked by the young military officers who had just been honored.

"I assume, Colonel Phinney," he said as he walked by them, "that next time you want to visit my country, you'll apply for a visa."

"Yes, sir. Absolutely, sir," Phinney replied as he watched the foreign minister sit down next to the secretary of state.

"By the way, Victor," the secretary of state said a while later as the two ate, "my intelligence sources have recently noted the lack of reference to Deputy Minister Aleksei Kalganov as well as to Grigoriy Pavlovich, the head of your Second Directorate. We have assumed, perhaps incorrectly, that they must have that terrible flu that is going around in Moscow right now and are not feeling well."

The foreign minister smiled, knowing exactly what was being asked.

"I understand that General Kalganov is on vacation," the foreign minister replied. "I believe he is in the process of being debriefed before taking another 'assignment.'"

The secretary of state noted the emphasis the foreign minister placed on the word "assignment" and wondered if the assignment happened to be a lifetime in Lubyanka prison.

"His replacement," the foreign minister continued with all pleasantness, "will be announced sometime next week, I believe. As to Pavlovich, I am afraid your sources are right. He did indeed come down with a terrible cold. He unfortunately passed away just last week. We will of course all miss him terribly."

"Of course," the secretary said, thinking that in some regards it is nice to see that Russia has at least a few remnants of their old style of doing things.

Phinney, standing at the opposite end of the room with the others, including Markham and Watson, thought it strange that such a ceremony would not include at least a photographer, and at least some press. He leaned over to Ike Watson.

"What was that signing all about?" Phinney asked quietly. Watson answered loud enough for Broughton and Konesky to hear as well.

"They just signed a secret protocol between our two governments allowing the inspection of non-listed sites, that is sites not listed in the annexes of the START treaty. There will be no more secret bases, not even the chance of a secret offensive base. It's a new world, gentlemen. A new world."

# CHAPTER 75

## Crystal City, Arlington, Virginia
## The next day

Phinney walked across the Jefferson Davis Highway at the cross-walk that paralleled 23rd Street. He had been staying at the Washington (now Reagan) National Airport Hilton at Crystal City until his flight that afternoon back to Minot. He assumed, until he had received the message from the front desk, that no one knew he was even in Washington, except of course the people at DTRA who had arranged for his hotel. The DTRA public affairs officer said he'd be glad to take him to the airport the next day, but his boss nixed the idea, mentioning that using the officer quarters at Dulles would make it too difficult to get him to the airport the next day, particularly given the weather report that predicted three-to-five inches of snow. Unlike Minot, where that small amount of snow stops nothing, in D.C. just an inch or two tends to shut the entire city down.

The unsigned message left at the front desk had simply said, "Meet me at Crystal City's St. Elmo's Coffee Pub, 551 South 23rd St. Noon." The clerks at the desk told Phinney that the coffee shop was just two short blocks away, just across the highway along 23rd Street. It took only a few minutes for Phinney to walk to the shop through the cold, wet snow that had begun to fall. He ordered a large "chai" and went upstairs where there was more seating overlooking part of the entrance area of the store, sitting down at the railing immediately above the entrance. Good, he thought, I can watch who comes in and try to figure out who it is that I'm meeting!

As he looked out through the upper windows to the other side of the street, Phinney observed the red-brick sidewalk and the various stores along-side that sidewalk. Being a Sunday morning—Phinney had come one-half-an-hour early—all of the shops across the street were closed. Having nothing else to do, Phinney studied the glowing neon signs of the Vietnamese restaurant, then the bright-blue sign of Alber's Valet and Shoe Repair, followed by the brick building housing G.B.S. Printers, and by the looks of it also housing the owners of the print shop in the back of the same building. Phinney also observed a dirt-brown older car, maybe a late-1950s Chevy of some sort, parked between the shoe shop and the print shop that clearly belonged to whoever lived behind the print shop, but he couldn't tell what make or model it was.

By the time noon came and went the snow had really begun to come down, now in big, moisture-laden flakes that melted when they hit the ground. And still no person showed up to meet him, just a few obvious neighbors grabbing a latte or mocha or whatever they call them. Phinney never did learn to drink coffee. He waited another five minutes sipping his *chai* and when it was gone he decided he had been there long enough and started to gather his coat to leave.

A familiar voice came from behind him. "Sorry I'm late," Tsinev said as he set his coat down on a chair next to Phinney. "I'll be right back. I've got to get something warm in me! You'd think it was years since I had been in Siberia! Here, while you're waiting for me to come back. I brought you something."

Tsinev handed Phinney a book and walked back downstairs to get his coffee. *I wonder how the hell he got in without me seeing him?* Phinney thought. *There must be a back door. These damn spies. They're always trying to play with your mind.*

Phinney looked down at the book. "The Catcher Was a Spy" the mid-portion stated in bold, typewritten letters. Below that it read, "The Mysterious Life of Moe Berg," and the author's name, "Nicholas Dawidoff." *Moe Berg*, Phinney thought to himself. *Never heard of him.*

Phinney opened up the book and began reading the author's prologue. The book was apparently about some guy who was graduated from Princeton, had played professional baseball in the 1920s and 1930s, and had spied for the United States during World War II. As he flipped back and forth through the first five or six pages Phinney read bits and pieces about students at Princeton who had written articles about Moe Berg in their college newspaper, about people who had known Berg and had turned the study of the man into an all-encompassing hobby, about a man who knew him and thought he was a fraud, and about relatives who knew him and never could understand who he was or what he did. His own brother had kicked him out of his house in 1964 as a good-for-nothing freeloader, and so Joe DiMaggio and others helped him out and made sure he had a place to live!

Phinney turned a few more pages and saw a reference to the CIA Exhibit Center and mention of its display of two of Moe Berg's baseball cards. According to the book, the display had the following caption to explain the apparent incongruity of the existence of the cards in a CIA exhibit case:

MORRIS (MOE) BERG BASEBALL CARDS
Following his 15-year career with five different major league teams, the Princeton-educated Berg served as a highly successful Office of Strategic Services (OSS) operative during World War II. Among his many missions on behalf of OSS, the former catcher was charged with learning all he could about Hitler's nuclear bomb project. . . .

Because of his intellect, Moe Berg is considered the "brainiest" man ever to have played the game. He spoke a dozen languages fluently and often autographed pictures in Japanese. These cards are from his playing days with the Washington Senators (1932-34) and Boston Red Sox (1935-39).

"What do you think of the book so far?" Tsinev asked as he sat down next to Phinney.

"Interesting. I've never heard of the guy."

"Hardly anyone has," Tsinev replied. "That's why I got it for you. How was your trip to Dulles?"

"Also interesting," Phinney replied, still trying to figure out what this whole thing was all about.

"Medals are OK," Tsinev said as he sipped his coffee. "But they don't mean shit. They help for promotions and things like that.

But otherwise they're just ornamentation as far as I'm concerned." He took another sip of his coffee. Phinney waited. Obviously Tsinev asked him to be here for a reason.

"I think you'll enjoy that book. It's not bad. It shows what living in risk can do to a man. For some of them it happens that way; they withdraw, turn inward. Maybe they just want to relax, not worry about things anymore. Me, I'm the opposite. I wish I could do it for another hundred years." He laughed at himself. "Not anymore, though. The whole spy world knows who I am now. Both sides. Nope, I'm done."

"What are you going to do then?" Phinney asked.

"Don't rightly know. Guess they'll change my name, who knows, probably my face too, not that that wouldn't hurt anything! Probably be an improvement! Then I suppose they'll give me a stipend, a little place wherever the hell I want, and then I disappear. Just like in the movies, but this time for real."

"So this is it, in other words?"

"Yes, my boy. 'This is it.' The odds of you ever seeing me again are about as close to nil as you can get. I heard you were in town, so I thought I'd give you my regards, as they say. Although I reckon they'll still be awhile de-briefing me for the next couple of months. Shit! I never thought that a life that was so interesting when I lived it would be so damn boring when you have to go over every little detail! I feel like an insect 'pinned and wriggling on the wall,' perfectly categorized and with a little tag below me giving my official scientific name in Latin!"

"*À la* T. S. Eliot?" Phinney asked, catching Tsinev's not-so-subtle allusion to "The Love Song of J. Alfred Prufrock."

"Absolutely, my boy! Professor Moore would be very proud indeed!"

"Yeah, right," Phinney said, clearly not convinced.

"Oh well," Tsinev continued thinking about the extended de-briefing session, "that's the deal, and it's a good one, so I shouldn't bitch." Tsinev looked out the window. "Nice car, huh?" he said referring to the old classic car parked across the street. He took another sip from his styrofoam cup, and then looked over at his former student.

"So, enough about me," Tsinev said. "What will you do now?"

"Go back to flying, I suppose."

"I bet they'd let you do anything you damn well wanted to!"

"Yeah, they've said words to that effect. But I'm just not interested right now. I'd rather just fly and relax, get back to some sort of normalcy."

"Well, that's understandable. And God knows you're due." Tsinev paused for a few seconds. "You thought you were dead there for a while, didn't you?"

"Yep," Phinney replied simply.

"It's quite a feeling to think you're about ready to check out, and then survive it. There's nothing like it, is there?"

"No," Phinney said simply.

"When did it hit you? When you were in the jail?"

"Yep. I decided right away that I wasn't going to let you put me on trial."

"So your plan was to try to escape, and if a guard was lookin' that would have been it, huh?"

"Yep. That was the plan."

"I thought so. That's why I never let you out of that cell. I didn't want you to muck it all up. Besides, someone had to fly that big contraption out of there, and it sure the hell wasn't going to be me!"

Tsinev stood up and started to grab his coat, but then stopped and turned back to face Phinney. "Let me see that book for a minute, then I have to go."

Phinney handed him the book that Tsinev had given him. Tsinev pulled out a pen and scribbled something on one of the inside front-pages.

"Don't spend your life alone, like I did, Jack," Tsinev said as he handed back the book. "And don't worry so much. Everything is going to be just fine. Just fine."

And with that, Tsinev picked up his coat and began to put it on. "You'll be good now, ya' hear!" Tsinev said as he finished putting on his coat. "I'm working on my 'good-ol'-boy' accent," he explained. "Gonna hafta blend in for a while, ya' know?"

"I'm sure you'll do fine," Phinney said smiling as he stood up to shake Tsinev's hand. "Thanks for everything, Professor."

"No, my boy, it is *me* that needs to thank you," he said looking Phinney directly in the eyes. "You got me the hell out of there, didn't you? You take care now," he said in a more serious tone, his hand resting on Phinney's shoulder.

"I will," Phinney promised.

And with that he was gone. Phinney heard him walk down the stairs, say "See you'll," and then walk out the front door, turning right on the sidewalk and out of view. He never looked back, Phinney noted.

Phinney leaned back in his chair and let out a sigh. What a weird man, he thought. No family. No life. Just memories of helping his country. And that's another thing, Phinney thought. Which country? Who was he really helping? Which side was he really on?

Phinney opened up the book. Maybe the book was a way to let Phinney see a glimpse of who he was. He looked down to his scribbling on one of the pages in the front, at an almost forty-five degree angle and barely readable:

Jack ———
    Thanks for the ride!
Take time to think.
Take a lover. Or two!
Rejoice in the moment you
    thought you were dead.
You will never be
    dead again!
                T.

"Do you mind if I join you?" a young woman said as Phinney finished reading Tsinev's note. Phinney looked up at a beautiful brown-haired woman holding a fur coat wrapped on her left arm and holding a cup of coffee in her right hand.

"By all means," Phinney replied as he began to rise.

"There's no need to get up," she said, but Phinney nonetheless continued to rise and pulled up a chair for her. "A gentleman," she said as she sat her coffee down. "How nice."

Phinney watched as the woman gently laid her fur coat over the top of another chair.

"I see that we have a mutual friend," she said as she sat down.

"Oh really?" Jack replied as he too sat down.

"Yes, the gentleman who was just here. I believe you call him 'the Professor'?"

Jack said nothing. He just stared at the beautiful woman and wondered what this was all about, finally noting her slight accent. English? Perhaps a glimmer of Russian? he thought.

The woman studied Jack for a moment, then continued. "About three weeks ago I sat in a KGB prison called Lubyanka," she said simply as she sipped on her coffee. "I was being held incommunicado. A general had arranged to have me placed there, supposedly under the charge of treason. Your professor friend, who turned out also to be KGB, apparently heard about me being held and bribed a guard to get in to see me. The guard assumed he was there to, I believe you say, 'take advantage' of me, and thought nothing of it. We visited for awhile about some information that he needed, and then he told me that in three weeks he would have me out of there, and that I would be here in the United States within four weeks." She smiled and looked directly at Phinney. "And here I am."

"Interesting," Phinney said noncommittally, realizing that Tsinev must have gotten the exact location of the missile site from this woman, and then the United States must have requested her release or perhaps traded her for a Russian agent in custody. That meant that either Tsinev only knew the general location when he sent the first message, or he was just confirming the exact location through this woman. Either way, he jeopardized the entire mission by going to visit her. "Very strange," Phinney said, not even realizing that he had uttered the words out loud.

"Yes, life can be very strange. One minute you think you are dead, and the next you are sipping coffee—or *chai*, in your case—watching the lovely snow fall upon a wet sidewalk." She sipped her coffee again as the two of them looked out the window.

"The Professor mentioned," she began again, somewhat shyly, "that perhaps you could show me around a little, if that would not be too much of a problem. This is my first time in the United States, and I admit I am somewhat lost."

Phinney laughed and smiled at the woman. "No problem," he replied thinking about all of the leave time he had saved up over the years. So much for that plane flight back to Minot this afternoon.

"My name is Jack," the man said as he put out his hand to shake hers.

"Yes, I know Mr. Phinney," the woman replied as they shook hands. "It is indeed a pleasure to meet you."

The woman's hands were warm and gentle, Jack noticed. She exuded an air of sophistication, and yet vulnerability at the same time. Jack waited a few seconds as they continued to shake hands, and then he finally asked, "And your name is?"

"I'm not sure right yet," she replied somewhat thoughtfully. "They are getting me a new one. But for now, we might as well use my old one. Riana. Riana Kovapiova," she said as she smiled and continued to hold his hand.

# Author's note as to factual details

As of this writing the Open Skies Treaty has not taken effect because three signatory nations, including the Russian Federation, have not ratified the treaty. Nor is the author aware of any agreement between Russia and the United States to allow inspection of non-listed sites under the START treaty or other formal agreements.

The fire at Biysk in 1986 occurred as mentioned in the text. Although the assumption is that all of the RSM-52 missiles were destroyed in that fire, it is indeed possible that some or all of the rockets survived the fire and were diverted elsewhere. The United States continues to attempt to assist the Russians in making their nuclear weapons and weapons-grade material secure. The proper security of these assets continues to be a serious problem, despite these efforts.

The intercept of the Russian "Bear" bomber by the 5th Fighter Interceptor Squadron by Evans and Sparkman actually occurred in March of 1987; the change to a date *prior* to the fire at the Biysk Rocket Facility is made for literary reasons only. Also, Zhukov's wonderful concert described in the text actually occurred on January 21, 1994.

To the author's knowledge, the book is otherwise factually accurate in all other respects.

# Specific Literary References and Allusions

p. 11: "The target is destroyed." Radio transmission of Soviet pilot after shooting down Korean Airlines Flight 007, Sept. 1, 1983. A detailed description of this event may be found in Seymour M. Hersh's book, *The Target is Destroyed* (1986).

p. 17 *Les Miserables* by Victor Hugo (1862).

p. 28 Sir Isaac Newton's letter to Robert Hooke (Feb. 5, 1675/6).

p. 29 Dante's *Inferno* Canto III, line 53 (1310-1320)(J. Ciardi, trans.); also, T.S. Eliot, *The Waste Land* line 63 (1922).

p. 104 *Othello* Act III, scene iii, lines 126-27.

p. 124 Reference is to Dr. Edward A. Ivanian of Institute of US and Canadian Studies, Moscow. An excellent description of the so-called Newburgh conspiracy, and Washington's quick response to it, may be found in Volume 2 of Page Smith's *A New Age Begins* at pages 1768-1772 (1976).

p. 145 "The end is the beginning." See *Revelations* 1:8 & 22:13.

p. 146 "Come up here, my friends, and I will show you what must take place after this." See *Revelations* 4:1.

p. 146 Command Center artwork, *Revelations* 4:4-8 & 19:15.

p. 152 Missile artwork, *Revelations* 6:2-12, 8:6, 9:21 & 11:15-19.

p. 178 Compare Fyodor Dostoevsky's *Notes from the House of the Dead* (1861-62) with Nikolai Pomyalovsky's *Seminary Sketches* (1862-63).

p. 207 Note intended parallelism to the encounter between Dmitri and Father Zossima in Fyodor Dostoevsky's *The Brothers Karamazov* Book II, Ch. 6.

p. 208 Reference to *The Universal Tarot of Salvador Dali* consisting of 78 tarot cards containing Dali's artwork.

p. 251 "I cannot forecast to you the action of Russia. It is a riddle wrapped in a mystery inside an enigma." Winston Churchill, radio broadcast (Oct. 1, 1939).

p. 252　　Valjean of course refers to Jean Valjean, the protagonist in Victor Hugo's *Les Miserables* (1862), and Portia refers to the wise judge's plea for mercy in Shylock's famous trial scene in *The Merchant of Venice* Act IV, lines 182-203.

p. 252　　Many books and articles describe the "Wilsonian" view of the "convergence" of the United States and the Soviet Union. As to the theory of convergence and acceptance by Roosevelt despite the contrary views of our representatives assigned to Moscow, I suggest Dennis J. Dunn's fine book, *Caught Between Roosevelt & Stalin: America's Ambassadors to Moscow* (1998). For the contrary view that Roosevelt had no practical alternative, I suggest Michael M. Boll, *National Security Planning: Roosevelt through Reagan* 28-31 (1988).

p. 271　　Jefferson's unfortunate comments are contained in the only full-length book he ever wrote, *Notes on the State of Virginia* Query XIV (1861). For a recent discussion of Jefferson's views on slavery and the subsequent use of those statements, see Joseph J. Ellis, *Founding Brothers* 99-101 (2000).

p. 272　　Reference is to Walter Laqueur, *The Age of Terrorism* 73 (1987) and Paul Wilkerson, *Political Terrorism* 23 (1974); for a concise review of the issue of democracy's relationship to terrorism, see generally Jonathan R. White, *Terrorism: An Introduction* 150-52 (1998).

p. 273　　For basic information on Amartya Sen's award and views, see *Time* 69 (Oct. 26, 1998).

p. 368　　Nicholas Dawidoff, *The Catcher was a Spy: The Mysterious Life of Moe Berg* (1994).

p. 370　　T. S. Eliot, *The Love Song of J. Alfred Prufrock* line 58 (1917).

# Acknowledgements

Literally hundreds of people have assisted me over the years in my work on this book. I hope I do each of them credit by accurately describing what it is like to be in the military.

At each base or government entity described in the book I received a superb tour of the base by either the wing commander or a public affairs officer. I have been privileged to have been the honorary commander for numerous persons assigned to Minot AFB, including Rick and Carolyn McDonald, Randy and Becky Spetman, Joe and Susan McNabb, Tom and Helen Goslin, Steve and Sarah Schmidt, Jim and Cheryl Ewing, Ed and Elise Dixon, Dave and Vicki Swafford, Greg and Elizabeth Ebensperger, and Keith and Anne Wagner. I have worked and became friends with many of the commanders and the wives of the 5th Bomb Wing and the 91st Missile Wing, including Bob and Jo Linhard, Bill and Melly Hodges, Ralph and Dolly Pasini, Dave and Ginny Young, Bob and Bess Elder, Greg and Mary-Ann Powers, Reg and Bev Rider, Denny and Dee Abbey, and Gerry and Debra Perryman. I have also received assistance and support from my Air Force friends Pat and Jean Travnicek, Jeff and Holly Boulware, David and Lisa Crockett, Colette and Preston Obray, Reed and Carol Heddleston, and crud master Keith Teister; members of DOCA (including John Ohlsen, Judge Herman Reviere, and George Wallace), and members of AFIO.

I received substantial information and support from the numerous persons who have worked on (or written about) the SR-71, including Marta Bohn-Meyer, Bob Meyer, David Lux, and Jim Greenwood. And of course I owe a great debt to those individuals who assisted me as translators or just good friends as I traveled throughout Russia, as well as Greg Stites, who was kind enough to accompany me during one of my trips to Russia and let me use the photos he took if they were better than mine.

Thanks also to everyone who reviewed the complete manuscript and provided editorial assistance and suggestions, including Mark Nelson, Alyssa Martin, Shonna Miller, Mike Gallagher, Greg Power, Marta and Bob Meyer, George Wallace, General Russ Dougherty, Jim Greenwood, Bob and Bess Elder, Kurt Saladana, and

Dale Elhardt. Any errors, of course, are attributable to me alone. Thanks too to Ian Stern of 16 SOW/PA for the special ops photos.

I am particularly grateful to General Mike Loh for asking me to serve on his Commander's Air Power Support Group and having the opportunity to work with and become friends with Steve Croker, Mike Gallagher, Karen Wilson, and each of my fellow members of that group.

Lastly, I am honored that General David C. Jones and General Russell E. Dougherty were kind enough to review an advance copy of my book and provide their kind words to the jacket cover.

Thank you all.

# Commanders of the
# 5th Fighter Interceptor Squadron
## 20 November 1940 — 26 February 1988

1st Lt Allan T. Bennett

1st Lt Ward W. Hacker

Capt Thomas A. Holdiman

Capt William J. Payne

Capt Edwin W. Fuller

Major Hadley B. Eliker

Major John M. Konesky

Lt Col Thomas D. Robertson

Major Adam Swigler

Lt Col Edward C. Heckman, Jr.

Lt Col Roland J. DuFresne

Col Hubert L. Williams

Lt Col Garland W. Eagle

Lt Col Donald J. Parsons

Lt Col Jack H. Sandstrom

Lt Col Thurman D. Cothran

Lt Col Dallas R. Hanna

Lt Col Richard L. Maki

Capt John C. Erickson

1st Lt James F. Whisenand

Major George C. Deaton

Capt Everett K. Jenkins

Major Ralph W. Watson

Lt Col William C. Bryson

Lt Col George D. Mobbs

Lt Col Robert M. Myers

Lt Col Theon Markham

Major Gordon H. Scott

Lt Col Jacksel M. Broughton

Col John H. Fowler, Jr.

Lt Col Vander L. Smith

Col Joseph L. Phinney

Lt Col Dennis M. Harper

Lt Col James E. Waddle

Lt Col Daniel L. Wodstrchill

Lt Col Richard E. Coe

Lt Col Thomas W. Dobson, Jr.